THE GALACTERAN Legacy

Galaxy Watch

Also by Michelle Izmaylov

Dream Saver

THE
GALACTERAN
Legacy

Galaxy Watch

Michelle Izmaylov

Mercury Publishing House
Atlanta, Georgia

The Galacteran Legacy: Galaxy Watch

For information address Mercury Publishing, Inc.
2526 Mount Vernon Road, Atlanta, GA 30338
www.mercurypublishinghouse.com

Library of Congress Catalog Card Number: 2008935154

ISBN-13: 978-0-977-87939-7
ISBN-10: 0-977-87939-9

Printed in the United States of America

First edition, January 2009

The text was set in Adobe Garamond
Book Design by Bart Dawson

To my mom, for believing in me.

To my dad, for standing beside me.

To my sister, Nicole, for revealing
that the world is full of magic.

And to the hero in us all.

Table of Contents

Prologue • 1

Chapter One
Discovery • 3

Chapter Two
The Phoenix • 9

Chapter Three
The River • 15

Chapter Four
Lily • 22

Chapter Five
The Various Doohickey Place • 33

Chapter Six
Dark Warrior • 49

Chapter Seven
The Galactera • 59

Chapter Eight
Darkness Descending • 65

Chapter Nine
Of Legends and Prophecies • 75

Chapter Ten
The Shazgor • 81

Chapter Eleven
Azimar • 92

Chapter Twelve
The Hatchling • 105

Chapter Thirteen
The Map • 115

Chapter Fourteen
The Kidnapping • 125

Chapter Fifteen
Predator • 130

Chapter Sixteen
Espia • 138

Chapter Seventeen
Coralian City • 144

Chapter Eighteen
Convincing Rayonk • 157

Chapter Nineteen
The Espian Treasure • 164

Chapter Twenty
Serrona • 175

Chapter Twenty-One
Blood on the Wind • 184

Chapter Twenty-Two
The Royal Guard • 194

Chapter Twenty-Three
Falkor's Tale • 201

Chapter Twenty-Four
A New Hope • 208

Chapter Twenty-Five
Plans for Rescue • 221

Chapter Twenty-Six
The Mission • 230

Chapter Twenty-Seven
The Omenra Secret • 243

Chapter Twenty-Eight
Connecting the Pieces • 253

Chapter Twenty-Nine
Escape • 267

Chapter Thirty
The Soul of the Universe • 281

Chapter Thirty-One
Preparing for Battle • 288

Chapter Thirty-Two
Engage • 297

Chapter Thirty-Three
War • 312

Chapter Thirty-Four
Lily's Sacrifice • 325

Chapter Thirty-Five
Unveiling the Past • 337

Chapter Thirty-Six
The Queen's Treasure • 346

Chapter Thirty-Seven
The Potion • 355

Chapter Thirty-Eight
The Core • 366

Chapter Thirty-Nine
One Last Chance • 380

Chapter Forty
Meeting Tibo • 391

Chapter Forty-One
Making a Bargain • 398

Chapter Forty-Two
Kyria Again • 406

Chapter Forty-Three
Fiery Pursuit • 415

Chapter Forty-Four
The Second Prophecy • 421

Chapter Forty-Five
Arli's Return • 429

Chapter Forty-Six
The Only Way • 438

Chapter Forty-Seven
Dawn of Destiny • 453

Epilogue • 461

THE GALACTERAN Legacy

Galaxy Watch

Prologue

Thorns and branches snared the fugitive's fur. Gashes cut the otter-like creature's paws as he splintered sharp twigs on the forest floor. Clearing a fallen trunk in a massive bound, he splashed chest-deep into a torrent of freezing water, lashing out at a drooping branch to avoid being swept away. Securing himself onto a gravely patch of shore with his claws, he ground his way out of the river and shook the water from his fur. Pausing for an instant, he listened for sounds of an approach. Something was crashing through the tangles behind him. Twisting about, he sprinted away from the sound.

The Omenra were near.

Ahead, just past the trees, lay a paved road. The runaway pelted towards it, but suddenly a gnarled root clutched his foot. He crashed onto the hard earth, the force of the impact throwing a compact, golden object from his belt loop. Scrambling up, he desperately scavenged the undergrowth for it.

Something slammed into the back of his head—a hard, metal something. He wobbled unsteadily and lurched forward, crashing face-first into dirt. The thing struck him once more, harder, and blackened his vision. Quickly, before he was hit again, he reached for a wrist strap and tapped a few buttons in sequence. Three blips sounded, but then the final blow came and he knew no more.

In remote outposts across the galaxy, a distress signal was detected. The call was traced to a small planet isolated on an outer spiral arm.

A planet called Earth.

Chapter One

Discovery

Nicole Sky wasn't having a good day, and the news didn't make things better.

"Record-breaking highs reaching into the hundreds have been documented worldwide—"

Yeah, thanks for the update. Hadn't noticed that.

"—and this rapid rise has sent global warming advocates swarming over Congress to demand immediate legislation."

Sure, try the political approach. Couple decades too late, I'd say.

"More on that at the top of the hour. Lisa, back to you."

Nicole brandished the remote threateningly. *More breaking news?* "Thanks, Jerry. In other news, highly unusual comet activity has been detected close to Earth."

Wow. Bright rocks in sky. Save us all.

"Abnormal satellite readings around the globe have fueled further controversy. Several days ago, a slight drop in the planetary gravitational pull—"

The television snapped off. Nicole flung down the remote control and tucked a strand of chestnut-brown hair behind one ear. "That's right," she drawled. "It's the end of the world as we know it." More seriously, she added, "End of my world, anyway."

It was hot. Dead hot. This was the global warming to the max, and it had hit the town like a fireball. Somewhere in the distance, a siren wailed pitifully. Temperatures were skyrocketing. Sunlight filtering through smoke from burning forests had dyed the world red.

Nicole's parents weren't helping. She could hear them now, roaring at each other in the kitchen. The argument went something like this:

"Honey," her mom said, "the plants outside are brown."

"You read the papers!" came her dad's voice. "We're on the Monday, Wednesday, Friday watering schedule. It's Tuesday."

"But I can't stand to watch them die."

"Then *sit*."

"Honey!"

And it went on. And on. And on. Until finally Nicole couldn't stand it. Instead of arguing about the stupid water, they could be calling someone to fix the AC that hadn't worked in two days—forty-eight hours of stifling heat in their airless trap of a home. Well, granted, they *had*, but they could be calling someone other than a company booked three weeks in advance. Unless, of course, every other company was *also* booked, leaving Nicole stuck in heat that probably couldn't be much worse outside than in.

"Mom, I'm going out!" she yelled and stormed to the front door. In sweaty frustration she snatched a thin jacket from the coat rack to screen her head from the blazing sun.

Outside was no better, but it also wasn't worse. Yellowed

tracts of dried grass and crinkled leaves lined the cul-de-sac. Drooping trees sadly hung their once-majestic heads. The sudden heat wave had devastated the whole city. But at least it wasn't nearly as bad here as in some of the towns out west. Fires weren't rampant here, for a start. *Good old East Coast,* thought Nicole grimly.

She hadn't stepped off the porch before a helicopter roared overhead, a tiny dot on its way to disaster. Sweat was already soaking her clothing, so she decided to find some shade. Half jogging, half walking, Nicole passed a beet-red bald man guzzling a sports drink and holding a large ice-cream bar. He stared at her accusingly, as if the weather was all her fault.

"So how come you're out? Day's a nightmare." He took a bite of the ice cream and licked some melted chocolate off his sausage-like fingers. "Maybe all them tree-hugging vegetarians were right. Them and that global warming guy."

"Yeah. Too late, though," Nicole mumbled, quickly walking away.

She checked by her best friends' houses. Danny was on vacation, she remembered too late. In Anchorage, Alaska, to visit some relatives. Lucky him. Lex was gone too, off on some horse-riding competition, as usual. Lex sure did love horses. But just thinking of riding in a thick uniform with the blazing sun beating down made Nicole sweat.

Taking a shortcut around a neighbor's house, she stumbled out close to a forest. *'Forest,'* she thought, tacking on quotation marks. The thing that lay spread before her was not a wild, untamed, breathtaking forest but a poor, ragged excuse for a woodland where campers dragged their complaining little brats to sleep under the stars, or whatever. If one was into that kind of thing. And Nicole wasn't. Getting eaten alive by millions of pesky insects, lying in a sweltering sleeping bag, trying to sleep with screechy animals sounds in her ears—not so high on her to-do list. Comfort was top priority. Past that, file in it her inbox and she'd get back to you. Maybe.

Nicole tottered to the shade of a giant oak at the edge of the forest to rest. She'd been out a whole ten minutes. Ten minutes too long. Throwing down the jacket, she sat against a twisted root and kicked at the dirt. Nicole hated heat because it made her grumpy and angry. Actually, a lot of things made her that way, but heat was close to the top of the list. *At least the shade is helping,* she thought. Sort of, anyway.

Rubbing her back against the root, Nicole listened to the sounds of the forest. Birds twittered overhead. The gentle rustling of leaves filled the air. There was a squirrel, scratching up a tree trunk. And that noise . . . that last one . . .

There was something wrong with the sound. It was a low, eerie creak in the trees. Nicole whirled around, throwing up a flurry of leaf litter, but the forest before her was empty. And, suddenly, strangely quiet.

Something swooped down from the trees. She scrambled to her feet, but it turned out to be just a bird. It settled on a low branch and watched her with wide, curious eyes. Nicole sank back to the ground, but her attention was fixed on the strange creature. It was a very large and ugly bird with grey, wrinkled skin. A few ragged red feathers stuck out in odd places.

"Well, you're a miserable sight," Nicole snickered.

The bird suddenly hopped down from the branch and

pecked about frantically in the leaves. It dug aside pebbles and scratched madly through dirt. Nicole leaned closer. For some odd reason, she was intrigued by the hideous creature. She reached out to touch it, but then, all of a sudden, the bird glanced up sharply and cocked its head. It soared skyward, settled onto a high branch, and chirped roughly. A single dull feather floated down and came to rest at the base of a nearby tree.

Then it sat silently upon its perch, watching. Waiting.

Nicole stood slowly, wondering why the air suddenly felt cooler than it had in days. She shrugged into her jacket and thought about going back; the edge of the forest was only a few feet away. But the feather was tempting, and at last she took a tentative step towards it. The bird's gaze followed her. Nicole knelt next to the feather and picked it up.

Then she noticed what lay beside it.

Tossing the feather aside, she gasped at what lay half-covered by a pile of brittle leaves. The small, bright object glittered even in the forest shadows. Nicole eagerly snatched what looked like a golden pocket watch and rubbed it against her shirt. Grinning, she leaned back against the tree and examined the strange watch more closely as online auction sites flashed through her head.

Fingering the long chain hanging from the watch, she wondered who had lost such a treasure. There was a single word inscribed on the front and four lines of text on the back, both written in strange symbols. The watch was double-hinged, probably so both the front and back cover could be opened.

Chapter One

Nicole's fingers probed along the sides of the pocket watch. There were two tiny buttons and a larger one. She pressed the latter.

The front cover snapped open. Instead of a clock face, a ring of sixteen faintly glowing blue buttons greeted her. Each button displayed a word in what looked like different symbols from those on the outside of the watch. Nicole's mouth dropped open in amazement. Curiosity lifted her fingers to the buttons.

Logic instantly sprang to her defense. *Drop it. Drop it now. Drop it and run.* But Nicole couldn't. It was as if the watch was glued to her hand. It was too tempting. She couldn't let go. After a second of hesitation, she pressed one of the blue buttons.

A flash of electricity sparked through the air. The bolt split and formed a solid ring around her. Nicole screamed, but the tremendous roar of the spinning light silenced her cry. She tried to get up and run, but she seemed to be rooted to the ground. Shielding her face, she could only look on in terror as the ring expanded into a closed sphere and sucked at her like a vortex. Faster and faster the light swirled until the entire oak was lit with an unearthly blue glow.

Just as quickly as it had appeared, the vortex vanished. With it went Nicole. Now nothing was left where she had been moments before, not even a scratch in the earth.

Far overhead, the ugly bird preened its feathers, chirped, and soared into the sky, disappearing in a flash of white light.

The Phoenix

A ir came in convulsive gasps. Nicole staggered; she shook her head to clear her thoughts. The bird, the watch, the blue light—what had happened? In a spasm of fear, she flung down the pocket watch and smothered it into the ground with the toe of her sneaker. "Stupid watch!" she screamed. "Stupid forest, stupid bird, stupid . . . stupid . . . where am I?"

One thing she knew for sure: she wasn't home anymore. It was much cooler, for one thing. The forest was gone. Then Nicole's mind flashed to a very different thought. This place seemed strange. Too strange. Where could she possibly be on Earth? And . . . was this even Earth?

At first her surroundings appeared to be a giant field of jellyfish. Another look revealed something much more peculiar. As far as she could see grew a field of transparent flowers with long, skinny petals. There was no wind, yet the petals waved slowly, reflecting sunlight off their liquid-like surfaces.

Nicole backed up. Fast. Her feet trampled a flattened path through the flowers until she brushed against something warm. She yelled, whirled, and froze.

Resting lightly on a bent stalk, its wings folded peacefully together, was the ugly bird.

Nicole lunged and thrashed a fist. The bird hopped sideways to another stalk and flared its grotesque wings. The movement dislodged more red feathers, leaving its wings completely bare.

"What've you done?" Nicole shrieked. Noticing a jagged stone lying nearby, she snatched it up and brandished it threateningly. "Where am I?"

The bird cocked its head almost thoughtfully. Then it burst into a soft, mystical song that seemed to flood the air with warmth. Its wings began to glow, and a hazy wave of fog wafted through the air, enveloping the bird in a swirl of crimson light. In incredulous disbelief, Nicole watched the fog lift on a transformed, red-gold creature that could only have been one thing.

A phoenix.

Lifting its magnificent, crested head high, the bird chirped and jumped to the ground, scarlet tail feathers trailing. Nicole stumbled backwards over her own feet and fell, cringing as the sharp rock bit into her palm. Throwing the stone aside, she clutched her fingers over the bloody gash, but a warm weight on her lap distracted her from the pain. The phoenix stared at her with strangely shining eyes that seemed to mesmerize her with their purity and power. Shaking violently, Nicole broke the spell by tearing her gaze away and shoved the bird off her lap.

Fluttering its now-beautiful wings, the phoenix brushed her hand with its feathers and she felt warmth seep into her skin. Nicole glanced at her palm and nearly cried out in shock—the blood was gone, and the cuts were healed over with fresh skin.

"Thanks," she said quickly.

The phoenix moved closer, absorbing her in its gaze. Then it spread its crimson wings, glided over several feet, and picked at something in the flowers. Nicole craned her neck to see, but before she noticed anything the phoenix was beside her once more, clutching the pocket watch in its beak.

"Y-you want it?" Nicole stuttered.

The bird dropped the watch at her feet.

"M-me? You w-want me to have it?" she stammered.

The phoenix dipped its head. After a moment it lifted into the sky, appearing as a brilliant flame against the blue. Piping strange music, it vanished into the distance.

Nicole was left alone, staring in amazement. She didn't know why the watch was important, but she jammed it into her jean pocket nonetheless. There would be time to worry about that later. Right now the phoenix's warmth was ebbing, and fear rose to seize her once more. Nicole still had no idea where she was, and now she dreaded what other creatures would be on the prowl, despite the kindness of the phoenix. Her eyes shot around for a place to hide, but all she saw were the flowers and the majestic sky.

Fluffed, silver-tinged clouds straddled a sapphire sky streaked with lilac. Like liquid metal, the clouds lazily trickled past two amber spheres hunched against the horizon. The twin suns' radiance blanketed the field. Nicole squinted, forced to shade her face against the intensity of light reflecting from the flowers. Hovering in the far distance where earth met sky, she made out a wisp of darkness. But it was too far away to see clearly.

Nicole stood shakily. The flowers around her waved peacefully, seemingly beckoning. Though still fearful, curiosity welled, and she touched the nearest flower. Like watery mist, the cool, damp petals curled around her fingers. She jerked her hand away. But the flowers were awfully beautiful. Nicole had to pick one. Just one. With a hard tug, she ripped a flower free.

The flower morphed into water in her hand and spilled through her fingers. Its liquid center hardened into a mirror, and Nicole only just snatched it out of the air before it broke against the ground. At first the mirror seemed to simply show normal reflections. Nicole twisted her face into a funny grimace, but the mirror didn't reflect it. Instead, the image changed to before she picked the flower, and she saw herself walking backwards. The phoenix glided back to its perch, healed her hand, and transformed into the ugly bird. Image by image, Nicole witnessed her own sudden appearance. The mirror was like a movie in reverse—an inverted record of time. It would have probably showed more but, overcome by fear, she smashed it against the ground. It melted away into water and seeped into the dirt.

Sheer terror bound Nicole till she could barely breathe. Her feet drifted and she went along with them, crushing flowers in her way. They burst into a liquid form and soaked her pants, shoes, and feet. The watch pressed and rubbed against her leg, but Nicole didn't mind. She might need the device—

or whatever it was—later. Because whatever was to come, she was almost certain she was no longer on Earth. She knew, too, that if the watch could transport her far from home, it could take her back. Somehow. Someway.

* * *

Night stalked silently over the field. Gasping, Nicole collapsed to her knees in exhaustion, unable to continue the trek. Hunger clawed at her belly, and her body felt hot and taut from strain. She had walked all day, but there was no break or end to the flowers. Nicole began to wonder if this whole world was composed only of them. They crumpled beneath her as she lay down to rest, but for the first time that day she was glad to be drenched by cool water.

A flurry of thoughts swept through her head. Adventure, mystery, and excitement lurked in this new world. Nicole shuddered nervously. But how could she handle danger? What about worse things?

Oh, great. Only now did Nicole remember her parents. *I've got to get home soon or Mom and Dad will freak out! They'll probably think I ran away, and I've got no way to tell them where I am.* She broke down, and her hot tears trenched the ground. Her parents would call the police and everything, but the search would be hopeless. She'd be stuck here on this desolate planet with nothing but the stupid watch that got her into this mess.

When Nicole calmed down at last, she rolled onto her back and stared up at the cold, lonely stars, feeling sleep edging on. For now, there seemed to be no way back. She was stranded out here—wherever 'here' was. Yet despite it all, a simple stroll turned into a breathtaking journey had always been Nicole's dream. If this was what it seemed to be, maybe things wouldn't be so bad after all.

Maybe.

Because somehow, as Nicole's eyelids drooped, she had a strange suspicion that there was someone, or something, waiting nearby and just out of sight. The very rustling of the petals prickled the hairs on the back of her neck. Forcing her eyes closed, she lay trembling in the flowers in the darkness and wondered if she was safe.

Or, at the very least, alone.

Chapter Three

The River

The forest echoed with hushed rustles as creatures began to stir for morning. Ancient trees with massive trunks and looming branches leaned across the sky, heavily laden with leaves and blossoms that spilled onto the earth. Vines twisted intricately in the canopy, obscuring the sky, filtering wisps of light. It was cold in the understory, and damp. Beads of dew quivered on the outstretched tips of leaves and fronds. Even the dirt was moist. Patches of the forest had gone years without light. Some of deepest layers would never see the sun.

It was to this world that Nicole awoke.

Her first reaction was a terrified jolt to a sitting position. Strings of meandering thoughts raced madly through her mind. First there was the phoenix, then the flowers, and the field, and night, and now . . . now . . .

Nicole leaned back to the ground. Her eyelids felt heavy, almost swollen. Numb fingers clumped wet soil. Stiff muscles complained at the thought of movement, but hunger and thirst forced her clammy body to sit again. She couldn't think of a single rational reason regarding how she had suddenly appeared in a forest so different from the flowers of last night, so she contented herself with a dazed glance at her surroundings.

The air was thick with moisture. And cold. Shivering, Nicole watched her breath form mist. Gradually, her ears caught the sound of water breaking over stone. She rose, hugging the sodden jacket closer to her body. Following the distant murmur, she slipped through the undergrowth, leaping over fallen branches, thickets of brambles, and dense clumps of some strange plant with long, tentacle-like leaves that smelled rather like honey. The rushing of water was louder now. Nicole ran ahead, slowing to a steady jog when the walls of trees thinned. Skirting a final layer of squatting bushes, she scrambled down a gentle slope to a river's sandy banks.

It was no mere trickle; the river was at least two, three hundred feet across. The current was swift, and the surface crested with whitecaps. Birds—bird-like creatures, anyway— flew low over the water, hopping between leaning trees, looking for a meal. They called to each other, their sharp shrieks rising above the river's roar. A number of large, angular rocks stretched from shore to shore. Nicole tested the nearest one with her foot, leaning her weight against it. The stone held firm.

The first thing she did was lap water from the river, scooping it up in her hands as a makeshift cup. It wasn't as good as diet soda, but it would have to do. Thirst satisfied, she focused on the beast of hunger growling in her empty pit of a stomach. Luckily, the opposite shore looked promising. There were several fruiting trees just within reach of the river's edge.

Nicole could eat, and then figure out what in the world had happened in the night to transport her to the forest. In her current state, it was hard even to concentrate.

However, getting food would mean crossing the river. It was not a trial she was eager to face. Only a snarl of her stomach convinced her to attempt the inevitable.

Nicole stretched her body over the water, scrambling onto the first rock. One down, a bunch to go. She leapt onto rock number two. And to think, just last week she'd been flipping through pages of school finals, chewing eraser tips. Number three cleared, on to number four. Her stomach grumbled weakly in encouragement.

Nothing much went wrong for the first half of the journey. She nearly slipped once. One of her sneakers was soaked through, but it would dry. Crawling onto the next rock, Nicole thought of the cinnamon raisin bagel she'd had for breakfast the morning she'd found the pocket watch. The heat had made her sick after just a few bites, so the trash got the rest. She'd give anything for just a couple of crumbs now.

Water splashed along the bank she had left minutes ago. Nicole twisted on all fours, clutching the rock, waddling around to face the receding shore. Sure, it was a river. Of course there were snakes and alligators—their alien counterparts, at any rate—and who knows what else lurking around in the depths. She'd simply been hoping they'd leave her alone. The wildlife seemed to have other plans.

Something pale blue slid beneath the river from the far shore and vanished. Nicole squinted into the rushing current, but frothing waves obscured what lay below. Her knuckles turned white squeezing the rock, and her body rocked precariously. If there was something dangerous down there, she had no way of knowing. Deciding not to hang around and find out, she wobbled around to face the next rock.

The water beside Nicole suddenly boiled up. A rushing wave smashed her into the river. She flailed her arms, barely managing to cling to a stone to avoid being swept away. Spitting water, she screamed as four slanted, amber eyes glared at her across the rock, two on each side of a long, pale blue crooked snout. A gleaming mouth hovered inches from her face. White, jagged fangs curved out from massive jaws, snapping for a taste of flesh. Two powerful flippers, spiked with thorny spines, balanced the creature against the outcropping.

The beast lunged. Nicole's fingers lost their hold as the creature barreled into her, flinging her into the torrent. They broke apart as Nicole went under, breathing water. She felt the slinky body coil against her legs and kicked off from it, breaking the surface. Managing a snatch of air, she was pulled below again, whirled sideways and deeper in. Nicole struck out to reach the surface, only to go farther down. The pressure was threatening to break her body and crack her spine. The current carried her away at its will. Her body felt lighter now. Her efforts at surfacing weakened. Water filled her lungs.

Cold air suddenly seared Nicole's face. A violent surge had forced her back to the surface. Fighting against seductive visions, she beat the water, searching for refuge from the roaring spray. Roaring, and much louder than before. Swiveling in the rapids, Nicole strained to see downriver. The water ahead rushed faster, faster, and all of a sudden was cut off. A waterfall—and there was nothing between her and the abyss.

The shores had retreated towards the forest, meeting the water at sharp angles Nicole would never be able to climb. The plunge was nearing with no chance of escape. Paddling against the current, she saw the water churn several yards away. A crested back seethed out of the river, sinking again into the depths. She wondered which would reach her first—the predator or the plummet.

Something smashed into the water beside her and snatched her at the waist, twirling her away from the beast. Nicole was half unconscious now, fighting just to stay afloat. She had little strength to understand what happened next. All she knew was that suddenly the water was dyed crimson, and then the deafening snarl of the waterfall fell away. Snapping rows of fangs clipped the water beside her, but following another surge of blood the beast drew back. The small cliff guarding the safe haven of shore was nearing. Nicole almost felt herself float over the top, though in a brief moment of sharp awareness she realized she was being dragged. Then her body met soil. Nicole didn't dare breathe.

She rolled over, chest heaving, crushing a patch of fern-like growth. Coughing up at least a lungful of water, she clutched at clumps of grass, afraid to let go, wondering if the last few minutes had been real. Trying to sit up right away was a bad idea. Her head reeled and throbbed, and Nicole began to vomit. When her stomach was finally empty, she fell back to the ground and scraped her weary body along the earth towards the shelter of nearby trees. A series of scarlet drips, bloody splashes, and torn strands of dark russet fur marked the trail. Her rescuer, whoever it had been, must have been hurt. How seriously, she couldn't tell.

With the cold shade of the forest blanketing her face, Nicole finally rested. As she slipped in and out of delusions, the world swirled in a mirage before her. Tired and exhausted, she at last gave in, filling her mind with dreams and drifting away to sleep.

Nicole woke up on her side, covered in blood, wet, dazed but alive, and suddenly aware that it was raining. Leaves stirred in soft rustles from the pulse of the storm. The river threatened to break its banks. She shook her head clear and stood unsteadily, still working out the details of the last few hours. Looking skyward, Nicole realized it had been longer than that. The twin suns were beginning to sink beyond the distant treetops. The river grew dark, and in the dusk creatures prepared themselves for the night. Retreating into the shelter of the forest, Nicole examined the damage. Her clothes were damp, but quickly drying. There was blood, but it was not hers.

She didn't like the idea of bedding down in a mysterious and most likely dangerous forest in the dark. Yet the trees held promise, with low-hanging branches in vast abundance. Hope for safety was greater the higher up she could get. Nicole thought so, anyway. Who knew what secrets this wayward world concealed?

As the amber light of the suns finally flickered out, she groped about among the high limbs of a tree leaning away from the river. There were several large fruits dangling from the branches, and these she picked and ate with great gusto. Warm, sweet juices trickled down her chin. It wasn't much, but at least her hunger and thirst temporarily abated. Nicole's famished stomach reveled in the meal, sucking every ounce of nutrition from the meager feast.

Wedging herself between two forked boughs, she sat awake for a long time, watching the rain, hearing the river, recalling what had been, thinking of what could have been.

Chapter Four

Lily

The brief storm had subsided by next morning. Only a few occasional drops still broke through the canopy through the night, and by dawn the rain was entirely beaten out. Clouds flitted across the sky, light and airy. The banks of the river were littered with leaves, twigs, and other debris. The air remained cold and damp.

Nicole stretched her body out and climbed down from the tree, glad that the night had passed uneventfully. Breakfast was a few more fruits and rainwater collected in the wide, bowl-like leaves of some low-lying bushes. Now, however, she was at a loss for what to do. This side of the forest looked exactly like the other. She was still lost, confused, and scared. And it didn't look like she was an inch closer to home.

Squatting in the shade of the trees, Nicole pulled out the pocket watch. It was so tempting to just throw it away into the river. But reminders of the misery it had brought were all around in the trees and grass and the waterfall murmuring somewhere in the distance. It was easy to close her eyes, think of home, pretend that nothing had ever happened. Too bad reality got in the way.

Lily

A burst of noise from the undergrowth startled Nicole into flight. She sprang towards the river, grinding to a halt on the balls of her feet. Stuffing the watch into her pocket, she steadied herself against the edge of the bank. No need to get wet again, or face the river creatures. Although maybe she'd prefer that to facing whatever was lurking in the thick forest growth.

The leaves nearest the ground swayed but quickly rustled back into place. Something was crawling along the bushes. Nicole snatched a glance along the length of the river. To the left lay the falls and rapids; to the right, sandy banks bordering water. She had just starting to plan an escape when she noticed the movements had gone. Was it safe? Silently, she crept forward to investigate.

The creature exploded from the shrubs, colliding with Nicole head-on. She bolted, not caring to look back. The open territory of the river flashed alongside her. Sand scattered at her feet, spraying in waves. She cleared a boulder in a single bound, skipped over a ditch, and then caught her foot on a fallen log as she tried to leap over it. Smashing into the ground, Nicole kicked at the tree to free herself, crying out as a spasm of pain rocked her leg. Wriggling her foot free, she felt for injuries. The throbbing of her ankle convinced her that it was sprained. Perfect. Just her luck.

Then Nicole realized she was being watched. A little purple-furred creature, the most peculiar she had ever seen, had found a perch atop the log. Large feet, tipped with tiny, milk-white claws, and fluffy tail dangling over the side, the alien cocked its large head and blinked enormous eyes. The round orbs were bright and misty, giving the creature a perpetually dreamy gaze. It swiveled its ears and squeaked musically.

Nicole pushed away from the log and tried to stand on her good leg. The balancing act failed, and she wobbled sideways and tumbled to the ground. The little alien squeaked again.

Are you laughing at me? Venting pent-up anger, Nicole scraped her way to the log, flailed her hands, and screamed, "Get out of here, will you?"

The creature flipped backward and remained somehow suspended in the air, even though it had no visible wings. Its eyes held fear and wonder. Nicole hissed air between her teeth again. Nothing was going her way.

"Hey, I'm sorry," she called out, knowing the alien wouldn't understand. "Come down, please. I won't hurt you." To make her point, she took out a fruit she'd been saving for later from her pocket and held out a friendly arm. A universal peace offering, she hoped.

Floating down slowly, the creature landed on Nicole's outstretched arm, standing upright. It took the fruit and nibbled cautiously, then bit with obvious delight into the snack. It stood no taller than a foot, plus or minus a few inches, and Nicole couldn't help but smile. "See, I'm not so bad."

"So you're from outer space, right? I hear the weather's choice. In some parts, at least."

She retracted her arm viciously, flinging the alien skyward, limping backward and terrified. It talked. The creature talked. In English, of all languages. How?

Levitating in midair, the alien finished off the rest of the fruit. "Got more?" it mumbled through a mouthful. Its voice was light and airy—a female's—but tinged with playful mischief.

"Y-you know my language?" Nicole stuttered.

"*All* languages. It's a gift. Of tongues. But you're from Earth, right? I've studied about aliens like you—humans, yeah?—and you're fascinating. Slow, and delicate, but interesting."

Study? *Humans?* Nicole only gaped in astonishment.

"Hello? Any of this getting through?"

"Wh-where am I?"

"Little place called Lunara, fourth planet from the Solea suns, and that's the Sepra River. Oh, and my name's Lily Solaria. Who're you?"

"Nicole."

"Nicole?"

"Nicole Sky."

Lily's smile widened. "Nicole, huh. I've heard your name somewhere. Can't place it though. Me, always been fascinated with names. Yours means something special, did you know?"

"I know what it means, but I don't think it's anything too special. It's a Greek name that means 'victory of the people' back on Earth."

"Greek?"

"They're a kind of Earth people."

"You mean there're different species of humans?"

"Not species, exactly, but sure. All sorts."

"Wow."

Nicole was starting to warm up to Lily. "I can tell you a lot about Earth if you want."

And then she caught herself. *Tell you about Earth.*

It was finally starting to register. She was on some place called Lunara. Not Earth. Her home could be light years away. Was this planet still even in the Milky Way, or was she halfway across the universe? It was a terrible thought, but worse was the fact that she might never get home and see her family and friends again. Lily, in the meantime was sitting upside-down in midair, watching Nicole think. Seeing the alien stare curiously, Nicole got a brilliant idea.

"Listen, Lily. This planet's great and everything, but I'm here by mistake. I need to get home soon, but I don't how. Do know a way back to Earth?"

Lily flipped over and shook her head. "No, sorry. Me, I've never even been off this world."

"But you said you've studied humans. Where did you learn?"

"From my parents. My adoptive parents."

"Oh." Not wanting to pry, Nicole tried to change the subject, but Lily guessed her unasked question.

"Don't worry, it's okay to ask. I never knew my real parents. They vanished one day. When I was really, really little. But my foster family couldn't care less about me, so we severed ties as soon as I was old enough to go out on my own. I don't have anyone now, really. I'm an orphan of the universe, I guess." All this Lily said matter-of-factly, as if it were something she'd long come to terms with.

"An orphan of the universe? What do you mean by that?"

"I've never known anything about my family or who I really am. Don't even know my real name. Lily was my own choice. My foster parents didn't care. They never cared, long as I didn't go off somewhere too crazy. But I've never met anyone the same species as me, so I don't even know what we're called. I don't even know if this is my home world."

Feeling miserable for the little orphan's plight, Nicole lifted her arm again. "I'm sorry, both for your family and for how mean I've been." Being an orphan was bad enough. But an orphan with no past?

Lily levitated over, ignoring the waiting arm and touching down on Nicole's shoulder. Oddly, the new weight felt comforting. Lily dangled her tail around Nicole's neck, kicking out her large feet. Then, suddenly, her face bloomed into excitement. "Maybe I don't know a way back to Earth," she said, "but that's not to say we can't find one. Me, I've always had a dream—a crazy one, sure, but a dream—to go on some wild, daredevil adventure to the distant reaches of the galaxy. And with a human! It'll be amazing!"

"You mean that?" Nicole said in awe. "You'll help me?"

"Yep."

"Really?"

"Really, really."

"But why? I'm just some stranger who showed up on your . . . doorstep, I guess."

"Me, I'm enthralled by names. And yours means something special, like I said. I'd like to see what kind of victory you're going to bring to your people. Not to mention we can have fun along the way. And me, I love fun. And you'll have time to tell me about all your Earth things."

"Well . . . thanks. I owe you one."

Lily giggled. "You're silly. Our adventure will more than make up that debt. For now, though, you hungry?"

"Sure. I mean, yeah, I am."

"Me, I'm starved. Let's get out of here and find some fruit. I know the choice groves!"

Lily made a flying dash for the forest and Nicole thoughtlessly gave chase, suddenly crying out and falling to her knees. The sprained ankle. She'd forgotten. Lily hovered over her with obvious curiosity. "You okay?"

"Yeah, fine. Just great."

Her new friend caught the sarcasm. "If you're hurt—"

"No, I just need something to lean on. A stick, something like that."

"I'll find one. Stay here." Lily zipped off into the woods.

"Hey, don't worry. I'll be right here. No way am I going anywhere."

Nicole leaned back, plopping down with a firm thud. Yawning, she stretched out her legs, wincing when the ankle wobbled slightly. The river bubbled behind her, splashing over stone and sand. She poked at a patch of grass, young, springy, and fresh from the recent rains. And so different from the hot nightmare of Earth. The bushes at the edge of the forest rustled, and Nicole glanced up lazily. "Found a good one?" she called out. Lily didn't reply. Assuming, of course, that it *was* Lily.

Suddenly Nicole was alert, struggling to her feet. If it wasn't her new friend that was lurking about, she was in a bad spot. Defending herself would have been hard enough at prime condition. A sprained ankle increased the difficulty ten-fold. Anything more than hobbling was painful. Running was out of the question. A sprint to safety? Maybe in her dreams.

Something flew out from the bushes, landing at Nicole's feet. She leapt back and crumpled to the ground, inches from the object. The rustling stopped, so she leaned closer to take a look. What lay before her was a tiny bundle made of leaves just small enough to fit in her palm. Nicole picked up the leaves and they fell apart in her hand, revealing a scoop of shimmering blue powder. Confused but curious, she rubbed a little between her fingers. "Lily, what's this?" she shouted. But still her friend was silent.

Wondering if it was meant for her ankle, Nicole rubbed some over the injury. Her skin glowed cerulean as the powder seeped into her flesh, warming her leg as it did. And then—magic. There wasn't another word to describe what happened next. As the glow faded, so did the pain. And the sprain. Leaning on her ankle, Nicole realized it was healed.

Lily rocketed out of the trees. Clasped tightly in her paws was a long, sturdy branch.

"Wow, Lily," Nicole called, seeing her friend. "Thanks. The pain—it's gone! My ankle's fine."

"Me?" Lily replied, stopping short. "I didn't do that."

"I mean your powder."

"What powder?"

They exchanged confused glances. Both turned to look at the forest. But everything lay still and quiet. No sign of anyone.

"Let's just go," Nicole said. She felt thoroughly spooked, and based on Lily's face, her friend was no less frightened.

They began their trek through the forest, Nicole stumbling and picking a path behind Lily. After a few moments of silent pondering, Lily burst out, "So where do you think the powder came from?"

"I don't know," Nicole admitted. "But I'm not sure I want to know. I've got bigger problems to worry about."

Lily nodded. "Like getting home?"

"Yeah."

"Me, I don't get it. How did you end up here, anyway?"

Nicole laughed halfheartedly. "Would you believe me if I said magic?" As proof, she took out the pocket watch.

"Wow!" Lily exclaimed. "What is it?"

"That's just it. I'm not sure. Whatever it is, this is what's responsible for sending me out here."

"Wow," Lily repeated, and then they lapsed into silence.

Nicole stored the watch away and let her thoughts drift. She wondered about her apparently inexplicable appearance in the forest. And about the blue powder. And about the mysterious rescuer who had saved her from the river beast (a creature Lily identified as a Klith) and the waterfall. Someone was watching out for her. But who?

And why?

He leaned out over the forest, easily balancing on a branch some thirty feet from the ground—not, of course, that he particularly enjoyed dangling from trees. Not these stubby ones, anyway. The tallest ones in this forest were maybe . . . *maybe* . . . three hundred feet high. He spat. A fool's challenge. But for now, this was the best way to follow the Earth child and her friend, who were both proving difficult to manage. Especially Nicole. She seemed to have a knack for putting her life in peril.

The otter-like creature grimaced as a pulse of blood trickled down his left arm. Klith bites—nasty business. Slow to heal, tough to stem. He glanced at the leather belt encircling his waist and pulled out a small pouch. A sprinkle of blue powder acted as a pain killer. Of course, he could probably have healed the same wound with a slightly larger dose. But the fugitive wanted a reminder of how dangerous impulses could be.

Granted, it wasn't like he'd had any other choice. Only he hadn't wanted to intervene so early. It wasn't time just yet. He released a hiss of breath. But he couldn't have left her in the open field at night. The night creatures that prowled those parts left nothing more than gnawed bones when they were through. As for the Klith, he had waited until the last second, pulling her from the sheer jaws of death.

The powder had been a mistake. A sprained ankle wasn't worth raising suspicion. But he just felt sorry for her, somehow. She was an innocent—so far. And it was the least he could do.

A fluttered of crimson wings signaled an arrival. He glanced at the shining, red-gold phoenix, Kyria, as she alighted on the branch beside him. She avoided him as he reached to stroke her. It was a test. For as long as he'd known her, Kyria had willfully accepted the touch of only one creature, her chosen owner, a man who'd raised her from an egg. For him she would sacrifice anything, as he would for her.

Chapter Four

The fugitive pulled back into the shelter of dense growth when Nicole and Lily passed beneath the tree. As Nicole went by, she suddenly stopped and glanced up. She seemed to look directly at him for a few seconds. He didn't budge, and she looked innocently away. As Nicole and Lily moved away, he tracked them silently through the trees, wondering if her glance had been accidental or if she had somehow sensed someone was there.

Kyria crooned to remind him of her presence. He whispered a request for her to fly ahead and scout the area. Night was coming, and it was essential that Nicole and Lily find a safe place to rest, even if he had to somehow show them the way.

Almost time, he thought as the phoenix soared away.

Almost.

Chapter Five

The Various Doohickey Place

They'd found a good place to stay until morning. A safe place, anyway. Nicole didn't like the thought of clambering up into trees, balancing between branches dangling half a dozen yards up in the air, and avoiding a fatal plummet for the second night running, but Lily promised that it was the safest option. And since getting mauled and devoured wasn't anywhere near the top of Nicole's to-do list, she reluctantly agreed. Sleep came quickly, and Nicole dreamed of the strange varieties of fruits Lily had gathered for them that day. The dream was silly, but she woke up refreshed, ready for a new start.

After a quick breakfast of more fruits and some tart orange berries, they trekked about half a mile to the edge of the forest according to some plan of Lily's. They started late and the going was slow, and as far as Nicole could tell it was about noon when they first caught sight of the sky and the suns through the thinning trees. Another hour brought them to the boundary where trees met grass, long, swaying, and brown-

33

yellow. Here they stopped, deliberating.

"Me, I think our best bet would be to cross over," Lily reasoned. "Beyond the plain's a wasteland, but we make it past that and we come out on some big cities. Someone there can get you home."

Nicole wasn't as confident. "You're sure about the cities?"

"Yep!"

"And you know where to go?"

"Sure. Now come on!"

"It's just, I . . . well, see—"

But Lily was long gone, flipping aerial cartwheels and humming a cheerful alien melody. Nicole followed halfheartedly. She was glad they finally had some sort of heading but worried about leaving the shelter of the forest. Prairies didn't lend themselves to protection if anything happened. Just the thought terrified her.

Not wanting to get left behind, Nicole chased after her friend. She soon caught up, and Lily bounced onto Nicole's shoulder. The tall grass waved playfully around them, a monotonous landscape of amber and copper stretching to the blue horizon.

The tranquil scene was not to last. Thick clouds, heavy with the threat of thunder, formed by the horizon and stalked across the plain. The storm swelled quickly. Lightning sizzled, matched by great claps of thunder. Gusty wind flattened the grass. The very air seemed heavy with dread.

"What's happening?" Nicole yelled over the howling wind and the roaring thunder. "I've never seen a storm come up so fast!"

"Looks bad!" Lily shrieked back.

"See, I knew going was a bad idea! We should've stayed in the forest!"

"Should have spoken up, then! We're stuck now! You—"

"Okay, fine, you're right, whatever! It's no time to argue. We need shelter, now!"

"But where—"

Lily broke off, wide eyes revealing she was frozen by fear. The dark clouds formed a funnel that reached down from the pitch-black clouds and tore at the wildly writhing grass. A second later it spun and roared across the plain in a wild fury.

"Twister!" Nicole screamed, breaking into a sprint. Lily gripped her shoulder, struggling to hang on. The frenzied winds sucked at them. Lily's terrified screams pierced the air. Cold and desperate, pummeled by wind and darkness, Nicole collapsed, clutching at the alien. She tore at the ground to stop them both from being pulled away. But it was hopeless, and she knew it.

A flash of scarlet amid the chaos drew Nicole's attention. Soft, echoing music flooded her ears. The sound gave her strength. Forcing herself to stand, she stumbled forward.

Nicole suddenly thought of the golden pocket watch. She snatched it from her pocket. Lightning streaked overhead, its fire reflecting off the gold cover. Nicole felt for the large button on the side. She pushed it and the cover snapped open, all sixteen blue buttons shining. She would push one of the buttons, any one of them. It didn't matter. Nothing and no place could be worse. The tornado was gaining. The sky pressed down upon them.

Chapter Five

Then lightning flashed across the sky, illuminating a single structure for a brief instant, etching it on the horizon. Realizing that the building was their only chance, Nicole jammed the watch into her pocket and broke into a flat-out run, Lily in her arms. The distant, soothing music still resounded in her ears, grower louder as the building loomed closer. As they approached, Nicole saw that the structure was a little stone cottage. She saw Lily's mouth move in a shriek, though the sound was lost in the storm.

Screaming winds and freezing rain whipped and tore at her clothes. Pelted by rain, swept by wind, and deafened by thunder, Nicole fought on. Thoughts of shelter, fear of the raging storm, and the echo of the music and the lingering feeling of warmth that came with it kept her moving.

Finally, her weary fingers grasped the doorknob of a massive and ancient wooden door. She wrenched it open with the very last of her strength. The door slammed inwards as she and Lily fell forward onto the floor. Nicole crawled forward, fighting against the sucking winds. But then the door swung shut of its own accord, muffling the sound of the storm behind its thick frame. A bell tinkled softly overhead.

Nicole mopped her dripping face with a sleeve and looked around. Surrounding her was a cozy shop with rows upon rows of goods. Some of the items she recognized, such as the warm-looking blankets and rugs piled high along the walls. Other goods, including a pile of wooden poles riddled with more holes than Swiss cheese heaped by the door, were so bizarre that Nicole couldn't even begin to fathom what they might be used for. The room was spick and span. And crowded. Even the crossbeams overhead were clean and wiped and draped with cloth for sale.

A squat and rather round human-looking woman with overlarge eyes made an appearance from a shadowy corner. Her black-brown hair was pinned up in a neat, fat bun. Voluminous silver robes swallowed her body. She tut-tutted impatiently as the two companions, weary from their narrow escape, rose shakily to their feet. As soon as they were up she ushered them towards the rear of the shop.

A wooden sign dangled at a crooked angle above the counter at the very back. Scrawled on the sign was a short phrase in what appeared to be about a hundred different languages, none of which Nicole recognized. Words written in thin, curvy script were squeezed into every corner, battling for space and crushed into one another.

The woman vanished through a beaded curtain and came back a moment later carrying warm, fluffy towels. Nicole eagerly accepted them, mumbling her thanks.

"Glad we got these!" Lily exclaimed. "It's too cold in here."

"Ah!" the woman said knowingly, rushing behind the curtain again and coming out with a scarlet-feathered quill. "English." Picking her way through mounds of goods, she took down the sign, scratched something in the top right-hand corner, and stuck it back up over the counter. The new phrase read:

The Various Doohickey Place

"Oh, you poor things," she said, setting the quill on the counter. "I can't imagine how you two got caught in that storm, but you can rest here until you feel ready to go. Would you like something to eat?" Without waiting for a reply, she continued, "Yes, of course you would. And you, dear, need a change of clothing. You're dripping wet, and your friend's right. It is freezing here. Wait a moment, please."

"Thanks," Nicole said, though she said it to the air because the woman had already disappeared through the curtain behind the counter. Turning to Lily, she added, "Well, *that* was weird." Staring for a few more seconds, she cracked up with laughter.

"What?" Lily asked, clutching the towel in her small paws.

"Your tail," Nicole choked out.

"What about my . . . eek!"

"Static electricity. Gets me every time, too."

While Lily tried to flatten the poof that was her fluffy tail tip, Nicole looked again around the shop. She was unable to shake a feeling of misgiving about the seemingly kindhearted shopkeeper.

A few minutes later the woman returned with cloth draped over her arm and two bowls of some strange berries glazed with thick syrup. Nicole didn't know what had been prepared for them, but she didn't bother to ask; she was too hungry and exhausted to care. She grabbed the bowls eagerly, thrust one at Lily, and immediately dug in. Her teeth crunched around the small, hard berries that prickled her tongue with a cold sensation like eating ice.

As the woman watched them shovel down the food, she said, "My name is Madam Banda, and I am pleased to be of service." She bowed low and gave her guests an unnerving smile. "And here's a fresh shirt, dear. Wouldn't want you to catch a cold, now would we?" Turning, she walked away and disappeared behind a row of shelves crammed with silverware. Her voice floated to them. "Once you're dry, feel free to look around. Maybe you'll find something interesting. You never know what will turn up around here."

Making sure Lily was busy with her food, Nicole pulled off her soggy jacket and shirt, glad to change into something warm. She pulled on the soft shirt and wrung her jacket till it was nearly dry. Preferring the cold of her own clothing to that of the chilly shop, she slipped back into the jacket.

Slurping up their last bit of food, the companions set about examining the strange shop. Curious objects lined the shelves. Intricate gadgets, funny doodads, fantastic weavings, quilts, clothing, decorations—but nothing that really interested Nicole. They drifted apart, and suddenly Nicole found herself at the back of the shop, staring down into the glass counter. There she saw something dangerously beautiful.

"Hey," Nicole called to Lily. "Check this out."

The display was packed with gems and jewelry, bangles and bracelets, decorated ribbons and rings. Among the tangle lay a single dagger. The silver blade, cleaved at the tip, was double-edged and serrated. The handle, black as night, bore crimson lettering. Through Nicole couldn't quite place it, the language seemed almost familiar.

The weapon was fierce, but tempting. "Madam Banda?" Nicole cried out.

The shopkeeper appeared with a stagger, her arms laden

with cans, canteens, a smooth brown sack, and a handsome leather belt. She dumped the supplies onto the counter. "There, that should be enough. You were saying, dear?"

"That dagger. It's pretty cool."

"This one here?" Madam Banda retrieved it. "Oh, yes, it's a wonder, this little dear. Saved my life once when I wasn't confined to this old cottage. Seen its fair share of adventure even before my time. Little story for you . . . it's been around long enough to have earned itself a name—*Cárine*, which means heart. It's an enchanted dagger and will bring help when you need it most. It can do extraordinary things. Trust me, I know. It was a gift from an old friend. He told me to keep it out of trouble, and I've kept that promise. Mostly," she added with a laugh.

Madam Banda offered forth the dagger. Nicole took it, surprised at how warm the handle felt. It reminded her of the phoenix and its mystical song. The spell was broken when a sack, filled to the brim with provisions, was thrust into her arms. "For the road, dear," the shopkeeper explained. "I see you haven't got any supplies."

"Thanks," Nicole mumbled, "but I don't have money."

"Don't worry, dear. I like to think that kindness always comes back to you. I always help friends in need, especially those like you. You're one of the few humans I've seen since I left home long, long ago."

"You mean . . . you're from Earth?"

"Of course. What did you think?"

"B-but . . . but . . ."

"A tedious story, dear. Too tiresome to waste your time.

You've got quite a job ahead of you, you know."

Nicole felt herself pull a face. "Um . . ."

Madam Banda's mouth wrinkled into a smile of pity. "I'm getting ahead of things. You'll see soon enough."

"Only job I've got," Nicole said, "is getting home. Speaking of—is there a city nearby? Some sort of town? A village? Anything?"

"I'm afraid not. The fastest way would be to head directly east, but that would lead you right into the Ayédru wasteland. You wouldn't like that, would you?"

"Guess not."

"What I suggest is bearing due south for a day or so before turning east. You'll avoid the wasteland that way."

"Sounds good. Thanks. Er . . . I think this belongs to you." Nicole tried to push the dagger back at Madam Banda, but she wouldn't take it.

"Tosh!" the shopkeeper said. "Though I never thought I'd see the day when I'd give it up, here we are, and now that dagger's yours. It's helped me countless times, and I hope it does the same for you. Take this belt too—there's a nice little loop stitched on where you can hook the dagger when you're not using it."

Nicole bobbed her head breathlessly. "Wow. Thanks!"

The woman smiled kindly and clapped her hands together. "But all those supplies are for later, dear, when you leave. Here . . . we can pile them all up back behind the counter for now. This shop is a refuge for wanderers, and you're welcome to stay here as long as you wish."

"Thank you," Nicole said again, "but I think we'd best go.

I've got to get home soon."

Madam Banda looked stunned. "You're sure? You look so tired, dear. Just a day, maybe?"

"Hey, don't worry," Lily said, jumping into the conversation. "I'll look out for her. Me, I'm tough when I want to be."

"I'm sure you are, but it can be very dangerous on this planet."

Nicole glanced towards the door. "Uh . . . we can handle ourselves, I'm sure."

"Perhaps you'd like some more food?" Madam Banda encouraged. "Actually, I've got a lovely little fireplace in the back—why don't you curl up there in the warmth and stay the night."

There was something very, very strange going on. Nicole wasn't quite sure what, but she wasn't planning on staying long enough to find out. "Thanks," she insisted, "but we really have to go."

But now Lily was hooked on the idea. "But what about the fire?" she groaned. "And the food? We could stay a *little* longer."

"Listen," she warned, "we can't. But thanks anyway."

Madam Banda's face creased in disappointment. "Never a problem, dear. Come back any time if you ever need anything."

Slipping the belt around her waist and clipping on the dagger, Nicole listened for sounds of the storm, but it seemed that the worst had passed. Pulling open the massive door, she peeked outside at a cloud-streaked but peaceful sky. The grass shivered around her as she passed, soaking her jeans and sneakers with raindrops. Lily took her usual place on one shoulder, and Nicole hoisted the sack up over the other. "Thank you again!" she yelled from a distance, waving.

"Goodbye, Nicole and Lily!" the shopkeeper called out. "Have a safe journey! I hope you find your way home soon!"

"Don't worry! We'll stay safe!"

"One more thing!" Madam Banda cried. "You're headed south now. Follow that way for a day or so, but remember to turn east!"

"I will!" Nicole called back and burst into a sprint across the prairie. She hadn't gone far when Lily made her stop.

"Why'd you make us leave? That woman was really friendly."

"Exactly. Wasn't it creepy how much she wanted us to stay? I just really thought something weird was up."

"You're overanalyzing," Lily snapped, but she didn't force Nicole to turn back. In fact, they went a long way before Nicole remembered something else strange.

"Hey, did you notice that she knew our names?"

"So?"

"I'm sure I didn't mention them. Neither did you. So how would she know?"

"Bet you did and forgot. Anyway, what's it matter? Got a journey ahead of us. Me, I think that's what's important."

But no matter what Lily said, Nicole couldn't help but think about the shop. She was certain she hadn't said their names, and besides—why would the woman give free supplies and the dagger she cherished? She felt there was a secret motive behind the shopkeeper's intentions. And no matter how long Nicole assured herself that all was well, she couldn't shake the feeling that their meeting had been very curious indeed.

Madam Banda cursed under her breath. As soon as the companions were gone, she rushed to the back of her shop. She flung aside the beaded curtain, hastening into a dusty room that was quite the opposite of the neat, packed little shop. A thin sheet of dust coated everything. The room was empty except for a low-burning fire, a pile of sticks for kindling, and a window that was slightly ajar to let in air.

The shopkeeper paused, glancing briefly at the curtain. The beads rushed together, clattered, and then were still. She squatted down on the cobblestone floor and fed the flames a few pieces of wood. Then Madam Banda drew out a sack and a metallic device from one of the pockets of her robe. A translator. Sprinkling a pinch of blue powder onto the fire, she fitted the device over her ear. The flames leapt up and turned a brilliant shade of violet. Leaning close to the fire, she hissed, "Rayonk!"

The sound of crackling wood was drowned out by a high-pitched, male voice. "I here."

"Sky's been to my shop. I couldn't stop her from leaving. I thought the twister would frighten her into staying, but I guess maybe I didn't make it strong enough. And there was another mistake . . . I shouldn't have given them supplies straight-off. But what's done is done. Here is what's significant: Sky's set off with her friend Lily. Watch for them. Warn the others. I'll see if we can intercept them while they're still safe. In the meantime, prepare yourself. With luck, she'll be traveling your way soon."

"I hear you loudly and clear. Considers it done! But I still don't know why we needs her help. Plan good before with no Earth girl, and plan still good without her."

"Rayonk," Madam Banda said in exasperation, "you know perfectly well what this girl means to us. What she means to the galaxy!"

"I knows, I knows, but I *still* thinks—"

"Please, Rayonk. We've been through this before. Tibo's never been wrong before. The important thing now is to act quickly. Get everything ready like I told you. If Tibo's right— as he always is—her quest will take her to you."

"Okay, okay. I on it!"

The shopkeeper pinched a bit of purple powder from another sack and threw it into the flames. Devouring the powder, the fire burned red once more. Madam Banda sat next to it for a long time, staring at the heart of the fire, and then called out, "Kyria, thank you for leading the girl. Who knows what would have happened if you hadn't found her."

In a blaze of light the phoenix seemed to materialize upon the windowsill, her red-gold feathers shining in the firelight. Kyria crooned, hopped down onto the floor, and strutted towards the fire. Madam Banda reached out to stroke the phoenix for a job well done, but Kyria evaded the hand, staring instead into the fire and piping a quizzical note.

Laughing, the woman added more blue powder to the fire. "All right, all right—Tibo," she said. "I have to talk to you. It's about Sky."

Chapter Five

The shadows just beneath the cottage window twitched when a creature darker than shade exhaled a soft, silent breath. Glinting, pearly fangs poked out from the beast's ridged jaws. Malicious eyes glazed with death glared from below crested brows. Dark green scales were slick with the rainwater that clung as beads to a black uniform, mark of the Omenra *Emprá*—Empire.

The Omenra soldier's legs ached. His arms felt heavy from remaining still for so long. But he dared not move. The words shared in the cottage, converted to a language he knew via translator, were too essential.

It was about the girl.

When the fire sputtered and the conversation died he moved away, thinking over what had been said. Then he eased a jagged-edged, oval disk from a pack slung across his back and flicked it into a solar-fueled JET Glider. When the Omenra hopped on, steel safety straps automatically locked over his feet. Entering a code into the flashing screen clipped to his wrist, he following its *blip* through the grass on the hovering Glider board.

Omenra General Malkior Taggerath had never been one for patience. This, however, was becoming ridiculous. The spy should be arriving soon . . . in theory. Malkior dug his shoulder blades against a metal edge. That's what you got for not buying the latest Glider models. He glanced back at the streamlined cruiser rearing behind him. Granted, not all old things were bad.

He'd had the *Aphelia* for almost longer than he could re-call, but she was a lethal beauty. The ship was wide, flat, and wired for speed. Her body was fused with narrow, slanted wings and a transparent windscreen which extended from the spiked nose and curved over the cockpit. Malkior absolutely adored her, and even though she was an aged model, she was the best. He would make do with nothing less.

A nearby noise alerted him to another presence. At last the spy had come. Good thing, too. Malkior's claws had started toying with the trigger of the Salvira Sigrá handgun strapped to his hip, hidden beneath his tunic.

The Glider swerved to a halt. Seeming intimidated by the fact that General Taggerath himself had come, the spy hopped down from the JET. He quickly dipped his head, his eyes fearful, yet hopeful. For a second Malkior's claws tightened around the Sigrá. It had been a boring day. Maybe . . .

"Permission to speak?"

Malkior sighed and loosed his grip on the gun—another time, perhaps. "What did you learn?" he snapped.

"General Taggerath, you were right. The girl had been there. It must mean what they say is true."

Malkior grinned. His dagger-like fangs glimmered mali-ciously in the meager light. "True? Perhaps. But the future is not set in stone. Does she have a heading?"

"Circumnavigate the wasteland."

"Then she is not far. Find and kill her. And make certain she is never found. There is enough trouble already. If this is traced to us—"

"Of course, General. I understand."

Chapter Five

"Perfect," Malkior hissed, watching the soldier mount the Glider. "The end is very near."

Chapter Six

Dark Warrior

Lush forest tangles were mere memories to Nicole now, lost somewhere beyond miles of rolling grassland. Following the shopkeeper's advice, Nicole and Lily had trekked south. Impatience had turned them eastward within half a day, each certain that turning a couple of hours early would create little difference to their journey. But the farther they traveled, the rougher the land became. Burning by day, freezing by night, and all the more difficult to find berries, edible roots, and water by the hour. Scrub and cracked earth became the norm. Hoping they hadn't made a terrible mistake by changing course early, Nicole forced them onwards, fighting the temptation to turn back. She wouldn't have them lose another precious day.

But the land was a nightmare—cracked, brutal, and merciless. Withered trees provided no comfort for scorched heads when temperatures spiked. Night brought cold so intense that it might have been warmer in a freezer. Never in all her life on Earth had Nicole been forced into such extremes. Even the dead heat of the summer hadn't been so cruel. Lily didn't seem pleased either, but by the time she forcefully insisted on turning back neither could recall the direction they had come from or which way they were supposed to go.

In the evening of their fourth night they ran out of water. Lily tossed the last empty canteen angrily into the sack. Nicole brushed her tongue—as cracked and parched as the dirt—over dry lips. By the light of the stars she could see a small grove of emaciated trees in the distance.

"Should we head there?" she asked.

"Me, I don't care," Lily sighed.

"Come on, I need your help now. Don't give up on this."

"Me, I'm not giving up! It's just . . . me, I'm tired."

"So should we head for the trees?"

Lily didn't reply.

Nicole made the decision for her, turning for the grove. They could spend the night there and figure out what to do. The situation was critical.

In half an hour they had reached the trees. Lily drifted lazily away, slinging her weary body across the lowest branch. Curling her tail around her tiny frame for warmth, she choked out, "Anything left to drink? Eat?"

Scrabbling around in Madam Banda's sack, Nicole jotted a list. "Couple of salty crackers, a can of food, a few canteens—"

"Full?"

"Empty."

Silence.

"We're in big trouble, Lily. If we don't find water or food tomorrow, then I guess . . ."

Nicole trailed off. Lily shuddered and flipped onto her side, refusing food. Though Nicole realized it would only make her thirstier, she decided to eat alone, tossing the last, licked-out can at a shrunken tree. The hollow echo of metal striking wood gave little satisfaction. Nicole kicked out a place on the rock-hard earth; she finally lay down to what she hoped wouldn't be her last night alive.

The icy steel of a Salvira E70 handgun felt good in the Omenra spy's grip. He inched forward, closer, careful to stay concealed behind the cover of the gaunt trees. The mark was tired, but one could never be too careful. Shoulders hunched, muscular legs bent, he crouched and aimed, ready to shoot to kill. Soon the Earth child would be dead. Then the Omenra would be free to lay claim to the galaxy.

The gun's shiny barrel, newly polished, glistened against the night. He drew his claw around the trigger, squinted into the clearing, waiting for a perfect shot. Then he was locked on—the girl, an open target, lying in the dust.

The trigger hardly creaked as he pulled it back.

The Earth girl was driving him crazy. And they hadn't even met yet.

The fugitive had almost lost her scent when she randomly turned the wrong way, despite Madam Banda's careful instructions. Lily hadn't stopped her, so off they'd gone, traipsing around a deadly wasteland. Ill-prepared, on top of everything. If it had been up to him, he would have left her there. Both of them. But no. He followed her out into the middle of nowhere. Good thing, though. If Nicole had seen some of the creatures that lurked around in the night, she would have fainted on the spot. And there had been quite a few. Hungry ones, too. His Mar blaster still bore the scars.

He waited until the two had settled down for sleep before edging towards the trees. It was finally time. But then, just as he was about to approach, he noticed a dense shadow concealed behind a pair of leaning trees. The flash of a gun gave away the second alien's intent. Knowing he had to act fast, he expertly drew his Mar, raised it and, barely taking aim, fired.

Nicole rolled onto her side, toying with the dagger. Sleep was out of the question. Tomorrow's prospect wasn't just bleak. It was terrifying. They were out of water. Out of food. They wouldn't last another day. Short of a miracle, she wasn't sure how they would survive.

Suddenly an electric-blue blast flared over her head. It burst against a nearby tree, burning a gaping hole. Nicole shrieked and spun sideways, dropping the dagger, trying to get out of the line of fire. Woken by the noise, Lily glanced up sleepily from her branch and yawned. "What happened?" she mumbled, but a moment later her voice broke into a scream as Nicole snatched her up and fled behind a tree.

"What's going on?" Lily cried.

Before Nicole could answer, a creature lunged towards them out of nowhere, a large, sleek weapon gripped tightly in his claws. He snorted, bared long, pointed fangs in a menacing grin, and aimed the gun straight at Nicole.

An explosive blast from behind stunned the creature. The

shot seared into his chest. The alien dropped his gun and staggered, struggling to breathe. Nicole squealed as he collapsed to his knees, blood flooding over his clawed hands. He fell forward, black uniform drenched with crimson, convulsing in pain.

A nearby crackle of branches caused Nicole to whirl around, just in time to see someone else leap out from behind a tree. Her first impression was of a tall, upright otter. He adjusted his grip on a silver handgun, well-sharpened claws tight around the trigger.

The otter-like creature curiously cocked his head. Nicole retreated fearfully, but he followed, footfalls silent. Suddenly, claws snatched her ankle, and she tripped backwards, dropping Lily as she collapsed to the dirt. Finding herself staring into the cold eyes of the dying creature, Nicole shrieked as the alien reached for his gun. A lightning flash of motion from her right was followed by another slight scream. Nicole's would-be killer gave a puzzled cough as he slumped over backwards, a knife buried in his throat up to its black handle.

The sickly stench of blood forced Nicole to her feet. Struggling against nausea, she purged her lungs clean with fresh air, clinging to a twisted tree for support. As she fought for breath, her eyes warily tracked the otter, but he ignored her, focusing on the dead creature.

"You were lucky," he muttered, drawing out his knife with a wet slash. He cleaned the bloodied blade on the alien's black uniform and slid the dagger back into his belt. Picking up the creature's fallen gun, he added, "Salvira E70. Nasty handgun. He meant serious business."

It was several seconds before Nicole realized the otter was speaking English. "How——" she started to ask, but he cut her off with a snarl, flailing his left arm. Nicole glimpsed Lily sink her tiny, milk-white teeth into his fur. He cried out and flung Lily away. She flipped over in the air and bared her teeth, stained red with his blood.

"You leave us alone! Got it?" Lily snapped, a soft growl rolling up in her throat.

The otter narrowed his eyes with humor. "Such kind words for your savior."

"Savior!" Lily spat. "Me, I saw you pull that gun on my friend! You'd have killed her if that thing hadn't dragged her down."

"Had you paid attention, you would have seen it was 'that thing' I was aiming for. I am here to help you, not hurt you."

"Right," Nicole muttered. With a flick of her head, she motioned for Lily to back down.

Leaving the otter behind, Nicole returned to the clearing, Lily perched on her shoulder. Their 'savior' seemed to be trust-worthy enough, but something about him seemed dangerous. She didn't like how viciously he'd killed that other alien. Sav-ior or not, the otter should have thrown the dagger to begin with. Instead he's cruelly let the creature suffer and bleed his life out after the handgun blast.

A loud crack split the silence. Nicole whirled around, only to see the otter-like alien snapping several twigs from the dried trees. She moved away, but he seemed to have completely for-gotten about them and was instead intent on picking out the choice branches. When he'd gathered an armful, he knelt on the ground and piled the wood together. Selecting two of the sturdier branches, he twirled them together expertly until a glowing ember sparked at the heart of the pile. The wood burst into flames, crackling with heat.

Holstering his gun, he sprawled out next to the fire. Nicole now noticed his slightly torn, dust-brown pants cleaved slightly below the knees and the strap slung over the shoulder, clipped to a broad leather belt.

Nicole was shivering from the cold of the wasteland night, but she'd doubted it was safe to share the warmth. Lily, too, was freezing, her fur erect, tiny teeth chattering.

"Come on," Lily said, "let's go get warm."

"It's not safe."

"Me, I'm too cold to care."

"Listen, he might have saved us or whatever, but that doesn't mean we should randomly trust him."

"Me, I'm not trusting *him*. Just the fire," Lily said matter-of-factly, "to keep me from dying in this cold!"

Tired of arguing, Nicole warily approached.

The otter noticed her coming and sat up. "Come on, don't be scared." Beckoning to the fire with one paw, he added, "I will not hurt you. And you have a cut over your lip, by way. Wash it off before any dirt gets into it. Infected cuts can be dangerous."

Nicole squatted next to the fire, rubbing her hands for warmth. Tasting blood, she wiped the back of her hand over her mouth. Her fingers were stained red. Suddenly, she felt the stranger's presence by her side. "Get away!" Nicole shrieked, kicking out instinctively.

Easily dodging, he held out a funny-shaped bottle. "Sorry. I just thought you were thirsty. And run some of that over your cut. It should help."

Nicole only managed to gawk. She didn't know whether she should thank him or throw the bottle away in case it was poisoned. But most of all, she was curious about who this stranger was, so she kept her silence and drained a few gulps of water. Her body welcomed it like the desert welcomes rain after months of drought. When Nicole had downed her share, she tossed the bottle to Lily and watched her friend take a long drink, finishing off the water.

With her thirst quenched, Nicole turned to the problem at hand. The alien otter seemed okay. Friendly enough, anyway. Even now he watched them calmly, firelight reflected in his deep-brown, almost black eyes.

She examined him more closely now. There was a sort of serene power about him that Nicole couldn't quite associate with anything she had ever known. But there was also an aura of vigilance and menace. And then there was the thing around his neck, a tight necklace of string and twine decorated with six beaded letters that spelled the word *Serena*. She doubted that could be his name. But what did the word mean, then?

He broke the silence first.

"You two okay?"

"Guess," Nicole snapped.

He noticed her dagger lying on the ground nearby. Nicole edged away a little when he picked it up. "You would not be taking that tone if you realized that I just saved both your lives," he said.

"By shooting at us, you mean?" Lily growled.

"By killing the Omenra that was about to murder you both."

At the word 'Omenra', Lily's fur bleached to white. Her body trembled, and she whimpered, "I-I thought th-that was an O-Omenra, but I-I wasn't sure. I can't believe it."

Still staring intently at the dagger, Nicole snapped, "What's an Omenra, if you don't mind me asking?"

"Terrible, horrible, monstrous tyrants," Lily squeaked, trembling paws linked on her lap. "Everyone fears them."

"So what do they want with us?"

Their rescuer turned the dagger over. Handing it back, he said, "Take care of that. You have no idea how helpful it might turn out to be."

Nicole wouldn't be thrown from the subject. "You're not answering my question."

"Anxious, are we? I saved you. Is that not enough for now?"

"Fine, so you saved us. Great. Will you at least tell us why? Who are you, anyway? Are you some kind of mutant otter or something?"

"First, I'm not the mutant. It's your Earth otters that evolved from my race. And second, I understand that you might have general paranoia, but there is no need for it now. I'm the 'good guy,' as you humans say."

Nicole wasn't convinced. "Listen, you've got to understand how I feel. A few days ago something really strange happened and now I'm stuck who knows where with no way of getting home. You're just some random guy who popped up out of absolutely nowhere and apparently 'saved' me from some even weirder guy who was apparently trying to kill me for no reason whatsoever. I'm still working out the details, but basically, I'm not in a mood to trust *anyone* right now, and I'm going to be as paranoid as I want to be until you lay down the line. So, let's start over. My name is Nicole and this is my friend, Lily. Who are you and what exactly do you want?"

"My name," the alien said slowly, "is Diu. And I'm afraid I have very bad news."

"Hey, whatever," Nicole drawled. "I seriously doubt my life could get any worse than it is now, so just lay it on me. What's the so-called bad news?"

"You can't go home, Nicole."

For a moment, she froze. *Home*. He had mentioned home. But something didn't seem quite right.

"Oh, that's not news," Nicole said, faking calmness when truly she was just barely managing to restrain from crying out. "We're probably going to be lost for a while in this wasteland anyway, so I'm in no hurry."

"I mean . . . ever. You can't go home, ever."

"Oh, really? Why's that?"

"Because in one month, your time, there won't be a planet Earth for you to return to. In one month, the Terranova will destroy Earth."

Chapter Seven

The Galactera

The words reached her. They took a long time to process. There was a faint roaring in Nicole's ears, a whisper of wind in the silence, but the meaning was insane. Impossible.

"Less, actually," Diu corrected himself. "Minus about ten Earth days, since that's how long the Terranova has been activated already."

It was too much to take in.

As Diu calmly fed another stick to the fire, Nicole's mind boiled painfully around his words. She would never be able to return home. Ever.

"Nicole," Lily said, but she didn't hear the little alien's words.

"If this is some sort of joke . . . some crazy, stupid joke—" Nicole cried.

"I hardly ever joke, and certainly not now."

His meaning was beginning to really hit home. Still, it was only when Nicole had played the words several times over in her head that they finally began to stick. Reality buried into her, piercing her soul.

. . . There won't be a planet Earth for you to return to . . .

Nicole wanted to do something but her body seemed to have shut down. No Mom and Dad, no Lex and Danny, no . . . anything. Her lips moved but no words came out. She couldn't breathe. Couldn't move. "Can't be true," she whispered. "It can't."

"But it is," Diu said. "And, I'm afraid, there is hardly any hope left."

"No hope?" Nicole echoed through tears.

"But that's where I come in. You see, I'm the one they send when there is no hope left. Because I can tell you that there *is* a way to save Earth."

Nicole's heart skipped a beat. "You're sure?"

"I would not be here if there wasn't. I have been following you for days now, but to tell you the truth, I'm surprised you have not figured part of it out on your own yet."

"Which bit?"

"Not so paranoid now, I see?"

"Well you know, if you'd just come quietly instead of bursting in and scaring us out of our wits, maybe we wouldn't have—"

"Distrusted me?" Diu said. "But I figured you would, regardless. I don't exactly look like a rainbow unicorn here to save the day, do I? But getting to the point, you have had both the way home and the key to saving Earth all along. Do you remember how you got here?"

"Sure. I pressed a button on the . . ." Nicole trailed off, suspicious. Instinctively, her hand darted to cover the pocket of her jeans where the gold watch lay.

"Don't worry; I know all about the pocket watch. It is not ordinary, as I am sure you have come to realize. It is a device called the Galactera. It functions as a teleporter."

Nicole thought back to the blue vortex that had transported her to this strange world. "I guess I already knew that," she said. "But, wait. If this is some sort of alien teleporter, how did it ever get to Earth?"

"A long story, but basically—you remember our Omenra friend?"

Nicole shuddered. "Too well."

"His species are the ones behind all this."

"What do you mean?"

Diu suddenly seemed distracted, focusing on one of Lunara's glittering moons over the horizon. "It's late," he announced. "I think you have been overloaded enough for one day. Let's cut the chit-chat for tonight. Tomorrow morning, I will tell you the rest."

But Nicole was eager to hear more. "Just one more secret? Please?" she begged.

"You know you sound like a pestering kid."

"Well, I *am* a kid."

"True. All right, but just one. That Galactera you have there, it's quite special. It actually used to be mine."

"Yours?" Nicole said doubtfully. "Yeah, sure."

"It's a long story—one I will reveal tomorrow—but I lost that watch on Earth."

"If it *is* yours, which I doubt, do you want it back?"

Diu seemed to consider it. At any rate, something strange passed across his face. Then he firmly said, "Keep it. We're going to need it."

"We?"

"Pardon me, but I doubt you would last half a second out there if I just told you what to do and left you alone to do it. Besides, I was sent here to help you."

Nicole nodded weakly. Guessing ahead, she wondered if she was about to take on responsibility for her entire planet and for all the people she loved. It was insane, the whole idea. Could it all be a joke? But the image of the Omenra's gun seemed to be burned into her eyelids, and every time she blinked, it flashed into memory.

What if it was all true? And if so, could she really save Earth? Where would she even start? For lack of anything else to say, she asked, "And just who sent you?"

Diu was about to answer when Lily interrupted the conversation. "Wait, wait, wait. Back up. You said we're going to need the Galactera. What're we going to do? Teleport our way out of this mess?"

"Yes," Diu said simply. Nicole wasn't sure if there was sarcasm in his voice.

"What?!" Lily retorted.

"Tomorrow, I will explain. It's late now and you two need sleep."

Lily growled. "But—"

"There is much to tell, but it must wait. Goodnight to you both. Try to get some sleep, regardless of the situation. You have to be ready for what I have to tell. It is imperative you understand, and quickly."

"Sure," Lily muttered, levitating to the branches again.

Nicole stretched out on the ground, breathing in the cold air. The fire crackled nearby, casting long shadows. Watching Diu lean back against a withered tree, she mumbled, "Hey, um . . . I'm sorry I was so mean before. I was just really scared."

He tilted his head back and looked skywards for a long time. "Don't worry about it. I seem to inspire that feeling." After a silence, he added, "But I will warn you right away that if you plan on surviving for very long, you are going to have to listen to my rules from now on, understand?"

"I will, promise. Though I still don't get why that Omenra thing was trying to kill me. I didn't even do anything."

"Yet," Diu said. "Tomorrow, you will understand."

His tone made it obvious that the conversation was over. Nicole flipped onto her back, staring at the stars, thoughts teeming. The destruction of Earth was always something she had associated with movies and videogames, not with real life. Then again, she'd never been a believer in aliens. Yet here she was, stuck with a friendly local and a not-so-gentle warrior— armed to the teeth, in the middle of a wasteland, on some strange and unknown planet in a mysterious galaxy. *Yep. Pretty much sums up my life*, Nicole thought.

As she dreamed about what the future held, her mind settled on the strange Diu. Although he pretended to be asleep, Nicole could see him guardedly scanning the surroundings for danger. His body was stiff, his eyes were half open, and his claws lay ever by his gun. He *seemed* honest enough. But there was something ominous about him. The fact that he knew English—good English, at that—was unnerving. And he had been sent for her. Why? And by whom?

She and Lily would have to be wary. That much was clear. There was something concealed beneath the surface of Diu's words, she just knew it.

Nicole sighed. Tomorrow would mark a new beginning. A dangerous, crimson dawn. But as she closed her eyes and listened to the gentle crackle of the fire, she knew in her heart that wherever she had to go, whatever she had to do, she would never, ever give up.

No matter where her path might lead.

Chapter Eight

Darkness Descending

Nicole bolted upright. She hadn't remembered at first, but at some point in her dreams the memory returned. And now she had to know.

The twin suns had long since peeked over the horizon. Nicole glanced over at Diu's tree. Ever vigilant, he was now warily perched among the branches. She wondered if he'd slept at all. Noticing her stir, Diu gave the Ayédru wasteland one final sweep and sprang down to land deftly beside her.

"Have a good sleep?" he smirked. "It is already high noon."

"Hey, if you don't value sleep, you be my guest." But secretly, she was grateful for his watching over them.

"Thirsty?" He held out his canteen.

"Thanks," she mumbled, guzzling water and patting some on her forehead. Already, the heat was rising. "So what were you watching for, anyway? Or do you just have a thing against sleeping?"

"I like the dark, for one thing."

"The dark? That's ridiculous."

"Why?"

"Because dark things are . . . I don't know . . . evil, I guess," Nicole finished lamely.

"Really? What about peaceful? Or mysterious?"

"I don't like shadows or night, okay!"

Diu smiled. "Just because *you* don't like something doesn't make it automatically evil."

"Whatever. I bet that's not the reason you stayed up."

"It is a reason, but not the only one. I feared they might come back."

"You mean things like that psycho Omenra? There are *more* of his kind around here?"

"Perhaps. Thought otherwise?"

"I guess not," Nicole admitted, feeling a shiver creep up her spine. She was starting to realize that there was something big going on, only she didn't know what. Yet. "But speaking of Omenras," she continued, "what did you do with . . . you know."

"The one from yesterday? Moved it for the night prowlers."

"Prowlers? Like the vicious animal kind?"

"Where do you think you are, Camp Sunshine?" he quipped. "Luckily, I think that meat was filling enough for them. For now, anyway."

Nicole smiled queasily. "Great. I'm . . . going to wake Lily, okay?"

Diu didn't respond, turning his back on her and looking out over the wasteland.

Seeking her friend out among the grove, Nicole finally

spotted her resting on a thick tree branch. She nudged Lily awake, and the little alien grouchily sat up from her makeshift bed and scratched her left ear. "Why so early?" Lily mumbled.

"Well, according to *someone*," Nicole said, "it's 'high noon' already."

Lily's mouth widened in a yawn. "You don't like him, do you?" she said plainly.

"I just don't trust him."

"Me, I think we should give him a chance."

"Sure," Nicole finished gruffly. "A chance."

Once they had all gathered, Diu offered Nicole and Lily some dried meat strips and tangy berries from a small sack. They dug in gratefully. As they ate, Nicole gauged the right time to ask her burning question.

"Diu, what's that?" Lily mumbled through a mouthful. Nicole, too, noticed it for the first time. The strap across his chest, loose last night, was tight now, burdened by something tied to his back.

"This?" Diu unstrapped a large, thin, circular disk and placed it on the ground. "I salvaged it from the Omenra. It's a Jyro-Magnum Electro Terracannon Glider. JET Glider, for short. These are very expensive to purchase and difficult to find. Must have had good funding."

Lily goggled. "What's it for?"

"Fast travel. Hovers over land, water, and air. Since these are so rare and not too heavy to carry, I didn't want to pass up the chance to have one. You never know when we might need it."

Chapter Eight

"Speaking of needing things," Nicole broke in, curiosity bubbling over. "I was thinking about what you said yesterday. You were following us, right?"

"Right."

"Since when?"

"Within hours of your first teleportation."

She just had to know. "Then was it you—"

"Who took you to the forest? Who dragged you from the river? Who tossed you the healing powder? Who followed you out here to the wasteland, risking his own life, just because you can't follow instructions properly and then get lost with no supplies, on top of everything?"

"Me, I think that sounds right," Lily giggled.

"Not funny," Nicole snapped. "But yeah. Thanks, I guess."

"I did not do it for you. I did it for your planet."

"Does that mean you're going to explain this all now?"

"Yes, but it's complicated, so listen carefully. I will not tell you twice."

Nicole bristled at his tone but bit her tongue to keep quiet. "Yeah, I'm ready."

"All right. Speaking in terms of Earth time, everything started about ten years ago on Ámroth, the Omenra home world. Historically speaking, the Omenra were always a powerful, intelligent race, but they were never cruel. They treated other species justly and were even members of the Ethári Council that once brought peaceful union to the galaxy. But ten years ago, that ageless tradition shattered with the crowning of a new leader.

"The Omenra *Krethor*—a title close to 'king'—is normally determined hereditarily, meaning that the throne is passed from father to son. However, when a king dies and leaves no heir, the Omenra will elect their next leader through popular vote. And unfortunately . . ."

"What happened?" Nicole probed.

"The old king disappeared under mysterious circumstance ten years ago," Diu continued. "No one knows what happened exactly, but what everyone does know is that the newly elected king was a very unpopular candidate. He was a creature who cared nothing about peace and only wanted power—at any cost. But as things would have it, every other candidate either dropped out of the running or vanished, until there was only one left to be chosen. The new ruler, *Krethor* Gavaron, gathered the Omenra and fed them lies about murder and domination, tales that would make your blood run cold. And because Gavaron knew his peaceful people wouldn't turn to his side without goading or pressure, the king promised glories such as wealth and dominance that could not be refused. Once he had full trust, he gathered an army and set out to conquer the galaxy.

"Gavaron's first lightning strikes were successful because no one had expected the peaceful, gentle Omenra to bring out guns and cruisers and embark upon a massive campaign of conquest. *Krethor* Gavaron's army took the planets nearest their Ámroth easily and with little resistance. What small forces tried to oppose his were easily cut down. The king taught the Omenra to love the scent and taste of blood until they lusted for it day and night.

"There was another matter that facilitated their speedy conquest. The king's hand-picked commanding officer, General Malkior Taggerath, was and remains one of the fiercest, cruelest creatures in the galaxy. The Omenra themselves are terrified of him, and his bloody word is law. He has been at the head of every major planetary invasion for the last decade, and he's a formidable foe at worst. At best, he is a killer who will stop at nothing to achieve galactic conquest.

"So at first, *Krethor* Gavaron got his way. But soon there was more resistance. Planets assembled armies to oppose the new threat. In retaliation, the king built up his army with slaves and prisoners from each planet he captured. Soon his force was greater than any a single planet could take on. Some started to make plans for cooperation, but most feared betrayal by their allies. This only helped to speed the Omenras' triumph. Those who attempted to resist on their own failed. If the Omenra wanted a planet, they always got it. Soon, it became obvious that, unless something was done quickly, the entire galaxy would fall under the rule of a single, bloodthirsty empire.

"That's when the first efforts of the Airioth began, named after their founder. The first members were mostly creatures from those planets taken by the Omenra, who wanted to free their homes. But others, fearing ruin, soon joined as well. A tiny, obscure effort at first, the Airioth has since grown into a massive alliance to end the Omenra rule. It is the single most powerful rebellion movement in years. It harbors all kinds of creatures, as long as they are against the Omenra."

"Yeah," Nicole interrupted. "We even have an Earth saying

for that. 'The enemy of my enemy is my friend'."

"It is more than that. There is brotherhood in suffering and brotherhood in revenge. That is what the Airioth provides: refuge from the former, an opportunity for the latter. And in recent years, after a long, grueling struggle, victory finally seemed to be at hand. Then, about a month ago, in your Earth time, everything shattered.

"A weapon that could destroy worlds was something many species wanted to devise but never could. Many have come close, but the weapons were so powerful they could not be contained. Some failed experiments created black holes that swallowed solar systems or even ripped the fabric of space-time. And so, until just recently, it was considered to be impossible. Impossible, that is, until the Omenra created the Terranova, a device that could do just that. They decided to test it before introducing it into their army's artillery, but they didn't want to draw too much attention. To be safe, they decided to test it on a vague, tiny, insignificant world that nobody really knew or cared about, a planet that would never prove useful to them."

Nicole felt her throat stick. "Earth, right?"

"Exactly. Airioth spies on Ámroth immediately sent word throughout the galaxy. The rebellion leaders set about devising a way to thwart the plan because every victory for the Omenra, even a small one, drives them closer to total conquest. And that is where I come in."

"Are you part of the Airioth?"

"Yes, but I'm nobody important," Diu answered quickly. "Just someone in the lowest ranks. And when the Airioth called on me to help, I was stunned. They required my assistance with a direct strike—a high honor. I was to infiltrate the ship that was headed to Earth with the Terranova and disable the weapon.

"I managed to board the ship without being detected, but the Omenra found me in the cargo storage vault and captured me. When they landed on Earth, I managed to escape. I tried to run but only got so far before they caught me again. That is when I dropped the Galactera you found. I didn't have time to retrieve it before they dragged me back with threats of punishment and death. I managed to get away later by means of an escape pod, but the point is that I failed to disarm the Terranova. And, therefore, I failed to save Earth."

The silence that followed filled Nicole with such dread that she wondered if she would suffocate under the weight of Diu's words. Omenra, Airioth, Terranova, Earth. Thoughts blended in a crazed swirl in her mind.

"Nicole?" a voice squeaked.

She forced herself to focus. "Yeah, Lily?"

"Did you hear him?"

"Hear what?"

"I can show it to you, if want," Diu repeated.

"Show me what?"

"The Terranova. But I need a fire. Get me some wood."

"Why?" Nicole asked, but she stood.

"Just do it. If you really want to know."

"Fine. Come on, Lily."

They picked out the driest branches from the trees, whispering to each other as they worked. When they returned,

Nicole watched as Diu untied a tiny, ragged pouch. "What's in there?" Lily asked.

"Never mind that. Let's just hope I still remember how to do this."

Starting a fire, he pulled a pinch of blue powder from the sack. Tossing it onto the flames, he whispered something Nicole couldn't quite hear, and the fire erupted into a black inferno. The air around them grew cold as if all the warmth of the world had been sucked into the suddenly freezing fire. Darkness swept a cloak around them, shrouding the suns. Nicole's breath frosted and she shivered, but she was drawn to the fire and the pale point of light that seemed to glow within it.

Suddenly the light morphed, twisting into a sleek, silver shape. The creature it became loomed from the darkness—a massive, mechanical, spider-like beast. It raised an enormous leg, slamming it down inches from Nicole's face. She screamed and rolled sideways, reaching for Lily, but realized with a pang that she was alone.

The spider leapt forward, pinning her down. Nicole kicked out, but the giant beast was overwhelming. It leaned closer, shiny metallic body quivering with a lust for murder. Then a voice called out from the shadows, luring the spider monster aside.

A creature Nicole recognized as an Omenra manifested from the dark. This one, however, was not quite the same as the one Diu had slain. His very stance was proud and haughty, and his uniform was not simply charcoal black but edged with silver. Heavy, booted feet stamped towards her. In a cold, cruel voice, the Omenra hissed something in a language Nicole could not understand.

A beep echoed through the darkness, followed by the creature's piercing laughter. Once, twice, thrice, faster and faster the beeping swelled until the tinny noise was overwhelming in Nicole's ears. A countdown. And the pitiless laughter amplified with it, searing the air.

And just as it became nearly all too much, an explosive wave of heat erupted in her face and her screams were blotted out by fire and heat and darkness.

Chapter Nine

Of Legends and Prophecies

"Nicole! Nicole!" Lily shrieked.

"Umgh," Nicole muttered, opening her eyes to the bright sunlight. She groaned, raising her body to a sitting position, trying to remember. There was something about darkness and the cold. And—the spider. She screamed and twisted around, but the wasteland, warm again, was empty.

"What's wrong?" Lily yelled.

"I don't know. Y-you did something!" Nicole cried, turning on Diu. "Something with the fire, and then it was cold, and dark, and . . . the giant spider . . ." She stopped, amazed at the blank looks on both their faces. "You two have no idea what I'm talking about, do you?"

"Well, there was a spider," Lily said quietly, "but it was small. The fire turned into a mini Terranova, but Diu put it out when you started shaking like mad and twitching on the ground. You were having a fit or something, but we couldn't get you out of it."

"Nicole, what did you see?" Diu asked, seeming concerned for the first time.

"I . . ." Suddenly she felt really stupid. Sure, she was afraid of spiders. But she didn't know her fear would go so far as to give her crazy hallucinations.

"It was nothing," she said at last.

"It was something, and I must know what," Diu insisted.

"Well, fine, but don't laugh when you hear it. When you did the fire thing, everything turned dark and cold and I couldn't see a thing. I thought it was all part of whatever it was you were showing us, but then the fire turned into a giant spider that attacked me. An Omenra intervened, at first I thought to save me, but then it said something and there was an explosion, and . . . and . . ."

"And?" he encouraged.

"That's it."

He sat down across from her. "Odd," he said offhandedly.

"Was the spider . . . was it the Terranova?"

"Yes."

"And the explosion?"

"An expression of its purpose, as imagined by your mind."

"And what does that mean?"

Diu sighed impatiently. "It means you don't really know how the weapon works, so your mind naturally imagined an explosion to symbolize destruction. The true weapon does not work in such an obvious manner."

"But you told us yesterday that there may still be a way to save Earth. You said it has to do with the Galactera. What did you mean?"

"I will tell you, but be warned. We enter now into the realm of legends and prophecies, tales that may or may not be true. In ages long gone, a weapon with such power was merely a myth and a favorite story among children. Part of the prophecy about the weapon's creation was a story about how to destroy it. It told of gathering four artifacts—four elemental crystals—of vast power, a power which, when united, would be strong enough to destroy the weapon."

"But it's only a legend?" Nicole groaned.

Lily snorted in agreement. "Yep, and me, I think it's a dumb one."

"But it is a legend rooted in fact," Diu said. "There *are* four crystals that harbor incredible power. They lie scattered throughout the galaxy. And it may be our only hope to find these crystals, get to the Terranova, and destroy it."

"Me, I don't get it. Don't you have any weapons that can do that?" Lily asked.

"Yes and no. With the strength to destroy the Terranova? Perhaps. But take any one of them to where the weapon lies and you will ignite a cataclysmic chain of events just as bad as anything the Omenras' weapon will do."

Nicole asked, "Just where is the Terranova, anyway?"

"The center of the earth. Where else?"

All her hope vaporized like a candle blown out by a gust. *Get to the center of the earth?* He was crazy! "But the center of the earth isn't hollow!" Nicole shrieked. "And besides, even if it *were* hollow, the temperatures down there are enormous, not to mention the force of gravity. We can't go there! We'll die!"

"The earth *was* solid—until the Omenra decided they

needed the center for their Terranova. You seem to underestimate the power of a king who is willing to do anything to get what he wants. But wait, let me explain:

"Several days before the Omenra arrived with the weapon, a separate ship blasted a rift straight through to the heart of your planet, carving a hollow in the core. Within this chamber, Omenra engineering specialists mounted a special insulating field. I know," he added, seeing Nicole's incredulous, blank face, "that it seems impossible. But believe me, every word is true. The Omenra thus created a void in the center of Earth, their force-field preventing the planet from collapsing upon itself. Then they launched the Terranova into the shielded core. There it lies now, dormant at the moment but soon to become the deadliest weapon in the galaxy."

Nicole's memory fizzled. She remembered watching television, the news, right before she went outside that fateful day. What had been the big story? Her heart skipped a beat. Unusual comet activity, record-breaking temperatures, a changing force of gravity—it finally all made sense!

"I still don't get one thing," she said uncertainly. "Why don't they just blow up Earth right now? Why do they have to wait a month?"

"Because the weapon is meant to torture, then kill. First it amplifies its surroundings. In heat, temperatures spike. Vice-versa for cold, and the Terranova's effects spread over a wide range. Now take that concept and imagine that such a weapon is placed where temperatures reach more than 8,000°F."

"My God," Nicole barely managed to whisper.

"Thus the Terranova will warm your planet by amplifying

temperature, particularly targeting the heat at large areas of cold. Oceans, ice caps, lakes, rivers—it will seek to evaporate water sources, causing shortages and global panic. Then, after a month of torture, it will trigger a massive internal reaction that will destroy your world."

Nicole opened her mouth to speak, but Diu cut her off. "As I calculate it, the Omenra are too powerful for us to just fight them off, if that is what you were about to suggest. If we are going to save Earth, we will have to deactivate or destroy their weapon. And that is where the crystals come in. Maybe it's only a legend, but if you are willing to ride on the hope that it might be fact, I am willing to help you find the crystals."

Lily snapped, "And if it *is* only a legend?"

"Isn't there another way?" Nicole begged.

Diu shook his head. "No way will guarantee success. This is merely the only one that does not guarantee failure. But Nicole, it is up to you in the end. Your world. Your quest. Your choice."

His words said she had a choice; his tone said it was already decided. For a moment Nicole retreated into her own mind, searching for an answer. Maybe she had known all along that there was no backing out, but now that the time had come she wasn't sure if she was really ready to face this. She saw the fear on Lily's face, felt foreboding in her own heart. But Nicole knew what she had to do.

"I'm in," she said. "Lily?"

"We-e-ell," Lily said.

"It's okay," Nicole replied sympathetically. "If you don't want to go, I'll understand."

Lily seemed to ponder this. "No," she said at last, slowly. "It's not okay. Me, I promised to help you get home. If you have to save Earth so you *can* go home, then me, I'm in."

"You sure? It'll be dangerous, so I won't blame you for not coming along."

"Danger! Ha! Me, I'm not backing out just because of that! Nope, you're stuck with me. Like it or not."

"Thanks, Lily."

"We will leave tomorrow," Diu said. "Today, I will make plans and decide how we are going to do this. You two can wander, but not far. Close enough so I can look after you. And Nicole, about the fire—"

"Forget it," she said. "Honestly, I'm not sure if I *want* to know what happened. I've got enough things to worry about. Come on, Lily."

"Remember, not far."

"Yeah, I know. And don't worry, we'll be fine. Just fine."

Chapter Ten

The Shazgor

"There's something weird about him," Nicole said as she walked out past the trees, Lily on her shoulder, out into the wasteland heat. The land spread in a smooth blanket before them, dry as cement.

"Me, I think so, too."

"Do you think he's lying? About Earth?"

Nicole's sneakers crunched across hard, cracked rock.

"Me, I guess it could be a trap. But what if it's not?"

"That's my worry, too. What if we don't trust him now and then . . . then . . . it turns out to be real?"

The ground had a softer quality now, not quite as smooth as sand but not like rock, either.

"I guess," Nicole said, "we should just be careful. You know what I—hey!"

Her left sneaker was trapped in a soft mound of squishy sand. She dragged it out with a barely audible suck.

"That's strange," Lily said, leaning to see. "Me, I thought the ground was dried solid."

Stretching before them was a plain of this same, half-wet, sandy substance. Quicksand? Nicole glanced back. The grove of trees hunched low over the horizon. "Maybe we should head back," she suggested. "I hadn't realized we'd gone so far."

"Me, I think—oh . . . Ni-Nicole—"

About fifty feet away, the quicksand-like ground shuddered. Sandy ripples combed across the surface, and the ground buckled slightly. Nicole twisted her body around and ran like living fire, pounding across the semi-hard earth. Lily was quick to follow, levitating at her friend's side. The sound of rock cracking under pressure ripped through the air like thunder. Suddenly, a massive, elongated bulge in the ground sliced a path around Nicole. Then, not ten feet from where she skidded to a sudden, dust-raising halt, a creature broke free from the earth.

The beast was enormous, a cross between a snake and a fish swelled to great proportions. It was sandy in color with dull, dirty scales. A pair of spiny, red-orange flippers thrashed in the air. The creature's head, grotesque in appearance, was a mass of rows upon rows of spinning teeth lodged within a gaping, pit-like mouth. Six dagger-sharp, crimson mandibles ringed the dark opening. There were no visible eyes.

Nicole stood still, terrified even to breathe lest the creature sense the movement. Lily, too, was immobile. They were like statues, silent and stationary. The beast probed the air with its glittering mouth, sucking in a breath with a deathly rattle. It did not strike. Instead it merely swayed, channeling scent through its body, still half-submerged in the ground.

But it was impossible to contain so much fear, so much terror, for long. After several tense, stretched minutes, Lily's body trembled. Once.

The beast whirled on them. It lunged faster than Nicole thought possible. She leapt sideways, and the lightning strike missed by a fraction of an inch. Making a dash for the trees, Nicole spun her head to see the creature arch over in the air, mandibles folding together and spinning rapidly. It drilled into the ground, blasting up a curtain of sand, its bladed tail vanishing in a flash. She scurried on, screaming for Lily to follow, eyes darting around in hopes of detecting the creature's trail. However, it must have tunneled deeper because it was impossible to tell where it would surface next.

Suddenly, the earth bucked like an enraged stallion. Nicole cried out as she was flung into the air on a rising mass of dirt. She barely managed to clutch a mandible as the creature reared up from beneath her. Lifted ten, twenty, fifty feet into the air, she screamed wildly, flailing to keep her legs away from rotating, serrated fangs. She screamed for Lily, but her friend didn't reply. *She went on without me*, Nicole realized with a pang. But she couldn't concentrate on Lily when the beast was intent on her.

The creature scraped its head against the ground, dragging Nicole across the dirt. Sharp stones and grit sliced at her legs but still she held on, realizing that it was her only hope to survive. Holding onto its jaw, she was in the one place where the beast could not reach her. Clicking its mandibles, the creature slashed its head through the air, weaving Nicole in a tangle, trying to fling her off. But she clung on, screaming, fighting for a hold. Then the beast's head shot up so swiftly that Nicole's fingers slipped off the slick mandible. Her body curved in the air and drooped in a sheer plummet towards the rotating, trembling mass below.

Two small, furry paws suddenly snatched her left hand. Nicole's gaze flashed to Lily. Hovering in midair, the tiny alien braced her whole weight against that of her friend, trying to keep them both suspended.

"Lily!" Nicole joyously cried. "I thought you'd gone back!"

"Me, I did, but—" Lily's voice broke off in a pant.

"What's wrong?"

"You're heavy . . . can't keep . . . hold!"

Nicole's sweaty fingers slipped through the small paws. She was falling again, shrieking, the spinning fangs rising to meet her. Lily screamed, too, but there was nothing they could do, nothing—

Another paw caught Nicole's hand, larger and stronger. This time her eyes met Diu's. He was hovering above her, feet strapped to the JET Glider, twisted upside-down to keep hold. One paw gripped her hand; the second clutched the board. Straining to drag Nicole up, Diu swung her onto the back of the Glider. She gripped his shoulders, easing away from the edge on tip-toe, watching the beast below writhe in disappointment.

In a flash, Diu whipped out his Mar blaster, grinding back the safety switch. Aiming the handgun at the creature's gaping mouth, he pulled back a little on the trigger. The inside of the barrel heated to blue.

"Don't!" Nicole shrieked, shoving the gun up. The sizzling blast nearly singed her hair.

"Are you crazy?!" Diu snarled, trying to aim again.

"You don't have to kill it. You don't."

Cross-armed, Lily blocked the barrel's opening with her body. "Me, I think she's right. It was just trying to find a meal."

"Please," Nicole begged.

The Mar trembled. "You're wrong. That thing is evil. It deserves to die."

Nicole shook her head furiously. "Just because you don't like something doesn't make it automatically evil," she reminded him.

Diu's eyes narrowed, but at last he holstered the gun with a slash of his arm. Far below, the beast flipped in the air, chiseling below the ground and disappearing with a flick of its tail.

"What was that thing, anyway?" Nicole asked.

"A Shazgor," Diu snapped curtly, turning the Glider towards the trees.

"Hey, listen, if you're mad about me not wanting you to kill the—"

"I said to not go far! And what did you do?"

"In *my* opinion, I didn't go far at all!"

"Should I just leash you next time?"

"The Shazgor was an accident, okay?"

"It only takes one."

"It won't happen again, I swear."

"It only takes one," he repeated.

The Glider swerved roughly between two trees, nearly clipping an outstretched branch. "Who gave you a driver's license," Nicole complained as she hopped off.

Diu didn't reply, but the moment the board was securely

strapped to his back he said, "I was originally banking on leaving tomorrow morning, but I doubt it's a safe idea to leave you and Lily to wander the rest of the day. I have some more rations that we will split and then we'll go."

Nicole gaped. "Right now?"

"Right now."

"Oh, that's brilliant. Let's just go off with no heading and traipse around the galaxy—"

"We do have a heading. I will tell you before we go."

Accordingly, they all ate quickly. Nicole swallowed the sweet, tangy berries and hard strips of meat as if they were air and guzzled down the water. Lily, too, stuffed her mouth so full that her cheeks bulged. Only Diu ate in moderation, and when they'd finished, he turned to Nicole and announced, "It's time."

She stared blankly. "For what?"

"To go."

"Okay."

Silence.

"Well?" Diu growled.

"What do you want? I'm ready, Lily's ready, you're ready— so let's go."

Diu snarled in annoyance. "Then get the Galactera," he said, fighting to keep his voice level.

Nicole took out the pocket watch and unlatched it. "Okay. Now what?"

He scowled and swiped the watch away. "I thought you'd already figured it out."

"Just randomly, you mean?" Lily snapped in defense of her

friend. "Like the knowledge just popped into her brain!"

"And why not? She's smart, I take it?"

Fuming, Nicole said, "Just tell me how it works, okay?"

"It's *simple*," he said, pointing to the sixteen buttons. "All you have to do is decide which planet you want to go to and press the corresponding button—the Galactera takes care of the rest. However, the watch can only keep fifteen planets in memory, so it retains data of the most recently visited worlds. The latest planet is the uppermost button—where the twelve would be on an Earth clock—and then it proceeds from newest to oldest in a clockwise direction. The button directly to the left of the top button is for new planets. The blue word on each button changes to reflect the name of the planet that's programmed to it."

"How do I use the new planet button?"

"Again, it's simple. Speak the name of the world you wish to visit and then press the button."

"Got it."

"And was that so hard?" he said, feigning sweetness.

"Now that you've *explained* it," Nicole said. She took back the watch, closed it, and turned it over in her hand. For a moment her mind flashed to a radical idea: why not just go back to Earth? The watch was here, right here, clutched in her hand. All those buttons . . . and it would only take one click . . . it would only take one—

But then Nicole remembered. She couldn't go back. Not now. Maybe . . . maybe not ever. Suddenly, she noticed that Lily was sitting oddly quietly. To distract herself from the terrible thought, she asked, "What's wrong?"

Chapter Ten

"There's something about that watch," Lily muttered. "Me, I don't know. Just makes me feel strange. What do those words on the cover mean?"

"I don't know," Diu admitted. "Those words," he went on to explain, "are text from a long-dead written language that, ironically, corresponds to the most commonly spoken tongue in the galaxy. But while it is easy to speak, the language is almost impossible to learn to write. Thus the written form has perished. Unfortunately, with no record of the writing, I am unable to translate what the script says."

Lily bobbed her head, but her face didn't change.

"Is something else bothering you?" Nicole asked.

"Well, actually—oh!" Lily cried. "I've been thinking about what we're about to do, and me, I just don't think it's possible. Completely insane, this whole thing! Out of all the millions of planets in the universe, how are we going to pick the right ones? And how—"

"I said that we have a heading," Diu interrupted, "and I was just about to explain. Part of the legend about the weapon is a prophecy to reveal the locations of the crystals. I have been able to track down the very beginning." Pulling out a yellowed scrap of paper from a pouch clipped to his belt, he held it out and Nicole read:

> **Be swift and be shrewd like water**
> **Be soft and be pure like air**
> **Be strong and be brave like fire**
> **Be hard and be cool like earth**

Quest far beyond mountain summits
Traverse the arctic plight
On Azimar, land of legends
Seek darkness mingled with light

"Is that it?" Lily asked.

"As I said, it's just the beginning," Diu said. "And I know one thing for fact. Somewhere on Azimar lies a map, and when we find it, that shall be our guide to the locations of the crystals."

Suddenly, Lily's face lit up like a star. "Wait . . . Azimar," she breathed. "Me, I know that planet."

"What about it?" Nicole asked.

"From the things I've heard, it's the most beautiful, magical land you could ever find. I've always dreamed of going there, but me, I never got the chance. Not with my foster parents."

Diu grinned. "You believe it's as nice as you say?"

"Absolutely!"

"Well, I'm glad the planet's pretty, but there's something . . ." Nicole trailed off.

"What?" Diu encouraged.

"What does it mean by 'arctic plight'?"

"It means that Azimar is a very dangerous place. Beautiful, perhaps, but deadly in the wrong weather."

"Whatever it means," Nicole said, "that's where we're going."

She looked over the buttons, wondering how she would ever be able to learn the strange language, but realized that the script was now in English. Her head shot up in amazement.

Seeing her funny look, Diu explained, "The language changed, right? That is because the watch reprograms to whatever tongue its master speaks best."

"Master? Me? But it's your—" Suddenly, Nicole remembered Diu's exact words. *Keep it. We're going to need it.* He'd given her the watch to keep, meaning . . .

"The Galactera's switched its allegiance to you," he said.

"Wow," she said, noticing that, strangely, Azimar was already programmed. "Hey, did you—"

"Yes, I have been there recently. Oh, and make sure we are all touching when you press or else the Galactera will teleport only you."

Nicole found the appropriate button. Then, curiously, she checked the inscription on the front cover. The words hadn't changed. "Diu, how come—"

"Because that text is a constant," he explained even before she'd finished the question. "When I got it, the inside changed for me, but not the outside. It was the same for the previous owner."

Though still curious, Nicole decided to ignore that factor for the time being, resolved to find out eventually. She touched the button eagerly, and then stopped. This would be the first time she had used the Galactera since Earth. And speaking of Earth . . .

The planet wasn't programmed into the watch. There was, however, that button Diu had mentioned; a button for new worlds. Nicole glanced at it longingly. All she had to do was press that button and she would be home, back with her parents and friends and everyone and everything she loved. Her finger hovered over the button. She could go home now. She could go home.

No. I can't go back.

Nicole forced her finger to the button for *Azimar*. If she went now, what would happen in a month to all those people she cherished? What would happen then? Going back was easy. Going on was tough. But then she felt Lily's warm presence on her shoulder and gripped Diu's paw in her hand. Nicole realized that there was no need to be afraid anymore, not when she had . . . friends. *Yes, that's what they are now. Friends. Good friends or bad, I guess I'll just have to wait to find out.*

When she finally pressed the button, it wasn't with fear, but with hope.

The air grew frigid and a crackle of blue electricity sizzled through the air. It was joined quickly by many other sparks, until the air fizzed and the light formed a vortex that enclosed them on all sides. As soon as the sphere was complete, a shower of snow drenched the companions and a gust of ice-cold wind slashed out with an intense chill. Nicole clutched Lily in fright. The ice and snow whirled faster and faster around them until it clawed at their arms and gnawed their legs. Thrashing gusts lashed their faces until Nicole was ready to scream. But then, just as suddenly as it had begun, the vortex hissed into nothingness. The snow stopped. And then there was nothing but silence.

Chapter Eleven

Azimar

Nicole took a wary step forward, her sneaker crunching into fresh snow. Lily hid in the thicket of her friend's hair to keep herself warm. Only Diu seemed unshaken by the deep cold. He glanced around the frozen tundra with a hard, impassive gaze.

"Teradru Valley," he announced.

Nicole could almost bet he was bluffing because she couldn't see even one landmark. What stretched before them was nothing but another wasteland—albeit a colder one—and not anything at all that resembled Lily's beautiful description.

Well, granted, there was landscape that *resembled* landmarks. Close by, a range of ominous, ashen cliffs rippled against the sky. Beyond, dark mountains jutted skyward, piercing the heavens. Vague, but hey. If one was good with geography . . .

Overhead, thick gray clouds blended together in a dark swirl, barely filtering through enough light to see by. Icy wind ripped through the valley. Nicole rubbed her hands together furiously to create warmth through friction, but that didn't help keep out the ferocious cold. Shivering, she untied the jacket from her waist and shrugged into it.

"We should get going," Diu said, a cloud of vapor steaming from his mouth. The surrounding air was so cold that his breath froze into tiny icicles. "We need to find a warm place to stay."

"Got to . . . find it before we . . . frr-freeze to death," Lily stammered.

"Hey, I thought you said this place was, and I quote, 'it's the most beautiful, magical land you could ever find'," Nicole said wryly. "All I'm getting out of the experience is cold."

"Me, I *did* warn you it was going to be cold! Just didn't know *how* cold."

"Might have been a useful thing to know, don't you think?"

Lily shouted, "Diu, you said you've been here before! Why didn't *you* warn us?"

"Stop the bickering, you two, and concentrate!" he snarled, shutting them both up. "We have to get to those cliffs before nightfall. We might find a cave there where we can stay overnight. I don't fancy our odds if we have to stay out here after dark."

The trio strode through the snow. *Crunch . . . crunch . . . crunch . . . crunch . . .* With each footstep, their feet sunk deep into the snow. The cold seemed to gnaw deeper into their skin with every passing second. *Crunch . . . crunch . . . crunch . . . crunch . . .*

Suddenly, Nicole pointed ahead. "Look!" she called out. Diu and Lily followed her finger skyward, staring at the high edge of the cliffs. Lily gasped and Nicole said, "Is that what I think it is, or am I randomly colorblind?"

Sprawled along the cliff's edge, winding down the jagged rock in fierce tangles, was a twisted patch of greenery. In the black and white world it stood out like a beacon.

"Let's head that way," Diu said. "There might be food there, and we have little left."

He pushed ahead, leaving Nicole and Lily to scurry after him. As they crunched on, Nicole noticed a dark line snaking through the valley far to their right. *Must be some kind of landform*, she thought, and soon forgot all about it.

The sky, in the meantime, had grown darker, shaded with a purplish, greenish cast. A single creature glided overhead, pure-white, with long, outstretched wings and a ribbon-like tail. Against the dark of the sky and the black of the mountains, Nicole thought she had never seen anything whiter.

As they stumbled across the snow, the heavy clouds broke, spewing great chunks of hail. "Run!" Lily cried, clutching her tail over her head.

Forced to tear her eyes from the whiteness of the flying creature, Nicole snatched Lily from her shoulder and hid her inside the jacket for protection. She staggered, blinded and lashed by hail. Diu called her name from somewhere far away. Trying to run, Nicole tripped over her own feet and crashed onto the ground. Lily squealed beneath Nicole's weight and squirmed free, screaming for help. Nicole suddenly felt someone beside her and Diu grabbed her wrist, jerking her upright. "Come on!" he ordered, pulling her along behind him.

She snatched Lily's arm and they bounded together through the blizzard, blindly following Diu. At last the cliffs loomed up before them, and Nicole saw him vanish into a dark crevice. She slipped in after him, relieved to find herself out of the elements.

The rocky walls flickered into sight. Nicole glanced towards the source of the light. Unsurprisingly, Diu, ever-ready, held a glowing mass that resembled a handful of flames. Leaning down, he drew a ring along the ground, forming a small circle of fire in front of them. She noticed him tuck the pouch of powder away into his belt.

"I think we will be safe here," he said.

The sides of the cavern swelled around them like a colossal mouth. Near the entrance, its roof was so high that Nicole could hardly see the top. Farther in, however, the ceiling sloped down so sharply that there was barely enough space for her to kneel. In the walls encircling them, jagged cracks were etched in sharp relief against the otherwise smooth rock—a surface that was so oddly flat and polished that it seemed it had been sanded down. Otherwise, the cave was as ordinary as any on Earth, complete with stalagmites and stalactites.

They huddled near the fire for warmth as the storm outside strengthened to a full-out blizzard. Hissing clouds of snow whirled in from time to time, forcing the trio to retreat as far back as they could into their makeshift shelter. Nicole slithered backward until her head brushed against the ceiling, and even then little flurries of snow managed to find her. Still, it was warmer in the cave than outside, and that already made their stay here worth it.

"Me, I think we better wait out the storm," Lily said at last.

"I guess," Nicole said.

They sat in silence for a few moments more.

"I'm hungry," Lily moaned.

Nicole glanced hopefully at Diu. "How much do you have left?"

"Enough for one more meal," he admitted.

"What?" Lily cried. "Nicole, what about Madam Banda's cans?"

"Well, actually . . ."

"Don't tell me we're out!" Lily whimpered.

"Okay."

"Then we have food?"

"No. But you just told me not to tell you that we're out."

Lily half-choked. "What're we going to do? We'll starve!"

"Hold on, hold on!" Nicole cried. She looked meaningfully towards the cave entrance. "Give me a minute to think."

"Not if it means going out into the blizzard," Diu said as if reading her mind. "We have to wait out the storm."

"Would you rather have us starve?" Nicole accused.

"We have enough to eat one more time, and storms on Azimar tend to not last long. And either way, if anyone's going, it will be me. I've had my share of dealing with rough climates."

"Then who'll protect us while you're gone?"

"Who will protect you if you go out there alone? You can't even begin to understand the danger that lies in the open valley."

Lily squeaked, "You can't go, Nicole, if that's what you're thinking! Me, I think it's *way* too dangerous! Storm's too rough!"

"Out there I can run. Here, we'll be cornered. If Diu stays, he could protect you."

"You're not going," Diu said firmly.

"Am too," Nicole insisted. "I'm not a baby, in case you haven't noticed. I'm almost fourteen, and as such, I bet I can brave a couple snowflakes."

"A *couple snowflakes*?" Lily shrieked. "That's the storm of the century out there!"

"I was sent by the Airioth to protect you, not let you go out in a blizzard and get yourself killed," Diu said.

"But . . . but . . ." Nicole muttered weakly. The matter seemed settled. "Fine!" she said at last, stomping the ground. "I won't go. But if we starve, it'll be your fault, Diu."

"We will not starve," he assured her. "As soon as the storm lets up, I'll find us something. It's lucky I brought this." He drew out his silver gun.

Nicole was still fuming, but she admired his sleek weapon, and said so.

"That thing's pretty cool."

"It's my trusty Mar. Not as powerful or light as some of the new Enfiros on the market, but it's reliable. Seen me through countless battles. And this gun will outlive all of us by a couple centuries. Nuclear power source means you never have to reload, plus a super-efficient internal cooling system means there's no chance of overload. In its day, the Mar was the most powerful production handgun in the galaxy, and I guess you can tell why."

"I see," Nicole said, which was mostly a lie.

Diu sighed. "No, you don't, but that's okay. Anyway,"—he

holstered the gun—"I'm waiting till the blizzard is over."

Lily yawned. "Me, I'm tired. Maybe I'll . . . nap."

Nicole had an idea. "Maybe we all should. It's been a hard day, and the fire should keep us warm."

Diu growled suspiciously. "You two can if you want. I will be just fine."

"But you were on sentry duty last night, I assume. Aren't you tired?"

"What are you planning, Nicole?"

"Nothing," she said innocently.

He looked wistfully towards the place where Lily lay curled up by the fire. "I'm fine," he repeated.

Nicole smiled. "All right. *I'm* going to nap with Lily." And she stretched out by the fire, facing the cave wall.

She waited for what seemed like hours, keeping her breath steady so as to appear to be asleep. As luck would have it, things worked out precisely as she'd hoped. Diu, after a long vigil, must have decided it was safe. He picked out a spot near the cave entrance and reclined against the wall. Soon, his deep breathing echoed through the cavern.

Nicole knew it was time.

She stood slowly and nimbly tiptoed to the entrance, careful lest she make even the slightest sound. Of one thing Nicole was certain—if Diu caught her, she was finished. Maybe not literally, but with a warrior like him, nothing would surprise her.

First things first—she needed a weapon. Nicole had the dagger, of course, but she needed something of real power. Something for defense. Maybe offense. She knelt next to Diu, sucking in her breath. One wrong move was all it would take. Carefully, she reached out. Grabbing hold, she tugged firmly, and the Mar was suddenly in her hands. Nicole had seen Diu almost use it on the Shazgor and had memorized his movements. She might not be an expert, but she knew how to work the gun.

As Nicole rose, she saw the pouch with the blue powder dangling from Diu's belt. On impulse, she snatched it and jammed it into her pocket. Her last glance was to the JET Glider. But there was no way to get it out without waking Diu.

Nicole paused by the entrance and turned to look at her friends. Diu might be angry, but they'd be in worse trouble with no food. Twisting to face the blizzard, she sighed in firm resignation.

And marched into the storm.

Sinking down instantly into the knee-high snow, Nicole shielded her face against the onslaught and craned her neck back to look at the ominous sky. Icy wind bit at skin where her jacket offered no protection. The gray glared darkly, and a fresh flurry struck her face. Shivering, she turned towards the cliff, squinting at the tiny patch of green far overhead. It was the only chance they had.

As Nicole stood thinking, she felt the winds easing at her back. The snowstorm was finally blowing itself out. At least for now. *Good*, she thought. The going would only be that much easier.

But she had a bigger problem—how to get to the top? There was no easy path to follow. With a sickening plunge of her stomach, Nicole realized she would have to scale the cliff itself. Sliding the Mar into her belt, she probed with her fingers, feeling out cracks that could serve as footholds.

Nicole pulled the dagger *Cárine* from her belt and gripped it tightly by the hilt. She glanced up one last time, peering at the greenery. For a second, she thought she saw a flash of red.

Finally, after drawing in a sharp breath, Nicole thrust her arm forward and plunged the split blade into the slippery slope.

Using the dagger to help pull herself up, she began her perilous ascent. Where there wasn't a natural foothold, she dug the blade into rock or more often ice and threw her weight against it. Then, shoes scraping against the stone, she forced her body up until her feet found another crack or outcropping in the sheer cliff. Each time, she was certain that the rock would crumble and she would fall to her death, but *Cárine* never let her down. In fact, the dagger even seemed to fill her with strength each time Nicole thrust it into the cliff, and she wondered if perhaps it had something to do with the magic it possessed.

The higher she climbed, the more confident she became. Soon her actions became almost careless. Whereas before Nicole would test each foothold for durability, she now merely assumed each would hold.

But suddenly, a crack splintered the air. Nicole turned her head sideways to catch the sound, but what she saw made her blood freeze. She had discovered a nice stone ledge jutting out from the cliff and, without even bothering to check it, had decided to use it as a support. But the ledge hadn't been stable, and now a deep fracture threaded along its length. Terrified, Nicole groped for another foothold, but the rock face was vertical and smooth. She tried to stab her dagger into a crevice again, but by the time she raised the weapon, the ledge had already shattered.

Nicole scrambled desperately for a grip on the cliff, but she was falling too fast and the rocks were too icy. Her mind writhed with fear and she shrieked, knowing it was too late, that she should have listened to Diu, that there was nothing left to save her.

Her right arm suddenly exploded with pain as her muscles tightened to their snapping point. Nicole threw her gaze up and saw, past knuckles white with strain, that the dagger had hooked on an outcropping and was jammed in a crack. She knew the little crevice wouldn't support her entire weight for long without breaking, so she quickly swung herself up, shoving her feet into two nearby footholds. She did not dare to believe her luck. The whole thing was impossible. No dagger could have caught just like that on a sheer rock face. *Except Cárine . . .*

For the rest of the climb, she regarded the cliff with caution, never sliding her feet or hands into an untested crevice. Her fall had taught her a powerful lesson. But, more importantly, the dagger that had captured Nicole's heart because of its beauty now held her respect as a formidable ally—something she could count on in a time of need. And the way her quest was going so far, she was going to need every bit of help she could get.

The cliff suddenly shook beneath her. Nicole barely

managed to hang on, swaying to and fro. An unnaturally sharp sound of rushing wind swelled, echoing from somewhere overhead. Nicole cowered against the rock. Something massive seemed to be approaching, and the noise of wind strengthened to a roar. With one hand still holding the dagger, she drew the Mar from her belt. She slid back a tiny silver switch which, she felt, had to be the safety. Her fingers tightened around the trigger, and she pointed the handgun skyward, wondering if she'd find the courage to fire.

This question was answered when a giant bulk soared out from beyond the overhang, casting a shadow darker than night over the cliff. Nicole could hardly keep from dropping the Mar, let alone firing. Whatever the creature was, it had an enormous wingspan, so wide she couldn't see the tips. An immense tail flashed into view and away just as fast, though it swiped down as it passed and nearly tore Nicole from the cliff. As it happened, the tail slashed just overhead and sent a shower of rock tumbling over her head. She kept silent, staring after the creature as it soared away.

Before she had a chance to change her mind about continuing, Nicole scrambled up and sprang over the top of the cliff. Catching her breath, she stood cautiously and peered out over the edge. The air caught in her chest.

Through the misty clouds rising from her mouth, she beheld a world more beautiful than any she had ever imagined possible. Teradru Valley lay spread before her, a sheer, white expanse, shining as if lit from beneath. The clouds overhead parted slightly, and through the gaps poured shivering beams of sunlight. The light bounced and echoed from the cliffs to the earth until the entire valley seemed to be on fire. *Lily was so right about this place*, Nicole thought wistfully. *Too bad she's not here to see this.*

Even more incredible was the lush bounty surrounding her. The air was warm and moist, and thriving in this rich climate was a myriad of fantastic flowering plant species, their blooms wafting delicious scents. A nearby tree, laden with green spiral fruit, seemed to bend its bows toward Nicole, offering nourishment, and she picked a fruit with delight. Twisting the tip to peel it, she was surprised to find the skin drop off of its own accord. She stuffed the fruit into her mouth and chewed slowly, reveling in its delicate flavor. Nicole tore down a few more and shoved them in her pockets for her friends. Tightening the handgun's safety back into place, she slid the Mar into her belt and wandered, picking at the various berry bushes and other plants surrounding the fruit tree.

This oasis of life was amazing, impossible, and Nicole loved every second of it. Her feet skipped along through the grass and bushes as she leapt and twirled with relief. All she had to do now was get back to the cave and tell her friends about this amazing place. They would survive after all.

Then something unbelievable happened. A warm, musical sound wafted through the air, a sound Nicole had heard twice before. She whirled, unable to believe it. There, perched on a drooping tree branch, surrounded by a wild tangle of intricately twirling greenery, was the scarlet phoenix.

"It's you again," she whispered, afraid that a loud noise would scare the creature away.

The phoenix sat perfectly still, staring curiously. Nicole

stepped forward, reaching to touch it. The mystical bird hopped to a higher branch, still just within reach. Creeping closer, she watched the brilliant creature in delight. It preened its feathers, crooning softly.

Nicole's foot suddenly hooked on a crack in the ground. Her fall was cushioned by a bush, but as she looked down at the offending crevice, she gasped. Snaking through the grass, cutting into the rock, was a deep gash in the stone face. Nicole knelt and felt a blast of warmth hit her face. Her sneakers kicked a few loose pebbles, but she took no notice. Wondering what lay within, she leaned closer, tilting her head to catch the warm gusts of air.

A blast like a gunshot brought reality back into sharp perspective. Nicole scrambled backwards, watching the crack beneath her widen and wind deeper along the rock. Her weight had been too much; even as she tried to escape the rock was giving way. She tore her gaze skyward and caught a glance of the phoenix as it soared away on the wind, singing its song. Nicole's cry of terror rent the air as she grabbed for a nearby bush, missed, and tumbled down, plummeting into the dark abyss.

Chapter Twelve

The Hatchling

Nicole hit a springy surface and bounced off onto rock. She groaned as she jerked to a sitting position, feeling juice from a smashed fruit seep through her jeans. "Great," she muttered, scooping out a few slimy pieces.

The ground was littered with some grass and long, supple branches, but mostly it was bare. Nicole looked up, realizing she had fallen through the ceiling of a cave of some sort. Its walls were painted by the flickering of an enormous pyre burning in the center of the floor. The flames spat sparks in all directions, illuminating the crevices and cracks of the circular cave and carving the rock into an illusion of dagger-like teeth. On one side, the sheer walls dropped away into an enormous passage.

The fire itself was magnificent. At its heart the flames were sapphire mixed with murky black, and around the edges flickering sheets of scarlet shivered and thrashed like waves at sea during a rough storm. But no sooner had Nicole glimpsed the powerful beauty of the fire than it was swept out of existence by a sharp gust of wind from the newly formed opening overhead.

The temperature dropped almost instantly. Snowflakes fluttered into the cavern, signaling the blizzard's renewed campaign. But Nicole didn't register the cold. She was busy scrambling to the edge of the cave, trembling in fear at what the fire had left behind when it had blown into nothingness.

At the heart of the fire's smoldering remnants lay a massive, red-gold egg flecked with onyx.

The egg was nearly as tall as Nicole and half as wide. It lay still at the center of the cavern, and as light poured in from the opening overhead, it was illuminated as if beneath a spotlight. Suddenly, the egg squeaked. Nicole pressed back against the wall and fumbled for the Mar with shaking hands, watching the shell as cracks snaked over its surface. The egg rocked back and forth wildly, the cracks widening. Heart thumping in a terrible frenzy, Nicole froze where she stood. And then, with one final surge of noise, the egg splintered. A red lump, covered in slime, tumbled to the ground. It stayed momentarily immobile, and then moved forward into an angle of light.

Nicole recoiled in absolute shock. Standing before her, staring straight back with sharp, thoughtful black eyes, was a dragon.

It was large, big enough for its shoulder to rise nearly to Nicole's waist. Its scales were deep crimson red. The dracling fanned its wet wings, squeaking. The wings were several times longer that its body and ribbed with lengths of bone that ended in widely spaced talons. A line of spines ran along its back from head to tail tip with only a small break at the base of its neck.

The dracling squeaked and thrashed its whip-like tail.

Its head snapped around towards the foreigner invading its shelter. But the hatchling quickly lost interest in the motionless Earth child and roamed to explore its home. Once, the creature yawned, revealing glistening, sharp fangs.

Finally Nicole moved sideways, just a twitch of motion, yet the dracling sensed it, twisting to face her. Flailing its tail like an excited puppy, it lurched towards her. Nicole broke into a dash, but she hadn't made it far when the hatchling skidded to an awkward halt before her and swung its head around to observe her.

Instinctively, glancing at the dracling when she felt its gaze upon her, Nicole was sure a second that, instead of eyes, she was looking into an endless universe of stars.

When the dracling turned away again and bounded over to a nearby rock, Nicole felt an excited thrill. Shoving the Mar into her belt, she followed the dragon, watching with laughter as it gnawed on the rock before realizing that rocks weren't food at all, and then sneezed, rolling playfully onto its back.

She noticed suddenly that the handgun had knocked Diu's pouch of powder to the ground. Lifting up the tiny bundle before the hatchling got to it, she scooped scattered grains into the small bag. A few sparkles stuck firmly to her hands. Ignoring them, she fitting the pouch into her pocket. In the meantime, the dracling had scampered to its feet, and Nicole felt a smile tug at her lips as she looked at the creature. "Hey, come here," she called, reaching with her right hand for the dragon's head.

A lighting strike ripped through her arm. Nicole screamed, feeling the fire shooting through her body. Throbbing jolts sizzled along her spine. She doubled over, sprawled onto the floor, ears reverberating with her own shrieks. Through half-open eyelids, Nicole snatched a glimpse of the baby, staring peacefully with its dark eyes.

Suddenly the shivering stopped. She pushed herself upright, gripping her hand, alarmed at the numbness she felt. The dracling's scaly body rubbed against her leg, and she jumped back. This time, however, there was nothing except a soft, inquiring chirp from the baby.

The rock beneath her suddenly trembled. Weakly, Nicole glanced up and beheld a breathtaking and fearful sight. The passage was now illuminated with flickering orange light, emanating from what seemed to be the stone itself. The glow intensified till it hurt to stare at it, and Nicole was forced to look away. Still, the strange sight was tempting, and finally she took another peek.

If only she hadn't.

The cave flooded with fire. Moments later, a pitch-black blur ripped through the tunnel, still blasting flames from its massive jaws. Even before Nicole could get a good look at the creature, she already knew what it was. The hatchling's parents—at least one of them—had returned.

The black dragon landed with a crash of earthquake magnitude. Nicole scrambled to the edge of the cave, watching as the dragon carefully nudged its little infant. The hatchling squeaked welcomingly. The adult made a sound between a roar and a purr and licked the dracling lovingly.

Nicole quickly formulated a plan. Since the parent was so involved with its child, she just might be able to remain unnoticed. She moved instantly, bolting towards the passage—her only hope for escape.

The dragon whirled on her. Pulling the hatchling to safety beneath its massive body, the parent lashed out its tail and caught Nicole round the legs, suspending her upside-down in midair inches from jagged rows of glistening, saliva-glazed fangs. Nicole struggled, but she couldn't free herself. She screamed as the immense jaws snapped towards her, knowing this was the end.

Then a single word blasted like a trumpet in her head.

No!

The black dragon snorted wet air, but its fangs came no closer. Nicole flailed aimlessly in the dragon's grasp until the tail unexpectedly loosened its grip. She collapsed in a heap and quickly scampered behind a craggy boulder jutting from the ground. Trembling, she peeked out and stared at the dragon. It appeared, however, to have forgotten her entirely and was now licking away the last of the membrane still clinging to the youngling. The red dracling lolled around beneath its parent's tongue, peeping cheerfully.

Nicole slowly crept out from behind the boulder. The tunnel was nearby. It was her only chance. Tearing her gaze from the dragons, she broke into a breakneck run.

A flurry of crimson flashed into Nicole's line of sight. The next moment she lay sprawled on the ground, staring up at the inky eyes bedecked with stars. The hatchling's outstretched wings loomed above her. The baby's shining eyes moved closer to Nicole's face. Its pointed snout brushed her nose.

Hi, Nicole thought, expecting no response.

The baby recoiled as if electrocuted. It cocked its head curiously.

Nicole giggled. Sitting up, she placed her hands on either side of the dracling's head. *There's nothing to be scared of. I don't have scary fangs like yours, or claws, or fire-breath, or anything else that could hurt you.*

The infant nuzzled her arm. Its enchanting gaze roved over Nicole's face.

"My name's Nicole," she said aloud. Then on impulse— "What's *your* name?"

The hatchling lay down on its belly at her feet. Placing its head on her lap, the dracling closed its eyes.

Arli.

The soft female voice flickered in the back of Nicole's mind like the light of a weak candle. It surged through her body, rocked her thoughts. Like the gentlest touch of flowing water on smooth rocks, the voice inundated her with an overwhelming sense of peaceful power.

But it terrified her, too. Nicole shrank from the baby, knocking its head from her lap. The voice played over and over in her mind, each time flooding her with strength.

Arli. Arli. Arli . . .

Then a different word.

Me.

The hatchling cocked its head.

Me.

Nicole goggled, unbelieving.

Me.

A wild shock ripped through Nicole as her fingers met the

dragon's snout. Her hand was caressed by a curious, probing tongue, but she was too amazed to notice. A frightening, impossible conclusion had formed in her mind.

"Arli," she breathed. The baby looked up and a ripple of emotion that was not Nicole's own passed through her. The dracling, she finally accepted, was acknowledging its name—a name the hatchling had mentally told her.

A sharp tingle of pain suddenly crackled up Nicole's arm. I bet this is all because of that stupid powder, she thought. "Which I guess I shouldn't have stolen," she admitted half-heartedly to no one in particular.

Nicole considered her options. There was no way she was getting out of the cave alone and alive, seeing as how the parent dragon was aggressively guarding the passage, so it would be best to just hang around and tackle problems as they came. Arli—who was, judging by its voice, a female—had in the meantime warmed up to her. As day dimmed into evening, the dracling even encouraged her to taste some of the flame-cooked meat her parent brought.

At last the infant was exhausted, having spent an exhilarating first day of discovery. Arli curled beneath the adult dragon's massive wing, and then encouraged Nicole to cuddle in beside her, offering her belly as a pillow for the night. Nicole eagerly agreed, but when she first approached the nervous parent snarled an angry warning. Arli convinced it otherwise with soft peeps, and at last Nicole lay down beside the baby and pulled its wing over herself like a makeshift blanket. The soft leather cradled her body in warmth, ideal for the cold cave.

Chapter Twelve

Nicole didn't fully understand everything that had happened, but she was too tired to think anymore. Maybe Diu would have the answers when she found her friends again. But in the meantime, for the first time since she discovered the Galactera, she slept at ease, her mind whirling with dragons, prophecies, and magic.

* * *

The following day was bursting with excitement. Nicole gripped tightly onto a spine on the black dragon's back, adjusting her body slightly in the hollow at the base of the neck. She watched as the dragon—a mother, as she had learned—gently lifted Arli in her jaws, taking extra care to avoid damaging the baby's delicate wings. Arli peeped in excitement. The baby couldn't speak complete thoughts yet, but she knew a few English words that Nicole had taught her and used them when she could.

Ready?

Yep. Thanks, Arli. I owe you one.

Earlier that morning when Nicole had woken, she explained to Arli about needing help to get back to the valley. Her newfound friend eagerly convinced her mother to help. And though the black dragon was still wary of the Earth child, she consented, but only because of her baby's strange friendship with the bizarre, two-legged alien.

Nicole had also been well fed. Leaving her child behind, the mother had left in search of food, bringing back a massive creature the likes of which Nicole had never seen—nor, probably, would ever see again. For her baby's pleasure, the mother had roasted the meat with her fire, toasting it to steaming warmth. Nicole had again been allowed to share in the meal at Arli's insistence, and in turn she'd shared some of the spiral fruit with her dragon companion. And when they were both full, it was time to fly.

Nicole felt massive wings stirring and pumping hard on either side of her as the dragon lifted heavily from the ground and took off through the hole in the ceiling. The already bruised cavern roof buckled as the mother slammed against the rock. Frozen chucks crashed around them as they lifted out. A shower of ice met them when they burst through, but the mother's wings shielded them from the onslaught.

Yelling as the ground dropped away, Nicole felt her stomach convulse. The breath was suddenly snatched from her and she sat silently, tightening her grip on the spine. It was only when they leveled off that she found the courage to glance away from the scales before her eyes.

The planet looked mystical in the wake of sunrise. The amber sun graced the horizon like a brilliant orb of fire. The valley sang with light. The land beneath them flowed like a pearly river on a winter day. Breathlessly, Nicole leaned sideways as far as she dared to revel in the fantastic view.

Beneath them, the land gave way as they soared over the cliff. In open-mouthed amazement, Nicole gazed at the wonders that spread out before her. Loosening her grip, she spread her arms to the wind. Rippling, cool breezes beat against her skin. Her jacket fluttered from the mighty force of the gusting winds. Snow caught in her hair and on her face.

The mother banked, spiraling close to the ground. Ice streamed in a rush beneath them. Rolling hills and crested peaks glowed from the morning light. Nicole shielded her eyes as the dragon swept towards the sky once more.

Then the black dragon dove—a vertical plummet. Nicole had no chance to grab on. Black scales slipped out of reach—she was caught in a void. A blitz of wind roared in her ears. The world spiraled in a jagged mass. One moment she saw the snowy ground; the next, a merciless, abysmal sky.

The wind slashed with fury.

The ground came closer.

Ice hammered at her skin.

And closer.

She was blinded by fear and nausea.

And closer still.

Solid ice was a few blurry inches away when Nicole struck something warm and sturdy. Laboring to draw a lungful of air, she fought against the darkness threatening the corners of her vision. Struggling against unconsciousness, Nicole tried to get up but found herself too weak to move. Her head flopped back. She panted for air. There was a purr like a kitten and a muted cry.

Those were the last things she heard.

Chapter Thirteen

The Map

"Nicole? Nicole, are you okay?"

Eyelids lifting heavily, Nicole groggily shook her head. An anxious and frightened Lily hovered over her, quickly looking somewhat relieved. High rock walls reared around her, so high that she could barely see the ceiling.

"I . . . guess so."

"Good," snarled a cold, sullen voice.

Nicole winced. She'd known there would be much explaining to do, but she had hoped there wouldn't be too much trouble. If *that* was her greeting, Nicole knew it meant danger. "Diu, I—"

"I told you to *stay put*," he roared, stamping into her range of vision. "But you went out into the storm! You could have died, Nicole! Do you even understand what that means?"

She fought tears of resentment. "I was only trying to help. I was afraid we'd starve."

"I said I would get food! I was only waiting for the storm to pass. But you disobeyed a direct order, Nicole. You put your life at risk!"

Chapter Thirteen

"I'm sorry, okay!" she cried. "Going out was stupid, I know. But if you'd stop treating me like I'm a baby, maybe I'd listen to you more. And what do you mean, a direct order? You're not my boss, you know. I'm not your soldier or something."

"If you want to live, you're going to follow *my* orders, understand?"

"Going out was *my* choice. It had nothing to do with you."

A growl welled in Diu's throat. "Your choice, my choice! This isn't a game, Sky!"

Nicole was taken aback. She'd never seen him so furious. "Of course not. I'm not pretending it is."

"Your actions don't say that. You risked your life! And for nothing!"

"Guys . . ." Lily squeaked, trying to intervene, but Diu wasn't finished.

"You don't understand yet," he said, pacing. "But right now, you are more important than anything else in the universe. If anything happens to you—" He cut himself off, realizing what he'd said. "Forget it," he said quickly. "It doesn't matter." But the mistake had been made.

"Diu, *what* are you talking about?" Nicole gasped.

"It doesn't matter," he repeated, suddenly defensive. "Forget it. The important thing is that you're safe."

"Anyway," Lily said loudly, glad for a break in the fighting. "Me, I want to know what happened. You were gone for so long, and we weren't sure . . ."

Nicole cautiously relayed her tale. Lily stared incredulously the whole time, and even Diu listened with some interest when she spoke of the dragons. "Arli and her mother must have caught me when I fell," Nicole concluded.

"So you can speak to the dragons," Lily said in awe. "Me, I think that's amazing."

"Just Arli, actually. But yeah, it is pretty cool. Haven't a clue how, though."

"I think I might know," Diu interrupted, his voice back, at least temporarily, to its usual calmness. "When the dragon family—or Drácar, the common term for your dragons—left you by the entrance and we had made sure you weren't hurt, I noticed that you had taken the powder and used some."

"I'm sorry, I shouldn't—"

"That's not important. However, you *did* use the powder, correct?"

"Only accidently. It just spilled and I tried to scoop it back—"

"Was it on your hands?"

"Yeah, a little."

"Did you touch Arli with it?"

"No!" Then, a few moments later: "Maybe." And then: "Yes."

"Then that's the answer. This powder isn't ordinary. It is infused with true magic. Usually it will only obey spells, but rarely—very, very rarely—along comes a creature with magic of its own."

"What do you mean?"

Whatever Diu might have answered, he never got the chance because there was a sudden startling crunch of noise near the cave entrance. Arli waddled inside, feet caked with snow, and huddled shyly near the entrance. Nicole beckoned to her friends to follow as she squatted down by the baby, stroking Arli's head. Lily goggled over Nicole's shoulders, giggled as the dracling cocked her head in a puzzled stare, and bravely levitated over to pet the dragon. Arli cringed away at first, but a soft word from Nicole calmed her, and she allowed Lily to stroke her snout.

"I still can't believe it," Nicole said. "A real dragon. I thought they were just legends."

"Earth legends," Diu corrected. "But where do you think your dragons came from? The Drácar were one of few races to try to make peace with you humans, but even in your more primitive days you refused that."

"Hey, don't accuse me. It's not like I told them to kill dragons."

"Me," Lily said, still petting Arli's head, "I think she's cute. Are we going to keep her?"

The dracling crooned cheerfully, pumping her thin, filmy wings and raising a cloud of dust.

"Stop!" Lily shouted. She tried to look angry, but Arli gave her such a silly look that she could only smile.

An earsplitting roar suddenly ripped through the cavern. Nicole slammed her hands to her ears, shutting out the blast. With a terrified squeak, Arli rushed outside in a flurry. She paused for a moment, tilting her head towards the sky. Then she snorted and flared open her wings, trying to lift up. But her wings—even at an impressive eight-foot span—were still too weak. Arli tumbled and landed headfirst in a snowdrift.

Diving out, she folded back her wings and, stumbling, scrambled across the valley.

"Arli, wait! Hold on!" Nicole pleaded. She ran to follow, but then Diu leapt out in front of her. She skidded to a halt at the sight of the Mar in his paws.

"You're not leaving," he snarled. "Again."

"Am too! Arli could get lost. Or hurt. Or worse!"

"*You* are the one who could get hurt!"

"I'm going."

"You are not." He made a point of raising the gun just slightly. Enough for her to understand.

Nicole suddenly hated Diu. Of course, she'd never taken a liking to him to begin with, but that had just been distrust. This was loathing. She stormed back into the cave, if only to hide her eyes. She didn't want him to see what was there.

"What was that sound?" Lily asked quickly, if only to delay what seemed to be the promise of another argument.

"Beats me," Nicole snapped.

Lily shrugged. "Whatever it was, it doesn't matter." As an afterthought, she added, "Nicole, want to eat? You must be hungry."

Guilt surged. Caught up in the excitement of meeting the dragons, Nicole had forgotten all about bringing back food. "If you mean the stuff I went out to get," she mumbled, "I don't have anything. I mean found some food, but . . ." She pulled out two fistfuls of splattered fruit.

"Don't worry about it," Lily said cheerfully. "The dragon mother brought her baby some meat, and Arli shared with us. We saved you some. It's here beside the fire to keep warm."

Then she giggled and added, "Well, actually, *I* saved you some. Diu wanted you to go out and find your own food after what you did."

"Would have served you right," he said. But Nicole noticed that he had holstered the Mar.

She squatted down the by the fire, warming herself and watching Diu. He leaned against the cave wall by the entrance, staring at some point outside. Lily dropped down onto Nicole's shoulder, wiggling her large feet.

"Me, I don't understand him," Lily whispered.

"I get one thing," Nicole murmured back. "He really hates me."

"Me, I don't think so."

"Yeah? What gave you that crazy idea?"

"He won't admit it, but he went looking for you. Right away. In the blizzard and everything. Without even that gun he likes so much. Gave me the Glider and told me to get away if something went wrong."

"So?"

"If he hated you, he wouldn't have done that."

Nicole had to admit that there was truth in what her friend said.

As she started to eat, Lily caught her up on everything she had missed. "After the dragon brought you here, Diu and I were both really scared. Actually, can't speak for him, but *me*, I was. Thought you were . . . you know. Then Arli left with her mother and brought back food. We ate, and then me, I stayed with you while Diu looked at that tunnel in the back of the cave. Guess what he found!"

"Wocks?" Nicole joked around the glob of meat in her mouth.

Lily grabbed her by the wrist. "Stop fooling around and come see! Me, I didn't believe it until he forced me to go look!"

Nicole shoveled down the last scraps of meat. Her heart fluttered anxiously as Diu moved towards them. He glanced first at the tunnel, then at her. His eyes betrayed nothing.

With growing fear, she followed Lily into the dark tunnel, Diu bringing up the rear. The walls closed in, forcing them to crawl on their knees. Tinny drips of water echoed in the claustrophobic space. An unnerving breeze hissed through the passage. Darkness deepened into pitch, and soon they were forced to grope to find their way. More than once, Nicole smashed into a wall where the tunnel veered sharply.

After what seemed like an eternity, the passageway began to brighten. "We're nearing the end," Lily whispered, and suddenly Nicole remembered something and understood. The dark of the cavern and the glow ahead blended together to create a scene of surreal beauty and wonder.

Seek darkness mingled with light.

The passage suddenly transformed. The ceiling swerved up, leaving them room to stand. The tunnel itself was now bathed in pale, cerulean light that poured from the rocks themselves. When Nicole faltered briefly, Diu took the lead, forcing them in farther. As the light became more vivid, the tunnel wider, the walls smoother, and the passage more level, Nicole saw that they had reached the end.

They emerged into a vast, spherical chamber. Fragile icicles drooped from the ceiling. Enormous points of ice jutted from the ground, each emitting a hot blue glow. But none of these things captured Nicole's attention. Her eyes widened, entranced by the far side of the chamber, and she breathed, "What is that?"

"A map, Nicole, and our last hope," Diu said.

Weaving through the ice points to cut across the chamber, Nicole ran her cold fingers over a rectangle of icicles that jutted from the wall. Carved within this figure was a series of sketches and strange symbols that she couldn't understand.

Nicole's breath misted in clouds. She forced herself to ignore it, feeling only a rising sense of optimism as she backed away to see the whole picture. Four circles probably meant to be planets were carved in each corner of the map. Above each planet was etched a diamond-shaped crystal and below the circle a strange word.

Most enchanting and astounding, though, was the center. A small metal disk was implanted here—a real artifact, not one of ice. And crowning the map were four lines of symbols curved in an arch.

"I can't believe it," Nicole whispered.

Lily touched the wall. "Me, I think it's weird. This ice isn't cold, but the air and everything else is."

Diu didn't comment, and Nicole took it as a cue to move on. "What do the words mean?" she asked, pointing.

"'Earth,' 'Water,' 'Fire,' and 'Air,'" he said, characteristically getting right to the point. Nicole started to roll her eyes, and then realized something. His voice was indifferent. *Bored*, almost. As if he'd known what to expect.

"Four crystals," Lily said. "Like in the prophecy. Me, I guess that makes sense. But what's this thing? In the middle."

Gripping Madam Banda's dagger in her fist, Nicole wiggled the blade around the disk. It dropped into her hand with a small pop. Her fingers probed along the sides of the artifact. There were four large holes, centered as would be the cardinal directions of a compass. But there was nothing else interesting, so she pocketed the disk for later.

Diu shook his head. "Whatever it is, it's not significant now. The text up there, above the map, *is*, however, important." Again, the same apathy. And the same uninterested tone, even as he recited the next stanza of the prophecy:

> "The sun gives way to the darkness
> And a world submerged by sea
> Surrounded by eternal walls
> Set Espian treasure free"

"That's it?" Nicole groaned. She had hoped that they'd find at least a few of the crystals here, but all they got was another mystery.

Lily sensed her disappointment. "Me, I think it's okay." she said. "We'll just follow the trail."

"Of bread crumbs," Nicole joked.

"What?"

"Oh, you know, the two kids who find their way back home."

Lily stared blankly. Nicole sighed. "Never mind," she said.

"But I'm curious. Me, I—"

"Now is not the time for this," Diu snapped. "We have the next clue. All we have to do is figure it out. So let's get out of here."

He looked towards the tunnel, but before anyone could make another move, Nicole suddenly cried out. She cringed, collapsing to her knees, eyes narrowed to slits. Her fingers scraped at the ground as searing pain churned her insides, sending fiery tendrils along her arms and legs. Diu grabbed her by the shoulders and shook her as Lily shrieked, "What's wrong?"

But Nicole hardly heard Lily. Barely felt Diu's grip. Acknowledged the pain of his claws digging into her flesh with only a slight gasp. Because her mind was focused on four words that beat a terrible drum in her head. Arli's voice, once gentle, was trembling with anger, and she kept repeating a single phrase, over and over and over again.

Kidnappers, murderers, thieves, liars!

Chapter Fourteen

The Kidnapping

"Arli!" Nicole screamed against the torturous throbbing echoing through her body. She knew she was feeling the dracling's pain, but she did not understand what could possibly have happened.

"What's wrong?" Lily pleaded again.

"Never mind me, Arli's in trouble!" Nicole cried. "We have to find her!"

In a mad scramble, she skidded across the icy ground, wobbling and spreading her arms to stay on her feet. She sprinted into the pitch-black passage, fighting blindly through, scraping her knees and arms on the craggy earth. But at last, she saw the light that soaked the end of the tunnel.

Nicole dashed out in a frenzy and tore to the cave entrance. They had stayed inside longer than she'd thought. It was already dusk.

Kidnappers . . .

Arli, where are you? Nicole called, running outside. She stopped short when the snow swallowed her up to the waist. *Arli?*

Here, here!

Then there the dracling was, shoving her way through the snow. Her neck bobbed fitfully. The rest of Arli's body was submerged. Her head was bent over, and tiny red drops dripped from her mouth, shining against the virgin snow.

Arli fell into Nicole's arms. *Kidnappers . . . murderers . . . .*

Nicole shuddered from the shock of the baby's trembling body.

Arli, what's happened? Your mouth—you're hurt! Blood stained her jacket, leaving a dark smear.

Come! Arli thrust out her wings, using them to carve herself a path in the snow. *I show you.*

Let's just wait for—

No! Come. Now.

Nicole could hear sounds behind her and knew that her friends were near. But Arli was desperate and already far ahead, half-vanished in the snow. Deciding to run before Diu could stop her, Nicole took off and followed in the dracling's tracks. She couldn't bring herself to imagine what they would find at the end of their journey. Arli had refused her help, refused to wait, refused to listen. Yet her injuries seemed extensive. Her mouth was bleeding harder now, painting a thin line in the snow.

They traveled on, long enough for the last patches of light to fade from the sky. Darkness swallowed the valley, and Nicole found that even the jacket was not enough to keep out the frost. She tried to imagine that Arli was a fire, but she was too cold even to think.

"Arli, you've g-got to st-stop!" Nicole stammered. "Please!

I c-can't keep up!"

But the dracling was determined. Regardless of whether or not Arli heard the desperate cry, she only sped up. Nicole stumbled and pleaded again, but this time to the air. Arli had vanished.

Sinking to the snow, Nicole clasped her arms around herself. Cold seeped through her jeans, nipping at her legs. The craggy cliffs were merely skinny lines hovering over the horizon. Though she couldn't see them, Nicole felt certain that dark creatures were lurking about, creeping invisibly around her. Twice, she was sure the snow moved. Wild beasts poured from her imagination and stalked the stone-still valley, hunting the unknown. It seemed as if hours passed in that lonely span of time.

Then a vast smear of darkness reared up before her and charged, taking her by surprise. Nicole kicked out and rolled away. Leaping up, she squinted and tried to make out the shape. Its dark red color was unmistakable.

"Arli!" She ran to where the dracling's neck showed above the snow. "You really scared me! I thought you'd left."

The baby shook Nicole off and glared skyward. Her teeth were bared, and her wings shook visibly. Her whipping tail slashed the air. She snorted so hard that tendrils of frosty smoke poured from her nostrils.

They come now! Watch sky.

Nicole followed the dracling's gaze. She saw a massive band of stars that reminded her sadly of the Milky Way. Ragged clouds flitted pitifully through the sky, shoved along by a breeze that only made the night colder. The moon hovered like a shining eye above the mountains, watching over the valley.

Suddenly Arli growled. A falling star slashed across the heavens. It soared away beyond the mountains, shimmering with pale, cold light.

Kidnappers! The dracling pounced forward and tried to roar angrily, but her young voice only produced a pathetic, whiny peep.

It's just a falling star!

Not star! Ship! Bad, evil ship! Mama say evil Omenra on ship. They comes and take her! The ferocity the baby's peeps could not express fought through in her snarling tone.

Nicole felt a thick lump well up in her throat. Then she looked down and realized what they were standing in. A flat expanse of snow, trampled by feet and torn apart by struggle. And blood. Blood dripping over everything. Hot and steaming, soaking the white snow.

Nicole had heard of destinies being intertwined, but not like this. The little dracling looked away from the sky and buried her snout in the jacket. *I want Mama. Want Mama!*

Nicole wasn't sure what to do, so she made a promise. *We'll find your mother.*

Ignoring her, Arli bounded away. *I find you, Mama, and I rip, tear Omenras!*

Arli, I know it's hard, but you've got to calm down! I promise we'll find her, but you have to come here now.

Arli wandered back slowly. *Mama.*

Ignoring the biting cold, Nicole sank to her knees in the snow and cradled Arli's head in her arms.

We'll find her, Arli.

The dracling pressed her warm nose into the folds of Nicole's jacket.

Mama.

A lump welled in Nicole's throat. She fought against tears.

We'll find her. I promise.

Mama.

The dracling's mouth was bleeding harder than ever.

Chapter Fifteen

Predator

They camped in the open valley that night. Nicole tried to mop up Arli's wound again and wash it with melted snow, helplessly wishing she had Diu's powder. But the dracling seemed to have gone wild, stalking and pouncing on invisible prey. Time and time again she spread her wings and raced off across the snow as if in flight. After a while, Nicole simply gave up and tried to sleep alone, but the cold kept waking her at odd intervals.

The third time she woke, Arli was curled beside her, one wing draped over Nicole like a blanket. Glad of the warmth, Nicole rolled onto her side, remembering Earth. Her parents must think she ran away or else had been kidnapped. And Danny and Lex? They must be back by now. What would they think?

She forced the thoughts away. There would be time for that later. For now there was a more pressing matter, namely wondering how much of the precious month was left . . . and just how much of *Nicole* would be left once Diu got through with her after tonight.

Not that she cared much. Getting him mad had become

somewhat of a game now. One at which she was an expert. Which that thought and a grimace, Nicole felt asleep once more.

They awoke just before dawn in the same position, save for the fact that Arli was pushing the snow around with her nose and licking her snout clean of blood. Nicole was at first hesitant to probe the dracling for information lest the baby be driven into a frenzy again, but Arli seemed to be calmer now than last night. At last, Nicole decided to find out exactly what had happened.

Arli, you need to tell me about yesterday. Who hurt you?

The dracling didn't reply.

Please, I'm scared for you. Tell me and maybe I can help.

Arli's head drooped. *I not know what happen,* she admitted. *Omenra attack from nowhere. Mama says hide, and I do, and she fight them. She does good, but they better. They drag her onto ship and take her away, and I left alone.*

Shaking off pearly tears, the baby began to drift away.

Nicole had to run to keep up. *I promised you help, and I won't break that promise. But we have to go back now. We can't do this alone.*

Arli agreed, thought Nicole suspected this was mostly because of a lack of any other constructive recourse. Nicole led the way back as best she could remember. At the rate they were going, she hoped they would reach the cave by sunset—if they could find it at all.

As sunrise blossomed over the mountains, the planet came alive. The sun played tendrils of fiery light across the valley, and the ice sparkled like scarlet diamonds. Flurries of snow danced red-gold in heavy gusts. Swirling clouds of orange and pink raced overhead. Arli herself seemed to glow, her scales shining.

A sudden sound of cracking rock burst overhead. They had been wandering close to a cliff for shelter from the wind. A mistake. Nicole whipped her head up in time to see a silhouette against the sun. The shadow slammed into the ground not twenty feet away and turned on them, advancing over the ice. It was massive—a shaggy beast with long, curving fangs, clinking spines along its back, and a coarse tangle of fur covering its eyes. Its body and four legs were armored with metal, leaving only its gray head and paws free. Icicles crackled in its fur like demonic harbingers of death.

The thing was nearing, snarling. Arli squeaked, terrified, and huddled behind her friend. Nicole gasped and swung out an arm to shield the dracling, struggling to breathe and think fast all at once.

Arli, stay close, she warned, backing slowly away. The creature snorted and took a massive leap towards them, closing in ten feet. "At least it's alone," Nicole muttered to herself, an attempt at reassurance. But she knew that even one was enough.

When I say run, you follow me, she said. Arli crooned in understanding.

The beast was very close now. If Nicole wanted, she could have reached out and petted it. There was a deadly *snick* as six-inch claws snapped out from paws the size of monster truck tires. But she waited a second longer until the creature leaned back on its haunches, the sure sign of a pounce.

"Run!" Nicole shrieked, pelting sideways just as the beast

leaped into the air, slamming down right where she had been moments before. It roared, enraged, but its prey was already gaining distance.

"Keep going, Arli!" she cried. "Come on, faster!"

Luckily the snow wasn't as deep here as elsewhere, and it was hard-packed. It crunched beneath Nicole's sneakers and Arli's legs, allowing them to run more quickly. But it wasn't enough. The beast had gone berserk with rage and pounded after them, tearing through the snow in a fury.

Nicole thought fast. A cliff was swiftly approaching. There could be a cave there. A place to hide. Their only chance. But the beast was closing in much faster than the cliff. And there was another problem. Nicole had noticed the dark line winding through the valley when they first arrived. She hadn't known what it was then. Now she did. And she regretted not asking before.

It was a chasm, a vast gorge that ripped straight through the heart of the valley. It was several hundred meters wide at its narrowest, and it separated them from the cliff. Nicole snapped her head left and right, searching for a way to cross. There was nothing.

She and Arli reached the chasm before the beast and turned to meet it. The creature slowed and approached at a trot. It paused with curiosity, a predatory growl welling in its throat.

I protect you, Arli insisted, snarling.

No. I've got a better idea. You run away from here, and keep running. No matter what.

Nicole, no!

Arli, go! Go now! Go!

The beast moved simultaneously with the dracling. Nicole dodged left as it pounced, its massive claws scrapping the ice. She ran in the opposite direction to Arli, hoping to give the hatchling a chance to get away. But the hunter saw the baby as a worthier prize and leaped after her, leaving Nicole behind.

Help! Arli squealed as the creature hurdled over her, turning to meet the dracling head-on.

I'm coming! Out loud, Nicole screamed, "Hey!" At the same time, she jerked out her dagger and nicked the palm of her hand with its tip. "How's that smell?"

The blood served its purpose, distracting the creature long enough for Arli to just barely scramble away and make a dash towards Nicole. But realizing what had happened, the beast moved like lightning and jumped between them. It snarled, snapping fangs at the baby. Arli was dumbfounded, unable to move. Nicole saw her stare in blank horror as the creature advanced.

In desperation, Nicole took a running leap, shrieking, and landed on the creature's back. She snagged onto two long spines. Feeling herself slip, Nicole dug the dagger into the beast's flesh. The creature howled in pain and scraped at the nuisance with its needle-sharp claws. Several slashes hit their mark, tearing through skin and meat. Blood soaked Nicole's jeans and jacket. Her legs slid on the armor. But still she hung on.

Then the beast stopped, sniffing the air. It gave a mighty shake and flung Nicole off. She tumbled across the ground, cringing. Arli was beside her in a heartbeat, but Nicole couldn't hear the dracling's cries. Burning jolts of pain swallowing all her senses. She could barely muster enough strength to sit up.

The predator was silently standing a short distance away. It seemed to be waiting. Nicole forced herself to stand, leaning against Arli for support. Her whole right side was pulsing, straight from her hip to her ribcage. Breathing was hard.

And it wasn't even over.

A blood-curdling roar suddenly ripped through the valley, echoed and amplified by the cliffs. The beast howled at the sky and bowed its head. Nicole watched through a haze as two other creatures leapt down into the valley from a nearby overhang. They were more massive than the first and looked wilder, as if born from the black heart of chaos. The larger of the newcomers wore an armored covering over his head, crowned with three metal spikes. The rest of his body bore armor as well. He snarled something to his fellows and they ran ahead, fiercely cornering Nicole and Arli, stopping them from fleeing.

The leader moved forward. The stench of blood seemed to rouse him, and he tore Nicole away from Arli with a massive paw. She fell onto her back, her blood staining the white snow crimson. Nicole watched, unable to move, as Arli got between her and the creature, flaring out her wings and squeaking to ward him off. But the two other beasts shoved the dracling away and restrained her.

Nicole was left alone for their leader.

She cringed, grasping at consciousness. There was too much blood. It pulsed onto the snow, pooling in hot puddles. Everything was blurred. Through the soupy mass Nicole made out the vague image of the advancing beast, mouth half-open, teeth dripping in saliva.

She heard an enraged cry but didn't quite register it. All she saw was a shadow as it fell over her face. Someone cried her name—a small sound, and very far away. Then a rougher voice spoke beside her in a strange, snarling language. Forcing herself to focus, a familiar face swept into view, a face Nicole was infinitely glad to see.

"Diu," she breathed.

"Nicole!" cried the first voice again, and this time she recognized it as Lily's. Before she could say anything, Lily was beside her, crying. And then Arli was circling around her too, crooning and licking her face. They helped her sit, and finally Nicole established a clear focus.

Diu was balancing precariously on the JET Glider, speaking to the armored leader in its own language. The two guards stood warily by. The beast listened, and then ordered his fellows back. He dipped his head in farewell, snarled a command at his guards, and bounded away over the ice.

Diu leapt off the Glider, securing it onto his back. His face twisted into a look of rage. Whirling, he roared, "Nicole, if you *ever* do that again, I'll—" Then he stopped cold, eyes fixed on her bloody jacket. "No!" he cried, all anger gone. "Nicole, how bad is it . . . *no!*"

Lily peeled away the tattered jacket and shirt. For the first time, Nicole snatched a glance at her wound. She turned away fast to keep from fainting. Blood poured steadily from a chunk of missing flesh. At least two ribs were torn away entirely. Several more had cracked.

Diu knelt, gingerly touching her side. She winced, screaming out in pain. He raised his paw, dripping in her blood.

"Nicole, Nicole!" sobbed Lily. "Diu, what can we do?"

"Only one thing, and I'm not sure it will work. Nicole, stay still."

"Wh-what a-are . . . you . . . g-going to d-do?" she stuttered.

"Just hang on. Here, I'm going to roll you over—"

Nicole shrieked as he gently tugged her onto her uninjured side.

"Hold still! Now wait." Diu pulled out the pouch of powder. He poured some onto his paw. "Lily, Arli—hold her still. I'm not pretending this is going to be pleasant."

Nicole writhed as he rubbed the powder over her ragged flesh. It stung like fire. She kicked out, nearly hitting him, but he dodged and shook more powder onto her skin. An acid splash would probably have been less painful.

"Stop it!" Nicole shrieked. "I-I c-can't . . . t-take th-this, I—"

"It's this or the wound!"

"Th-the . . . I'll t-take . . . the wound."

"And risk death?"

"N-not th-this! N-not . . . not . . ."

The pain swelled to suppress her voice. Every word was a struggle, and Nicole barely managed to stay conscious.

But as the powder began to glow, she felt what she was certain was her last breath hiss out. A shadow glossed over her vision, coupled with another tear of lightning pain. Then she fell away into nothing.

Chapter Sixteen

Espia

"Nicole . . ."

Someone was calling to her, close by. Nicole stirred faintly. Her vision was soaked in darkness. The air smelled of the cold. Her memory was fuzzy, but there was something . . .

And then she remembered. Her fingers flashed instinctively to her side. She touched unbroken skin.

Nicole tried to sit up, but it was a few groggy moments before she could fully lift herself to that position. The high walls of the familiar cave reared around her. Before she could speak, two creatures barreled into her head-on.

"You're okay!" Lily exclaimed. Arli licked Nicole's face in excitement.

"No clue how, though," she groaned. "That creature nearly tore me to bits."

"You are lucky we found you in time."

Nicole was shocked to find Diu's voice gentle, worried, and, above all, entirely friendly. He squatted next to her with no apparent signs of rage.

She burst out, "Look, I'm sorry, okay? The first time was bad enough, but this time was insane! I don't know why I didn't wait for you two. I went out by myself, into the cold, nearly got myself killed, and—"

"It's okay," he said softly. "Just be glad the Korrak king is an old acquaintance of mine. I managed to cut his hunt short."

Nicole stared as if he'd started break-dancing. "You're not . . . *mad*?" she gasped.

"You're safe. That is all that matters."

"But . . . but . . ." she trailed off, utterly confounded. Talk about major mood swings.

He didn't let the subject linger. "I want to know what happened last night. Everything right up until we found you."

Lily and Diu listened with rapt attention as Nicole relayed her adventure. Only once did Lily look away, casting a pitying glance at Arli, who lay curled up at Nicole's feet. But Nicole herself could barely keep her focus on Arli's story. Her mind was locked on a single instant.

"I owe you my life, Diu," she finished in awe.

"There was nothing special involved. Just a Glider and a lucky guess."

Then he changed the subject entirely.

"Any idea who took Arli's mother?"

Nicole flinched. The one thing she hadn't revealed was the identity of the kidnappers. "Yes, I know," she said slowly. "The . . ." she stopped, frightened to speak.

"Who was it, Nicole?" Lily chipped in.

Silence. Then:

"The . . . the Omenra."

This revelation was followed by a dark stillness that stifled all conversation. It was Nicole who finally broke the silence.

"What do you think they want with her?"

"I can't begin to imagine," Diu said solemnly. Nicole was sure he knew more than he was letting on, but before she could probe further, he said, "I think our best bet would be to start our search for the crystals. Nicole, I know you want to help Arli, so before you start arguing, I think our only hope for finding her mother is getting the crystals. Why? Because we need to find the Omenra. If they know about the crystals, they'll be after them, too. And I have a feeling they know."

"Just remember I made her a promise to find her mother. I won't break that."

"I understand. You *will* keep your promise. Just not immediately."

"Fine!" Nicole barked. She knew Diu was right, that they were running out of time, that Earth was the critical problem, that her home, life, and people were in danger. Yet even after everything he had done for her, there was still something strange about him. Nicole almost felt as if she was begin pulled into a trap. What kind of trap, and why, she wasn't sure. But she wasn't about to blindly trust or openly follow Diu, and she wanted to make sure he knew it.

"Me, I think that sounds like a plan!" Lily exclaimed. "Just as soon as we solve the next stanza—"

"Already done," Diu said. "We are given a reference, and then it's just trivia. 'Espian' refers to Espia."

"What's it like there? On Espia?" Nicole asked curiously.

"Espia is a water-based world, completely submerged. But you will see soon enough for yourself."

"Me, I guess we're ready for the Galactera, then!" Lily said.

Nicole nodded. "We'll leave right away." And looking meaningfully at Arli curled miserably in a trembling ball, she added, "All of us." The dracling squeaked half-heartedly.

Nicole pulled out the pocket watch. And stopped.

It was stupid, being afraid of the device. Twice it had teleported her safely. And Diu had used it even before then. So what was she so scared of?

There was something even stranger about the watch, if that was possible. Nicole felt it. She couldn't name it, this strange thing, but it was there, and strong, and growing. Maybe she was just crazy. Paranoid. But sometimes, she wasn't sure.

And what Nicole did know was that, just now, she had felt that something again.

She realized that everyone was staring at her. Lily at the watch, Arli at her hands, and Diu . . . at her face. She wondered why. He answered before she could ask.

"Your eyes, Nicole. I can read you flat without you saying a word. Fear, excitement, doubt—it's all there. You need to learn to control yourself. You must control what you show, what you feel—"

"Hey, I'm not a robot. Not a soldier, either, in some crazy boot camp."

"No, you're right. You are not those things. But you *are* in a war."

She chuckled. "I'd hate to see what your commanders are like."

Chapter Sixteen

"My . . . what?"

Nicole rolled her eyes. "Since you're just some guy in the lowest ranks and totally strict and serious and whatever, I'd hate to see what the Airioth leaders must be like."

The corners of Diu's mouth twitched. "They are strange, all right."

Suddenly Lily broke in. "Me, I want to know if we're leaving anytime soon. We can chat later. When we're on Espia."

"Fine, fine," Nicole laughed. She found the button labeled *Espia*. "All right everyone, grab hold," she instructed, stretching out her arm so the watch would teleport them all. And then, trying to control her fear, Nicole tapped the button. Regret, she hoped, would come later, if at all.

Later was immediately defined as a few seconds.

The blue vortex swelled with water. A massive torrent blasted against Nicole's head, pounding against her body, coiling around her legs. She barely had time to swallow air before she was submerged and struggling. Judging by the darkness of the water, they were deep below the surface—wherever they were.

A furry paw brushed Nicole's arm. Lily floated into view, hovering limply in the water. Nicole grabbed the little alien's paw and clutched her close. Arli churned the water several feet away, choking for air. Nicole's own lungs felt like they were about to burst. She begged for some miracle that might save them.

Then something pulled at her, and the water churned violently. She thrashed around to see what was going on. Her mouth dropped open in a silent scream. *Not again*, she thought.

Propelled by giant fins, a massive fish swam towards her. It was completely black except for a few yellow stripes that ran horizontally around its body. Bristling spines struck out along its back, and when the fish opened its mouth, Nicole saw jagged teeth jutting from its gums. But far worse than anything about the fish itself was what the monster did next.

Arli was whipping about madly in the water. Her eyes were bulging in fear, and when she tried to snarl at the fish, she only produced a few wispy bubbles that floated away like a last hope. The creature, which was many times larger than the little dragon, swung its great bulk up next to her.

Its jaws snapped open and swallowed the baby whole.

Nicole felt her stomach turn over. Arli, a newborn in the world. Gone. Just like that.

But the fish didn't stop there. It turned on the only creature that seemed to be completely calm, even considering their dire situation—Diu. He seemed to hover in a surreal state for the longest moment before the fish's teeth clamped down on him, too.

When it turned for her, Nicole didn't even try to swim away. She'd escaped from the Klith and the tornado, from the Omenra and the spider, from the Shazgor and the Korrak . . . only to find her grave below the ocean. She hugged Lily one last time and felt purple fur tickle against her arms. The fish beat its gigantic tail one last time, closing the few remaining feet between them. Lily's fur brushed her arm again as the fish's gaping jaws swallowed up the sea.

And the world was gone.

Chapter Seventeen

Coralian City

Nicole felt her eyelids flicker open. At first, she couldn't remember where she was or what had happened. She sat up. Her line of vision began and ended in an oval-shaped room. Wooden benches stood in two rows, and there was a long window along each wall, below a high, curved ceiling. There were two doors, one at each end of an aisle that ran between the benches. Standing, Nicole looked down to see a marble-like floor shimmering beneath her feet.

A sudden jolt nearly threw Nicole to the floor. Grabbing onto a bench for support, she quickly sat. She hadn't noticed it before, but the room was swaying slightly. Even better, her companions were nowhere in sight. Confused and frightened, Nicole pressed her forehead to the cold window.

She tried to piece things together. They'd teleported to Espia and had been . . . eaten? Then where was she now? Why was she unharmed? And where were the others?

There was something strange about the window. The sky seemed to be the wrong shade of blue. It was dark, but not black; it almost had a purple hue. A fish flew past the window.

Flew? No, swam!

She jumped to her feet as if electrocuted. What was going on?!

The door near the front creaked open and Nicole spun towards it. Lily meekly peeked inside, but when she saw that her friend was awake, she burst forward in a blur.

"Nicole!"

As the little alien squeezed out a hug, Nicole, the victim of utter confusion, stared blankly. She couldn't believe that they were still alive. When Nicole spoke, her words were slurred. "Lily? You're okay! How? I thought . . . we . . . for sure, I . . . and, well . . . we were eaten!"

"Me, I thought so, too. But turns out this isn't a real fish at all! I was told to tell you that we're on a kind of *taxi*. Whatever that means. The driver saw us in the water and rescued us."

Nicole opened and closed her mouth wordlessly. A taxi? But before she could speak again, the slightly ajar door slammed open, and Arli barreled in. *Nicole!* The dracling skidded into her, and when they were sprawled over the marble floor, Arli licked Nicole's face all over. *Safe!*

Good thing we all are. But when Arli finally got off and Nicole climbed up onto a bench, she noticed someone was missing. "Where's Diu?"

"Up front with the driver. They've been chattering away since we got here. Like best buddies."

"Did they say where we're going?"

"Yep. Coralian City. About half an hour away. Diu told me to tell you to just stay put."

"Like I've got any other choice this time," Nicole muttered.

Lily made a face and went off to play with Arli in the aisle.

Half an hour drifted by in silence. After a while, Lily grew tired of her game with Arli, crawled onto the bench across from Nicole, and promptly fell asleep. Sometime after that, Arli drifted off to sleep as well. She lay spread out on the floor, dreaming, her feet twitching madly as she chased imaginary prey.

Nicole leaned back, too, but just as she was beginning to feel sleepy, a speaker hanging over the front door crackled and a voice announced something in a squeaky, completely foreign language.

Whatever it was, it sounded important.

"Lily! Lily, wake up," Nicole shouted, hoping Lily would be able to translate.

"Ugh . . . wha—?" the little alien groaned. She leaned forward slowly and rubbed her eyes, blinking out the sleepies.

"Oh, never mind now," Nicole said, looking up at the now silent speaker. "You can go back to sleep."

"Except me, I'm not tired anymore," Lily said happily. "Going to look around." She hovered to stare out the window. And gasped.

"What's wrong?" Nicole yelled. She was beginning to expect just about anything.

"Nothing's *wrong*," Lily said breathlessly. "It's just the most amazing thing! Coralian City looks awesome! It looks like . . . well, kind of like . . . or maybe . . . oh, just look outside!"

Nicole pressed her face against the window. Blinking, she continued to stare until it all soaked into her mind. She could believe it, but she couldn't manage a word.

Spread out as far as Nicole could see was a most incredible world. Coralian City was not comprised of buildings as she'd expected but instead of seaweed and spheres made of some clear substance. Thousands of these spheres were attached to twisting stalks that were each taller than the greatest skyscrapers on Earth. An intricate structure of clear tubes linked the city together. And the closer they drew, the more mechanical fish she noticed swimming about outside the seaweed city.

As the taxi neared the great metropolis, Nicole made out hundreds upon thousands of creatures milling about inside the spheres and tunnels. They appeared as tiny dots from where she stood, all rushing and pressing together in wave after wave of motion.

Not the least incredible thing about the city was the way to enter it.

The taxi suddenly jerked roughly, signaling an end to the ride. Traffic, probably. At any rate, several lines of fish vehicles snaked towards the city, all waiting to get inside.

"This is so cool!" Lily exclaimed.

The taxi pulled forward again. Nicole craned her neck and saw that they were approaching an enormous sphere the size of several football fields. The problem was that she couldn't see how the taxi was supposed to get inside. There weren't any openings, although that made sense since the spheres were obviously full of air. No doubt the aliens who lived in the city couldn't afford to flood Coralian every time a vehicle entered. But then how *were* they supposed to get in?

The fish in front of them appeared to magically pass into the glass sphere, and it was only when it was their taxi's turn to enter that Nicole understood the secret. The spheres—this one, at any rate—were made of some kind of membrane that allowed them to pass through. Once their taxi was inside, the membrane sealed behind them. They made a bee-line for a vacant space and parked by a particularly fearsome-looking mechanical eel with red flames splattered along its length.

A sharp whine blasted Nicole's ears as the cabin door reluctantly groaned open. Diu walked through it, conversing in a strange language with a bizarre creature. The alien, roughly humanoid, had lightly tinted green skin and shoulder-length braids of kelp-like hair laced with beads. It had a wide, pleasant smile. When it gave them a wave, Nicole saw that the alien's fingers were linked with thin membranes. Exchanging a final word with Diu, it stood quietly and goggled curiously.

Diu stepped between them. "Nicole, Lily, Arli—this is my friend Rayonk."

The alien immediately launched into an eager babble of which Nicole understood exactly nothing. "Umm, Diu . . ." she said.

He held up a hand to stem Rayonk's stream of words and unclipped a circular device from his belt. "I've been meaning to give you this for a while now. I have had to learn your language but, with the very rare exception, few other creatures are going to know English." Indicating the mechanism, he explained, "This is an automatic translator. Fit this around your ear and see if that is any better."

Nicole swiveled the device tightly in place, noticing for the first time that Diu and Rayonk both wore one too. "Sure it works?"

Rayonk burst into speech again. At first she couldn't understand a word, but suddenly the translator hissed in her ear. ". . . is bestest pleasure meeting you," he finished.

"Pleasure's all mine," Nicole said warmly.

"Me, I'm Lily," her friend said, grinning. "Cool hair."

Rayonk replied with a terrified squeal. Nicole pounced forward in time to pull a very grumpy, snarling Arli away from his leg. He backed away very slowly, braids jangling wildly. Arli lunged again, and Nicole only just managed to restrain her with Diu's help. At first she thought that Rayonk had just stepped on the dracling's tail, but then Arli fiercely explained, *I no trust him. He no good, I sense it!*

What are you talking about! We haven't even known him for five minutes!

"Nice animal . . . thing. Stay back, please." Rayonk threw a pleading glance at Diu.

"Nicole," Diu hissed in her ear. "Get Arli under control!"

"I don't know what's wrong! She just went berserk for a second, but she's fine now." *Aren't you?*

Rayonk slipped back into the cabin, and a moment later one side of the fish slid open towards the top. He jumped out and motioned for them to follow. Still wary of Arli, Rayonk said, "Diu tells me all about what's happening. I takes you to my house, we discuss there. Okay?"

Nicole glanced at Diu. He dipped his head in approval. "Do we have time for a quick tour?" she added. "This place looks amazing!"

"Me, I'd love one!" Lily exclaimed.

As would I, but not with him.

Ignoring the last part of the dracling's statement, Nicole said, "Arli agrees. What do you think, Rayonk?"

"If it okay with Diu, I be glad to!"

"Please?" Nicole begged.

Diu shook his head. "We don't have a day to kill."

"Oh, come on!" Nicole cried. "Please, please?"

His gaze hardened, but he relented. "Very well. One day."

Nicole hopped down first from the taxi. Lily secured her favorite shoulder spot, and Arli scampered out, keeping beside Nicole. Diu came last of all, slamming the taxi door shut.

All around green-skinned aliens dispersed among the fish cars. There was noise everywhere as they chatted and swapped gossip, fish throttled towards parking spaces, and vehicles swam in and out of the city through the membrane. For Nicole, it was surprisingly almost like being home on Earth again.

Lily draped her legs over the side of Nicole's shoulder, eagerly looking around. Arli made small, frightened noises. Diu walked ahead of them, looking quite at home.

"This is welcome center and parking place for visitors," Rayonk explained, swinging an arm overhead for emphasis. "Two sides of bubble made of membrane so metal fishes can go in and out. But is special, so only robot fishes can go through."

They moved on to the central city, the grand metropolis of Coralian. Enclosed in one massive sphere, it was just like New York City—bustling, loud, and breathtaking. The city also held the charm of Nicole's own hometown. Lush (though strange) vegetation flowered on every corner and along every road. They passed soaring stalks of seaweed sprinkled with spheres and caught a ride on a serpent-shaped bus.

Later in the day they ate at an alien-style restaurant. It was an interested experience, considering that alien food *period* was strange enough. Undersea alien food was even odder. But Nicole didn't want to miss out on anything, so she ordered some of everything that was offered. The table before her ended up piled with more things she wanted to try in one place than she had ever seen in her life. And still, the best part was yet to come.

To finish off the day, Rayonk showed them a dealership where the fish cars were sold. Nicole particularly enjoyed browsing through the sporty sharks.

"Care to try one out?" Diu asked halfway through, grinning mischievously.

Nicole stared as if he'd gone crazy. "You mean . . . drive?"

"Sure. You keep telling me you're not a baby. So care to get behind the wheel?"

His playful remark was enough to get her into an open-top, two-seat tope shark, motorcycle-style. There was only one device on the dashboard, a built-in green pad with a pale glow. Diu slid in behind her. He leaned forward and pointed at the pad.

"Touch your finger to it."

Nicole prodded the pad with her forefinger. The car roared into life, rising a few feet off the ground.

"Now place your hand on the pad. Gently. Very gently."

"Okay, gently. Got it."

She slapped her hand down and screamed as the car

screeched forward, nearly slamming into a group of shoppers wandering in the lot. Diu only just managed to pull her hand off in time.

"I said gently!" He looked up and waved at Rayonk two rows over. "Hey!" he called in a strange language that Nicole's earpiece quickly translated. "Hang around with Lily and Arli and let the dealer know we're taking this tope for a ride."

Nicole twisted around in her seat. "Are you serious?" she cried, half laughing.

"Care to trade places?"

She let him onto the driver's seat and climbed in behind.

"Um, Diu?"

"Yes?"

"There aren't any seatbelts."

"But that would ruin half the fun," he said, touching down on the pad.

Nicole shrieked as the car roared onto the parking lot. Diu swerved expertly, tearing past a terrified group of locals. He maneuvered the vehicle flawlessly into a main tunnel, throttling it down a notch as he zoomed over the heads of pedestrians. Nicole grabbed onto the sides of the car to avoid being thrown off.

There was a traffic jam ahead.

"Slow down!" she screamed.

"Hang on," Diu muttered.

"What're you—aghhhhhh!" Nicole screamed as the world flipped over. She clutched her seat as they sped upside-down beneath the other cars. Passing the traffic, Diu righted the car again, slowing to a crawl. Nicole peeled her fingers away from the seat and took a shaky breath. "Okay, let's go back," she said.

"Go back?" Diu mocked. "Why, are you scared?"

"No way!"

"Then I'm only just getting started. I have been keeping to the rules so far, but it's time to go off-road."

Nicole looked around, recognizing the welcome center. Craning her head forward, she saw that they were at the back of a line. A line leading straight . . .

"Outside?" she squeaked.

Diu eagerly tapped his claws on the dash. "You bet."

"Uhh . . ."

"Yes?"

"You know there's no top on this thing."

"So?"

Nicole was sure she had heard wrong. "How am I supposed to breathe underwater?"

They were next in line.

"Diu, you're not serious!"

"I am."

"How are *you* supposed to breathe?"

"Let's work that out *after* we get outside."

"Are you insane?!"

"Slightly," he muttered, slamming down on the green pad.

Nicole screamed again as the car lunged forward through the membrane. But it didn't fill with water. A transparent shield slid tightly over the top of the tope. Diu smirked, pointing at a lever hidden under the dashboard.

"Not funny!" she retaliated, laughing.

The shark sliced through the ocean like a knife. Whispering motors drove them deep below the surface to where it was nearly pitch black. Mysterious sounds echoed around them. Strange shapes lurked in the water, shadows in a dark mass. But for some reason, Nicole suddenly realized she felt safer than she had ever felt in her life.

"Would you like to see something incredible?" Diu asked.

"Yeah," she replied softly.

Diu revved the engine, and they sank deeper. Even in the darkness, Nicole could see a faint glow approaching from below. Skirting along the sea floor, Diu drove them into a clump of tall, waving shapes. He throttled until they reached a clearing. Then he slowed the car and removed his paw from the pad.

They stopped.

"Where are we?" Nicole whispered. It felt strange to break the absolute silence.

In reply, Diu reached beneath the dashboard and shifted another lever into place, igniting a series of electric-blue lights on the outside of the tope.

The world around them burst into a wild bloom of life. Bright colors vibrated with thousands of species. The shapes transformed into lush stalks of multicolored seaweed. Fish darted all around, a rainbow of sparkling light. Giant jellyfish with wisp-like stingers drifted lazily by. Tiny animals skittered along the vivid yellow-orange sand below.

The sands glowed with their own mystic light. Nicole

glanced over the side of the car just as a large snake-like fish squirmed out from a narrow tunnel, pursued by an enormous crab animal with four hefty pincers. A low, echoing call wrenched her attention away.

A pod of gigantic creatures floated overhead, moving like wraiths through the water. Black serpent heads gave way to gray spines and ribcages. Resting in the safe clutches of the skeleton-like bodies were large sacs of what seemed to be blue fire. One creature glanced briefly at the car before gliding on with the group.

The smallest of the pod showed more than passing interest and dived towards them. Nicole looked into its wide amber eyes as the creature turned a loop above the car. An annoyed bugle from the pod leader called it back.

The whole scene was a swirl of beauty unlike anything Nicole had ever seen. Nor, she thought, unlike anything she would ever see again. She didn't know what the rest of her journey would bring, but this one moment made everything so far worth it.

"This place," she whispered, "is amazing."

"I thought you would like to see it."

"How did you know it was here?"

"This is not the first time I have been here."

"When was the last time?"

"A long time ago," Diu answered slowly. "Nearly ten Earth years back." He let Nicole enjoy the scene for a few moments longer. "We should be getting back," he said at last.

"We should," she echoed reluctantly. She wondered if she'd ever get the chance to come back.

Chapter Seventeen

Diu placed his paw back on the pad, and the engine whispered to life. "Consider yourself lucky," he said as he tilted the car into a climb. "You're one of only three non-natives to have ever seen this place."

"Who were the other two?"

"Me," Diu said. He paused. "And Serena," he said at last.

"Serena?" Nicole repeated. She was sure she'd seen the name before and thought back. And then she remembered.

"That's the name on your necklace."

Diu did not respond.

As the tope whispered off into the shadows of the ocean, Nicole felt the significance of this simple, quiet day. She wondered if it was a prelude for what was to follow. A day of peace, followed by a dark future. But somehow, Nicole felt sure in that moment that, no matter what was coming, she could face it.

They could face it. All of them.

Together.

And that was a comforting thought as they set off for Coralian.

Chapter Eighteen

Convincing Rayonk

The first thing out of Lily's mouth when the tope shark car veered into a parking spot was a string of very uncharacteristic and angry words directed at Diu. He waited patiently till she was through. Then he smiled in a very calm, irritating manner and asked, "Your point?"

Lily made a choking sound. "You randomly go off with Nicole and leave me and Arli here all alone and think that's *okay?*"

"You were not alone. I left Rayonk with you."

"Fine, so *technically* not alone. But Arli wouldn't get near him! Kept trying to run off to look for you two, so me, I was stuck all by myself—" She broke off, and her eyes narrowed in anger. "Are you even listening?" she cried.

Diu jumped down from the driver's seat. "'Course," he said absentmindedly, wandering off to find Rayonk.

"Me, I can't believe him," Lily growled as Arli greeted Nicole with a rub against the legs. "He thinks he can just go and do whatever he wants with no consequences." Then curiosity overcame anger and she whispered, "So, where'd he take you?"

Bending to pet Arli, Nicole grinned. "Nowhere."

"But you were gone for so long! Me, I know you must have gone somewhere cool."

Nicole glanced at the lights lining the edges of the floor near the membrane sphere. They were dimmer than before—artificial night, she reasoned.

"Come on!" Lily begged.

Nicole opened her mouth, and then closed it. For some reason, she didn't want to tell Lily. She kept her mind innocently blank altogether for fear that Arli could hear more than just direct thoughts. It felt silly, though. The place had been beautiful, but that was all. What, then, was she hiding from her friends? And why?

But she knew the answer even as she wondered. Excluding the natives of Espia, only three creatures had ever seen that place. Being one of them made her feel strangely special, and she liked that feeling of power. It was a guilty feeling, but a good one.

"There wasn't anything interesting where we went," Nicole said firmly. "Diu just got something into his head and decided to take a drive."

Lily wasn't satisfied, but she dropped the matter.

At last the whole group gathered and set off. Rayonk led them away from the main part of the city and down a winding tunnel that let out at another seaweed stalk, this one covered in spheres that, as he explained, were homes. They rode up on an 'elevator' made of a polished chunk of coral and tugged by long strands of kelp. When the platform jerked to a halt before a large sphere, Rayonk gently stroked the entrance diagonally with one long finger and a door slid up, allowing them passage. Inside was a giant space that served as several rooms at once. The center was a living room, complete with a plush sofa and chair made of some oddly seaweed-textured, dark green material. To the far left of the entrance was a large bed with a fluffy blanket draped over a pillow, and to the right was a kitchen and table.

Nicole found herself unable to stay awake. She was utterly exhausted and waited only long enough for Rayonk to direct her to the bed with Lily and Arli before curling up beneath the soft, delicately woven covers, made of the same seaweed-like material as the living room furnishings. Rayonk lay down on the sofa, using the armrest as a makeshift pillow. Diu leaned against the chair but didn't sit, seemingly never tired and always alert. Nicole was glad of it.

The covers gracefully folded around her, swallowing her in comfort. The bed itself was a wonder—the material wasn't water but felt just like it, bending slightly yet holding her firmly. Arli's warm weight settled in beside her. Lily draped herself over the pillow, wiggling her large feet. Nicole stared up through the domed ceiling. Dozens of tiny fish darted around just beyond the transparent walls. They flashed every color of the rainbow, some in hues that were too beautiful and fantastic to describe. The colors began to lull her into sleep . . .

Suddenly, Nicole jolted wide-awake. She hadn't thought

about it before, but now the whole thing was curious. They had randomly teleported to Espia but had conveniently appeared almost right next to a taxi whose driver just happened to be one of Diu's friends. Or was it random? Nicole snuck a glance at Diu. He seemed innocent, but more than ever, she wasn't so sure.

More so even than the ocean and fish and brilliant colors, the thought remained with her as she drifted to sleep.

* * *

After a very long night—it felt at least several hours longer than an Earth night—Nicole woke up to stare at a large pair of black eyes inches away from her face.

"Ahhhhhhhh!" she shrieked and fell sideways off the bed.

"Ha! What, you `fraid?" Rayonk asked slyly.

"Of course I wasn't scared," she mumbled. "Just surprised. You shouldn't sneak up on people like that."

Rayonk snickered rather unkindly and walked to the kitchen. There, a partially assembled group sat around the table. Nicole joined them but immediately saw that their circle wasn't complete. "Where'd Diu go?" she asked, sitting down.

"Diu, this! Diu, that!" Lily growled. "Me, I think Diu is insane! We told him we were going to have breakfast. He looks happy and pleased about it right until we put the food on the table. Then he runs right out the door, going who knows where!"

"You're still mad about yesterday," Nicole pointed out.

Lily didn't reply. Instead, she pushed a plate across the table. "Try this. It's good."

Piled high was some sort of wiggly food that resembled

seaweed dancing a jig. Nicole poked it with her finger, but when the food hissed at her, she suddenly didn't feel very hungry anymore. Nicole found satisfaction in a bowl of fruity-tasting orbs.

There was a knock at the door. Rayonk stood to open it, and Diu marched in, grinning. He was clutching something eagerly.

"Very proud of yourself, are you?" Lily said. "Leaving us alone. Running off somewhere. Coming back with . . . hey, what is that?"

"This," he said, setting down the object—a flat rectangular box—on the table, "is a map."

"For what?" Lily asked, but Nicole already knew.

"To find the crystal," she said.

"Yes," Diu said. "I thought there was no sense in wasting time more time when we running out of it. Look here." He tapped a tiny button on the side of the rectangle, projecting a three-dimensional holographic map of Espia over the table. Touching a tiny dot on the map, he magnified the image of Coralian City.

"We are here, see?" Diu indicated. "Now, I have just been to the city archives. I remembered reading something there once about an elusive treasure but, because I'm not much of a treasure hunter, I never gave it attention. But then I thought back and realized that maybe it is not a real treasure at all—not like gold or precious gems, but something very different."

"Like a crystal," Nicole said, jumping ahead. Then, realizing what she had so openly blurted out, she glanced warily at Rayonk.

Diu picked up on her concern. "Don't worry," he said. "Rayonk is a friend. He knows about your quest. And yes, you are right. I think it might be the crystal, so I mapped a location; it wasn't hard because so many have tried to reach that place. And if what I've learned is accurate, the crystal should be in a cave somewhere around,"—he prodded another point on the map, and a glowing line connected Coralian to the new location—"here."

Rayonk slammed his fist hard on the table, cutting the conversation short. The wiggly plate of food overturned and bits scattered all over the floor. He cried, "You can't go."

"And why not?" Diu asked coolly.

"Because I tries to find cave myself, but it not worth it! Treasure in very terrible, dangerous place where many creatures go but none comes back!"

"Rayonk," Diu said kindly, but firmly. "I hope you haven't forgotten some of the things we've been through before. Whatever is in that cave can't be even near the worst."

Rayonk looked away.

Diu waited.

Groaning in resentment, Rayonk snapped, "When I involves myself in mission, I not know it means this." Then he sighed and bobbed his head. "But fine, I takes you. But I only do it because it against Omenra and their Terranova."

Nicole blinked in surprise. Surely Diu wouldn't have revealed so much! Unless . . . what if Rayonk was somehow involved with the Airioth force as well?

Suddenly Rayonk jumped clear onto the table. He wound himself into a frenzy. "I hate Omenras! They try take Espia before, but we no let them, remember! Now I gets even with them! We teach them to mess with Rayonk and friends! You following me, I show you the way!" He leapt down, picked up a few pieces of the wiggly food from the floor, and popped them into his mouth. As Rayonk chewed, a determined grin blossomed on his face, and then he was making plans, telling Diu to pack that, Lily to do this, and Nicole to fetch that.

Nicole happily listened and did as she was told. But when she asked Arli for help and the dracling refused, she recalled the hatchling's warning words. Thinking back to Rayonk's grin, she wondered why he hardly needed any serious convincing to help them. There was something strange about the whole thing, starting with the coincidental rescue and ending with the all-too-quick agreement. But Nicole just wasn't able to pinpoint it.

Yet.

Chapter Nineteen

The Espian Treasure

After breakfast, the morning—artificial, like the night—was spent equipping the taxi. Mostly, Rayonk and Diu geared up the mechanical fish, hooking up things that looked like lasers and bombs, while Lily, Nicole, and Arli stared in amazement and fear. Watching their flawless teamwork, Nicole's conviction about them being teammates in the Airioth deepened. At the same time, watching them load enough hardware and ammunition to take out half of Earth made her more than a bit queasy. Rayonk *had* said that the cave was dangerous, but *that* dangerous?

The early part of the afternoon found them seeking the cave. Diu's holographic map led them to the general vicinity, but because no one knew the precise location of the treasure, it was up to them to guess correctly where to look.

The map led them down to a part of the ocean floor that was cracked all over with hundreds of caves and crevices. They were forced to go down into every likely cave—which was all of them, because they hadn't the slightest idea what their cave looked like. And after several hours of hopeless searching, even Nicole was ready to call it quits.

"I think is enough," Rayonk said over the intercom at last. "We's turning home. We can trys again tomorrow."

Nicole sprawled across a bench, miserable from the lack of results. Based on Lily's vicious facial expression, she was barely keeping herself from spouting off a list of complaints. Arli licked Nicole's hand to enliven her, but she didn't even respond. Even Diu seemed to be a little discouraged.

Slowly the taxi began to turn.

Suddenly Nicole felt something strange. Lily's image seemed to grow sharper as the rest of the world blurred over. The little alien became everything, and then Nicole was on her feet, by the window, her breath misting on the cold glass. A shadow of Lily, a semi-transparent little ghost, levitated up next to her, giggling musically. Then they were both in the water, swimming towards a jagged-edged cave. Inside it. Through a twisting tunnel. Into a spiraling chamber . . .

"Nicole!"

She felt someone shaking her shoulders. "Yeah?"

"You okay?" Lily squeaked.

"Am I . . . what?"

She sat up. From the floor. And by the terrified looks of everyone, something was very wrong. "What happened?"

Diu quickly explained. "You went into a convulsive fit and fainted."

"Where are we now?" Nicole asked.

"Still in the taxi."

"And the caves?"

"Not far behind. We had just turned for Coralian when—"

"We have to go back!"

"Go back?"

"I know where to look now! Trust me, Diu. I can't explain how, exactly, but I know."

"Rayonk will not be happy. But . . . are you sure?"

"I'm sure."

"Then I'll be back."

As Diu left to convince Rayonk, Nicole crawled up onto a bench, catching her breath. She struggled to retain what she had seen. The cave, tunnel, and chamber. And the ghost Lily. She wondered what that could mean. The very thought left her cold and distressed.

The taxi veered as they dived back towards the caves. But this time, Nicole was looking, searching for what she had seen. *Maybe it was crazy*, she thought. *Maybe . . .*

"Wait!" she cried, running to the cabin. "Rayonk, see that one there. Yeah, that's it. It's where we've got to go." She paused, then: "I'm certain."

The taxi swerved as a serrated ring of rock rose to swallow them. The dark, craggy walls of the cave drew closer together, and the passageway threatened to crush them. As the tunnel narrowed, Arli's tension rose, until at last Nicole and Diu were forced to return to the passenger area to comfort the little dracling. She snarled and nuzzled Nicole's hand. *Not safe. Enemy and danger ahead.*

Nicole swallowed. Hard. *Then I guess it means I was right.*

Lily climbed onto Nicole's shoulder. Her tiny body

shuddered. Even Diu stiffened. Rayonk ignited a chain of electric-blue lights to see outside. But the light seemed to have virtually no effect in the pitch darkness of the cave. The same was true of the interior lights, which were as bright as fireflies at midnight.

The cave walls were now so close that Nicole could have touched them. Screechy, scraping sounds and hefty jolts became common as Rayonk found it nearly impossible to maneuver. Then there was a solid thirty seconds in which Nicole heard nothing except the groan of metal against rock. She was sure they were about to be trapped.

And then, almost as if the cave felt it had put them through enough, the walls gave way. They came to a veering halt. The taxi's light faded over smooth walls but didn't quite reach the seemingly abysmal bottom.

Lily squished her face against the window. "Me," she squealed, "I think we're in big trouble."

Nicole half-choked as she stared down into the cave. The electric-blue lights slid over dozens of scaly bodies spattered with spikes and spines. Curving fangs poked out between folds of flesh piled beneath massive, closed eyes. By body form and size—at least three times as long as the already gigantic taxi—the alien creatures resembled sea serpents, only much deadlier than those from any Earth story.

"There's another tunnel branching off this one," Nicole said, closing her eyes to draw back the memory. "But we have to clear those things out of the way first. Ideas?"

Suddenly, and for no apparent reason, the cave was in turmoil. The serpents churned and transformed the cave into an uproar of frothing bubbles. They blindly smashed head-long into each other, fighting for the exit. One slammed into the taxi, rattling the floor. But then they were gone, leaving behind an empty cavern and a gaping hole in the ground.

"Rayonk equipped us with ultrasonic," Diu explained. "We can't hear it, but they can."

"Now what?" Lily whispered, almost as if afraid of the sound of her own voice.

"We dive," Nicole said.

They dipped and fell through another passage. It was growing very cold, very quickly—nearly as cold as on Azimar. Nicole rubbed her stiff fingers together, but even that didn't help.

At last the taxi emerged into a giant, enclosed chamber. The outside lights revealed twisting, spiral walls. Rayonk directed a beam of light towards the bottom. Nicole gasped. At last she found just what she was seeking. Sort of.

A rough rock slab thrust crudely into the center of the floor was the only structure in the sweeping cavern. Sprawled limply across the rock was a creature that looked like a mutated octopus with several dozen arms instead of the usual eight. One of its many tentacles held a dull chunk of blue rock that could only have been one thing.

"That's the crystal," Nicole whispered, a sinking feeling in her stomach.

"And we are going to get it . . . *how?*" Lily squeaked.

The taxi shuddered as Rayonk settled them onto the bottom of the cave. He joined them in the back. "We here," he said rather coldly. "Now how we get it?"

There was a very brief silence in which they all stared at Rayonk. Diu voiced what they were all thinking. "You know I would go if I could. But since we're underwater, you are the only one who can go out there."

Rayonk stood watching them in gloomy silence. For a long moment Nicole was sure he'd refuse. She couldn't imagine what would happen then. There was no alternative.

But luckily it didn't come to that.

"Fine," Rayonk said at last. "I go. But only because it's you, Diu."

He pulled open the rear door and stepped forward. For a brief moment, he lingered in the doorway as if thinking something over. Nicole was about to wish him luck when he shut the door tightly behind him, securing himself in a sort of air-lock. A moment later, they all watched Rayonk glide through the dimly illuminated water outside.

Nicole was terrified. She knew the sort of risk Rayonk was taking. And as usual, the only one who seemed entirely unmoved was Diu. He seemed, in fact, almost suspicious as he watched his friend through the window.

"I have known Rayonk for a long time," he said at last, "and he's never been like this."

"What do you mean?" Nicole asked.

Diu's mouth compressed into a thin line. "He was always the first one into a brawl, always the first to want to go off on some adventure or other. Kind of like you."

"That's a bad thing, you mean," she snapped.

"No, not bad. But now he is different. He is still my friend, but colder than I remember."

"Maybe it's just been a while," she suggested.

Rayonk was now only a few short strokes from the crystal. He paddled around the enormous octopus and hovered beside the prize. Reaching out, he grabbed the crystal in his webbed fingers and tugged hard, trying to free it from the octopus's suctioned grasp.

It was enough of a disturbance.

The creature jerked awake. It spiraled upwards, thrashing its many tentacles down towards Rayonk. There was a breathless moment when he was almost struck down, but he maneuvered out of the way, diving below the taxi. The rear door slammed open as Rayonk sprinted inside, a stream of water following him all the way up to the driver's cabin. "Diu," he cried, "we're going to need firepower!"

"I'm on it," Diu snarled, pulling out the device he'd shown them earlier. This time he clicked a different button and two panels snapped out, one on either side, each bearing a variety of buttons. "Little added bonus to the map," he commented. "This is linked to all those weapons we hooked up this morning. Now just as soon as that thing gets in range I'll—"

A grinding burst of noise cut him short as the walls of the taxi groaned inwards. Nicole screamed as she fell sideways against a bench and was thrown onto the floor. Pushing herself upright, she saw a massive tentacle wrap around the taxi, crushing it like a can. Diu rapidly tapped a sequence of buttons and suddenly a fierce blast of electricity sizzled along the vehicle's surface, forcing the octopus away. The water clouded red as Rayonk propelled them forward, veering sharply through winding tunnels.

The taxi scraped its way through the last narrow passage. Then they were free, speeding through open ocean. The octopus kept a hot pursuit. Diu started to key another sequence into his device, but Nicole cried for him to stop.

He snarled, "If you think I will relent as I did with the Shazgor—"

"No, look!" she cried, pointing through the window.

One of the serpents had lingered behind, close to the cave opening. Now it smelled the injured octopus's blood. The serpent struck in a blitz of fangs and spines, slicing into the octopus's flesh. The latter spun away, spiraling behind a rocky outcropping in the distance. The serpent, drawn by the scent of blood, followed, and soon the dark water was empty.

"Yes!" Nicole shrieked. "We did it! We actually—" She stopped, staring as Rayonk entered the room after grinding the taxi to a halt, still dripping wet. He held out his hands.

"The water crystal," Diu said.

"Rayonk, you got it!" Nicole cried as he handed her a chunk of cold, blue rock the size of her fist. The crystal piece was strangely ordinary, like a regular rough rock. Nicole stumbled backwards breathlessly, not sure how she could ever repay him.

"One down," she breathed.

"And only three to go," Lily finished, squeezing Nicole in a hug.

Diu held out a paw. "Now give it here. Let's get the next clue."

"What do you mean?" Nicole asked.

"Just watch." Diu flipped the crystal upside-down,

pointing out symbols scratched into the surface. "The next piece of the prophecy," he explained.

"How did you—"

"It reads," he loudly interrupted:

> "In the sky land of Serrona
> Upon islands lush with green
> The claws of a mighty empress
> Hold the crystal in-between"

Now, Nicole had never known Diu to be afraid. At least, not in the true sense of the word. Sure, he'd been worried occasionally, but that didn't count. And, granted, he wasn't really scared then, either. But when he went on to speak, there was something strange in his voice. Almost, but not quite, like fear.

"Air—the invisible, 'in-between' force that drives all worlds—is our next target. But planet Serrona . . . Nicole, there's something you need to know."

Lily looked taken aback. She broke in, asking, "Did it say the *claws* of an empress?"

"I guess we'll soon find out," Nicole said.

"And we will leave as soon as possible," Diu said. "Just as soon as you let me tell you—"

"Meaning now," Nicole agreed without waiting to hear him out. She dropped the crystal in her pocket, right next to the mysterious metal disk she had kept from the map, and took out the pocket watch. Snapping open the lid, she ran her fingers over the buttons. "Rayonk," she said, looking up, "thank you for all you've done."

"It was nothing," he muttered, looking pleased.

"It was a lot more than nothing." Nicole hugged him, smiling. "I don't know what we would've done without you!"

Rayonk nodded and moved out of the way so Lily, Diu, and Arli could crowd around the Galactera. Diu gave Rayonk an almost imperceptible nod. The Espian returned a smile. Nicole chose to ignore it, giving them their right to secrecy, though she hoped that, one day, when she truly earned Diu's trust, he would tell her how they knew each other, among other things.

"Goodbye, Rayonk, and thank you!" Nicole said cheerfully. "I won't forget what you've done for me. I'll pay you back someday, somehow. I promise." Then she found *Serrona*, strangely enough already programmed, and pressed the button. The familiar vortex flashed into sight as they were swallowed by a heavy blast of wind.

The last thing Nicole heard was a soft chuckle from Rayonk, and then they were gone.

Rayonk stood back, watching Nicole pull out the Galactera. She thanked him, and then pressed the button for Serrona. He laughed to himself as she vanished, and the moment she was gone, he pulled her dagger from his pocket. Nicole hadn't noticed, but he had nabbed it from her belt when she hugged him. Now he looked it over carefully to be sure. This was not a game in which mistakes were forgiven.

He withdrew into the driver's cabin but didn't start the taxi. Instead, he activated a button on the dash that projected a holographic image of a cluttered desk. There was no one sitting behind it, so he decided to leave a message.

"They headed to Serrona, sir," Rayonk said. "And I have prize for you from Sky. Her dagger. *The* dagger. I leave it with your guards."

"Very good, Rayonk," a cold voice suddenly said. A shadow glided into view from the right and sank into the chair behind the desk. "To Serrona, then? Good. We'll be ready."

"I glad I could help," Rayonk said and terminated the connection.

Chapter Twenty

Serrona

They had only been on Serrona for about five seconds when Nicole decided it wasn't the planet for her. The whole world seemed to be one massive soup of fog so dense it was hard even to breathe. There was also a sense of utter weightlessness, as if gravity had no bearing here. And there was no ground either. They floated endlessly through the mist.

Then Nicole realized that the Galactera was gone. She whipped her head around—a slow, lazy motion—and saw that Diu now had it, holding down two tiny buttons on the sides.

"I noticed those before, but I never figured out what they were for," she said. Her voice was a low moan.

"I will explain," Diu said. "But grab Arli and Lily first or else we will separate."

They held on to each other as they drifted. At least Nicole assumed they were moving—the sameness of the place made it seem as if they were hovering in place.

Diu indicated the thick soup. "This is not Serrona," he said. "This is not anything, exactly. It is an in-between world, a place with neither time nor space. A place that, technically speaking, cannot exist. The Galactera can bring us here, but it can't keep us long. In Earth time, about three minutes, maybe. Probably less."

"How'd we get here," Nicole asked.

"And why?" Lily chipped in.

"The why is easy. The how? Not as simple. As a matter of practicality, these two buttons pressed simultaneously and held down teleport us here. As a matter of principal? Even I'm not certain. But as for why, you tried to transport us, Nicole, before I could warn you. We can't go to Serrona by foot. We need the JET Glider there."

"But the Glider's so small," Nicole complained. "We can't all fit."

"Small for storage," Diu explained, "but it expands. Just watch."

He unstrapped the Glider, tightened a series of levers along the bottom, and let go. The Glider floated beside them, at first unchanged, but then two side panels and a rear platform slid out and clicked into place, wide enough to accommodate them all.

Diu got on first, locking his feet into the Glider. Nicole bravely climbed on next, tightening her hands around his shoulders. Then Lily chose her shoulder spot, and Arli came last of all, tail wrapped around the Glider.

"Ready?" Diu asked.

"Yeah . . ." Nicole said, not at all sure if she liked his mischievous grin.

"Then hang on."

"Diu—"

He let go of the buttons on the Galactera. They ripped forward and pulsed through the fog. Then the ground was below them again—sort of. It was far, far below. Miles below. Many miles. And they were plunging towards it, spiraling uncontrollably through the air.

Nicole shrieked as they fell, her mind bursting with her own fear and Arli's. Lily snatched Nicole's hair, tearing it back, searching for some secure hold. Only Diu seemed to enjoy it, leaning against the wind as it ripped past them. One of his arms rippled against the sky. The other clutched the Glider tight.

Suddenly Diu kicked the JET into gear, blasting them sideways. Nicole clasped his shoulders tighter than before, forcing down screams. Serrona was more fantastic that she had imagined it would be. It was even more majestic and imposing from this angle, from miles and miles above the land.

Serrona sprawled below them. At least, parts of it. The planet seemed to be shattered into separate chunks, sort of like continents. But there was no ocean, no force that bound the pieces together.

Diu, ever the mind-reader, said, "Serrona used to be a single planet. Clearly not anymore, but it once was."

"What happened?" Nicole asked.

"Serrona was an Airioth stronghold of old. Not only did the planet itself feed rebels to the force, but this world is also located on what you could call a galactic crossroad. Perfect to rest up, refuel, and launch major rebellion strikes to any corner of the galaxy. After a while Serrona became too much of a hassle for the Omenra to deal with, so they used an early trial version of the Terranova to try to destroy the planet. As you can see, it didn't work perfectly. The main species of this planet, the Aereons, gathered a group of brilliant technicians to rebuild and unite the pieces under a single gravitational field, orbiting at varying levels around an artificial planetary core."

"So it's basically just a bunch of planet pieces floating around together?"

"Exactly. But although every piece is entirely self-sufficient—food supplies, a certain level of government, and all the rest—they are all controlled by a monarchy operating from a palace isolated on the largest stretch of land."

"Is that where we've got to go?"

"We are headed there now," Diu said, throttling the Glider's engine.

From what Nicole could glimpse through Lily's paws over her face, the planet was a wild collage of the high-tech and rural. Desolate villages on smaller planet pieces clashed violently with towering buildings and hovering satellites on larger land masses. She supposed that the Aereons abandoned their villages when Serrona broke apart, and yet those eerie, empty, pinprick-sized houses were somehow frightening, even from high above.

As night closed in—semi-dark, anyway, for it was clear that the rotating nature of the pieces never allowed true night to settle—Diu veered them to a halt on a small floating island, several hundred yards from a little village. He insisted on camping out in the open. Apparently, he didn't trust the vacant buildings any more than Nicole.

She didn't mind because Serrona was truly beautiful. The grass was deep, lush, and rich with young, tender shoots. The wind, a ceaseless, gentle gust, played delicately over their faces, soft and cold. More incredible was the sky—a clear, swirling medley of azure and periwinkle.

They feasted on berries that evening, fresh from springy bushes scattered over the land. They drew water from a crystal-clear lake by the village. And as they lay down to rest at last, Nicole felt that there was nothing that could destroy that perfect night. Nothing.

And then Diu bolted upright in the grass.

His fur was slightly ruffled, half erect. Nicole carefully elbowed Arli away and leaned on her arm. Lily quietly snored a couple feet away.

"Diu, what's wrong?" she whispered to avoid waking the others.

"We need to move. Now."

"Right now—"

"Right now! Hurry up, wake them. We need to get out of here. Fast!"

Nicole shook Lily awake, mentally yelling the warning to Arli. She took off in the direction Diu pointed, grabbing Lily's arm. Occasionally, she fell behind to allow Arli to catch up.

Diu at first stayed behind. He waited until Nicole could barely see him in the distance. She slowed down to wait, and soon he caught up to them at a steady jog. He was much calmer now.

"What was *that*?" Nicole gasped, huffing to catch her breath.

"Nothing," he said. "I just thought I heard something."

"Like 'grass' something?" Lily squeaked. "Or like 'wild animal' something?"

"Don't worry. It was nothing. But we should make camp here."

Nicole moved to block his path. "You heard something, and it wasn't nothing."

"Nothing you need to know," Diu growled warningly, pushing past her.

He was keeping another secret, and this time Nicole had had enough.

"Okay, listen!" she yelled, advancing. "I know we haven't known each other for that long, but we're in this together, so we have to trust each other. Right?"

"Right," Diu said coldly.

"Mutual trust?"

"Right."

"Well it's not working out that way. We trust you! Why can't you trust us?"

Diu did the exact opposite of what Nicole expected. Instead of backing down, apologizing, and promising to trust them from now on, he started to advance on *her*.

"You think you're clever, Nicole," he roared. "So brilliant for defying me and surviving. You think that is the way to earn my trust? If anything, you're only proving that I have every right to be careful with what I say around you."

Nicole felt her face flush. "I only disobeyed because you insist on treating me like I can't make my own decisions," she hissed. "If you'd just treat me like an equal, I'd listen more. I don't like being treated like a baby."

"That's the problem with you," Diu snarled coolly. "You think you are so brave and so smart now, but if you knew everything I knew—even a fraction of what I know—you would have given up on this quest and returned home long ago. You think you're not afraid of anything. You think you're ready to face the galaxy. But that does not mean you are."

"If you can say that with any sort of conviction, then you don't know *anything* about me! I'd never just go home! And what do you mean, I'm not brave? I'm plenty brave!"

"Are you certain?"

"Why wouldn't I be?"

"Because," Diu said, "being brave means standing up to what you're afraid of. It means doing the insane. The impossible."

"You think I wouldn't?"

"I'm not sure."

Nicole's heart thumped painfully when she realized his words were sincere. "You can still trust me," she said. "Please, Diu?" Then her voice turned hard. "I won't beg again."

"It's not that I do not trust you. But for your own sake, for your family's sake, for your planet's sake—I cannot tell you everything."

It was the last straw. Whatever restrains Nicole had been forcing upon herself shattered. "Then I'll force you to!" she screamed.

She threw herself forward, smashing headlong into Diu, and sent them rolling and thrashing in the grass until they reached a sharply sloping hill. Nicole's heart skipped a beat when she felt open air at her back. The next thing she knew they had both fallen probably ten feet. She smashed into the ground and lay sprawled there limply.

Diu got up first. He didn't look upset or angry, just disappointed. But before he could speak, Nicole spat out a mouthful of grass. "You know what?" she cried. "Fine! You want secrets, you can *keep* your secrets!" Standing in a huff, she stomped in the opposite direction. "I don't *need* your help saving Earth, anyway. I'm going on my own. I can take care of myself, all *by* myself! I'm not afraid to be alone!" But even as she said it, she felt a sob rise in her throat

Diu shook his head. "Nicole, this is not a good—"

"I don't *want* to know what's a good idea anymore. Not from you. Not from anyone. Because I've had enough." And with that she stalked off. Lily and Arli caught up soon enough, but all the convincing and pleading in the galaxy couldn't have made Nicole go back.

She aimlessly led them for about an hour until they approached another village. Here, Nicole at last forced herself to calm down. "We should go look for blankets," she suggested. "We'll camp out here."

Leading the way again, Nicole made a bee-line towards the buildings at the very edge of the settlement. A hollow sort of silence rested over the village.

"I don't like this," Lily whispered, hunching down on Nicole's shoulder.

Something feel wrong, Arli said.

The more they explored, the more Nicole felt she had to agree. The small, rickety, long-empty buildings seemed to have been the arena of a vicious struggle. Floors were stained with dark red splotches that could only have been one thing. Walls were scraped with claw marks and riddled with smooth, blood-rimmed holes. There was an aura of terror around the place beyond anything Nicole had ever known. She had a growing fear that she should have heard Diu out. Maybe stayed with him. Because she was past wondering whether there was something dangerous on this planet. The only question was what. And where.

When it was finally time for sleep—in the open rather than the shadowy homes stained by death—Nicole and Lily agreed to take turns staying up as sentries to protect themselves from whatever had decimated the villages. Lily took first shift. Arli fell asleep almost immediately. Nicole stayed up longer, thinking about Diu.

And when she finally fell asleep, it was with tears sprinkling her dirty cheeks.

Chapter Twenty-One

Blood on the Wind

Hours later, Lily shook Nicole awake.

"Your turn for the watch," Lily said, barely stifling a yawn. "Me, I'm dead for sleep."

"Yeah, no problem. I'll wake you if I see anything suspicious."

Watching Lily tuck herself warmly beneath Arli's wing, Nicole sprawled out in the grass. She leaned back against her arms, watching the clear sky. Two moons were sinking and a third was already a sliver above the horizon. There was a misty quality to the night at the edge of the sky—the onset of dawn. Nicole smiled, finally beginning to see a little of what Diu liked about darkness. Night had a sort of peaceful quality to it that wasn't at all like the fearful suspense attributed to it on Earth. A cool, steady breeze whipped the grass, tickling Nicole's face. She sighed, reveling in the feeling.

Something crackled nearby, and she was instantly alert. At first Nicole wondered if she had just imagined it. They had picked a flat spot to sleep, and she couldn't see anything out of place around them. Then she squinted into the distance. Tight against the ground not more than a few hundred feet away was a strange lump she hadn't noticed before. A hill?

A huddled body.

Nicole suppressed a gasp and shoved her friends awake. Lily started to complain but Nicole pressed a hand over her mouth. "There's something sneaking around," she whispered. "I don't know what. Just stay down." *You too, Arli.*

She ran through their options in her head. They could stay put and hope the creature was no threat, or they could try to run.

No threat? Yeah, right. But if the creature was armed with weapons—natural or otherwise—would it pursue them? Her own arsenal was nonexistent, except for the dagger, and melee combat was the last thing she wanted. If Diu had been there . . .

Nicole cut herself off. *If.* But he wasn't there, and it was all her fault. No use going down that track. She had to think of a different plan. Fast.

The sky was beginning to lighten. Maybe if they could hold out till daylight they would stand a better chance. Nicole knew she was hardly any use when she could see, but at night? They were finished.

The creature began to slink forward, a shadow in the darkness. Then Nicole noticed light glimmering as it moved. Was it coming from the creature itself? She strained to see and recognized a weapon. Not an ordinary weapon. She'd seen it once before. Only once, but that single time had been enough. Because that time, she'd nearly been killed.

It was an Omenra Salvira. They had found her. Again.

No use waiting now that Nicole knew what she was up against. But any sudden movement and the Omenra would blast her down. It was worse than the Klith, Shazgor, or Korrak. At least those had been beasts which could be out-smarted.

Not this enemy. Not this time.

The Omenra stopped suddenly, still hunched over. Nicole couldn't understand why. They were all open targets, sitting there on the grass. The light was growing. They could easily be seen. Why, then, would it stop?

Then she realized it was taking aim.

"Run!" Nicole screamed, rolling sideways just as a blast hissed by her ear. She pelted away, and her friends followed, keeping low to the ground. The Omenra leapt to its feet and aimed again, firing several blasts in their direction. The shots barely missed. The last would have struck its mark if Nicole hadn't half-tripped at just the right moment.

For some odd reason the Omenra didn't pursue them once they were out of range. It just stood back, watching them run. Nicole didn't have time to wonder why.

"Let's get to the village," she cried, changing direction. "We can hide there till it's safe."

The village was a deserted ruin, but it was better than being out in the open. Nicole rushed into the nearest house, and as soon as Lily and Arli were inside, she slammed the door shut. There was no furniture inside, almost as if this were a place that had never been meant for habitation, so they used their bodies to press the door shut. They waited in utter quiet, taking in the bloody stains on the floor. The darkness of the hushed room made the blood look black.

"That was an Omenra, right?" Lily whispered.

"Yeah."

"Me, I don't get it. Why didn't it follow us?"

"I-I don't know," Nicole stammered. In the silence, she could almost hear her heart pulse against her ribcage.

How long we stay? Arli asked.

"I don't know," she repeated, sinking to the floor.

There was a rumble like thunder outside. Something was stirring out there, and it didn't sound like just a few Omenras. Nicole peeked out through a crack in the wall. She bit her tongue to keep from screaming. She finally understood why they hadn't been pursued.

It had been a trap.

The tiny village was surrounded by a team of Omenra warriors. Two pitch-black cruisers hovered ominously in the background. One was a large carrier, spitting forth armored soldiers. The second was a small ship, inky as night, with sharp wings fused to the body and a sleek frame. Leaning against this ship, somehow distinguished from the rest, was a single Omenra, clutching a striking silver weapon unlike the ordinary Salviras carried by the troops.

An order was snarled somewhere along the lines and waves of Omenras charged forward, blasting down the doors and storming inside. Soon they would be at their hiding place. And still none of it made sense. The soldiers were looking for something, and it seemed like that something might just be the trio. But why? Because of the crystals? Because of Earth and the Terranova? From the looks of it, an army was gathering in the village. What could be so important?

"We need to leave," Nicole whispered, scanning the single room. There weren't any other doors. Just a single half-broken window on the opposite wall.

"What's happening out there?" Lily squeaked.

"I don't know, but it's not safe here. Just follow me," Nicole hissed, shoving her leg through the fragmented shards of some glass-like material still clinging to the frame. Her plan was to sneak away unnoticed or at least to buy some time.

It almost worked. At least until Arli found she was too large to climb through.

"Come on!" Nicole begged, peeking around the side of the house. The Omenra were almost there. They had about thirty seconds. After that it was over.

"Hurry!" Lily cried.

Arli thrust her head through, dangling her front legs over the sill. But her wings wouldn't fit past the narrow frame. She tried to shove through, and the frame cracked slightly. It wasn't enough.

"Arli!" Nicole hissed, but suddenly there was a rattle at the door. It was too late. Two Omenras barreled into the house, shouting for others to join them. The dracling was jerked back through the window as Nicole and Lily tried to run, but several guards rushed around the side of the house and pinned them against the wall. Something cold and solid jabbed into the back of Nicole's head.

She didn't need to turn around to know it was a gun.

The Omenras dragged her and Lily around to the front of the house where several other guards had Arli cornered. Nicole wanted to run to her, but the thought of the Salvira against her head stopped her. One twitch of the Omenra's claw would send a blast shattering through her skull and into her brain. Just the thought made her sick.

They were herded to the small cruiser. The guards closed in, blocking all escape. Nicole's guard kicked her in the back of the legs and pressed his foot into the small of her back, forcing her to her knees. Lily cringed beside Nicole, her frail body shaking with terror. Arli managed a snarl, but a vicious smack against the side of the head silenced her.

A heavy boot planted itself firmly beside Nicole's head, and she was forced to stand again. She found herself looking into the shaded eyes of a killer, an Omenra who knew no fear and no mercy. His very stance, outfit, and angle of the ferocious Salvira in his claws echoed vicious pride. Up close, the gun Nicole had seen from far-off was truly extraordinary. It was different from all the others. Sleeker and streamlined. More deadly.

The Omenra walked around her, dark eyes roving hungrily. Finally he halted and spoke, his voice ice-cold with venom.

"Nicole Sky," he said. "Weak. Defenseless. Alone. It's a pity. I expected more."

It took her a full minute to realize that the translator was not hissing in her ear. Like Diu, this alien, strangely enough, knew English.

"What are you talking about?" Nicole asked sincerely.

"Please, don't insult me."

"About Earth?" she snarled. "Yeah, I—"

"No. Not about that speck of a world you call home.

About the greater thing."

"*What?*" She truly had no idea what was going on.

"You think you can beat me, *child?*" He spat the last word. "You have no idea what you are up against. *Who* you are against."

"I'm not trying to do anything to you! I don't even know who you are! All I want is my home."

The Omenra laughed cruelly. "You are very good at lying, did you know? If I didn't know better, I would say you were telling the truth."

Nicole gaped. They were out of options, and she didn't even know how deep in trouble they were. But if she had a guess, it was very deep.

"What do you want from me," she said at last, voice tinged with what she thought was just the right shade of defeat.

"What do I want?" he mocked, smirking. "Only one thing." He pressed the gun to her forehead. "Your blood, Sky, spilled over the ground at my feet."

Nicole choked on her breath. What was this insane psycho talking about? She'd done nothing wrong! But she saw the faint glow at the back of the gun's barrel. It was charging. And in seconds, it would all be over. She heard Lily shout something and felt Arli's anger burst like flames in her chest, but there was nothing left in the universe except that gun and its glow and the bloody sun rising against the horizon behind them.

An explosion shuddered through Nicole's body as if trying to rip out her heart. But it wasn't the Omenra's blast. His gun spiraled through the air and landed several yards away. In livid anger, he whirled to face a point somewhere behind her. Nicole turned too, staring in blank shock. There was a shadow against the sun, holding a smoking handgun. It ran, gun blazing, towards them. Several Omenras folded over where they stood, clutching their chests. Other guards returned fire, but their adversary dodged expertly, squeezing off several more blasts. The Omenras crumpled, shot down by the seasoned warrior. The remaining guards sprinted forward, blocking Nicole's view.

But she didn't need to see to know that it was Diu.

She thought fast and reached for her dagger. With a start, she realized it was gone. There wasn't time to wonder where she had lost it. All she could think of now was to run. Lily and Arli were already ahead of her, sprinting across the grass. Nicole made a hard effort to reach them, not realizing until Lily whirled and screamed that someone was behind her. Turning, she saw the chief Omenra retrieve his gun and raise it, aiming at her chest.

Diu intercepted him before he could fire, barreling into his side. They struggled for a few moments until what remained of the Omenra force wrenched Diu away, striking him to his knees as they had Nicole. Their leader stood and snatched his gun. He shoved it against Diu's head.

Nicole didn't hear the conversation that ensued. All she could hear was the sound of her own thundering heart as Lily and Arli restrained her from running back to the fray. But she could make out one of the words that Diu mouthed— *Malkior*—as the Omenra grinned and lowered the gun from Diu's head to his chest.

Chapter Twenty-One

The shot fired. The blast was long and resounding, followed by a spray of blood and a hollow stare on Diu's face. He slumped forward and hit the ground with a dull thud. A guard dragged his body onto the large carrier, leaving behind a thick smear of crimson on the silver ramp. Lily forced Nicole to press herself flat against the grass when the Omenras looked around for them, and sheer luck prevented the trio from being noticed.

At last the Omenra leader signaled the carrier to take off. Even from where she lay, Nicole could see his grin of triumph as he boarded his small ship. The two spacecrafts lifted off, roaring into the distance.

Nicole's brain had shut down. She allowed her friends to lead and followed with mechanical footsteps. The sunrise painted the grass red as if the whole world had died and spilled its blood over the field.

She couldn't reason through what had just happened. It didn't seem real, any of it. It couldn't be true. There was no chance the Omenra could have found them. There was no reason for Malkior Taggerath—the general himself—to come after her. There was no way the three of them could be left alone in the universe to complete an impossible quest in pursuit of an impossible mission.

But Diu had died to save her. There was no path around that fact.

There was a hill nearby. Nicole struggled on until she reached it. Then her legs ceased to obey, and she stumbled aimlessly, finally sinking to her knees at the base of the hill. Her friends did not force her to go on. Arli curled up next to her, trying to comfort her. Lily, in spite of her own grief, tried to console Nicole, too.

Nicole tried to think of something, anything, besides the single image that seemed to have been burned into her eyes—a slow-motion memory of Malkior blasting Diu's life away. She might have stayed at the base of that hill forever, reliving that terrifying memory again and again, if it wasn't for a sudden shrieking cry from overhead. A mass of dark shadows fell over her, and she looked up, expecting the Omenra again.

What Nicole saw was worse.

Crouching over the rise, their leather wings and scaly bodies dark against the sun, ranged a line of pterodactyl-like aliens, clacking beaks with gleaming teeth in her direction and snapping long, whip-like tails through the air. Nicole backed away on her knees, but she didn't go far before one of their rank broke free, soared into the sky, and pounced down in front of her, wings spread wide and teeth flashing. She didn't know what they wanted, but in her heart she had a sinking feeling.

Diu's death had been for nothing. With this new threat, it was over anyway. But maybe it wouldn't have mattered. What could she have done on her own? Bravery? Courage? Diu had been right about that, too. He had been right about everything, and she couldn't go it alone. It was now that Nicole realized it. Too late.

The alien took another step forward, and she squeezed her eyes shut. She imagined Diu beside her, together in death.

Chapter Twenty-Two

The Royal Guard

The creature stopped before her, folded back his imposing wings, and glared intently. Nicole peeked through her eyelids and stared back, not sure if this was a sign that, hopefully, the alien meant no harm, or if he was simply looking for the best place to bite in. Dark gold scales flashed in the sun as he began started to pace around her.

Nicole was distracted by a sudden shriek as the apparent leader, clearly bewildered, leapt away and scrambled back up the hill. A second later, Arli dashed past her. She snapped her fangs and fanned her wings at the retreating creature.

"Arli!" Nicole hissed. *Come back. Let's see what they want first.*

The aliens crooned strange words to one another that were too quiet for the translator to detect before the golden one flew forward and landed about a meter in front of her. His body bent in a quick bow. Nicole wasn't sure what to do, so she just stared back.

The leader flashed a smug look and tittered. In his strange language, he said, "Clearly raised by savages, one would think."

Nicole felt her cheeks burn as the others broke into sniggering laughter. She had expected hostility, not sheer obnoxiousness. Not bothering to keep a certain inflection from her tone, she said, "Not really. And anyway, I haven't done anything yet to deserve that."

"Precisely," he said with the air of one talking to a clueless three-year-old toddler. "You *haven't* done anything. But I would think that even the youngest Aereon would know to pay respects to commanding officers."

"Hey, I'm not exactly a local." But she bowed, realizing suddenly that these creatures must be equipped with translators as well.

"Better," the alien remarked in a much kinder tone. He now seemed to be satisfied and was waiting at ease, ready to hear her out. "We were flying a patrol and heard sounds from over here," he explained.

Nicole wasn't sure what to say so she looked down at the ground—a mistake. The sunlight on the ground, now brightening from deep red to scarlet, looked more like blood than ever. She burst into tears again, and the startled aliens jumped slightly. Lily tried to comfort her, landing on her shoulder and whispering, "Nicole, we did all we could for Diu. There were just too many Omenras. We couldn't have fought them all away!"

"We could have done something! I just—"

The alien leader cut her off. "Diu, did you say?"

Nicole was puzzled at the inquiry. "Yeah," she said slowly. "That's right."

"Of the Airioth?"

"That's what he said."

"What did you say happened?"

"Why do you care?"

"Is that an actual question?" He was staring at her like she'd gone completely out of her mind. "If you're his friend, as I assume, or even an ally or acquaintance—or, come to think of it, even an enemy—you know the answer to that already."

Nicole had no idea what he was talking about. All she knew was she was on the verge of tears again. Unable to restrain herself, she cried, "If you *must* know, he was killed by Omenras! B-by Malkior Taggerath. He shot him. I saw. I . . . I-I . . ." She couldn't go on and fell to her knees, her body shaking from great, racking sobs.

The golden alien's scales bleached to white. An instant wave of utter silence descended.

"Are you certain about what happened?" he asked when Nicole finally calmed down enough to speak.

"Completely."

"And you saw this yourself?"

"Yes."

"Then you must come with us to warn Queen Tári."

"Tell her yourself!" Nicole barked. "I've got more important things to do." When he gave her a 'like what?' sort of look, she added, "I have to find—"

As she said the words, something clicked in her memory. According to the prophecy, an empress had the crystal. Empress was roughly equivalent to queen, which might mean . . .

"On the other hand," Nicole said gently, "it would be

better for me to come. You know, as an eyewitness to confirm the story."

The alien leader scanned her with a suspicious glance. "Oh, I see. Sudden change of heart," he sneered.

Nicole's cheeks flushed in anger. "You've got no right to talk to people like that!" she cried.

The golden alien puffed out his chest and gave a pompous salute. "I very much do have the right," he proclaimed. "I am General Falkor Avalar, captain of the Royal Guard and second-in-command of the Aereon forces of Serrona."

"Oh," she mumbled. "I'm Nicole Sky. Of Earth."

Falkor's eyes grew large. "Nicole Sky?" he repeated, slightly awed.

"Yep, that's me. Why?"

Falkor quickly regained his composure. "I always knew Earth creatures were rude and ill mannered, but I never imaged they were *such* savages. I guess you proved me wrong." But something in his face told another story.

Lily waved. "My name's Lily Solaria."

Arli strode to Nicole's side, head raised high in pride. Nicole placed her hand on the dracling's taught neck muscles and said, "This is Arli."

Falkor nodded and came a step closer, looking to Arli for approval. She sniffed and approached cautiously, staring him down. He neither blinked nor backed away, and at length, Arli bowed her head so he could pet her.

I feel kindness and strength. Can make good ally.

Nicole was unsure whether she could trust Arli's judgment after her conclusion about Rayonk had proved to be false, but she, too, felt that Falkor was on their side. Snide and smug, perhaps. But he could make an ally nonetheless.

Falkor scratched Arli's scales and rubbed her nose gently. She crooned softly at his touch. He didn't look at the dracling with fear or greed for her power, but with simple benevolence.

But there was something else that made Nicole determined to befriend the general. He held the power to command the Aereon armies. She didn't like the feeling, but revenge almost seemed like a pleasant thought in wake of Diu's death. It was time to show the Omenra who *they* were dealing with. Because if they thought humans were weak and pathetic, Nicole would be the one to prove them wrong.

Diu's life would not be given in vain. If nothing else, she would make sure of that. Nicole would save Earth, not only for herself but for him, too.

"When you're ready," Falkor said, "we can take you to the palace. You and your friend Lily can ride on my back, and two of the guards can carry Arli. Please," he continued, speaking directly to the dracling, "take no offense. I mean nothing against your flying abilities. I just think you're too young to fly on your own."

Tell him I understand.

Nicole relayed Arli's words and voiced her own concerns. "You're sure I won't be too heavy for you?"

Falkor snorted at the very idea. "Oh, of *course* you will be," he said. "How silly of me to offer! Obviously I can't carry a scrawny girl like you and a fluffy little chew toy. Who would ever think that?"

"Funny," she muttered, barely restraining a bristling Lily.

"I try."

Falkor stooped low for Nicole to climb on. There was a hollow near the base of his neck, similar to that of the dragons. Gripping a wing for support, she clambered on and slid into place. Lily clung to Nicole's shoulder, and Falkor glanced at the two guards, busy preparing Arli for flight. One clutched her shoulders with his foot claws and the other held her tail.

"Ready?" Falkor asked.

"Ready, rav," one called back.

Rav. The translator chewed over the word and spat it out in the Aereon's language, untouched. Curious, Nicole decided to ask about it as they took off, soaring high above the rolling hills.

"Hey, I thought you said your name is Falkor."

"It is."

"So how come the guards called you rav?"

"Because rav is not a name, but a title. It's accepted in almost all languages and cultures, and it means something close to boss or commander, but there's more power behind it. Occasionally, it's used to respectfully refer to elites, as that guard did just now. More commonly, royalty uses the phrase in naming their children, although sometimes families with high aspirations do the same. For example, you mentioned Malkior earlier. His full name is Malkior Rav Taggerath. Makes sense, I suppose."

"Yeah. Suits him just fine," Nicole snarled.

Soon, the first land island was far behind. The next one was larger, and they passed sprawling villages and navigated through towering metropolises. The Aereons banked using wind currents, flying on and on. Nicole vaguely marked time by the sun as it sank, finally dipping below the horizon and showing blood red when they crossed the pitch black open space between the planetary masses. After the first few times, however, she mostly closed her eyes for the parts over empty space. No reason to feel needless vertigo.

With the sunset came a smell of ash and sulfur that stained the wind and air. The scent reminded Nicole of the abandoned village they had left behind, and she summoned up the courage to ask Falkor about what had caused it. His answer allayed none of the fears that dawned with the coming of dusk.

"Our planet is at war."

Chapter Twenty-Three

Falkor's Tale

"At war?" Nicole echoed.

"As is the rest of the galaxy."

"Why?"

"Because the Aereons side with the Airioth."

"I know that. But I figured Serrona's war would be over when the Omenra failed to destroy your planet."

"That was just the beginning. Serrona was an Airioth stronghold even then, but we were typically passive and mostly aided in matters of trade. Now, for what they have done to our world, we have taken the offensive and struck against the Omenra with our own forces. This is not to say that we are winning, necessarily."

"What do you mean?"

We are winning in the military aspects We have pushed the Omenra out of our cities, away from our villages, and to the planetary outskirts and the smallest land islands. But psychologically, they are winning. The Aereons are strong, but they are tired. Soldiers refuse to take up arms. Civilians refuse to accept rationing. Wherever Omenra claws rake the earth, lives are destroyed. The Aereons are tired of it all."

"I can imagine. Diu told me that the war's been going on for ten Earth years. I can't even think about ten days of warfare."

Falkor nodded. "There is also the matter of the queen's daughter, Arvia."

He veered sharply to the left; the rest of his guard followed suit. They soared in silence, watching the last lingering rays of sunlight fade.

"What happened to Arvia?" Nicole finally asked.

"At the start of the war—as you said, ten Earth years ago," Falkor continued, "the Omenra regime changed hands. That year, the new *Krethor*—king, in your English—withdrew the Omenra from the Ethári Council, an interplanetary organization once designed to promote galactic peace. He then initiated a reign of terror. Once he was sure of the Omenras' loyalty, he began to send out scouts across the galaxy to capture anyone important that might be useful in a bargaining situation. One of those taken was the queen's only daughter and heir apparent to the throne, Arvia. Queen Tári tried to retrieve her daughter by promising the king glory, riches, incredible things he'd never dreamed of, but *Krethor* Gavaron only wanted power. He demanded rule over Serrona in exchange for Arvia. The queen refused."

Nicole did not understand. "Why? Didn't she want her daughter?"

"Of course she did. The queen loved Arvia with all her heart. But she knew that giving up Serrona would only make the king demand more." Falkor sighed. "Arvia was roughly twelve years old in Earth years when she was kidnapped.

Today, if she's still alive, she will be twenty-two and a mature princess. A day hasn't passed all this time when the queen hasn't tried to find her daughter, but the Omenras have enough power. They don't bargain anymore. They just take whatever they want, and nobody can stop them."

The smell of ash rose up again until Nicole's eyes watered. They were flying over another rural section, barren except for a few scattered villages. But below them the fields were covered with dark stains. In the dark, Nicole couldn't tell if it was blood she was seeing or something else.

They flew on and soon it was so dark that she could hardly see anything at all, let alone the ground. Lily had long since fallen asleep in her arms, and even Arli was growing drowsy. Nicole felt overcome by sleep, but just as she was drifting off, it grew very light, very quickly.

It was far too bright for night.

Over the horizon streamed billowing clouds of flame-streaked smoke. Falkor looked taken aback. "They haven't been so near the palace in years," he muttered. He swerved his company to the right to avoid the smoke.

Although their course ran parallel to the one they'd been on, they still passed close enough for Nicole to see a blazing bonfire, once a village. Aereons glided aimlessly overhead, watching the remains of their homes collapse into ruin, or else huddled on a ragged ridge of hills. Parents cradled infants while others cried over deaths.

"Please, can't we stop?" Nicole cried. "We should help them."

"No. We can do nothing."

Her voice hardened. "How can you say that? Don't you care what happens to them?"

"I do," Falkor said. "But just as the palace is not a refugee shelter, so is their suffering best left alone."

"And then you wonder why the Aereons are tired of the war," Nicole muttered. "I'd be, if I were them."

Falkor stiffened. "Don't judge us before you know us."

"I know people like you well enough, back on Earth."

"Enough!" Falkor snapped, suddenly vicious. "You are a guest on *our* world, not the other way. Learn to keep your silence."

Nicole literally had to bite her tongue to keep from commenting. She hated this Falkor already. Hated his cruelty. Hated his formality. Hated the fact that he couldn't bend the rules.

She sighed and stared blankly at the horizon. He was right, in the end. It wasn't her place to complain. And either way, besides Lily and Arli, he was the closest thing to a friend she had in this place.

They streaked across the amber sky until the fire fell behind. Then the island dropped away and they were soaring over an empty expanse of space. Soon another land mass rose before them, a huge technological structure of revolving satellites, arching glass-like bridges, and levitating buildings. This city was more fantastic than any they had passed before, and Nicole figured they must be getting close.

They ducked past the sheer walls, spiraling to avoid light night traffic—both Aereons flying solo and cruisers—and soaring over the needle-points of skyscraper-like buildings.

They were finally forced to land outside the city at the base of a squat, ten-foot wall guarding an empty stretch of grass. There was a single gate in the wall, and piled before it was a short line of Aereons and others waiting to enter. But Nicole didn't get it. Why couldn't they just fly over the sad-looking wall?

Then Falkor explained that the palace lay beyond and that the wall was just a diversion for foolish enemies, as the Omenra once learned well. The whole of the palace complex and its grounds was defended by a completely invisible force-field. "Undetectable," he said, "unless one smacks directly into it. Or," he added with a chuckle, "unless an entire fleet of your Farrider Infiltrators gets blasted apart by some seemingly imaginary force."

Nicole sighed as they waited for clearance from the tired gatekeeper. Falkor prattled on. He sure did like that force-field.

As they took off into the sky once more, Nicole gasped at the utterly transformed world beyond the wall. She almost checked the Galactera to make sure they hadn't teleported. Because, at the heart of this technological flowering, lay a peaceful valley of old times, an ancient place unlike anything Nicole had ever seen. It was utterly untouched, a virgin land of lush reds and violets and flowers tossed about by the wind.

Ahead, a single rise was crested by amber light.

"Beyond that hill is a valley," Falkor said, "and within it lies the palace. It can be a little overwhelming at first, but you'll get used to it."

Nicole almost openly disagreed. After everything she had

seen, after the Klith and Shazgor and Korrak, the horrors of the Omenra, and the wonders of that place beneath the sea, she was sure that nothing could surprise her. But when Falkor's wings cleared the hill, she was forced to take back her words.

Maybe it was the fact that the palace was lit up from the outside by red-gold light that made Nicole draw in her breath. Or perhaps it was the way that the light shimmered and skidded across the translucent glass surfaces of the structure, lighting up the night like a powerful beacon. Whatever it was, the twisted spires and towers that pierced the air like crystal daggers and the smooth, beautifully clipped lawn that surrounded the palace captivated her. It struck a glorious pose against the night sky, clean and fresh and beautiful. It also finalized the contradictory nature of Serrona. The palace was simple in comparison to the intricate cities, like a relic from a forgotten world.

Falkor circled around the courtyard once before slanting into a slight dive, landing gently on the grass. The rest of the guard collapsed beside him looking completely worn out, especially the pair bearing Arli. The moment the dracling herself found a soft spot on the grass she curled up to sleep, wings folded back and tail curved around toward her head. In a minute, she was quietly snoring away.

Lily was still asleep in Nicole's arms.

Falkor dismissed the guards and led Nicole away through an open doorway beneath a crystal entrance arch. He told her that Arli would be fine outside and that he'd personally see to it that she was fed well in the morning. As for her and Lily, he called for a servant to find them a nice, private bedroom to share for the night. Nicole hardly paid attention to where they were going—left, right, down the hall, through a clear door, left again, another door, an arched passageway . . .

But at last they reached the bedroom, a suite better even than any hotel room Nicole had ever stayed in on Earth, sweetened with vases bursting with fresh flowers. A four-poster bed dominated the room; it was decorated with a draping red curtain woven with flowers and bird-like creatures. The floor was silver marble inlaid with precious red gems, sparkling as if newly polished. Nicole threw off her shoes and crossed the length of the room, gazing around at beautifully crafted paintings hanging from walls misted just enough so one couldn't see fully through them. Pulling away the curtain, she crawled up and sank into hand-woven silk sheets of exquisite colors. A silken pillow made of fine golden fibers cradled her head.

Nicole gently spread Lily on the bed next to her and rolled over onto her side. She heard the servant instructing her on how to get to the dining hall in the morning, but she paid no mind. Nicole was far too tired, the bed far too comfortable. In an instant she had drifted into sleep, not even dwelling on the fact that the room seemed perfect, so close to what she would have desired on Earth, complete with an Earth-style bed and amenities. There was even an Earth-style bathroom, she noticed.

Almost as if it had been prepared that way and had waited all this time for her.

Chapter Twenty-Four

A New Hope

Nicole woke the next morning to cheerful sunshine. She sat up and flung off the covers. Seeing that Lily was still sleeping, she decided to leave her that way.

Feeling strangely invigorated, Nicole splashed her face at a washbasin—just the sort she would find on Earth, except that it was made of crystal. Strange, she thought for the first time, but decided to ignore it. Desiring a walk in the courtyard before breakfast, she tiptoed to the door, pulling it open quietly so as not to wake Lily. After finding her way through the winding hallways of the palace, she ventured outside through the crystal archway and found herself surrounded by a garden overflowing with fragrant flowers. Nicole wondered why she hadn't noticed it last night—the courtyard had seemed rather ordinary then—but disregarded the oddness of it. The flowers seduced her with delicious smells and bright colors, and soon she was traipsing around in their midst.

Then, Nicole noticed a particular type of flower that was all too familiar. Rather, it was mostly ordinary, except that it was composed almost entirely of watery mist. She remembered the same type of plant growing on Lunara, and when curiosity got the better of her, she picked the flower to see what the mist would show.

Her surroundings warped into a dark, scorched plain. Steam rose from the ground as if the very soil were on fire. The liquid center of the flower hardened just like before, but this time the mirror reflected a compass whose arrow spun around and around unceasingly. Nicole was about to throw down the mirror when the compass arrow jerked to a halt, pointing straight.

Hunched against the pulsing red sky several hundred yards directly ahead was a charred hill. Nicole ran towards it, following the compass arrow. Breathlessly, she rounded the top of the hill and stopped dead in front of a scene that could only be a horrible instance of déjà vu. She dropped the mirror. It shattered into water against the ground.

The grass was streaked by blood, but Diu was still fighting, still dodging, still carving a path towards where he thought she was. He didn't know that somehow Nicole had escaped Malkior's clutches, that somehow she was safe. He had no weapons except his claws and the faithful Mar, but although he could still maneuver well, his fur was lashed and brutally torn. Blood dripped into his eyes from a cut on his forehead. His fur was stained red.

"Diu!"

He pivoted towards her voice and headed to the hill, firing a final shot over his shoulder. Nicole met him halfway to the top, and together sprang over the hill and slid on their backs to the base. The sounds of the Omenra faded away.

"I can't believe you're okay!" Nicole cried.

Diu's mouth twitched into a demon grin. "That is because I'm not."

Her heart thumped painfully. "What do you mean?"

"I'm dead, Nicole. Remember?"

She cringed away, sneakers scraping at the grass to gain distance. He laughed, a cold, merciless laugh, and suddenly raised the gun Nicole recognized as Malkior's unusual weapon. But it wasn't Diu anymore. A nightmarish crimson swirl had morphed him into Malkior Taggerath, and now he pulled back the trigger to spill her blood at his feet.

Someone nearby yelled Nicole's name, but she paid the voice no mind. She screamed for Diu, screamed for herself, screamed for the cruelty of a world in which Malkior could be allowed to command.

"Nicole!" The voice ripped though her mind like a blasting current. "Nicole! Nicole!"

She jerked to a sitting position, panting. Her hair was plastered in a sweaty mass over her forehead. Salty sweat stung her eyes. Lily was beside her, trembling. Looking around, Nicole saw woven birds gazing kindly at her with periwinkle eyes and realized she was still in the palace bedroom. She gathered her head in her arms and sobbed. Lily tried to comfort her but at last left her alone in sorrow, and Nicole was glad her friend understood her need to be on her own, at least for this short time.

After some time, Nicole pulled back the curtain to let in the glow of the sun. She recounted her dream to Lily, who cried through most of the tale.

"What're we going to do?" Nicole asked as she leaned over the washbasin, the same as in the cruel dream. The slap of cold water felt good against her face.

"There's nothing we *can* do," Lily admitted.

Nicole sniffled. Tears crept back into her eyes. "Remember the day I first met you? You said my name meant 'victory of the people', and you wanted to come along to see what kind of victory I'd bring."

"Me, I remember."

"Well, you were wrong! I can't even save my own friends, let alone Earth. I might as well give up. Might as well just go home and wait for the inevitable. At least then I'll get to see my family one last time."

Then Lily did something completely unexpected. The little alien levitated up and struck Nicole across the face. Hard. Nicole stumbled back, rubbing fingertips over her smarting cheek.

Lily puffed out her chest and shouted, "Don't ever say that! Diu's death was *not* your fault!" Voice lightening, she added, "You *will* bring a victory to Earth. Me, I'm sure of it. Now come on. Shoes on. We'll go to the dining hall for breakfast. Me, I'm starving. My stomach feels as if it's eating itself. And hurry up, or I'm going without you!" Hovering towards the door, Lily muttered, "There better be a huge feast laid out, or me, I'll eat one of the Aereons. Maybe that mean Falkor."

Nicole smiled weakly. Now that Lily mentioned it, she was ravenously hungry, too. Slipping into her shoes, she shoved open the glass door, followed Lily outside into the hallway, and found that she absolutely didn't remember one word of the directions the servant had given last night. Nicole went down a hallway with an arched ceiling and pushed open the door at its end, but when they got to the end of the next hallway, she found herself faced with three identical glasslike doors facing off in different directions. Lily stared her down like a vulture and, since Nicole felt like she was about to get one of her arms gnawed off, she pointed left. "Uh . . . that way?" she said.

Nicole could almost see steam shooting from Lily's ears. "You don't remember the way!" the alien cried.

"Like you know where to go!"

"Me! I . . . er . . ."

Of course.

"So we're lost," Nicole summed up, picking a door at random and madly stomping through.

"Not my fault! Me, I've been following you the whole way!"

"Hey, look out!" a new voice cried, and suddenly Nicole was being helped up off the ground by a slight, young Aereon male. "Sorry, I'm sorry. I didn't see you in time, sorry."

"It's okay," Nicole said cheerfully, glad to have escaped a Lily who looked ready to explode. "Where're you headed?"

"Dining hall. Late for breakfast again," he quickly stammered. "But that's me, always late. My name's Sorill, by the way."

"I'm Lily," Lily said.

"And I'm—"

"Sorill!" someone called out behind them. Nicole turned to see Falkor running towards them. "Sorill, you're missed at breakfast. Get down there, now."

"Going, going," Sorill squeaked. "See you there, rav." He rushed away, darting around a corner.

"Nicole," Falkor hissed as they wound their way through a maze of hallways. "Where have you been all morning?"

"Sorry. We just got a little lost," Nicole apologized.

"Figures," he said. "It's lucky I found you in time. There's something important I must tell you. You can't say your name here, understand?"

"Why?" she asked, dumbfounded.

Falkor ignored her. "I'll let you pick an alias," he continued. "Whatever you want. But you can't be known here as Nicole Sky."

"*Why?*"

"Because we can't let the Aereons have hope if it all proves false."

"If *what* proves false?"

Falkor stared as if she'd lost her mind. "Surely, you can't be serious?"

Nicole suddenly realized that they had come to an enormous pair of doors like sculpted ice. She was about to yell at Falkor, to tell him she honestly had no clue what he was talking about, when he pushed open the doors and shoved Lily and her inside.

"We can discuss this later," Falkor said as he abandoned them by the door. "I'll be back. Just wait here in the meantime."

Nicole's eyes darted everywhere at once. The dining hall was a giant, lively chamber filled with Aereons chattering.

Chapter Twenty-Four

Servants bustled about carrying fresh platters loaded with food of all colors and varieties—mountains of meat, heaps of fruits, piles of bread, and mounds of bizarre things Nicole had never seen in her life. Three long, wooden tables covered with colorful, patterned tablecloths ran along the length of the hall; these hosted most of the feasting Aereons. There was also a fourth table, much smaller than the others, standing by the far wall. Seated behind it, at the very center, was a red-purple Aereon who could only have been the queen. She was dressed elegantly in purple silk. A shining silver crown ringed the crest on her head.

Lily tugged Nicole's sleeve. "Can we sit and eat?"

"Falkor said to stay put. He'll be back for us, and then we can—"

"Me, I'm hungry *now!*"

And so Lily dragged Nicole away to the center table before she had a chance to complain. The little purple alien pounced on the food, shoveling in enormous mouthfuls, much to the disgust of the Aereons around her.

Disgust? No, the cringing expressions of their faces showed more than that. Fear, Nicole realized, and anger. But why? Surely a cute little Lunaran and a scrawny human couldn't do them harm.

Nicole was startled by a flurry of wings at her side. Falkor had come up alongside her, and they both looked down at Lily, now spread out on her back with a bulging belly. Nicole laughed out loud but was quickly silenced by the fiery stares of the nearby Aereons.

"Get Lily and follow me," Falkor hissed in her ear.

Nicole hoisted up her friend and Falkor them away down the aisle between two tables, straight towards the high table where the queen sat.

"I don't get it," Nicole whispered, all too aware of the many distrusting stares following her. "What's *their* problem?"

"Don't worry about them," scoffed Falkor. "I'm sure the way Lily barged in on the meal and shoved half the platters into her mouth had absolutely nothing to do with it."

"Hysterical," Nicole muttered, "but I was being serious!"

"So was I."

"Falkor!"

His expression softened. "There are just so many creatures working against the Airioth these days that we don't know who to trust anymore. The only way they'll trust you is if Queen Tári approves of you, so remember to act your best, and keep that fat, little piggy under control!"

"I heard that," Lily burped.

Falkor paid her no mind and swept around the table to the queen's side. He whispered something and waited until she nodded, then came back and shoved Nicole rather roughly until she stood directly across the table from the queen.

Queen Tári linked her claws and glanced appraisingly at the child before her. The other Aereons, seeing that the newcomer was about to be judged, lapsed into silence. A nervous wave of tension descended upon the chamber.

In the absolute quiet, the queen rose majestically. The purple silk cascaded gently around her movements. She glided slowly around the table and came to a halt before Nicole.

Unsure what else to do, Nicole bowed awkwardly.

To her great surprise the queen laughed musically, and the chamber itself seemed to sigh in relief. The Aereons appeared to accept that Nicole was, at the very least, not a threat, and they returned to their meals. The subject in question noticed that she had been holding her breath and sighed as soft chattering began to rise from the surrounding tables.

The queen held up her wings for silence. "Rise, child." Queen Tári commanded. "There is nothing for you to fear in my court."

"I'm not afraid, Your Highness," Nicole said as she stood obediently. "I just don't want anyone to think I'm—a savage."

"Very well," the queen laughed again. "But tell me, child, what is your name?"

Nicole paused. Was she supposed to lie to the queen too?

"My name," she answered, "is Danni Alexander." Combining her best Earth friends' names didn't seem to be so much of a blatant lie. And yet her voice, strained and tentative at best, turned the statement into a question. She prepared for the queen to challenge her, to correct her, to banish her from the palace and Serrona.

But Queen Tári gladly accepted it and motioned towards Falkor. "General?"

He was by her side in an instant. "Yes, Your Majesty."

"Please see to it that our guest, Danni, receives all she needs for her comfort. Then bring her to my private quarters after this meal is through. We have much to discuss." And with that the queen was gone, sweeping down the center aisle and vanishing through the crystal doors.

Nicole and Falkor were left staring in her wake. "That went—well," Nicole said.

"I guess you have brains after all, not saying your name here," he said. "As for the queen, I mentioned that you were a friend of Diu's and have important news about him. I'll leave it to you to break it to her."

"Thanks for being so considerate."

"Oh, you're quite welcome."

Lily, as usual, couldn't let the conversation go on without thrusting a word in edgewise. "Can we just go eat and worry about the queen later?"

"Lily!" Nicole hissed. "You just shoved your face full of half the stuff on the table and you're *still* hungry?"

"How dainty," muttered Falkor, but he led them to a table nonetheless. When Nicole sat down, the Aereons tried to goad her into speech, but without translators they couldn't understand a word of what she said and so the conversation lapsed into silence. Nicole instead focused on the food and piled her plate with some of everything and ate until she was full to bursting. Flavors burst inside her mouth—sweet, bitter, creamy, tart, velvety. All the food was strange yet fantastic, and definitely more delicious than Rayonk's wiggles. It was only when most of the other Aereons had left the tables and the servants marched in to clean up that she finally stood and managed to drag Lily out of the dining hall. Falkor was waiting outside with his usual smug look.

"Are you ready yet?" he muttered. "Or is your little friend looking for another platter to vacuum up?"

"Lily's finished," Nicole said. She hesitated. "But I was just wondering if I could please see Arli, my dragon. I want to make sure she's okay."

"You will see the queen first and then play with your pet. Now hurry up! I have more important matters to attend to than babysitting you all day."

Nicole was starting to become annoyed, but there were too many Aereons bustling around for her to do anything right then. She logged dealing with Falkor away on her to-do list and followed, fearing she'd lose him in the crowd. Nicole ran up to him just as he was turning a corner, but then she stopped while Lily caught up, and by that time, Falkor was already gone.

She sprinted all the way to the end of the hall, Lily dangling from her shoulder. Unfortunately, that hall led to yet another hallway that was split in two directions, left and right. And, of course, she had no idea where to go.

"Great," Nicole muttered. "He couldn't have waited half a second for us to catch up. *Now* where'd he go?"

Falkor's head poked out at the end of the hallway to the left. "Are you always so stupid or are you just trying extra-hard for me?"

Fuming, Nicole dashed after him, hardly pausing for breath. Finally, after a seemingly endless number of twists and turns through hallways that grew steadily quieter, they found themselves standing before the most intricately carved set of doors Nicole had yet seen in the palace. Falkor pushed one open and motioned for Nicole and Lily to go inside.

"Aren't you going to let her know we're here?" Nicole asked.

"You had a tongue last time I checked," he said calmly and pushed them forward. The heavy door slammed behind them, leaving them in pitch darkness.

There was little light in the room and, seemingly, no crystal walls. Nicole couldn't see anything at all except a bed, and that was only because of the tiny candle that flickered on a bedside table. She wasn't sure if she was supposed to wait for Queen Tári, or leave, or if the queen was already here, hidden by the dark, so she just stood stupidly near the door. "Well, at least Falkor's not here," she whispered to Lily.

"I see you have met his brighter side," said a soft voice, and the next moment, the bedroom was bathed with light as velvety curtains pulled smoothly away from the walls and let the sunshine in. Nicole noticed Queen Tári hovering in the far corner, tugging on a leather cord.

Nicole quickly backtracked. "I'm sorry, Your Majesty. I didn't mean anything against him."

Queen Tári laughed softly. "Child, if you think that General Avalar doesn't fluster me sometimes, then know you are wrong. I've always told him that his sharp tongue will get him into trouble one day. But he's a loyal friend and a powerful ally, and I am glad to have him as captain of the royal guard." She let the cord swing free and crossed the room towards Nicole, stopping a few feet short of her. At length, she added, "But we are not here to discuss Falkor, are we? You are here on a matter far more urgent, Nicole Sky."

Nicole was taken aback. "My name's—"

"Yes, Falkor told you to lie about your name . . . per my instructions. I know who you are, Nicole. You have nothing to hide from me. And now, what is it you have come to say about Diu?"

Nicole couldn't speak at first, couldn't retell it all again. At last she cut it short and brief.

"He's dead. He was killed by the Omenra. By Malkior Taggerath."

There was a long, trembling silence that soaked the very air. Then Queen Tári smiled sadly.

"Diu is not dead. Not yet."

Chapter Twenty-Five

Plans for Rescue

"*What?*" Nicole and Lily yelled.

Queen Tári sank onto her bed, precariously balancing on the edge. "The Omenra wired a message via our satellite system this morning," she explained sadly. "A message from *Krethor* Gavaron himself, stating that only one thing will be accepted in exchange for Diu's safety—the unconditional surrender of the Airioth."

"You won't do it," Nicole said. It was not a question.

"Not only do I not have the authority, but I personally doubt if he will ever be set free. The Omenra will wait for the Airioth to break and then shall kill Diu anyway."

"Me, I don't know," Lily broke in. "What if they're lying?"

Nicole nodded. "Yeah. What if he's dead already?"

The queen shook her head. "The transmission included a holographic disk recording of Diu. At least at the time, he was very much alive."

"And Arvia?" Nicole blurted out. "Is she involved?"

Queen Tári examined her curiously. "Why would you think that?"

Chapter Twenty-Five

In truth, Nicole herself had no idea what drove her to mention the princess. A strange feeling bubbled up inside her, a feeling she'd never felt before, a feeling of intense certainty without actually knowing. "I just . . . know, I guess," she said weakly.

"You are correct. My daughter . . . she is part of the bargain." The queen paused for a moment, and she suddenly seemed very tired. "As one of the Airioth's most valuable allies, the Omenra are determined to spur us to their side," she finished.

"You can't give in!" Lily cried. "Me, I might not know everything about this galactic war. But me, I know enough. If the Airioth fall, the Omenra . . . they'll take over everything!"

"Do you believe I do not understand that?" the queen said. "But I am afraid the Airioth will have no choice. Without Diu, there isn't an Airioth."

Nicole's wall of patience was finally breached. She was so tired of not knowing anything when it was *her* home that was in danger.

"Your Majesty," Nicole said firmly, "can I ask one question and be promised an honest answer?"

"That depends. I do not wish to lie."

"Who *is* Diu? I mean, who is he really? Everything seems to come back to him, but I can't figure out why."

"Please," Lily begged eagerly.

The queen regarded them with wonder. For a second Nicole was sure she'd tell them, but then Queen Tári stood. "I do not wish to lie to you, child, and this is not my knowledge to give. It is Diu's secret. When he so wishes, he will tell you himself. Now stay. I shall be back." And with that, the queen slipped from the room, her footsteps silent on the marble floor.

"I knew it!" Nicole said as soon as she and Lily were alone.

"Knew what?"

"That Diu was keeping stuff from us. You heard what the queen said: 'Without Diu, there isn't an Airioth.' What I don't get is why he didn't tell us and what exactly makes him so important."

The door slipped open silently as Queen Tári returned, carrying a small, flat, rectangular box that Nicole quickly recognized. "A holographic projection of Serrona," Nicole said with a smile.

"Yes," the queen said slowly. "How did you know?"

Nicole thought back to the city deep below the sea and a taxi ride seemingly so long ago, although it was really only a few days back. "Long story," she said.

The queen tapped one of the buttons, projecting the three-dimensional image between them. Nicole gasped at the incredible sight of the many planet pieces floating in space. Queen Tári studied the map briefly, and then clicked off the projection and moved towards the door. "Follow me," she said. "I have to speak with General Avalar."

"About Diu?" Nicole asked, running after the queen into the hallway.

"Yes."

"Are you going to convince the Airioth to surrender?"

Queen Tári shook her magnificent head, the purple silk

garments fluttering about as if tossed by an invisible wind. "No."

"Are you just going to let him die?" Lily squealed.

"No. Neither of those are real options. Because there is a third, but it is very dangerous. That is why I need Falkor. At the moment, I'm not certain my plan is feasible without extreme causalities."

Nicole drew in a sharp breath. Her heart thumped against her ribs. "Casualties?" she repeated.

"We are in a war, child. You should remember that."

They found Falkor in the courtyard, spouting reprimands to a pair of obviously newly recruited guards. When the young soldiers saw the queen, they literally collapsed to the ground in a shaky bow. Smiling, she released them from the day's training and sent them away to bring more meat for Arli, who was basking in the sun nearby.

Arli seemed as overjoyed to see her again as Nicole felt. The dracling bowled Nicole over and they rolled in the grass while Lily laughed.

Falkor chuckled. "Fitting behavior," he muttered.

Luckily, Queen Tári seemed to be in a good mood. "General Avalar, at least pretend to pay attention."

Nicole was glad to see him flinch. "My humblest apologies, Your Highness. It won't happen again."

You know, Arli, Nicole thought. *I think you were wrong about him. He's the meanest, nastiest creature I've ever met.*

Only to you. He himself bring me most delicious food I ever have this morning.

You've only had about five decent meals, you know, Nicole

replied, chuckling to herself. Suddenly, she remembered her conversation with the queen. *Arli, I found out something really important, but I bet you won't believe me.*

Again, it turned out that Nicole was the only one who was clueless. *About Diu? I know.*

How?!

You were thinking loudly.

Cheater, Nicole replied gruffly.

Arli ignored her. *But Diu still in danger. We must help somehow. Omenra murderers can do terrible things.*

I know. Wait—shh! They're talking about him now. She focused in just in time to hear the end of Queen Tári and Falkor's conversation.

"Prepare the most elite guards you have, general. We need the best of the best for this rescue mission. I hope you understand what depends on it."

"I do, Your Highness."

And then Nicole had a very strange idea.

It was dangerous and foolish, but she knew Diu would have done no less for her. Besides, it was time to learn what being brave was all about.

"Your Majesty," she said, standing and patting grass off her jeans. "With all due respect, I overheard you were planning a rescue mission. With your permission, I'd like to be part of it. I know I'm just a human without the ability to fly or do anything special, but Diu's my friend. His capture was my fault. I'd like a chance to reverse my mistake."

Falkor stared blankly at her. "You know, I'm sincerely beginning to think that you're depriving a village somewhere of an idiot."

He was really getting on Nicole's last nerve. "And why's that?" she spat.

"Because the fate of the galaxy rests on the outcome of this mission. We can't mess it up by letting you tag along, now can we?"

Nicole felt ready to explode, but Falkor was saved from a disaster when Queen Tári stepped between them. "General Avalar," she said calmly, "I expected more from you. Hers is a kind offer, and you must respect that." Before he could say anything back, she added, "Nicole, you must have patience, too. Understand, child—our foes are not to be taken lightly. They are very dangerous and very powerful. Take this advice from a mother; reconsider your offer. Friendship is a strong force, but if you go on this mission, you must accept the risks that go with it. Risks that include the most terrible fate of all."

"Death?" Nicole asked.

"No, child." The queen had turned her face away, and her voice seemed to be coming from a great distance now. "Capture. Enslavement. Being able to only watch helplessly as your family and the world you love goes on without you. Being forced to confront and fight against those you cherish. That is the world my Arvia must live in. I do not want it to become your world as well."

"I understand," Nicole said, "and I don't care. My life's not the most important one at stake." As she said the words, her thoughts flashed back to Earth, her friends, and her parents. But most of all, she remembered Diu.

"Plus," Lily said, "you can count on me to keep Nicole safe. Me, I won't let those stupid Omenra come anywhere near her. I'm a raging ball of wild fur when I want to be!"

"Do tell," Falkor growled.

"Hey, don't talk to Lily like that!" Nicole snapped.

The queen parted them once more with her wings. "Patience, child," she said. "It would do you no benefit to harm General Avalar. After all, if anything happens to him, who will watch your back?"

Falkor's jaw dropped open. "With all due respect, Your Highness, you are joking, correct? You are not actually going to let her come?"

"I'm afraid I am." She glanced at Nicole and said, "There is something very special about you, child. To be willing to risk all you know and love for the sake of friendship is a rare and precious trait. One day you shall make a powerful ally and the greatest of friends."

Lily shook her head. "You're wrong, Your Majesty. Me, I don't think she has to wait until one day comes around. Nicole's already the greatest friend I've ever had!"

Nicole blinked away joyful tears. "You too." *And you, Arli,* she added, kneeling and rubbing the dracling's head.

As are you.

Falkor was still stuttering, trying to overcome his own disbelief. "Y-Your Highness," he cried, "if Nicole is to come, I'll have to train her, prepare her, everything. We want this done as fast as possible, but I can't ready her fast enough."

"I trust you, Falkor. You will think of something. You have always come through for me."

"Yes, but—"

"Then the matter is closed. Nicole Sky goes."

"What'll happen to Arli?" Nicole broke in. "She's too young and defenseless to go with me." Arli snorted angrily, so she added, "Okay, maybe not defenseless. Just too young."

Queen Tári petted the dracling's head. "She will be quite welcome to stay here. I will make certain she is kept comfortable and well fed. And don't worry about her being lonely. The young ones will fight amongst themselves just to marvel at this beautiful creature."

"And Lily?"

Lily drew herself up to her full height. "What do you mean, 'And Lily'? Me, I'm coming with you! You and Diu are both my friends, and there's no way in the world I'm letting you two run off on a dangerous mission without me to cover your backs."

"Don't I get any say in all this?" Falkor complained, trailing after the queen as she glided towards the crystal archway entrance. "After all, I am the one leading the mission."

"With regards to soldiers, weapons, armor, strategy—you may have all the say you wish. But our guests' fate is settled. However, my general, the Omenra have not given us much time. Train Nicole and Lily as quickly as you can, and then we shall strike under cover of night." Turning briefly to Nicole, the queen added, "And remember, the fate of the galaxy rests on Diu, and his life rests in your hands. Train well, child."

"I will, Your Majesty," Nicole said with determination. "I will."

As Queen Tári and Falkor vanished into the palace, Nicole

fought through her suddenly contradictory feelings. Friendship was, of course, the foremost reason she had to go on this mission. At least, that's what she convinced herself it was. There was a second reason she had to save Diu. It was a selfish reason and she knew it, but Nicole could not press it from her mind.

Diu had a secret, something that made him essential to this galactic war. He had been the previous owner of the Galactera. He was the one sent after the Terranova. He tracked her down, followed her, relayed the disastrous Earth message, and saved her many times. Now he had been captured as a hostage. For a tyrant who no longer bargained, Diu seemed to be the ultimate prize. But why? And how, she wondered, could the Omenra believe that one creature could be traded for the Airioth's surrender?

Diu was essential to this galactic war. And Nicole had to find out why.

Chapter Twenty-Six

The Mission

The pale orbs of the triple moons hovered above the dark ground. Soft silver light gleamed over small knolls and bumps in the otherwise smooth ground. The night, splashed with stars, spread like plush fabric across the sky.

The dark was suddenly clipped by a lightening blast, followed by a rippling detonation from the far edge of the field. Nicole ducked as debris hurtled over her head with enough force to cleave metal walls. She peeked over the top of a force-field, the only defense strong enough to withstand an explosion of such magnitude. Watching tiny bits of her target flutter helplessly through the air, she shifted the weight of the Gyrosnare Embalizer in her hands.

In the past week, something had changed. Nicole couldn't name it exactly, but maybe it was that she was a soldier now, in a way. Weapons training, tech infiltration, military maneuvers—she'd been led through the basics. Even her new uniform conveyed her status. Nicole let her fingers glide along the cool, smooth surface of a specially designed tunic and pants, feeling the sturdy curve of the dense, flexible alien fiber;

it was light, maneuverable, and able to withstand substantial damage. Strapped to her hip was a holster for the Embalizer, and suspended by the golden chain around her neck, warm against her chest and concealed by the folds of the tunic, was the Galactera.

But of course, that was secret. None of the Aereons, not even the queen or Falkor, knew about the galaxy watch.

The microcom communicator she'd been wired with days earlier—basically, a microphone attached to an earpiece—hissed static in her ear. It was Falkor requesting a status check.

"Clear," she said. It was a word she'd never used before with that sort of meaning. Nicole unstrapped a pair of night-vision goggles as artificial darkness lifted from the virtual training field. A holographic sun, too bright, stung her eyes. Holstering the Embalizer, she waited for the room to shift to normal, wondering how Lily was doing down the hall.

After tonight, it would be over, for better or for worse. The plans were laid out and ready, and finally it was time to strike. Satellites orbiting Serrona had detected a wave of unusual activity in an isolated planetary sector; digital imagery revealed a fleet of Omenra carriers. From other Aereon sources, probably from within the Airioth, Diu's whereabouts had been uncovered. Temporarily, he was imprisoned in one of the carriers, waiting for the Airioth's reply of surrender. But Gavaron's patience was running short, and if the right answer was not forwarded soon, Diu would be transported to a prison outpost in the farthest reaches of the galaxy where he would most likely be held until the king needed further leverage against his foes. So the Aereons had to act fast.

The rescue team would venture out as soon as it grew dark, hence the night training. They would have to act quickly because they had a long way to fly, and if they weren't done before daybreak and were caught, they were finished.

Queen Tári also harbored hope that since Arvia was part of the bargain for the surrender of the Airioth, she might be on the same ship as Diu. Maybe even the same prison. And although Diu was the more important of the two according to the Airioth, Queen Tári had, Nicole knew, instructed Falkor to keep watch for the princess. She would not risk losing what might be their final chance to save her daughter.

And so Nicole had been given a thorough training. Lily too, a little, but especially Nicole and for a reason she couldn't quite fathom. How to handle a weapon, lock on target, run, duck, and fire. And once, on a beautiful, cloudless evening, how to pilot a small Aereon fighter craft called a Scythejet. Falkor had shown her the ropes, taught her everything and more than she would ever need to know.

And finally, it was almost time.

"You did well," Falkor said when Nicole stepped through the holoscreen door into the central training complex. "I was watching."

She glanced back at the one-way mirror. "Since I'm so good, think I could upgrade this?" she asked, indicating the Embalizer.

Falkor chuckled, moving towards another holoscreen. "Standard-issue is good enough for our purposes. Now let's see how Lily's doing."

Nicole obediently glanced into Lily's room. The Lunarian was also training, but not in weapons combat like Nicole. Her skills would be honed in infiltration. At the moment she was busy with an obstacle course, skirting a range of tight traps.

"But Falkor," Nicole pressed on, "your gun's so much better."

He laughed again, patting the hefty blaster strapped to his hip. "My gun? That's an Enfiro 3000. Baddest little handgun this side of the galaxy. Stick to the Embalizer for now—hey!" He slapped the techie in charge of monitoring Lily on the shoulder. "Are you blind? Her pulse and blood pressure are spiking—get her out of there!"

The virtual room was suddenly blank, and the next moment the holoscreen flickered as Lily rushed out, breathing hard. "What was that!" she cried. "Me, I thought that was supposed to be training, not scorch-my-fur-off insaneness!"

Falkor snickered. "You think it's easier out there? In a real battle?"

"Hey, hey!" Nicole broke in, moving between them. "How about," she nobly suggested, "a temporary truce. We can't waste time on bickering tonight."

"Fine," Lily snarled.

"With reluctance," Falkor said stiffly. "But that's enough for now. We should have an early meal, and then off to bed until dusk. It'll be a long night."

He led the way to the dining hall. It was early, so the chamber was mostly empty except for a few servants who were setting up tables. Nicole and Lily sat with Falkor at the center table in silence. Nicole hardly paid attention to what she ate, and even Lily, normally a voracious eater, only picked at her food. Both were relieved when Falkor sent then off, but when a servant showed them the way to their bedroom, neither was able to catch a wink of sleep. Nicole stared at the woven curtain and watched as it darkened from rosy red to dark crimson, the color of blood. Sick to her stomach, she tried to push the image out of her mind. But all she kept seeing were flashes from her nightmare of Diu and Malkior.

Nicole must have fallen asleep at some point because the next thing she knew, Falkor was shaking her awake. Water was already splashing in the washbasin, meaning Lily was up and about. Nicole got up slowly, trying to adjust to the darkness.

Falkor was decked out in full military garb—body armor, wing guards, and of course the Enfiro. He waited outside while Nicole got dressed. She felt a slight surge of something like regret as she strapped in her Embalizer.

"Ready?" Falkor called from behind the door.

"Almost." Nicole closed her eyes, thinking about what she was getting herself into. "What do you think, Lily?"

"'Bout what?"

"This whole thing. The war, and this rescue, and the Omenra, and everything else."

Lily, ever astute, said, "You're afraid of that Embalizer."

"Am not!"

"Not the gun. What it does. Me, I think you're afraid of killing."

Nicole thought about denying it. "Yeah, I guess," she admitted.

"Don't worry. Me, I am, too," Lily said. "But sometimes

we have to do bad things for good ends, like saving Diu."

"Hey!" There was a sharp rap on the door. "Are you both asleep in there?"

"We're coming, Falkor! Hang on!" Nicole yelled. But there was one more thing she had to do.

She walked to the table beside her bed and tugged open the top drawer. First she placed the water crystal and the small metal disk from the map inside, just for safekeeping. Then, lifting the chain off her neck, Nicole dropped in the Galactera. There were two reasons she had to leave the watch. The first was the possibility of a capture and frisk. She couldn't lose the galaxy watch. She couldn't. Losing it would be the end of all hope.

The second reason was one Nicole didn't want to admit but knew was true. If she had the possibility of escape from a tight spot, she knew she would take it. But now was not the time for cowardice. And so before she could change her mind, Nicole slammed the drawer shut, called Lily, and joined Falkor in the hall.

The atmosphere was charged with tension. Nicole felt it the moment she set foot in the courtyard. For once, even Falkor wasn't joking or flinging insults as they moved towards a single waiting Aereon. He was light brown, fitted with armor and a holstered Enfiro. But even from far away and in the dark, Nicole could see that he was trembling. His scales were dull and his claws looked like they had been chewed several times over. Slung sloppily over his back was a bulging leather sack. His head was bowed, and he twiddled his claws and glanced nervously around. How *he* ever got to be an elite guard, Nicole had no clue. He looked like a kindergartener worried about getting smacked by the scary bully on his first day of school. But he somehow looked familiar.

"Sorry we were stalled," Falkor said. "Though I'm surprised we made it here at all at the rate these two were moving." The brown Aereon cracked the tinniest grin but mostly continued to shiver.

"Ha, ha," Nicole said, "that was hysterical. Man, Falkor, I thought we agreed to a truce! Keep your end of the bargain."

"Dreadfully sorry," Falkor apologized. "Won't happen again, promise. Now then," he added when he saw her looking like she was about to erupt, "let me introduce everyone and briefly review the operation, and then we had better head off. We have a hard night ahead and can't waste any time. Nicole, Lily—my second-in-command, Sorill. He's the best of the best at what he does, and yes, Nicole, we can trust him with your real name. Sorill, I've told you about these two—the genius and her piggy pal!"

Scared and shy Sorill waved at them and beamed a genuine smile. He still seemed familiar, and Nicole picked her brain for why. Suddenly, she remembered where she'd seen him.

"Hey, you helped me that first morning in the palace," she said.

"Yes, that was me," Sorill said, smiling.

Falkor sighed with feigned annoyance. "Now listen, we have no real idea of what we're getting into, so it's going to be a lot of communication via microcoms and quick instinct. Keep your channels open, at least till we infiltrate. Omenra carriers typically have systems to disable tech not operating on their frequencies, so we'll be virtually alone inside. But keep your heads and we'll all get out alive, understand?"

Nods bobbed around the group.

"Good. Now Nicole, one thing before we set off. I doubt you realize precisely the sort of danger you are getting yourself into. Those carriers are going to be bursting with Omenras, and they're fierce warriors at their worst. On a good day, they are an unstoppable force, and with the number of defeats they've inflicted recently, they are all in mighty high spirits. There could be casualties, Nicole. Deaths, understand? Right here, right now—this is your last chance to say no. Are you still in?"

Nicole took a deep, shaking breath. "Yeah."

"You sure?"

"I'm sure."

"Then climb on and be quick about it or we're leaving you behind."

Nicole did as she was told, making sure Lily was gripping tightly to her shoulder before hailing to Falkor that they was ready. Sorill took up the right flank.

"Ready, everyone?" Falkor asked.

"Locked 'n loaded," Nicole said, trying to sound cool.

Sorill squeaked, "Ready as ever, rav."

And then they were off—soaring high over the palace walls and away over the rolling landscape, thrust on by gusting winds. Nicole leaned forward and watched as the hills rolled by. They slowed only once to cross the force-field wall. But they made up for lost time, flying ever faster. Falkor flew steadily, cutting a straight path through the wind. Sorill, however, wasn't holding up as well. Not only did he seem to be frail, but there was also the matter of the heavy-looking sack slung over his back. The gusty currents kept him twirling like a ballerina to keep from falling behind.

Nicole whispered, "Couldn't you have found a better fighter than Sorill? He looks like the first hit he gets will knock him out for good!"

Falkor sighed with much exaggeration. "First of all, you and your pal look twenty times worse than Sorill. Someone will *breathe* on Lily, and that'll be the end of her. And second, he is not meant to be a fighter. He is the cleverest Aereon in the entire force. Designed and patented the Enfiro series, the Embalizer, and that Mar I'm sure Diu's shown you, plus a hefty number of other weapons. Half the galactic fleets are populated with his ship designs. This whole planet—the new Serrona after the Omenra blasted it—was his idea, too. The planetary core was his design, and he built most of it as well. So if we hit a trap or need a door or cell unlocked, he will be the one to take care of it. Brilliant at tactical plans, too. That's why he's my Lieutenant."

Nicole glanced over with new respect for Sorill. Still, if she had to get stuck with just one of them, he wouldn't be her pick. As clever as he was, there were just some situations that called for raw strength. Survival in a ship packed with evil aliens who wanted nothing more than your blood definitely made the list.

They glided from one island to another, following a blipping radar attached to Sorill's wrist. Nicole quickly noticed they were passing empty space more and more often as land masses grew farther apart. They were climbing higher towards space, the artificial atmosphere thinning, the air becoming harder to breathe. There was little technology on the islands they passed now. Nothing but grass and rolling hills.

Then Nicole saw them. The carriers gleamed against the horizon, a range of massive, streamlined bulks rearing against the sky. The pitch-black ships hovered silently, hanging still in the night. Sorill's radar guided them to a ripple of hills behind which they could hide and formulate an approach.

Falkor landed first, settling lightly in the shadows. Sorill zipped along behind them, shaking slightly as he peeked around the hillside. He snapped back immediately, looking flustered and terrified.

Nicole slid off Falkor's back, and she and Lily looked on as Sorill explained what was happening.

"Looks pretty bad, rav," he squeaked. "I can't see too well from here, sorry, but those cruisers look like they have motion sensors, armed turrets—rapid-fire, large caliber, probably—force-field shielding—"

"Don't tell me," Falkor snapped, "what those ships have. Tell me how we can get around the defenses and which cruiser to try."

"The try bit's easy, rav. The Farrider there, in the center. Omenra favorite. Minimal friction framework, hyper-speed capabilities, aggressive turrets like nothing—"

"Sorill," Falkor growled, annoyed. "Cut the tech talk. We're on a tight timeframe, remember?"

"Right, rav. Sorry, sorry—right, the cruiser, rav, on it!" Sorill's voice lapsed into a whisper, spouting calculations, projections, maneuvers, and tactical strikes. Then at last he admitted, "Only way we're getting even close is clandestine infiltration, rav. Farrider's aren't under my patent, but I've studied models, and there's a storage hatch we can access from underneath. From there it's a straight shot to the ventilation systems."

"Perfect," Falkor said. "But how are we going to get close without being seen?"

Sorill hoisted up his leather bag, fishing around until he dragged out four thin straps. "New tech, rav. One-time use only, so we have to make these count. These make the wearer invisible for a short period of time. But so far, short means *really* short. Maybe enough to get us under that ship. Maybe not. But that's the only way I see, short of a straight-up assault on the patrol guards."

"No, we can't have that," Falkor said. "I'm not delighted by the time limit, but these bands are our best shot. Tell us what to do, Sorill."

"Right, rav. Just strap one on your wrist—like this, see—and just keep it on tight. I suggest a quick run, to be on the safe side, but keep quiet and out of the way of the patrols. The tech makes you invisible, not a ghost, so if you run into someone you'll still be solid."

As Sorill passed the bands around, Nicole thought again of what she was about to do. She tried to tell herself that she wasn't afraid, but that didn't turn out too well. She *knew* she was scared, more afraid than she'd ever been in her life. Diu's life was on the line, but maybe he'd been right all along. Maybe she *wasn't* brave. And now she'd met something she was too afraid to face.

But it was no time to retreat, not when they'd gone so far. So when Sorill gave the signal, Nicole strapped on her band with the rest, instantly feeling a cold, wet shiver run down her spine, a sensation like sliding egg yolk. A convulsing crack spiked through her muscles, but suddenly the pain was gone, and when she looked up, she couldn't see anything—not herself, not Lily, not the Aereons.

The microcom hissed in her ear—Falkor ordering them to move. Silently, they sprinted out from behind the hill, pelting towards the Omenra cruisers, the giant carriers rising towards them and then falling behind. Now only the Farrider lay before them, its massive hulk swallowing the sky, revolving floodlights underscoring its black shadow. Ducking past several guards, Nicole made a dash towards the cover of the ship's belly, wondering how much longer the strap would hold out.

She felt yolk dripping down her back again and realized in a jolt that Sorill's band wouldn't stand much more. Her madly pumping arms reappeared first, initially as a haze but soon with well-defined outlines, followed by her legs and body. Nicole collapsed to her knees, breathing hard from the run, flinging aside the now-useless strap. But she was safe. Just barely, she had made it to the Farrider.

Falkor and Sorill were beside her, the former still waiting for his left wing to reappear. Lily was toying with her band, trying to jerk it off. As she helped Lily, Nicole watched Sorill tinker with a small panel inset on the ship and fiddle with something from his pack. Small sounds echoed around them.

Chapter Twenty-Six

The noises suggested danger, but Nicole tried to ignore them and focused on staying silent.

Minutes dragged by as Sorill worked. They were all restless and itching to proceed. For Nicole, it was terrifying to think that she was in the eye of a storm, that a single twitch might alert the Omenra, that they could easily die, right here. Right now.

At last, Sorill signaled them and lowered the panel onto the grass. They stared up into complete darkness. A metal ladder led up into the bowels of the ship, probably set there for maintenance work. Falkor climbed up first, his claws clicking on individual rungs. Sorill came next, followed by Lily. Nicole brought up the rear, snatching a glance back at the receding ground.

She hoped it would not be the last time.

Chapter Twenty-Seven

The Omenra Secret

"Sorill, where are we?" Falkor spat.

"Somewhere over the core generator room."

"Very helpful, Sorill."

"Sorry, rav, that—hey, careful!"

"Sorry," Nicole whispered, removing her knee from Sorill's wing. She was beginning to get tired and careless. Crawling around a ventilation shaft for what seemed like hours certainly wasn't her idea of a rescue mission.

"Are we still on the right bearing?" Falkor said.

"I need to drop into a hallway to see what's going on," Sorill said. "I've lost my heading a little."

"Wonderful. Just perfect. But fine. That's a vent grate ahead, I think."

"We've been here forever," Lily groaned from somewhere in the dark. "Are we close?"

"Quiet," Falkor hissed. "Sorill's removing the grate."

There was a soft clatter of metal as hot yellow light spilled into the shaft. A shadow moved against the light—Sorill dropping into the hallway below. Falkor and Lily moved forward and Nicole was able to take a peek, watching as Sorill examined a series of small red blips on his radar. She leaned forward, a little too far, but she wanted to see . . .

Then, suddenly, her body lurched. A small sound burst from her throat as she fell forward through the grate and smashed into the steel walkway below. Nicole's hand shot to a sharp splinter by her ear—a piece of the now-broken microcom. Luckily, she quickly noted, the translator was still safely in place.

Sorill ran to her and helped her sit up in the hallway lined with pale-orange light. Nicole glanced up, rubbing her head and wondering how stupid she must be to fall from the vent. She could see Lily staring down at her, eyes round first with panic, then relief.

A distant click of claws against metal sent an icy spike through Nicole's spine. Lily hissed at her to hurry up, that an Omenra patrol was coming. In a flash Sorill was up inside the shaft, but Nicole had no way up.

The click of claws against the floor was faster. Maybe, Nicole realized with a jolt, the guards had heard them. She stood, ready to bolt but not knowing where, when suddenly one of the Aereons—she didn't notice which one—dropped from the shaft and shoved her into motion.

Nicole ran until she reached a split in the hall. She tore to the left. The orange lights were glowing more intensely, burning like fires. Her breath came raggedly. The claws were closer . . . but whose claws? There was a door ahead. She had to get there. Had to.

There was fire everywhere.

Nicole smashed into the end of the corridor, groping

about with her fingers until she found a door handle. She pulled. Locked. Scraping at the door and jerking the handle, she pleaded for a miracle. But the fire and claws were coming closer—too close, far too close.

The Aereon pushed her out of the way and twiddled the handle with a sharp thing in his claws until the door burst open. He dragged Nicole inside, away from the fire, and slammed the door shut. There were no lights in this room, and the darkness swallowed her up. She could make out nothing except the clatter of claws on metal in the corridor past the door.

Soon the sounds diminished and quiet engulfed the dark room. The hallway lay silent. Nicole fumbled about with her hands and felt a leathery wing. She was still afraid, still breathless, but at least she wasn't alone.

"Falkor?" Nicole asked.

"Me," came Sorill's squeak.

"Oh. Well, guess I expected that," she admitted. Sorill sure wasn't her choice of a companion, but he was better than nothing.

"Falkor's not all bad, you know."

"I know. He's not bad to everyone. Just to me. But anyway, what's the plan? How do we get out of here?"

"Not via the hall. If that patrol heard us, there'll be an ambush waiting. Hold on, I know . . . there might be a ventilation shaft we can access from here."

Nicole heard him sift through the supplies in his leather bag. Suddenly, a pale white glow swept the room. Shielding her eyes, she squinted to see Sorill attaching a flashlight device to his Enfiro. He pointed it up to the ceiling and grinned. "That's right. Like I thought." Passing Nicole the Enfiro, he instructed, "Hold this. Keep it directed at the ceiling so I can unscrew the bolts holding that grate." He fished out a screwdriver-like instrument from his bag and got to work.

The white light bathed the room with a pale glow. It swept the walls and ceiling, tentatively illuminating the darkness. It was a good thing Sorill was good with locked doors. But . . . a locked door? Unless the Omenra were afraid of someone getting in, why would they keep secrets from each other?

Stranger still was that the room was utterly empty. Unless something invisible was stored here, Nicole saw no reason whatsoever for keeping the room locked up. She went so far as to blindly stick out her hand and wave it around just to make sure. And there was also the matter of the room being pitch black. Was it dark so no one could see? But what *was* there to see?

Nicole shivered, though not from cold. Somehow, though the room was empty and eerie, she almost felt as if there was something there, something hidden. The silvery light pooled on the floor, revealing a flat surface. Smooth, sleek, and empty.

Except for one spot.

She aimed the light at a patch of floor roughly three by three feet. Running the length and width of this space was a silver outline in the metal. Nicole heard Sorill complain, asking her to raise the light, but she ignored him and kneeled to take a closer look. There was just enough light for her to see a latch in the floor.

"Sorill, come down. I think I found something."

In a flash he was across from her, following the beam of light. Nicole brushed her fingers along one edge of the square. Her fingers slid along a sharp ridge till they reached an inset. Sorill felt it too and gasped. He pulled up on the latch, and the door smoothly pulled up from the floor, revealing a descending staircase.

"It's unlocked? Weird," Nicole said.

"That is strange."

"I wonder where it leads."

"Wherever it goes, we need to get back to the team."

Nicole shuffled her feet. He had a point, but . . .

"Please, Sorill. Let's at least take a look. It could be something cool, you never know!"

"Sorry, but please, let's take the vent," he said. "I know for sure where those shafts lead, but we have no idea what's down there. It could be something dangerous."

"Or," she reasoned, "it could be where they're holding Diu. Why else would this place be locked like it's off-limits?" After a silence, she added, "If you're not coming, then you're on your own. I'm going down."

Falkor, she knew, would have just left her. Sorill, however, was the more sensitive kind. His conscience wouldn't let him leave. Nicole felt guilty and manipulative at using him in this way, but it was the only chance she had.

Sorill hitched up his leather bag. "All right," he said. "I'm coming."

"Thanks." Nicole looked down the dark stairs. "I'll go first and light the way."

Chapter Twenty-Seven

The beam scattered coldly on the metal staircase, not quiet dispersing the dark. The stairs seemed to plummet into an infinite abyss bent on swallowing them. Nicole waited for a moment on the edge. Then, feeling a rush, she sprinted down, glancing back only once. She wildly flashed the Enfiro around, bouncing its light off the pitch-black tunnel, till at last the beam skittered across a place where the steps melted seamlessly into the floor.

"Come on," Nicole whispered, aiming the gun along a narrow, deserted corridor. "I think the coast is clear."

She jumped down the last two stairs, landed cat-like on the floor, and pointed the beam back up the stairs so Sorill could see. He came down quickly, shivering and jittery. He was twiddling his claws again, barely restrained, ready to run at the slightest sound. Still, Nicole was glad to have someone by her side.

A cloud of frost rose from her breath. She shivered visibly, and the Enfiro trembled in her icy hands. They must have reached the deepest bowels of the cruiser, a place that had never felt heat, never seen light. Whatever was down here was probably top-secret; something not meant to be found.

Not by the Omenra crew. Not by anyone.

Although the sound was smothered slightly by the leather-like pair of shoes she'd exchanged for her sneakers, Nicole's footsteps swished softly against the floor. Sorill's claws scraped the metal, screeching so loudly that she was sure they'd be heard. But there was no one here. No one to hear them. No one to find them. They were alone in the semi-darkness, following a hallway that seemed to stretch forever.

Only of course there was an end. Nicole sighed audibly when she saw the door, releasing a breath she hadn't even realized she was holding. The door was arched and massive, looming and terrifying, but lacking ornamentation. A solid metal door, leading to some secret.

Nicole tugged on the handle. To her surprise, it slid open easily. She slipped through, followed closely by Sorill. Neither closed the door.

They came out in a wide chamber—a private deployment dock, it seemed. There was a single cruiser stationed here, one of the pair that had cornered Nicole in the village. It was the one Malkior had used, a small ship stamped with strange, silver letters. "It says *Aphelia*," Sorill translated for her benefit, but Nicole ignored it, moving around behind the ship to see another door on the far end of the room. She called Sorill over, realizing this door was not so easy to unlock. It was protected with a keypad bearing symbols.

"Looks like we have one shot," Sorill said. "We get the code wrong, and this thing will signal a breach."

"So what do we do?" Nicole asked.

"I think I can crack it. Here, let's see."

Sorill rummaged through his pack and came up with a handheld device dangling wires. He hooked the wires to the keypad and tapped some buttons on the device. The wire tips sparked momentarily, and the next moment a series of symbols ran over an inset display, finally projecting a row of five characters on the screen.

"Got it," Sorill said, repacking his supplies. He typed in the code and backed up as the door swung forward. Now they were in a sort of office, a room decorated with an assortment of guns, and not just Salviras. Otherwise, the room was empty except for a cluttered desk and a high-backed chair of some leather material. Papers spilled out sideways from drawers, littering the floor. Sorill picked through the desk drawers, having holstered his Enfiro after flicking on a series of pale lights that rimmed the ceiling.

Most of the papers were documents written in strange languages Nicole couldn't understand. There were also some metallic disks flung over the floor, and these she examined. At a tap of her finger, the disks projected holographic images and recordings, the latter lasting from a few seconds to a minute or more. A few were enhanced with sound bites. They mostly showed Omenras—soldiers and scientists and military technicians. One particular Omenra appeared in almost every image. Nicole recognized him as Malkior. With a violent shudder, she flung those disks aside in revulsion. But she kept searching, not knowing what she was looking for exactly, yet knowing there might be something here.

Nicole stopped at an image of a spider-like robot. The Terranova, she realized with a jolt. About to discard the disk, she suddenly realized there was more coming. It was a digital rendering of the machine tunneling into a holographic world, establishing base at a hollowed-out core, a fast-forward—thirty Earth days. All the while, the planet was stripped of water, of comfort, of life. As the recording fizzled out, the disk clattered to the floor from Nicole's shaking hand. The test had shown her some of what could happen to her Earth. And that probably wasn't even the half of it.

"Something wrong?" Sorill asked innocently.

"No, I-I'm fine," Nicole said, her voice quiet. She turned her face away so Sorill wouldn't see her expression.

She left the disks, shuffling now through the strange papers on the table. Then her hand hit something totally different; it was a small, cold, slender object. She shoved several thick stacks of documents aside, revealing a dagger with a split-tipped blade, jagged edges, and a black metal handle.

A handle with a word inscribed into its side.

Nicole stared blankly. There had to be a mistake. She flipped the dagger around, mouth open. This was *her* dagger. Her *Cárine*. But it couldn't be. There was no way.

How could the *Omenra* have it?

She pocketed it and looked around for Sorill. He was turned away from her, but when he heard her coming, he whirled around, clutching another disk. He tried to hide it behind his back.

"Let me see," Nicole said, snatching at it.

Sorill shook his head. "It's not the best idea."

"Come on!" She made a grab for the disk and wrenched it from his claws, but her mouth dropped open when she pressed the button. It was a short recording, but it was insane.

Impossible.

The image showed a group of three human kids on an ordinary Earth cul-de-sac. It was a group Nicole knew well. There was a boy named Danny, a girl named Lex, and . . . another girl. Danny and the second girl were busy climbing a tree while Lex stood below, looking on in awe. They had climbed halfway before Danny stopped, resting on a branch.

There was a crack as the branch gave way and he fell down onto the grass, laughing. The girl kept going and reached the very top, balancing delicately on a high branch, looking out over the street, waving to her two friends below. The image zoomed in on the girl's face and held the shot for a few seconds.

The recording terminated.

Nicole gasped. She dropped the disk. Her hands grabbed the desk for support.

"God," she breathed, "that was me."

"Precisely," whispered a cold, harsh voice. The arched door slammed shut behind them.

Chapter Twenty-Eight

Connecting the Pieces

The voice was terribly familiar. Nicole clenched her eyes shut, and her fingers curled into fists on the desk. Her mouth became a thin, jagged line. She didn't have to turn around to know they were in big trouble. Because she knew who had caught them.

Sorill almost fell backwards over the leather chair. He shook so hard it was as if he'd been dipped in freezing water and made to swallow ice cubes. His head bobbed furiously as he choked out, "Gen-Gen-General Taggerath!"

Claws clicked on the floor behind her. Nicole drew the Embalizer, knowing it was useless in her hands because she could never use it, and then ran around the side of the desk to Sorill's side. Malkior approached directly across from them. His cold eyes flashed to the Embalizer. He laughed. Nicole's eyes darted towards the door, and Malkior moved to stand between her and the only exit. They were cornered.

"It's rather ironic, Nicole Sky," Malkior said smoothly,

"that I've ordered out half my Omenra forces to scavenge the galaxy looking for you, and you end up in my private quarters."

"What do you want from me?" she cried. "I've done nothing to you!"

"I should be saying the same thing."

"What do you mean? You've done me plenty of harm!" When Malkior didn't respond, she snapped, "What about Earth?"

"What *about* Earth?"

Nicole clenched her fists. "Remember the Terranova?" When he didn't reply, she cried, "You're going to destroy Earth!"

Malkior tittered impatiently. "I'm going to take a wild guess," he said. "Did the Airioth tell you about the Terranova?"

"So?"

"And of course they told you about the terrible intergalactic war that we evil Omenra started."

"Yes," she said slowly.

"And do you know exactly why we started the war?"

"I—"

"Or did the Airioth not tell you their little secret?"

Nicole stopped cold. "What secret?"

Malkior grinned, ignoring Sorill's protesting stutters. "When, Nicole, did the Airioth form?"

"After the Omenra rose to power."

"The main bulk of it, certainly. But the original Airioth— today, the core leaders—were around long before the war."

"That's not . . . it's not . . ." Not true, Nicole wanted to say. But now she wasn't so sure.

"Who do you think started the war? The Omenra?"

"You're not saying—"

"Nicole Sky," Malkior said, grinning cruelly, "the *Airioth* started this war. The Airioth leaders allowed our galactic take-over. They even helped us. To cover their tracks and make up for their wrongs, they later gathered an army of rebels to combat the evil that they themselves spawned."

She couldn't believe it. He must be lying to her. He had to be. But there was a strange look of sincerity in his eyes, and Diu had kept so many secrets. Was there truth to Malkior's terrible words?

"You're still responsible for creating the Terranova!" she yelled.

"Me all alone?" Malkior asked innocently. "Or did your little Airioth friends give me the plans?"

At that moment, the door slammed open and two Omenra guards stormed into the chamber. They wrestled Nicole and Sorill against a wall and chained their arms to-gether with shackles. Nicole tried to wriggle out of their grasp, but one enraged guard twisted her arm until her eyes blurred with tears of pain. She bowed her head in wretched sub-mission and watched glumly as the guards tore away Sorill's bag, the Enfiro, and the Embalizer.

"Search them," Malkior ordered.

Nicole was infinitely glad she had left the Galactera back at the palace, but fury seized her as one guard pulled out her dagger and tossed it to Malkior. "Give it back!" she cried, although she knew it was futile.

Malkior carefully looked her over. Then he did an unthinkable thing. He walked across the room and slid the dagger back into her belt. "All right," he said calmly and turned away, leading the way out, followed by his two prisoners and the guards.

Sorill looked everywhere except at Nicole, but she barely noticed. Why had Malkior so willingly complied? Didn't he realize he had just armed her? Unless, of course, he meant to confront Nicole later and wanted an opponent who could fight back. Either way, she knew he realized she could never escape now.

And there was the second question—was Malkior lying, or had Diu not told her the half of it?

Nicole and Sorill were thrust up the stairs and jostled along through the hallway. Malkior led them through a narrow series of passages before they came out in front of another door. He typed a code into a keypad, turned the handle, and shoved them both into a well-lit room. Before he left, Nicole cried out, "I still don't understand. What did I ever do to you?"

"Why don't you ask your Airioth pals?"

The door slammed shut in her face, and she heard the computerized lock click into place. But she hadn't even had time to turn around before a warm, furry body hit her face. "Nicole!" Lily squeaked. "You're safe! Me, I was caught with Falkor, and we've been waiting . . . for . . ."

It didn't take a telepathic connection to sense Nicole's vicious rage.

"What's wrong?" Lily asked.

Nicole whirled on the balls of her feet. Her face was contorted in anger. She glared around the prison chamber in a fierce swipe of her eyes. Falkor slouched in a sitting position on the floor. Sorill quickly joined him. He trembled visibly and avoided Nicole's explosive gaze.

"Nicole."

The voice was soft and warmly familiar. For a second she forgot her anger.

"I thought you were dead," Nicole said.

"I thought I was, too."

She choked back a sob. "How'd you make it?"

"Malkior forgot about the powder. And when he realized what I had done, he said it was for the best I survived."

Survived. The word triggered a flash of memory: the Terranova on the disk. Earth's survival was on the line. But maybe, just maybe, the Omenra were not the cause. Nicole tightened her fingers into fists again. Now that Diu was alive—was alive for sure—it was time for answers.

"Malkior told me things I didn't know," she said.

"Really?" Diu said calmly.

"Lots of things. About the Airioth."

"What did he say?"

"That the Omenra didn't start the war. That the Terranova wasn't their idea."

"And?"

"Is that . . . true?"

Diu laughed coldly. "I'm surprised you even ask. Of course Malkior lied to you. He just wants to turn you against the Airioth and against me."

She might have believed him if it wasn't for Sorill. He was staring at the floor, avoiding her eyes. Diu could keep a straight face, but Sorill wasn't one to lie.

"Okay, fine," Nicole said evenly. "I'll buy it. The Airioth have absolutely nothing to do with starting the war. Just tell me one thing, then. How come Malkior sent out half his army to look for me when I haven't even done anything?"

"Yet," Diu admitted.

"Yet?"

"It's not what you have done. It's what you will do."

She stiffened. "What do you mean?"

Diu remained silent, but Falkor spoke up. "I think we should tell her," he said.

Nicole viciously dug her fingernails into her palms. "You're in on this, too?" she yelled.

"Actually," Sorill corrected, "we all are." Diu was staring murderously at him, but for the first time since Nicole met him, Sorill did not back down. "Sorry," he said, "but she deserves to know. She's at the heart of all this, so if *she* shouldn't know, who should?"

"We both deserve to know," Lily chipped in. "She's my friend, and if she's in any danger, me, I ought to know too so I can help."

"Come on, Diu. Give her a chance," Falkor said, for once on Nicole's side.

Diu could probably tell that he was going to be outvoted. "All right, all right. She can know," he said.

"Everything?" Nicole snapped.

"Everything. But you must understand one thing."

"What?"

"Every good thing has a shadow."

Nicole didn't like the sound of that, but she sat down across from Diu, Lily on her shoulder. A long, ominous silence spread, covertly slipping into every nook and cranny of the room. It dampened the air for a long time before Diu finally began.

"For a long time, there was just me and my best friend, Malkior Rav Taggerath. Yes, Nicole, my best friend. It's what has stopped me from killing him all these years. It's why this war has lasted ten Earth years.

"But to start at the beginning, the Omenra weren't always evil. In those days, there was a famous academy for brilliant students from across the galaxy. That's where Malkior and I met. I was there because I wanted to escape from my home world and Malkior because his parents—father, actually, his mother was dead—expected the best of him. In human terms, I was eight and he was seven. And there we met a young female of my age and species, a child named Serena Lutára Katang.

"The three of us ate together, attended classes together, studied for and cheated on exams together. Serena was brilliant and perfect in every way. On the other hand, Malkior and I were never model students. At least, not academically. We were, however, prodigies in virtual gaming rooms. War simulations, mostly. We both had a knack for military strategy, he even more than I. As a team, we always managed to outsmart opposing players. Our skills only grew as we advanced to higher levels in the academy, skipping quickly to upper classes. We soon graduated with honors, Serena with us. But we were all still young . . . he fourteen, she and I fifteen, and both ages equivalent in maturity to their Earth counterpart; our two species age at roughly the same rate as humans.

"We first sought reckless lives, traveling the galaxy in search of danger and adventure. We bonded more than ever then, making vows to be friends forever. That worked well for about six Earth months, but we soon grew tired of our games. We had found danger, coming close to death on several occasions, but we wanted something greater. A higher purpose. Serena left to return to the academy. For me and Malkior, the solution was the Ethári Galactra Force, an army the Council upholds in case of warfare.

"At that time, there were no severe conflicts. Scattered disturbances between planets did, however, occasionally surface. Through training and missions, our skills were tested, honed, refined. Malkior and I fought our way to the top, and soon we were allowed to lead missions. As at the academy, the generals thought we were brilliant military strategists, allowing us to draw up plans along with the experts. In those years in the army, I also met the first love of my life, a beautiful female of my kind and age named Máyra. And at that point, Malkior and I thought we were the kings of the universe. Nothing could have spoiled our perfect lives.

"Then tragedy struck. One day, I received a message from my father via disk recording. Rogue groups have always wandered my planet, pillaging what villages they can find. I had always been afraid of an attack from such a group on my family, knowing that my home world was isolated and a rural wasteland in comparison to the rest of the galaxy. Yet I'd never acted on that fear, and that day things caught up with me. A local band of simple thieves had broken into our house, taken everything, and killed my mother, who was simply in the wrong place at the wrong time. My father had been away then, finding out only hours later when it was too late.

"I had thought I was invincible, but here I was, about seventeen in human years and my life shattered. I went into a rage, wanting to find my mother's murders, yet knowing I might never get the chance for revenge. I was scheduled to partake in a mission that day, but I tried to run from the truth, refusing to fight until I could come to terms with my mother's fate. It was my grave mistake not to go that day.

"I found out the following morning that Máyra had been sent out in my place. In that battle, she was killed. My mother's death had not directly been my fault; Máyra's was. Before, I had always lived my life heedless of the consequences. Only then did I begin, on some level, to understand that things are not always so simple."

"In my blind rage and anger, I fled from the Force and hired myself out for mercenary work. I thought at the time that maybe if I killed other's enemies, I would somehow fulfill my personal lust for revenge. I soon became a full-fledged assassin, taking more lives than I could ever remember. Even worse, I had a terrible condition to my killing. I never shot until I could see the eyes of my victims so I could feel the force of every fleeing life.

"The longer I trained, the better I became. Soon, I received a contract from an underground group that rented out hired guns for those seeking personal vengeance. It paid better money, and I got the finest deals, the most powerful targets, and I climbed to great power. Yet there was a price.

"The leader of the group, a creature of my species who went only by the title Rav, had a daughter. Anira was a little younger than me. She was sadistic and had a tendency for malice and perfection, and I despised her. But she took a liking to me, and her father warned me that to stay, I had to please her. You can imagine, of course, that following Máyra's death I was unwilling to ever love again, much less so soon. I pretended well, enough so Anira was satisfied. Yet the longer I stayed and the more I came to know her, the more honest my affection became. At last, I felt something like love for her as well.

"Through all of it, Malkior remained with me. Ever my faithful friend, he joined the group as my primary partner. He worked more behind the scenes than on the field and was mostly responsible for researching the targets I struck down. However, he didn't like what we were doing and questioned me often in my actions. Yet he didn't make me stop. He just let me go on until I realized myself what I was doing.

"I finally broke in the end when my assigned target became someone I had always kept at the back of my memory but had rarely considered in the past few years: Serena. What happened between me and her is another story, one that has no bearing now. The important thing is that as a consequence, I resigned from the group; it nearly cost my life, as well as Malkior's. It was only because of Anira that we were allowed to survive, and even then Rav promised that I lived only to one day regret it. It is a promise still unfulfilled. I hope it will remain that way.

"At that point, I was about eighteen in human terms, and Malkior and I returned to serving partly with the Force. Before we left, we had amassed a sizable gang there, and now what remained of it returned to our side. Our team was unstoppable, and we became the Airioth, taking my name, since I'd unofficially long held the position of leader. You never asked, Nicole, but my full name is Diu Orior Airioth.

"We did not remain long this second time. Malkior and I had our fun, but as young adults we now needed a constant. In human terms, I was almost nineteen and Malkior was seventeen when we left the force. We were, of course, followed by our loyal Airioth friends, three of whom you've already met—Rayonk, the oldest, Falkor, slightly older than me, and Sorill, Malkior's age. But before we went our separate ways, Malkior asked me for two favors.

"Because my assassin skills were legendary, he first warned me he suspected that the current Omenra king was planning a terrible war against the galaxy. He asked me for my help in stopping him. Malkior said he knew the perfect Omenra to take his place, one who would be a fair and kind ruler. Second, he asked if I would be interested in helping him devise a legendary weapon—a weapon that could destroy worlds. Swearing never to use it against anyone, Malkior said he only wanted to see if it was possible. And because he was my best friend, because he had stuck with me all these years, I blindly believed him.

"We pooled our resources, Malkior and I, and purchased

a cruiser where we could work in secret. Our Airioth friends joined us, and we made a fantastic team. We devised the two plans simultaneously. Sorill was, and still is, a genius at technology, and he had schematics for the weapon worked out in no time. But while he set to work building the weapon we would eventually name the Terranova, Malkior and I laid out the final plans for the Omenra king.

"The Omenra ruler was assassinated at a public rally, much to the horror of his people. The perpetrator was said to have been a wild lunatic, and the murder . . . a tragedy. Omenra officials searched for the assassin for years, but it was a perfect job. No leads, no evidence. They never found the killer, and so only the Airioth knew the truth.

"As the king had no heirs, there were many candidates for election, but we took them out one by one, either by bribing them or by intimidation or, when it was called for, elimination. Finally, there was only one Omenra left. Gavaron ascended to the throne and in no time began his evil reign. Malkior swore that he'd had no idea of the new king's true intentions. He was my best friend and the only one who had stood beside me all these years, and so I believed him. Again.

"In the meantime the Terranova was nearing completion. Sorill just had to work out a few kinks, and it would be ready. But at that time, another member of the Airioth, one called Tibo, had a terrible vision. We would have ignored it, but Tibo has certain gifts, powers we can only guess at. He fights with what you humans call 'magic', not physical strength. And he warned us that, if we finished the Terranova, we would know no end of chaos until a child mended our broken galaxy.

"I had never meant any harm to come to the innocent and ordered Sorill to destroy his creation. Either way, we had achieved the unachievable, which is all Malkior had, in theory, wanted. We had created a weapon with the power to destroy worlds. We burned all the plans, and Sorill began to dismantle the Terranova, but we woke up one morning to find the weapon gone, along with a jet named *Aphelia* that Malkior and I had earned as elites in the army. It was only then that I realized Malkior had betrayed me.

"He left a note explaining everything. He had struck a deal with Gavaron even before we had left the army. According to the terms of this deal, if Malkior could create a weapon as in the ancient legends and make Gavaron king, Malkior would be made a general and second-in-command of the most powerful galactic force in history. Malkior was counting on my blind friendship and Sorill's incredible technological talents, as well as the undying faith of our Airioth friends, to help him get it done. He bet correctly.

"Luckily Tibo had never trusted Malkior. Maybe he knew what was coming. He stopped us from finishing the Terranova and left the Omenra to tinker with it for ten long Earth years before they could finally use it.

"Still, Malkior had always been my best friend, and I was not eager to confront him. Looking back, I admit that I might never have acted if it had not been for a rash act on his part. When I tried to convince Malkior to give up his power and help us elect a new Omenra king, not only did he refuse, but he also ordered my father killed. He wanted to break my spirit, and he knew how important family and friendship were to me. But this time he bet wrong.

"Instead of extinguishing it, he ignited my spirit. I was determined now to be the last of us standing. To avenge my father's death and my foolishness in following Malkior, I gathered my Airioth friends, and we began to fight back. Slowly but surely, we gained galactic fame for our small acts of courage. Other rebels joined in. Soon the Airioth and the Omenra were the two most powerful forces in the galaxy.

"Now, everything hangs in the balance of a conflict that began with a single betrayal, and the only hope for survival rests with a child whose fate is intertwined with destiny.

"That child, Nicole Sky, is you."

Chapter Twenty-Nine

Escape

Nicole was shocked beyond speech. Diu, her friend and ally—a trained assassin, leader of the Airioth, and Malkior's former best friend? And the bit about her? Impossible. How could she, a nobody from nowhere, mend the galaxy? What did that even mean?

Suddenly, Earth seemed like a tiny speck of dust in a giant galaxy, and she was destined to protect it all.

Before she could say a word, Diu cried out furiously, tearing a livid Lily from his arm. The Lunaran spat out blood and fur, raking the air with her claws. Nicole snatched Lily away, barely managing to restrain her. "Lily, are you crazy?" she yelled.

"It's your fault!" Lily shrieked, fighting against Nicole's grip.

"What's his fault?"

"Everything!"

"Breathe, Lily," Nicole said. "I know you're mad, but—"

"Don't pretend *you're* not! Earth wouldn't be in danger if it wasn't for him!"

"I understand," Diu said quickly. "It is my fault, and I don't blame either of you for thinking it. But as I said before, every good thing has a shadow. What's past is past. We can't change history. Only the future."

"Unless it's already been decided for you," Nicole said. "But at least one thing's cleared up."

"What?" Lily muttered, still fuming.

"Now I know why Diu's been so worried about protecting me all along. At least there's one secret revealed. And another, actually. I was wondering why Falkor and Queen Tári didn't want the Aereons to know my name. It's all because of that prophecy."

There was a bitter silence.

"What if I don't fulfill it?" Nicole snapped spitefully.

"You always have that option," Diu said. "Even prophecies are not set in stone. But if it's not true, then it shall be the end of us all. The Airioth can never surrender, and the Omenra shall never stop. Know this—we are equally matched except for one thing. Malkior and I both know about your destiny, so whoever has you has more control. We both need you. I have to protect you, and he has to kill you. Whoever gets you first wins."

"So I'm a *prize* now?"

"Nicole—"

"The way I see it, whoever wins, I lose. And anyway . . . *how* am I supposed to fulfill this prophecy thing? What am I supposed to do?"

"I think there's only one creature in the galaxy who can answer that question. Only Tibo himself knows."

"Tibo this, Tibo that! I don't care what he knows! Why can't *I* know things for a change?" She glared at the floor. "Whatever. It's too late either way. We're trapped in a prison chamber on Malkior's Farrider. There's no way we're getting out."

Falkor suddenly chuckled. Nicole blinked at him as if he had gone mental. "What's so funny, I'd like to know?"

"I told you we should bring Sorill," he said, and only then did she notice that Sorill was busy fidgeting around with a thin band around his wrist, the same color as his skin. The Omenras either hadn't noticed it or hadn't considered it a threat. But now she could see that there was a little pocket-knife built into it, and he was using the knife to unscrew a grate in the ceiling.

"Just give me a little time. We'll be out of here soon, rav."

"Good," Diu and Falkor said together.

But the time stretched into long minutes. The bolts were too large for the little blade to budge. At last Sorill stood back and stared at the metal grate, considering. Nicole figured that since the guards had taken his bag, he didn't have his usual supplies, and that left him in a bit of a rut. He was probably still considering his options when she remembered Madam Banda's dagger. Maybe, just maybe, *Cárine* could save all their lives. She whipped the dagger out by its black handle and tapped the needle-sharp tips with her fingers. They were large enough to easily twist out the bolts.

"Sorill," Nicole called out, "try using this. It might just be what we need."

He curiously took the dagger, but he hadn't held it for

three seconds before he threw it at the wall like it was on fire. It clattered loudly to the floor, and everyone looked at Sorill like he'd gone crazy. He ignored them all, suddenly trembling as if he'd been slapped hard in the face.

"What's wrong?" Nicole asked, retrieving the dagger.

"I won't use it!" he shrieked, his voice high and squeaky. "Not that dagger."

Falkor glanced at Diu, and so did Nicole. "Another relic of the past?" she asked coldly.

Diu crossed the room and took up the dagger in his paws, staring blankly at his reflection in the shining blade. "What else."

"What's the dagger's story?" Nicole asked, but she had a sick feeling she already knew what he was going to say.

Diu paced the room, tossing and catching the blade expertly. "This was one of my key weapons during my mercenary career. When long-range weapons would not do the job, this was supposed to be a last resort. One I used often. And one, now, that I think you will have to use often."

"I'm not taking that thing."

"What harm has it done you?"

"Not what's it done to me. What you did—"

"Exactly. What *I* did. But you are not me, Nicole. And *Cárine* is no longer mine. You will decide its future. It can continue to be what I made it. Or you can make it into something new. Something different. Something good."

Diu pressed the dagger forcefully into Nicole's hands. Her fingers tightened weakly around the handle, and her thoughts flashed to Lunara. Madam Banda had seemed so strange then in giving up the dagger. Only now did Nicole understand.

She glanced up at the vent shaft. "You're right, Diu. And now's the time to start. Sorill," she said, pushing the dagger into his claws, "things can change. You just have to give them a chance."

Sorill stared at her for a long time, his hand shaking. Then his claws stiffened around the handle. "You're right. Thanks," he said quietly, only loud enough for her to hear. To the others he shouted, "All right, rav. We'll be long gone before the Omenra know what hit them!"

As Sorill worked on the bolts, Diu took Falkor aside. But Nicole was still close enough to hear.

"Falkor," Diu said, "I know where Arvia is."

"On the ship?"

"Yes."

"How do you know?"

"I overheard the Omenra. She is captive, just like us."

"Do you know where?" Falkor asked.

"I think so, and I might be able to lead us there through the vent."

"Then we'll do that," Falkor said, "and then get out of here. I don't know about you, but I'm ready to go home."

"All right, rav," Sorill interrupted, his words broken by a resounding clatter as the grate crashed and skidded across the metal floor. "We're ready to go."

Falkor grasped Diu by the shoulders and lifted him up first through the hole in the ceiling. Lily followed, and then Sorill took Nicole. Yet all of it was suspicious, Nicole thought.

The fact that there were no cameras. No chains. No guards or defenses.

And the dagger. Malkior had given it back purposefully. As if he meant for them to escape.

Nicole shook the thought from her head and crawled after the others towards freedom.

Hopefully.

"We're close," Diu said.

"Me, I hope so," Lily moaned. "Been stepped on twice already."

"Just keep going," Falkor snarled.

Sorill whimpered, clearly upset by the growing tension.

Nicole was almost last in line, followed only by Sorill. She squinted ahead, wondering what Arvia would look like, unable to image how happy the princess would be when she returned home for the first time in ten Earth years.

With no Enfiro to light the way, they had been treading through near-pitch darkness for the last half hour. The only light was the faint glow from grates where they opened on lighted rooms and hallways. The team had encountered insect-like creatures, extremes of hot and cold, and dead ends.

In short, everything except the princess or a way to escape.

Now Diu crawled ahead, peering through another grate. He glanced back, shaking his head. Nicole paused as they moved ahead, briefly laying her forehead against the cool metal wall. She was exhausted, suffered from severe claustrophobia, and wanted nothing more than to go home.

Suddenly she jolted, raising her head to listen. A soft sound echoed to her from somewhere very nearby. The sound of musical laughter. "Hey, everyone, wait," Nicole called.

Diu was first to glance back. "What?"

"Listen."

Silence. Then: "To what?"

She couldn't believe he couldn't hear it. "That sound. The laughter."

"What laughter, Nicole?" Falkor asked.

"Me, I can't hear it," Lily said.

Sorill agreed. "Neither can I."

The laughter was louder now, seductive, moving closer along the shaft. It ripped through Nicole's body and seized her in a struggle. She pushed past her friends. She knew they were shouting for her, but she couldn't hear them. Her world became the cold, tight walls of the vent and the music of the laugh.

Nicole twisted her way through the shafts until at last she met a dead end. Ahead was one final grate. She poised her body above it but suddenly collapsed, shaking, onto the thick bars. Through sudden darkness she heard Diu's voice. He dragged her aside and rubbed something over her forehead. Her mind suddenly seemed to clear of chaos. When she touched her fingers to the spot, she felt powder.

"Are you okay?" he asked as she rolled onto her stomach.

"Yeah, now I am. I didn't know the powder could do that."

"It does just about everything, but that's beside the point. What happened?"

"I don't know. I just heard the laugh, and I followed it here. Now it's gone."

"I wonder—"

"Hurry up!" Falkor cried out.

"What?" Diu asked, looking away.

"It's Arvia. I don't know about the laughter, but Nicole led us right to her," Sorill explained, hastening to unscrew the grate with the dagger.

"Arvia?" Diu repeated, glancing at Nicole. She only shrugged.

There was a shriek and an explosion of noise as the grate hit the floor below. Falkor swept down first. His entrance was followed by another yell. Sorill jumped down next, then Lily, and finally Diu and Nicole.

The room was empty except for a small cot set against the wall and a tiny table in the corner. But sitting on the make-shift bed, mouth open in disbelief, was the Aereon Arvia.

The princess leapt to her feet. Her red-purple scales glowed regally even in the dim light. Her outfit was black and edged with silver. Her tail was sweeping, touching down gracefully on the floor. But her most incredible part was her eyes. They were the most expressive eyes Nicole had ever seen, but she didn't like what she saw in them. There was darkness there. Shadows, and fear. Maybe ten years of being with the Omenra did that to a girl.

Arvia stared at them. Then she screamed. "I knew I heard something in the vents!" she shrieked.

Falkor leapt forward and clamped his claws over her mouth. Her face contorted into a look of indignation, and she kicked him in the stomach and leaped away across the room.

"Arvia," Falkor groaned. "What're you doing?"

She looked startled. "You know my name?"

"Is it really you, then?"

"Who *are* you?" she asked sincerely.

"You . . . don't remember?"

"Should I? I've never seen any of you in my life." Suddenly, her eyes grew distant and terrified, and she muttered to herself, "What am I even talking to you for? He's warned me all along about something like this, and he's been right, and now—"

Diu moved towards her in a flash. He shoved her against the metal wall and clamped his paw over her mouth. "Keep quiet," he warned. "We're not here to hurt you. At least, they're not. Get me mad and maybe I'll break the rules."

Arvia lividly pushed him away, but she seemed to have taken the warning to heart. Across the room, Falkor made a choking sound.

"Aereon Princess Arvia, daughter of Queen Tári of planet Serrona," Diu said. "Any of that sound familiar?"

"I don't know who you are," she hissed viciously, "but if you don't leave now, I *will* alert the guards, and then you'll be sorry, and nothing you say or do will stop me."

"Arvia, what have they done to you?" Falkor muttered, leaning against the wall. "What have they done?"

She seemed sad now. "At least they care about me," she cried, "unlike the Aereons who never loved me."

"Did the Omenra tell you that?"

"Malkior himself."

"He lied, Arvia! He lied!" Falkor reached to grab her. "And now you're coming with us, so I can explain the truth."

Arvia backed away. "Don't you dare touch me!" she cried.

"Falkor, stop!" Diu yelled in vain.

The princess halted, grinning mischievously. "Wait, you're Falkor? General Avalar?"

He froze. "Do you remember me, Arvia?"

"I remember Malkior telling me about you."

"What did he say?" Falkor snapped.

"That's no way to talk to a lady," Arvia crooned.

Nicole realized with a flush of anger that the princess, who they were risking their lives to save, was toying with them now. For a moment she found herself half-hoping they would just leave the insolent Arvia there. But then the princess added, "But I might as well tell, it's not much of a secret. Shouldn't be, anyway."

"Arvia," Falkor asked, "what do you mean?"

"Silly Falkor," she hissed. "The day after tomorrow, the moment dawn touches Serrona, Malkior will finish off you and your pathetic army. He says you Aereons have been playing with the Omenra for too long. I begged him to be part of it, and he said he'd be glad to arm me for battle. It'll be fun, I think. Maybe I'll get to confront you. Maybe even kill you." The revelation was followed by a long silence, broken only by Arvia's soft, melodious laughter.

Diu took the news without as much as a twitch. Nicole was sure he was already strategizing in his mind. At any rate, he immediately took charge again.

"We have to go. Arvia stays—Falkor, wait, hear me out—

but only until the Omenra siege. Arvia, we're going to find out what they did to you. We're going to bring you home." He looked up at the ceiling. "Come on, we have to move. We have to warn Queen Tári before it's too late."

Arvia looked furious. "Warn the queen all you want, but you can't stop Malkior. And you will never take me. This is my home."

"For now, princess. Come on, let's go."

"No!" Falkor cried. "We can't just . . . leave."

All the while, Arvia had been edging closer to the cot. Diu suddenly noticed, flipped out the Mar, and pointed it at her chest. "Don't make another move, princess," he growled.

Arvia only laughed. A gentle, cruel laugh.

She smiled a mouthful of neatly filed teeth, the pearly-white points as sharp as daggers. "Too late," she whispered with a deadly softness. A tiny click sounded through the silent air, and Arvia lifted a foot to reveal a small, silver switch on the floor.

Nicole's brain flashed to two things at once. Diu still had the Mar . . . how? She could vaguely understand the challenge in Malkior's arming *her*, but . . . leaving the weapon of his worst enemy? It was a ridiculous notion at best, especially considering that the Omenra had taken the Glider, as she now noticed. The JET over the Mar? What was Malkior thinking?

There was no time to figure that out because there was a second problem. Suddenly, a burst of noise swelled in the hallway. The door to Arvia's room blasted open and a pair of guards rushed in, wielding Salviras. Diu instantly gunned them down, wounding both guards in the leg. Dashing across the room, he brought the Mar down on each head, knocking the guards unconscious.

There was still noise in the hallway. More guards were coming.

"We need to leave," Diu cried and motioned to the vent. "Right now."

Falkor shook his head. "But we can't just go!"

"Be reasonable! If we stay, we're finished! I cannot take care of all of the guards this way."

"That's right," Arvia hissed. "Go, and good luck till the battle. I'm looking forward to roasted Falkor, skewered on a stick."

Falkor's eyes flashed lividly, but Diu's word was final. Nevertheless, he was last into the shaft, waiting with defiance to the last. Sorill quickly remounted the grate, twisted the bolts into place, and returned Nicole's dagger. Diu signaled for them to move. Again, Nicole took her place just ahead of Sorill and behind the others.

She glanced back once at the square of light from the grate. A sound echoed towards her, but not one of angry guards. It was almost like weeping. Almost. There was something strange about the sound. Most likely, it was maniacal laughter of a daughter who no longer knew her home. Wondering if they would ever see Arvia again, Nicole started on the long crawl to safety.

And to war.

Malkior sat at his desk, watching via a concealed camera as Diu knocked two guards unconscious. The 'escapees' were doing very well, but worse than Malkior had expected. He would have thought the Mar and dagger to be enough to get them out of here faster. Maybe he overestimated his old friend and the Earth child. Diu certainly seemed off his game. Surprisingly, he'd barely wounded the two guards.

Suddenly, an Omenra burst into the room. "Permission to speak, General?" he panted, trying to catch his breath.

"Permission granted," Malkior replied, tapping the desk impatiently with his claws. Always so formal, these guards. Even if the ship was about to explode they would take ten minutes just to start speaking.

The guard took a moment to catch his breath. "The prisoners are escaping. Permission to retrieve the fugitives?"

For the longest time, Malkior did not speak. Finally, he ordered, "No. Let them go. Call in the perimeter patrols and launch the arming sequence. I want my Septagliders ready by morning."

"But . . . sir . . . the fugitives—"

"Are none of your concern. Do you dare defy orders?"

"No, General."

"Then let them go. You are dismissed." Malkior swiveled his chair so its back faced the guard.

"But Diu Airioth is with them!"

"I believe I said you were dismissed."

The guard's eyes widened for a second. Then he nodded and disappeared, closing the door behind him.

Malkior swiveled his chair around. He reached into the lowest drawer in his desk, one he typically kept sealed under lock and key. Groping with his claws, he picked up a single disk from among a stack of papers. He clicked the button to activate a projection of a single image frozen forever in time.

The scene was drawn from an evening long past, but from one Malkior remembered well. It had been a celebration of reunion after so many years. Diu, Serena, and himself—the eldest two eighteen at the time—were sitting together beside a beautiful, wild, untouched lake and watching triple moons hover high in the vast black sky. Diu was in the center, his feet dipped lazily in the silver water. On one side of him sat Serena, feet tucked beneath her, head resting on his shoulder. On the other side and about a foot away, a Malkior of seventeen relaxed, sighing mist into the cold night.

Ten years in the future, the image's counterpart sighed as well. The snapshot had been his idea. Shortly afterward, Diu and Serena had realized that Malkior had set up a recording device and lunged playfully at him, shattering the moment. But he hadn't let them destroy the disk, and now this was all that remained of a past he could not forget.

The hologram vanished, and Malkior shoved the disk back into the drawer and slammed it shut. He gazed longingly at the place where the image had hovered moments earlier. But that was all behind him. For now, he needed to focus on the present.

And everything was going according to plan.

Chapter Thirty

The Soul
of the Universe

"Any bright ideas?" Nicole asked, staring glumly at the night sky. It flashed in slivers through slashing blades. They had found a way out at last, but unfortunately, the only escape was through a whirring fan fitted into the end of the shaft.

Falkor watched the blades spin. "If someone doesn't mind having a paw or wing cleaved off . . ."

Diu shoved him. "Come on, now is not the time for jokes. Any serious ideas? Sorill?"

"Here's one," Falkor interrupted. "If my Enfiro would magically reappear, I could just blast that fan right out of the vent."

"That wouldn't work even if you had your gun," Sorill said. "The blast would ricochet."

"What do you suggest we do?"

"If I had my bag of supplies, I'd stop that fan and pry it out. But with the way things stand now, we only have one choice." Sorill was shivering again.

"What?" Diu asked.

"The best I can do is jam the fan for a little. Someone small could slip through and then we could route supplies or help from outside."

Lily fumed and poked her paw at Sorill's chest. "Me, I think I know just where you're going with this. If you think you're going to get me to go, you're wrong, pal."

"That's okay, Lily," Nicole said. "We'll just wait here until the Omenra figure out where we've gone and crawl up here looking for us. Then they'll drag us back to the prison cell and Malkior will come in, and I bet he won't be bringing flowers and chocolates."

Lily looked between the spinning blades and the depths of the shaft. "Sorill, are you sure you can stop the fan?"

"Absolutely."

"Then me, I guess I've picked my poison." Lily sighed. "Me, I'll go."

Sorill beckoned with his claws. "Nicole, may I have *Cárine* again?"

She tossed it over. "Why?"

"If I wedge it in right, I should be able to stop the fan for a little. Lily, as soon as I say, you have to slip through. I'll jam the fan, but I can't give any guarantees on how long."

Lily sauntered over to the lighting-fast swirl. Her purple fur reflected in the silvery blur. "Me, I'm never going into espionage," she moaned, ready for Sorill's signal. "But me, I'm glad for the virtual training."

Getting flat on his belly, Sorill crawled to the whirling fan.

He sucked in his breath and looked over to make sure Lily was ready. She nodded, and he twisted the dagger forward, shrieking, "Move!" the moment the blades screeched to a halt. Nicole hadn't even had time to see if Lily was safe before the pressure spiked and the dagger was blasted out across the shaft.

"Lily?" Nicole called out anxiously. "Lily, you okay?" The fan blades continued to turn over, spinning in an eternal cycle. "*Lily!*" Nicole cried again. But the night was silent.

She'd almost forgotten about the others and started when a paw touched her shoulder. Diu crawled up beside her. "Don't worry about her," he said, holding out the dagger. "Lily's tough. She'll come back even if she has to fight to get here."

"I know," Nicole said, taking the weapon. "If she needs to, she'll be fierce." She flipped her feet around and sat up, bowed head just barely scraping the ceiling. Gripping her knees with her arms, she pressed her sneakers against the sides of the shaft. Then, looking up, she noticed for the first time silver streaks in Diu's fur, highlighted by the faint moonlight. Though maybe she had imagined it.

Sorill and Falkor had, in the meantime, descended into hushed whispers. They were deep in conversation about three feet away. Falkor laughed, and Nicole remembered back to a time when she had been happy. Truly happy. A time—all the time—she had spent on Earth with her friends and family. Tears swelled in her eyes.

"It's not really the right time to be thinking about this," she said quietly so only Diu could hear. "But I've been gone for so long. Mom and Dad must be worried sick. They probably have cops all over the place looking for me. And I'm thinking, what if I don't come back? What if . . . if . . ."

Her cheeks were wet now. Tiny droplets sparkled on the gray floor. Diu pretended not to notice. "You're strong, too," he said. "You have to believe that. And you have something I've never seen in anyone else, not even in me."

"What?"

"Pure, unconditional love for the world. Since I've met you, you haven't done a single thing just for yourself."

She chuckled. "Right. Listen, I don't need lies to make me feel better. Honestly, I can't think of a single time when I *wasn't* selfish. Remember our fight? When I decided to go it alone, I was putting my pride above the mission . . . or whatever it is you commandos call it. And when I went out to look for food against your orders, that was just me trying to prove myself and you know it." Her mouth wouldn't let her stop there. "And even now," she added, "I'm here for you. But I'm here for me, too."

"True," he said. "But whenever you put yourself in danger, it wasn't only for personal gain. When you went to look for food, you were afraid we would starve. When you went out after Arli, you were worried about her. When you almost died fighting the Korrak, was that pride? And even the quest you are undertaking is not just for you but for Earth and those who call it home. The essence of this war is a fight between old friends. But you, you have the soul of the universe within you, the very soul of love and friendship. When people like you come around, they are treasured. The universe itself will conspire to keep you safe."

She smiled. "Thanks, even though I doubt one word of that's true."

"I don't, and I think I can even prove it."

"How?"

"Explain to me, Nicole, what those lapses are you seem to keep having."

"You mean those vision things? Hey, I don't know. Magic, I guess. Aren't you the expert in that kind of stuff? You and that Tibo?"

"Think about this," Diu said. "Do you remember how you saw the Terranova and the Omenra in the fire before you even knew what they were? How about when you used the blue powder to connect to Arli? And just now, when you led us to Arvia, even though you didn't know where she was?"

"Yeah. So?"

"Don't you realize that you know things without actually knowing, that you can feel things without them being close? Nicole, except for Tibo, that is as close to 'magic' as I have ever seen anything come. So tell me now that the universe is not behind you. Tell me now, with conviction."

Nicole instinctively opened her mouth to argue but couldn't find the words. Not any, she realized, that would sound believable. Because now she was starting to think that there really was some truth to what Diu said.

Suddenly Sorill cried out and Nicole looked up just in time to dodge razor-sharp fan blades. The fan screeched along the metal shaft, trailed by smoke, and Lily hovered into view. "Miss me?" she asked, panting, struggling to hold up a Salvira.

"Lily!" Nicole called out, laughing. "You're okay! But how'd you get that?"

"Me, I sneaked up on a patrol. Didn't know what was happening till I was long gone."

Diu swung his feet over the side of the shaft, caught and holstered the Salvira Lily tossed him, and jumped the couple yards down, landing smoothly on the grass. "Hurry up!" he yelled. "It's nearly dawn, and the Omenra attack tomorrow. We have to get back now so Queen Tári has time to prepare a counterstrike."

"You heard him," Falkor said. "Come on—move!" With a powerful stroke of his wings, he was gone. Sorill scampered out after him, leaving only Nicole and Lily.

"You go on," Nicole said. "I'll be down in just a sec."

"Okay. Don't be too long."

Nicole threw her feet over the edge of the shaft and watched Lily hover down. The hills beyond were blue-black, but as she watched, the light rose and washed the hills red. She looked skyward where the light grew colder and darker until it merged with the shadow of night. The grass waved with the pale orange of dawn.

You're strong, too, Diu had said.

She jumped down and landed cat-like on her feet. Diu was already astride Falkor, waiting patiently. Sorill beckoned to Nicole, and Lily took up her usual shoulder perch.

Pure, unconditional love.

She clung tightly to Sorill's neck. Falkor lifted off first, followed closely by Sorill.

As close to 'magic' as I've ever seen.

The Soul of the Universe

The hills sang as dawn graced the land. The fire of light blended with the ice of darkness, and day won over night. The sun crested the hills, a fiery dome against the sky. And all the time, Nicole kept her gaze straight ahead, looking at something past hope, past fear, past courage.

The soul of the universe shimmered in her eyes.

Chapter Thirty-One

Preparing for Battle

The scalded hills cooled to green as the sun climbed higher. The two Aereons cut a straight path through the air, gliding along wind currents. There was desperation to their movements, and they raked the sky with their wings whenever the wind died down. Because, somewhere beyond the hills, Omenra warships were gathering.

Every beat of Sorill's wings pulsed through Nicole's body. She strained to see ahead. If they didn't get back in time, there was no telling what would happen.

The sun had reached its zenith by the time palace shimmered into view. Turning on a wind current, Falkor led his team into a dive and swept into the courtyard, settling on the silky grass. Diu jumped down first and vanished without a word beneath the crystal arch.

"Finally!" Lily cried in delight. She rolled over in the grass, reveling in its lush warmth. "Safety! Comfort! Food!"

Nicole began to laugh but was cut off as something large

barreled into her, knocking her over. A rough, wet tongue streaked her face. Cheerfully, Arli wagged her tail like an oversized, scaly dog. *You back! I worry.*

I've missed you, too. But I've got so much to tell you, but not now. The Omenra—

I know. I hear what you think. Murderers want attack Aereon friends, but I no let them! Arli bared her fangs and snarled, lashing her tail. *I protect friends, and I protect you!*

Nicole cupped the dracling's snout between her palms. *Just don't go getting yourself in trouble. Promise?*

Arli shook her head. *I do anything to protect you.*

Nicole squeezed out from beneath the large body. She hadn't noticed it before, but the dracling had grown since her hatching. But it hadn't been that long—had it? How much damage had the Terranova done to her Earth? How much of the precious month remained? Before Nicole could calculate, a soft voice rang through the courtyard, channeling grief.

"Is it true?"

Queen Tári seemed to hover in slow motion as she crossed the courtyard. Diu followed close behind. The queen's voice, so strong before, now sounded close to breaking.

Falkor bowed before her. "Is what true, Your Highness?"

"The Omenra attack."

He nodded curtly. "We have very little time left. My team flew with all possible speed to warn you. Tomorrow, at sunrise, they will launch their final assault."

"Tomorrow, the war for Serrona ends," Diu said. "No matter which side claims victory."

"And what of my daughter?"

Falkor paused and looked away. "We found her, Your Majesty."

"Then where is she?"

"Still on the Omenra Farrider. She doesn't remember. Anything."

Nicole felt a pang of pity for Queen Tári as the latter stared blankly, confused, at Falkor. "No. How can that be?" the queen muttered, half to herself. "She wasn't kidnapped as a little girl, she was so much older, she has to remember, she has to."

"They have done something to her, Your Highness, but I don't think it's too late," Diu said. "Arvia will fight in the war. Against us, but she will fight. If we can capture her and take her to the palace, we can figure out what the Omenra have done and hopefully reverse it."

Queen Tári nodded, but her eyes were blurred with a wounded look. "Very well. Falkor, raise our armies. We need to clear the wall and keep the Omenra from infiltrating these grounds. Evacuate the city. That shall be our central battle-ground. As for you, Sorill, run a check on the force-field. If the Omenra breech it, I don't know what we shall do. And Falkor," she called to his retreating back, "make certain that the Aereons understand that this determines our future." She paused, and her expression hardened. "And tell them that I shall fight alongside my people."

"Your Majesty!" he gasped. "What you're proposing is far too—"

"Dangerous?" she snapped. "Falkor, they tore my child away from me. They destroyed her memory. Now they order her to fight against her own people. If you think for one moment that I shall not directly confront the Omenra, then you are a fool. Whether I have an army at my back or if I must stand alone, I will *fight.*"

"My forces are engaged with the Kronar Trade Federation," Diu said. "But you always have me, Your Highness."

"Me, I might look like a little scrap of fur," Lily exclaimed, "but I'm plenty tough. If my friends are in, then so am I."

From where she lay in the grass, Arli peeped her support.

"Very well," Queen Tári said. "Lily, Diu—I shall have a servant bring an early dinner to your rooms. Arli can stay in the palace tonight if she so chooses, and—"

"For me, too."

"Excuse me?" the queen asked, turning to Nicole.

"Dinner. Bring some for me, too," she repeated. "Because I'm going with you."

"No," Diu said.

Nicole laughed. "No?"

"You are not coming."

"You're going to stop me?" she snapped.

Quick as lightning he drew his knife. "If I must, I—"

"Enough!" cried Queen Tári. "We cannot have this fighting. Not tonight. Diu, you should know that better than anyone."

"Then tell her she cannot go," he barked.

"And why not?" Nicole yelled. "Because of the prophecy? Is that it?"

"Yes, if you're too stubborn to understand yourself!"

"That stupid prophecy—"

"Enough," the queen said again, more firmly. "Nicole, he is right. You are too important to risk your life in this battle."

"But . . . but . . ."

Her weak stutter was heard by no one except Lily and Arli. Diu, the queen, Falkor, and Sorill were already gone beneath the arch.

"It's not fair," Nicole snapped as they ran to follow. "If they think I'm going to live in a protective bubble from now on . . ."

Lily shook her head. "Me, I think Diu might be right this time. It really is dangerous."

It not safe outside palace walls, Arli agreed. *Evil Omenra murderers want your blood.*

Nicole didn't reply, angrily brushing past her friends, leaving them standing alone in the empty hall. She blindly stalked to her assigned room, not bothering to undress, crawling up on the bed and crying into a pillow soon soaked with tears. When Lily and Arli entered, she pretended to be asleep. Nicole didn't feel like talking to anyone. Not even to them.

Soon she actually fell asleep, waking towards late afternoon to the sound of activity in the palace. Lily was gone, and from Arli she discovered that troops were already gathering for a final rundown of plans. The dracling, too young for combat, watched her from the bed as Nicole left to at least say goodbye.

Strolling through the winding hallways she had begun to memorize, she watched the sun sink beyond the palace walls. Sorill's reinforced force-field cast a slight blue tinge across the crimson orb, melting the sun to violet. Thinking about that alien glow, she felt tears rise again. Diu just didn't understand. She could fight. "And I can win," she muttered to herself. If only she could get around that force-field.

And then Nicole had a brilliant idea.

Half-jogging, half-running, she sprinted down the hall in search of Sorill. Certainly he, of all creatures, wouldn't refuse her. Not this request.

When at last she found him, he was tinkering with a smoking handgun. Sorill noticed her and waved, calling, "Nicole, what are you doing out here? It's almost time for us to move out. I thought you'd be in your room."

"Listen, Sorill. I'll go to my room and stay there, promise. But I need a favor first."

"What kind of favor?"

"Do you have a . . . spare JET Glider?"

His eyes narrowed to slits. "You're not planning on sneaking out after us, are you?"

"Don't worry. I just want to practice. Need to get my mind off things, you know? Plus, it's a useful skill to learn."

She held her breath as he thought. "Fine," he said at last, "but stay within the grounds. Diu will have my head for this if he finds out I gave you a way out."

"Thanks, Sorill! I owe you one."

As Nicole followed him through a new set of hallways into the military sector, guarded with plasma-screen keypads and codes, she found that it didn't feel terrible, what she'd done. After all she'd only equivocated. That wasn't exactly outright lying, so it wasn't nearly as bad. Because she would return to her room. She'd go back and even stay for a while.

Till morning, that is.

On the way back, she passed by the dining hall, just in time to hear a snippet of Queen Tári's final inspirational message to her soldiers before an early break for the night. She was saying something beautiful, but Nicole would later remember only one thing.

"There is no such thing as being half free. Freedom must be held entirely, or not at all. And for too long, the Omenra have suppressed the Aereons, the Airioth, and the galaxy! Tomorrow, at sunrise, a new era dawns."

Half free. It was the perfect word to describe what Diu had forced her to become by clipping her to a leash of subordination. If he believed in his stupid prophecy, fine. But that didn't mean Nicole had to be his slave for it. And it didn't mean he could make decisions for her.

She stormed violently into her room, blasting open the door with a powerful shove. Arli looked up sleepily at the sound, startled by Nicole's sudden wave of furious emotion. The dracling followed her as she crossed to the bedside table in several brief strides. She threw the Glider onto the bed and jerked open the top drawer, taking out the Galactera but leaving the water crystal and the disk as she feared she might lose them. She had the dagger, which was good, but she needed another weapon if this was to really work.

"Nicole?"

She turned, recognizing the voice. "What?"

Diu leaned against the doorframe, arms crossed. His mouth was an angry slash. "Sorill told me you asked for a Glider."

"Did he tell you why?"

"Yes. But neither of us believes it."

"Straight to the point, aren't you?"

"When am I not?"

"Listen," she said, tired of playing. "What do you want from me?"

"Stay in the palace, understand? If you follow us you could be killed." He uncrossed his arms and stepped through the door. "Does that even mean anything to you?"

"Back off, Diu."

"I can't do that."

"You're going to have to!"

"Nicole—"

"Don't you get it? I'm not listening to you anymore. So back off and *leave me alone!*"

Nicole twisted away, seething, trying to hide the tears in her eyes. Shoving clenched fists into her pockets, she bit her lip to keep from crying. The door behind her softly slapped shut, and Nicole sank onto the edge of the bed. Her hands pulled up and the backs of her fingers wiped her cheeks dry.

She knew Diu only meant to protect her. She knew that it was her fault for being difficult. She considered running after him and apologizing and making amends. But then she remembered Queen Tári's words.

Half free.

Suddenly the door creaked open. Nicole's head shot up.

"Diu?"

"No, it's me. Sorill."

"What do you want?"

Something hard dropped into her lap.

"It's an Enfiro 3000. Top-notch weaponry."

"Why?"

"Because if you're coming, you need a weapon."

"Thanks, Sorill."

"If Diu finds out—"

"Forget Diu. I'm tired of being half free." Nicole stopped, not sure if she wanted to say the last of it.

"And for me, it's not just a war for Earth anymore."

Chapter Thirty-Two

Engage

Nicole stood in the shadows of the courtyard walls, clutching the Glider between clammy arms. Slowly, her mouth chewed over the last crumbs of a moist, bread-like substance she'd begged from a servant. Her fingers groped towards the Enfiro strapped to her hip, checking to make sure it was still there. What she was about to commit was the ultimate act of defiance. She knew, of course, that Diu meant only the best for her and the galaxy. But Nicole was tired of always being subject to his commands.

With the vast majority of able-bodied Aereon forces concentrated beyond the force-field, the palace was nearly empty, allowing her the perfect chance to sneak away. Arli had tried to stop her—in vain. Nicole's mind was set. No matter what, she had to go on with the plan now, before she was caught.

Nicole was glad she had seen Diu use the Glider. She jumped onto the board, wincing in fear when the Glider locked her feet into its mechanism. The board hovered a few inches up from the ground, waiting for the slightest twitch. Nicole leaned left and the Glider leaned with her, and when she slightly lifted her toes the board shot up, clear over the courtyard walls.

For perhaps the last time, Nicole took one last look back. The palace was beautiful, sprawled out in the pre-dawn hours. Its translucent walls glowed with interior lighting. She drew the serrated, razor-sharp dagger from her belt, gripped the handle tightly for a brief instant, and then thrust it back into place, turning back to where the triple moons lined against the horizon. Now was not a time for doubts.

Leaning forward, Nicole felt wind rip past her in a cold blast. The ground rolled smoothly below her, thrusting her into wild rage of freedom unlike anything she had ever experienced. This Glider gave her the chance to do anything. In fact, she could veer aside now, fly elsewhere, and not risk her life in a battle that had little bearing on her fate.

Only it did matter. Even as Nicole thought of turning away, she knew her future lay with the outcome of the fight. Lily was there. So was . . . Diu. And no matter how much she tried to convince herself and others, she knew she cared about him more than she wished to admit.

Nicole shook the thought from her head. All that mattered now was getting to the battlefield in time. Only now did she regret not asking Sorill for a new microcom; at least then she would have some sort of status check. This way, she was literally on her own.

The stubby wall lay just ahead. Nicole realized with a pang she hadn't planned this part out entirely. There was just one way past the force-field and that was through the single guarded gate. The central city lay just beyond, so close yet now impossible to reach. She thought fast, wondering if the guards might let her through.

Then she remembered the Galactera.

Pulling up the watch by its chain, Nicole touched the button labeled *Serrona*. Sure, she was already on that planet, so there was a chance it wouldn't work. But on the other hand, perhaps it would take her to the same place as that first time. She could find her way back from there. Maybe.

Thinking about the city, Nicole tapped the button with a slight dread. She hoped nothing terrible would happen. The vortex sizzled and flashed her to a new location. She twisted the Glider in a circle, trying to pinpoint her position. Recognition came almost instantly.

By some insane stroke of luck, the watch had taken her straight to the heart of the fantastic metropolis. Nicole giggled as she spiraled higher through the twisting tract of towering structures, gazing in open-mouthed amazement as buildings seemed to slant and fold over beneath her. Sunlight reflected from soaring towers and glittered on metal and glass.

The sun? Nicole swerved the Glider till the light was full in her face. The sun was a rounded hump against a far-off horizon. It was dawn. She was running out of time to find the Aereons.

A distant roar startled her, but Nicole recognized the sound. It was the engine growl of a Scythejet Infiltrator gearing for liftoff. Falkor had taught her to fly that small, versatile craft, designed by Sorill. She'd heard the engine, and Falkor's sharp reprimands, enough to have memorized both.

The roar died away, and Nicole realized the Scythejet had

switched to stealth mode. Nicole rotated the Glider towards the source of the sound, hoping the Aereons were somewhere in that direction. But something else was prowling towards her between the buildings, reflections of it flashing in the glass. She squinted to see, wondering why the thing was silent. Too late she remembered that the Scythejet could operate in supersonic—faster than sound—flight.

A sharp boom blasted through Nicole's head as the craft slashed past. Involuntarily, a terrified jolt tore through her body. The sudden flinch drove the Glider sideways towards a level plane of glass. She tried to swerve but couldn't. The window smashed into a million jagged shards that buried themselves in her arms and legs as she fell to the floor on the other side. The Glider scratched across the ground, letting Nicole's feet go at last, and she lay there, breathing hard, tasting blood on her lips.

A soft whisper swelled nearby. She turned onto her side and felt glass crack beneath her. The Scythejet had turned back and was approaching in ordinary flight mode. Wondering what it could possibly want and praying that it wasn't an Omenra craft, Nicole realized it was coming straight towards her.

Just as she twisted her face down, glass rained onto her back as the Scythejet's long and narrow wingspan ripped through the side of the building. The craft flashed over her head and landed on the far side of the large room, crushing an array of expensive-looking machines into crumpled pieces. The cockpit screen hissed up and someone leaped out, running across the glass toward Nicole. She tried to sit up and cried out as splinters bit deeper into her skin.

"Nicole! You were supposed to stay at the palace!"

It was a hard effort just to move her head. "Yeah? Well, you're supposed to be with the Aereons," she said to the familiar voice. "It's sunrise, you know."

"I was flying reconnaissance."

"And I'm out here to help. I'm not your slave, Diu. You can't tell me what to do."

He helped her stand, rubbing the blue powder over her torn skin to quickly heal the wounds. As the cuts closed over the glass fell away, breaking on the metal floor. Diu reached down to rub his own footpads, using the last of the powder. Angrily, he threw away the empty pouch.

"Even this one time," he snarled, "you didn't listen to me. Not even now. What if it hadn't been me on the Scythejet but an Omenra? You realize you would have died, Nicole? And just now, the shards from the window could have killed you. Do you understand that?"

"Are you going to take me back?"

"Take you back? I should run you through where you stand!" Diu roared, whipping out his knife.

Nicole stumbled backwards, crushing glass beneath her shoes. "I'm sorry, okay!" she cried. "I just wanted to help!"

Then she noticed Diu wasn't listening. His head was cocked slightly to the sound of a static-filled voice in his ear. Tapping the microcom, he said, "It's too late to take you back now. Just stay here until all of this is over. Can you manage that?"

"No," she insisted, "and I can try to explain why. I guess

it's two things. First, you told me on the Farrider that this isn't about me proving myself. I think I understand that now, and that's not why I'm here. I have to be here because of something else." She took a step toward him. "There's a reason I have to fight this battle. Kind of like how I knew about Arvia and the cave on Espia and the rest of it. You just have to trust me." Another step. "Please."

Diu sighed out a murmur of air. He closed his eyes as if in thought and pressed a paw to the beads tied around his throat. Then, stepping over a patch of shards, he picked up the Glider from the ground and strapped it to his back to replace the one Malkior must have confiscated.

"You really want to fight?"

She nodded. "I have to."

"Then we had better get to the Aereons. Fast."

As he pulled away from her and stepped towards the ship, Nicole realized for the first time that he had changed his outfit. Diu was an awesome sight to behold—a symbol of supremacy, the climax of what it meant to be a true warrior. The very air around him seemed to be charged with power. Like Nicole's outfit, his was woven of durable, resistant microfiber. He also wore metal plating over his shoulders and along his arms and thighs, and his feet sported heavy, clawed boots. Attached to his right wrist was a retractable set of serrated blades for close-quarter combat. And, as always, his trusty Mar was holstered at his side.

Nicole hopped in behind him in the two-seat cockpit and pressed back as the craft blasted off at supersonic speed. The craft veered at the gentlest stroke on a touchpad, searing vertically through narrow openings between buildings and spiraling past peaked summits. For a brief, giddy moment, it felt almost like being together in the tope shark again, only this time they weren't playing. All the while Diu murmured something into the microcom—a final set of instructions as the Aereons tightened their position and waited for his command to engage.

"Where are we going?" Nicole asked.

"We are launching our core operation from the open-air central plaza. It's wired with an electromagnet hover system for altitude adjustment. It was designed for massive rallies and so will allow a wide dispatch point."

Nicole blinked. "In English?"

"We're meeting at a giant floating platform so we can easily launch ships all over the city."

"Thanks."

"Not a problem," Diu growled.

"Hey, nix the sarcasm, will you?"

"Nix the stupidity, will *you*?"

Nicole leaned back in the seat, rubbing her eyelids. Why did she even bother?

At last the Scythejet blasted out into an open expanse of space enclosed by towering buildings. As Diu swung the ship around, Nicole peered out at the massive platform seemingly suspended in midair beneath them. A long line of ships—mostly Scythejets—was positioned at one end. Aereons mobbed the various cruisers, taking up position. Three Aereons, each paired with a Scythejet, stood alone in the center of the platform. Diu swerved in for a landing, and Nicole recognized the queen, Falkor, and Sorill. Lily, who had found a place on Sorill's shoulder, waved to the descending ship.

The Scythejet banked and landed, facing the other ships. The cockpit screen lifted open and Diu jumped out, followed quickly by Nicole. Approaching the group, she felt panic swell in her chest like a creature clambering to burst out. She had the Enfiro and *Cárine*, but would they be enough? And what if something went wrong?

Lily transferred to Nicole's shoulder, talking. But Nicole barely noticed the warm weight. *What am I doing here*, she thought, *risking everything? What kind of help can I be? I'll just cause trouble. Worse than trouble.*

"Scouts report enemy sighted," Diu said for Nicole's benefit, as she lacked a microcom.

"Just the *Aphelia*," Falkor added. "But I doubt that's a good sign."

Diu nodded. "We're probably circled by now. Septa-gliders, if I had to guess."

"Below radar?"

"Most likely."

"Well," Falkor said, drawing his Enfiro, snapping off the safety, "I dare them to try. Sorill's Scythejets have those things beat by a couple decades, so let's just see them fight."

"Nicole!" Lily cried.

"What?"

"Did you listen to anything I said?"

"Yes. Maybe. Okay, no, not really."

"Me," Lily sighed, "I wanted to know, what're you doing here? Weren't you supposed to wait back at the palace?"

"Supposed to," Diu spat.

"Long story," Nicole said.

Sorill cleared his throat. "Rav?"

"What?" Falkor snapped impatiently.

"It's the Septagliders. There's something odd going on. I would think if not those then at least the Omenra would have something below radar. But I'm getting a scan that doesn't make sense. Not from Malkior's point of view. His entire fleet is within radar."

"Position?"

"Classic, boss. Circling tactics, like Diu thought. But if they're within radar, that's not a smart move."

"What are the chances," Falkor asked hopefully, "that Malkior's finally made a mistake? Or if he didn't have enough time to prepare?"

Diu shook his head. "No to both. This fight was his call, and he was the best tactical planner the military had. He was better even than me. There's something under radar we just can't see."

He broke off as the queen, who had been listening carefully, raised a wing, silencing them all. "General Airioth," she said. "The *Aphelia*."

A hazy patch of air suddenly rose over the rim of the platform. Silently, it stalked to a landing near the far edge and spiraled down. Nicole began to pull her Enfiro but Diu held out a paw, flicking out his wrist blades experimentally and checking that his knife was in place. His claws moved over the Mar's trigger guard.

Red morning light finally found a hold on the pitch-black

cruiser as it threw off its cloak. Diu stepped back as the bulk of the ship shimmered into view. The canopy hinged open, revealing a single armored creature, Salvira Sigrá in hand. Malkior grinned viciously and jumped down, booted feet thumping hollowly against the metal platform.

Diu tensed, retracting the wrist blades, tightly clutching the Mar. Malkior approached with equal determination, Sigrá raised. He stopped his advance several feet before them, slanting his dark eyes over Diu in a once-over. Poised against each other, they stood immobile. The morning sun dyed Diu's fur crimson and Malkior's scales blood red.

Suddenly, the Omenra clicked his handgun's safety in place. He dropped the Sigrá and backed a few steps. Diu uncertainly raised his Mar.

"I propose to end this battle," Malkior said, holding up empty palms, "before it begins."

"I'm listening," Diu replied.

"I'm not armed, and my soldiers won't attack without my orders."

"And?"

"Here is my offer. I will give you, Diu, a choice. Kill me now and save countless lives, or let me live and allow Aereons to be killed in my place.

Nicole's stomach lurched. If Malkior wasn't bluffing, if the offer was real . . .

"Easy enough," Diu said. "Control," he said into the microcom, "patch me through to Cryo Team One—"

"I'm not finished," Malkior interrupted. "My offer is to you, old friend. At this moment, we are being closely monitored. If anyone but you touches me, my soldiers will fire on your Nicole Sky."

Nicole started. Her eyes flashed towards the sky. Were there invisible Omenra cruisers hovering over them now, just waiting to gun them down?

Diu's paw twitched angrily on the Mar. "Fine. I don't need the Aereons to finish you."

Malkior smirked. "Then proceed. Kill me. End the war."

"If you think I will not shoot then you are wrong, Taggerath!" Diu snarled.

"Prove it. Prove it to me and all your friends listening at the end of that microcom."

"Don't push me. I swear I will!"

"Come on! Shoot!"

"I will!"

"Come on!"

"I—"

"Fire!"

Diu dropped the Mar. He screamed at nothing and everything, furious as the world and at himself, unable to overpower either. And opposite him, Malkior chuckled and picked up the handgun that lay at his feet.

"Figures," he said. "Ten long years haven't been enough to teach you. We both know, Diu, that this war will only end with one of our deaths, and the only one who will ever have a chance to kill me is you. You're living in the past, old friend, in a life that's dead. And unless you accept me for who I am now, your Airioth are undertaking a foolish cause." Laughing coldly, he started to turn away, adding, "And I hope your

Aereons heard every word."

There was a rush of wings as Queen Tári moved beside Diu. "He has done nothing wrong in refusing to kill you in cold blood, General," she said. "Only savage Omenra assassins would slay an unarmed creature, even a foe. We Aereons have come to justly defend our kingdom. Remember, this is your challenge, General Taggerath. Fight a fair battle."

Malkior's lip curled in disgust. "As you wish, Your Majesty," he snarled. "But first, I think there's someone you want to see." He turned and beckoned with his claws towards the *Aphelia*. A second creature jumped down from the cockpit, twisting her head towards the group. The queen gasped softly, hardly able to maintain her composure.

"Arvia," she breathed.

The princess strolled elegantly towards them, hands clutched behind her back, sporting a black and silver jumpsuit. She paused beside Malkior. "Mother," she said quietly.

"Arvia, my daughter, my love," Queen Tári whispered. "You have come home. You have come home at last!" She ran forward with tears in her eyes and open arms. Arvia waited till the last and then sidestepped, raising a Salvira to the queen's head.

"Don't think I believe it, *mother*." The princess chuckled. "If my real mother were a queen, she'd be a much more fitting ruler than you. You're a weak creature. I see that even now. You would crawl on your knees to beg for mercy in the face of death. My true mother would never be as pathetic as you."

But before Arvia even had the chance to disengage the safety, Diu had jabbed the icy ring of the Mar's barrel against her temple. "If you make one more move," he whispered coldly, a claw over the handgun's trigger, "I'll kill you."

"Diu, stand down!" Queen Tári cried. "She doesn't know what she's doing!"

He didn't budge. "Drop the Salvira, princess."

Arvia whirled towards him, leaning forward. "Make me," she cried, squealing as his wrist blades extended with a deadly snick and curved to within an inch of her flesh.

"Care to test me?" Diu growled, his voice like ice.

"No need yet, Arvia, my dear," Malkior interfered, stepping between them. Diu retracted the blades and raised the Mar again. "And as for you, old friend, you had better decide soon whose side you are on."

Malkior retreated to his ship with Arvia trailing behind. Nicole ignored them, moving to block Diu's path. "He's right," she snapped. "Whose side *are* you on?"

"It's more complicated than that."

"Yeah? Well, I don't see anything hard in you ending this war. Just now you could have done it!"

"After you kill someone for the first time," Diu said. "After you look into eyes brimming with life and realize that you are the one who will snuff that out, tell me then how easy it is."

Nicole didn't know what to say to that. It was true that she'd never killed. She never intended to. Which was ironic, she realized, glancing at the Enfiro.

The *Aphelia* lifted off, blasted into the distance, and arced in a half-circle over the city. The Omenra cruisers rallied behind it. Nicole trailed Diu to the Scythejet, and Lily followed them until he said, "You stay with Sorill in the med squadron."

"But me, I want to stay with you two. It'll be safer."

"Hey, I'll be okay," Nicole said.

"Promise?" Lily begged.

Nicole voice caught in her throat. "Yeah," she choked out.

Reluctantly, Lily obeyed. When Nicole looked back, the platform was empty.

"What was that all about, anyway," she asked. "The meeting with Malkior, I mean. Some sort of procedure?"

"No, not formality. Malkior's request."

"Why? Seems pointless to me."

"No, it's brilliant tactics. Luckily, Queen Tári, Falkor, Sorill, and I kept the conversation on a closed channel so the soldiers don't know what has been said, but it has stirred anxiety for them because they know something private has happened. And they realize it was something we didn't want them to know."

By now the Scythejet was hovering, surrounded by several dozen identical, pure-white crafts, each piloted by two Aereons. Diu pressed a fighter helmet and headset into Nicole's arms, which she fitted over her head. They pressed a little too tightly against her skull. She snapped a visor over her face and strapped herself into the ship. A microcom built into the helmet hissed simultaneously with the translator.

"Control to Mark One. Control to Mark One."

"Copy," came Diu's voice. "Proceed."

"Breech on Del Perimeter."

"Clear to engage?" Falkor's voice said.

Engage

"Stand by to engage, Mark Two."

"Are you crazy?" Nicole yelled. "We should go now!"

He ignored her. "Not till I see the sun gleaming off their ships."

The *Aphelia* rose in the distance, a predator locked on its mark. It was the single pitch-black speck across a sea of gray Septagliders. For a moment, time hung still. Then Malkior blasted his cruiser forward, catching its windscreen in a blaze of crimson light.

"Engage," Diu said, slamming his paw on the touchpad. "*Engage.*"

Chapter Thirty-Three

War

Diu swerved the Scythejet into a vertical climb, allowing his fleet to rocket by underneath. Nicole clutched at her seat, terrified of touching anything until Diu's voice said through the headset, "Falkor taught you to fly this thing, right?"

"Yeah."

"Then get on missile fire."

"*What!*"

"I told you to stay at the palace. But you're in this now, so you *will* make yourself useful. Grab the sidestick controllers and aim. Keep your thumbs on the weapon release."

"Are you insane?" she screamed, but he didn't reply.

"Mark Two," he said.

"Copy, Mark One."

"Tag my position. Form your squad behind me." Diu dodged a volley of laser fire from an incoming Septaglider and spiraled out of the way of a flack assault, waiting for Falkor to pull up behind him as the shells burst just out of range.

"On your tail, Mark One," Falkor said, leading three Scythejets.

"Mark Two, Magna One, on my right. Magna Two, Three, flank left. We've got incoming fighters, three coming down the left."

"Add two on the right," Nicole said.

"Target them, Nicole."

"Uh . . . how?"

"You said Falkor taught you!"

"He did! But not under this much pressure."

"Switch to seeker infrared mode on your headset. Flashing red means an enemy frequency."

She tapped a button on her headset as Falkor had taught her days earlier, though it seemed like years now. Her visor automatically cycled through several frequencies until she stopped it on the right one. Now her vision was haze of blue with several areas highlighted in shades of red-orange. A few flashed rapidly.

"Now what?"

"Use the side-scroll on your dash to lock crosshairs on the target. The left sidestick weapon release launches auto radar homing short-range missiles, and the right sidestick launches semi-auto radar homing long-range missiles."

All the military terminology was giving Nicole a headache. Even the translations weren't helping because she didn't know a thing about Earth tactics or weaponry. "Side-scroll what?"

A flashing icon on the visor screen indicated that Diu had linked them on a private channel. "Look down," he said impatiently.

There were so many shiny buttons and flashing displays to look at. "Okay."

"The blue switch on your left. Flip it."

Nicole did so and a screen on her left projected a three-dimensional image of the Scythejet. Simultaneously, a camera outside the cruiser flashed a display across the inside her visor. "Cool!" she said.

"See the touchpad below the switch? Slide your finger around it."

She circled her index finger on the touchpad and the Scythejet projection rotated. At the same time, the display in her visor changed to allow her a full three hundred and sixty degree view outside the ship, letting her zoom in on one of the Septagliders.

"Locked on?" Diu asked.

The crosshairs tightened on the target.

"Yeah."

The Omenra cruiser rocketed past them and spun around.

"Then fire!"

The display blinked fast to indicate that the twin blasters on the sides of the enemy craft were heating.

"Nicole, what are you waiting for?!"

The Scythejet rocked violently as the Omenra gunned down on them. Diu veered the ship sharply and pivoted around, firing a massive volley on the target. The Septaglider shuddered past them, flaming. Somewhere far back, Nicole heard a resonating explosion.

"Why didn't you fire?" Diu spat. "I gave you a direct command."

"There was an Omenra in there," she said quietly.

"And?"

"I can't kill a living thing."

"If you want to survive, you must! Don't you understand? This is not a game! It's a war. One I've been living for ten Earth years."

It hit her then. The microcom hissed in her ear, but she didn't hear it. The visor flashed with red, but she ignored it. There was utter silence around her. Because all of a sudden, Nicole understood.

Ten Earth years. It had sounded like a long time before. Now she knew what it meant. She couldn't even kill one Omenra. Doing it daily for ten years? She had always been glad Diu was with them. Yet for the first time, she felt something more than respect, something bordering admiration . . .

They were back on the open channel. "Mark One!" Falkor's voice screamed. "Right flank!"

A second Septaglider shot towards them. A sizzle of energy channeled across the windscreen as the Omenra gunned down on them. Nicole's eyes widened, reflecting the blood-red flashing light of the visor screen. She couldn't kill. She couldn't. She—

The Septaglider burst into a fiery blast. It spun off and tore into a sheer glass building, collapsing the massive structure in a cloud of shards and debris. But Diu hadn't touched the weapon release.

Nicole had.

Her fingers peeled away from the sidestick controllers. A cold sweat slid down her forehead. Her heart beat a terrible rhythm against her chest. Nicole Sky of Earth had . . . had . . .

"Mark Two, stay on my right," Diu snapped. "Magna

Squad Two, break to Cryo Squad One."

Falkor moved into position while the rest of the squadron veered off. "So this is where the fun begins?"

"Blast high and left. Let's see if we can't find the *Aphelia*."

The two Scythejets accelerated, looping around enemy fighters and shuddering through maelstroms of laser fire. They cleared the tops of the buildings, throttled towards space, and then suddenly plummeted, searching.

Then a dark black ship flashed into view below them.

"Mark One, target sighted," Falkor said.

"Nicole," Diu asked, "are you locked on?"

"Yeah," she gasped, forcing herself to concentrate. Maybe she could just gun down Malkior once and for all and be done with it.

"Mark One!" a new voice ordered. "Disengage."

"Queen Tári?" Nicole asked in surprise.

"Don't fire at Malkior," the queen cried, dropping the military slang. "My daughter is on that ship!"

"Clever," Diu growled, angry yet impressed. "I wondered why he needed Arvia for the fight. He's bought himself safe passage." The *Aphelia*, meanwhile, had vanished in the fray.

A Septaglider suddenly pulled up directly behind them. It cracked several heavy volleys at them before Diu accelerated, slammed on the brakes, flipped the Scythejet around in a gut-wrenching grind and blasted the Omenra from the front.

"That was . . . nice," Nicole admitted, barely breathing in terror as the ship bounced through the debris.

Diu chuckled, then tensed as Falkor said, "Mark One, I think I just figured out why the Septagliders were within radar."

"Repeat, Mark Two."

Nicole half-choked as her whole infrared display filled with massive, flashing splotches against a sea more red than blue. Falkor explained, "They baited us out with that first wave. Now they know what they're up against. And now they can engage with those."

Tearing off her headset, Nicole stared out at what seemed to be nothing. Fitting the gear back on, she again saw the flashing red. "Diu, what are those things?" she asked.

"Rotorippers. Nastiest ships on the Omenra fleet. Just three, it looks like. But they're on stealth mode. Invisibility."

"Doesn't matter," Nicole said cheerfully. "We've got infrared to see them."

"Infrared is great for targeting, not flying."

She felt the ship jerk violently through a scatter of debris. "Watch it!"

"You try to dodge and pull through a needle-length gap when everything's the same color and then talk."

To Falkor he said, "Mark Two, change of plans. Break left and round sweep. Engage the Rotorippers at will. I'll find Malkior."

The Scythejet slowed significantly, rising above the city. Diu maneuvered in ample swings, allowing Nicole a wide range to target. But below, the battle wasn't going well. Screams of Aereons spiraling out of control, downed by enemy fire, screeched hollowly through the headset. Mechanically, Nicole plugged away at Omenra ships, the reality of what she was doing starting to dawn. She faltered. She was killing real creatures, with real lives and friends and families and a home they would never see again. Of course, they had done this to countless others. But if she was fighting back in this way, was she any better?

Nicole's momentary lapse was enough. The Scythejet buckled violently as a projectile clipped the left wing, spewing debris. Fast action on Diu's part kept the ship in the air, but there was bad news.

"Nicole," he said, isolating their channel again. "Keep watch on the left flank. I powered down that system, but one more hit and we're grounded."

"As in fall out of the air in screaming death grounded?"

"If you cheerfully put it that way . . . yes."

"Why me," Nicole moaned, scrolling the visor readout. "Hey!" she said suddenly. "There's something coming up behind us. Right flank."

"Malkior," Diu growled.

She removed the headset and twisted her head sideways to stare at the lethally stunning *Aphelia* climbing towards them. "What do I do? We can't shoot it."

"I know."

"Then should—"

"Just hang on."

"What—"

The words were torn from her lips as the Scythejet ripped forward. The *Aphelia* jumped with them. They accelerated, side by side, everything else melting into a swirl.

"How fast are we going?" Nicole barely managed to squeak.

"Approaching transonic."

"Why?"

"The queen only said not to fire. I've figured out another way. The *Aphelia* is an old cruiser and not built for speed. Malkior knows that, but he won't drop us. He'll tag along till one of our crafts breaks down.

"At nearly supersonic? Won't that be suicide?"

"Nearly supersonic?" Diu laughed coldly. "If I can, I'll breach hypersonic."

"Which is?"

"More than five times the speed of sound."

"Are you crazy!" she shrieked.

"No, just a gambler. And I'm betting the *Aphelia* gives out first."

"And if it doesn't?"

For a moment, Diu remained silent. Then he admitted, "I don't know. But this is our chance."

The injured left flank was beginning to protest. Bolts popped under sheer pressure. Nicole could barely tell what was going on. As they approached the speed of sound, by chance they lined in a certain orientation to the sun, and she could see a shock wave form around the ship. The light was finely dispersed in some manner, casting a shadow through the shock wave. Diu adjusted their angle slightly, briefly holding speed to check on the left wing, and then Nicole watched the shock wave move back around the wings.

Then they were building altitude, speeding again, the *Aphelia* close behind. The cockpit lining groaned, buckling inward. A warning blip rang in the headset, warning them to decrease speed.

"Diu, we can't keep this up!" Nicole screamed.

The Scythejet accelerated, and the whole ship rocked violently.

"We have to stop!"

The blip grew louder, more frequent.

"We're gonna—"

It all happened in a few brief seconds that stretched forever. The left wing gave in to pressure and shattered into debris. The Scythejet ripped forward and blasted sideways, spiraling towards the ground. Nicole's mouth moved, and her lips formed a small sound as an emergency force-field enclosed the ship in a protective bubble. It was too late.

The Scythejet slashed into pieces upon impact, smeared over the ground like jelly. The force field took some energy from the impact, enough to keep Nicole alive, at least for a while. Her body arched lazily through the air, was battered in a skid across the ground, then came to rest in a small heap. Fingers curling along soft grass and twisted metal, she blinked blood out of her eyes. Her mouth was full of something warm. The one arm she could see, coiled awkwardly around her head, was half-skinned. Raw flesh pulsed blood. Nicole tried to roll over but at last resigned herself to just lie still in the grass as it was slowly painted crimson.

They were far from the city and the protective heights of soaring towers. The sun was high in the blank sky, and it baked Nicole's exposed skin. She moved her legs a little. Scorching pain seared her muscles. Her palms clutched at the grass. At last she pushed herself up, catching a breath in her lungs. A centimeter at a time Nicole crawled, knees scraping curled metal. Blood trickled down her face from a gash on her forehead. Breathing almost became a voluntary effort. Nicole stopped, arms shaking to hold her body up. In a fleeting thought, she wondered if Diu had survived.

An engine purr whispered nearby, neatly looping overhead. Soft as silk the ship hovered down towards the wreck. It took every remaining ounce of strength in Nicole's battered, bleeding, beaten body to look up.

Black as the heart of shadows, the unharmed *Aphelia* glided gently into a landing.

For a moment there was no sound, no movement. A break in time bordered by nothing. Then Malkior and Arvia jumped down from the cockpit, the latter approaching Nicole with a musical laugh while the former stood back, studying the Earth child. Arvia nudged Nicole's body with a foot, pulling back bloodied claws. Still laughing, she glanced at Malkior. "She's finished."

"Already?"

"No, not quite. Still a bit of life in her. Strange, how some creatures just won't die."

"Then I'll take care of her. See if you can find Diu. Hopefully he's alive too so I can have a little fun, though after a crash like this . . ."

Giggling like a little girl, Arvia moved off to search among the pieces of the Scythejet's carcass. Malkior, in the meantime, held Nicole down with his foot on her chest. He drew his Salvira Sigrá. She didn't care, though. It was over. That had been clear long ago, from the moment she first touched the

Galactera. Everything else had just been a game, testing how long she could hold out. The only thing different now, she thought, staring up the Sigrá's barrel, was that reality had caught up.

"So ends Nicole Sky of Earth, who would have destroyed me," Malkior said, pulling back a little on the trigger.

A scream distracted him. He turned toward the wreckage where Arvia had shrieked, now silent with a handgun pressed to her temple and a paw over her mouth. Diu's fur glittered with blood, more red than brown. Flesh showed in some places, and a few jagged shards of metal clung to open wounds. Yet he stood in defiance, Mar in paw, clamping the princess to his side. "Let her go," he warned, "or Arvia dies."

Arvia bit Diu's paw on a bleeding gash and shoved him hard in the side, and when her mouth was free she cried, "Kill him now!"

With a smooth motion of his arm, Malkior flipped the Sigrá from Nicole to Diu.

An insane power rising inside her, Nicole kicked out. She launched her body at Malkior and beat him to the ground. He pushed her away and ran to join Arvia as another engine roared down beside them, a small med ship that had received a distress call from the downed Scythejet.

"Nicole!" cried a familiar voice. She turned her head to see Sorill fly across the few yards separating them.

"Forget me," she said. "Diu—"

"Is dead," Malkior snarled, "just as soon as one of you makes a move." Diu was pinned between Malkior and Arvia, both with drawn weapons, the former's Sigrá pointed at Diu and the latter's Salvira E70 directed at Nicole. "It's finished," he continued, grinning savagely. "You three are dead!"

Diu's eyes darted along the ground. He beckoned with his now-broken wrist blades. Nicole followed his motions and suddenly understood. "No, Malkior," she said. "You're wrong."

"How so?"

"It's not over." She pounced forward, rolling past a blast from the E70, and snatched up the Mar that lay abandoned between them. "Not yet." Standing on bloody, shaking legs, she pointed the gun straight at Malkior. "So get away, because I'll never let you hurt him."

"How sweet," Arvia crooned.

Malkior burst out laughing—a cruel, mocking chuckle. "Do you remember, Diu?" he hissed. "Just like Serena! And we both know what happened to *her* when she tried to protect you."

"You can't intimidate me," Nicole barked. "And you know what? I'm surprised. You two ganging up on him, and when he's injured. Malkior, I thought you'd want a one-on-one fight with him, just you two alone."

"Then you misunderstand my purpose. I'm not trying to prove that I'm stronger. I'm showing that he's weaker, has always been weaker."

"This torture," she screamed, "shows only that *you're* weak."

She was suddenly overcome by a wave of pain. Her senses were slowly starting to shut down. There was only one thing left to do.

Nicole raised the Mar to Malkior's chest.

"What are you going to do, shoot me?" he sneered.

"I will."

"Oh, really?"

"Look into my eyes and tell me I won't."

"I know your kind. You think you're so good. So pure. You don't have the strength to kill me. Even Diu doesn't have the courage for that."

"It's not about strength. It's not about courage."

"You won't shoot," Malkior sneered.

Her fingers tightened around the trigger.

"I *will* shoot. And you *will* die."

She pulled the trigger. There was a hollow click.

"Such a shame," Arvia said scathingly.

"The one creature with the guts to kill me," Malkior said, "doesn't have the brains."

Nicole fell to her knees. The Mar clattered to the ground, and she felt with her fingers for the safety. It was on.

Diu tried to break free then. He lunged forward and lashed Malkior with his tail. But Arvia struck Diu on the head and forced him to his knees, digging the gun against his temple. "Kill the brat, will you?" she barked. "Maybe it'll calm him down some."

Malkior snapped off his own gun's safety and wrapped a claw around the trigger. "You came close, Earth child. You wished to kill me. But it is *you* who will die!"

He pulled back the trigger. The blast exploded through the air.

Chapter Thirty-Four

Lily's Sacrifice

Something hit Nicole, but it wasn't a gunshot. A warm mass of wet, sticky fur dropped by her knees.

"Lily!" she screamed.

Roaring in rage, Diu threw himself headlong at Malkior, striking him to the ground. He flung the Sigrá out of reach and grabbed his Mar.

Nicole swept Lily up and felt where the blast had pierced her. Her brave little friend had taken the shot. But at what expense?

"Lily!" she cried again. To Sorill she screamed, "What was she doing on the ship?"

"She was with me on med squad. I told her to stay behind when the Scythejet crashed, but she wouldn't listen!"

Lily sucked in a shuddering breath. Her whole body shook with the effort. Her mystical eyes moved in Nicole's direction but didn't seem to find her. "Bring victory to your people. Me, I always knew you would. Too bad I won't see you when you do," she said, her voice calm and quiet.

"Don't say that!" Nicole pleaded. "Sorill's here. He can

help you!" Then she turned to Sorill, her eyes filled with tears. "What can we do?" she begged.

"At this point," he admitted, feeling the little alien's fur, "not a thing. The shot went right through a major artery, and—"

But Nicole wasn't listening anymore.

Lily's eyes sparkled as they drew in the sun and misted over with light. Her words were quiet, but her voice echoed pride. "Me, I can imagine you .... Your face, glowing like . . . a solar fire! You're," she coughed wetly and Nicole grasped her paw tightly, "you're special, Nicole. A human with the power to . . . shake the galaxy to its roots! You have . . . great destiny . . . great future." Her trembling paw touched Nicole's face. "And me . . ." Lily's tiny body rippled with pain. "I won't be gone . . . if . . . remember . . ."

Her voice choked off, and she slumped back. Her paw slipped and hung limply in the air. Nicole hugged the little alien tightly and screamed, blinded by tears.

Then something incredible happened. The sight of mangled Lily thrust the world back into sharp relief. All the pain was gone. Struggling to her feet, Nicole drew the Enfiro Sorill had given her in what seemed another lifetime and ground the safety off.

"Malkior!" she yelled. Clutching Lily's limp body in one arm, she raised the handgun in the other. "It's *over*!"

Malkior kicked Diu away and scrambled up, grabbing his gun. "For now, Sky!" he shouted, running towards the *Aphelia*.

But Nicole moved with inhuman speed. The insane power

was back, driving her. She squeezed off a few blasts in Malkior's direction, and he fired a shot back at her over his shoulder. His shot missed, but the Enfiro was true. Malkior staggered as the blast grazed his arm. Clutching his wound, he climbed up to the cockpit, and the moment it hinged open he jumped inside.

"Wait! Don't leave!" Arvia shrieked, sprinting towards the craft. But Diu jumped just in time, slamming her to the ground. "Don't leave!" she yelled again as the canopy began to lock down over the cruiser.

"Sorry, princess," Malkior said, switching on the ignition.

"You can't leave me! You dirty—" The princess's words were severed in midsentence as the *Aphelia* roared away.

The shadow of a half-crazed smile flickered over Nicole's face. Then she collapsed to the blood-stained ground in a convulsing heap. Still holding Lily in her arms, she fought to stay conscious. Sorill was screaming something and trying to pry away Lily, and there were more ships throttling down beside them. Though she resisted, Nicole soon felt the little body torn away, and then she was alone. But it barely mattered. She was losing too much blood to live.

It's over, she managed to piece together as someone lifted her in his arms. *It's all . . .*

"Nicole," Diu whispered.

"Y-yeah?"

"You're going to make it."

She felt his tears on her face. It was the first time he'd cried since she'd met him.

"I hate false hope."

"Nicole, the Aereons are magicians at healing. You'll be fine. You'll—"

"Diu, what's happened?" Falkor's voice broke in. "You're torn to pieces and—no! Is that Nicole?"

"Nicole Sky?" came a second surprised voice.

"*The* Sky?" said a third Aereon.

"I can't believe it!"

"Hey, is it true?"

"Did you see—"

"Get out of my way!" Diu roared, with more anger than Nicole had ever known.

Bodies swarmed everywhere. She was taken onto a carrier ship, pricked with needles and injections, and blasted back to the city. Vague, swimming outlines of medics led the way out to a makeshift tent in a secured location. Diu carried her the whole way, his fur wet with his own blood and hers.

He finally let Nicole go when he laid her gently on a cot inside the private tent. The medics rushed to him first. As the commander of the Airioth, Diu was first priority. But he wouldn't let them touch him. So they worked on Nicole, slathering her body with gauzes and applying ointments to speed the healing. Their medicines burned at first, but a few anesthetics soothed the pain away.

All the long hours, Diu hovered beside her anxiously, ignoring his own bleeding wounds even though most were worse than hers. In the beginning, Nicole slipped in and out of consciousness, but she later learned that it was not until the head medic assured Diu that she would live that he would allow any care to be applied to himself, and even then he took only a single shot in the arm to stem the blood flow from his injuries. All else, even the pain, he left unattended.

When she was fully able to stay awake, Nicole couldn't let go of her final burning image of Lily. She was unable to believe that her friend was truly dead. Even after the medics had left her alone, she lay still for a long time, listening to her own heavy breathing as she chewed over some food that had been brought for her. Each breath, each sigh, each motion was now a gift, a precious treasure whose cost had been too high.

"She gave her life for me," Nicole said at last. "She gave her life . . . *for me!*"

"Only because she loved you," Diu said. He had remained in the tent even when the last of the medics had dispersed. "You were her best friend, Nicole. You meant more to her than anything else."

She rolled over to face him, her face wet with tears. "She still shouldn't have done it."

"If you could rewind time and tell her what was coming, I guarantee she would change nothing."

"You should've killed him when you had the chance."

"Who?"

"Malkior," she sobbed.

"What would it have changed?" Diu asked, suddenly sounding tired. "The Omenra would have still attacked, and—"

"I don't mean now. I mean ten years ago. You should have killed him them. Then there wouldn't have been a war."

The dark truth was followed by a cold silence broken only by an occasional voice outside and the howling of a sudden heavy wind.

Diu buried his face in his paws. "We have to get you back to the palace where there's a proper medical ward," he said at last. "The Aereons can take care of you there."

"And where will you be?"

"I'm not going back to the palace tonight. You haven't heard yet, but Malkior called a retreat."

"Why?"

He shook his head. "That is precisely what I have been trying to figure out myself. Retreat isn't just unusual. It's impossible. Malkior has never backed down before, not even when he was the last one standing. This time, the odds were definitely in his favor. Back in the city, the Omenra had the Aereons virtually cornered. And if they come back, as I think they will, the Aereons will need every bit of help they can get."

"I'm staying with you."

"You are not. We need to get you to a medical ward and—"

"I'm staying," Nicole said firmly. Then, half pleading, she added, "Please. I can't be alone tonight."

Diu looked away. "All right," he said at last.

And so he took Nicole with him when he left, albeit reluctantly. Via Glider he lifted them both to the highest tower in the city, microcom open to all channels for the slightest hint of attack. The intricate, beautiful, technological metropolis unfolded below them. An occasional satellite orbited far overhead, bright like a second sun, or rather like the setting one, for Nicole had been treated for longer than she thought.

As the magnificent scarlet orb bowed low in the sky, a sea

of darkness grew against the horizon. It gathered first in the low gaps between buildings, rising till it seemed to overflow, till finally it buried the city beneath its mass and, flooding higher, swept over the stars, washing the day from them and freeing them to shine through the dark waters of the night. Nicole wondered if Lily, the orphan of the universe, was somewhere there, among the stars, forever watching over them.

Eventually Diu suggested that he take her down to the palace for the night. Nicole was desperate for sleep but refused. She didn't want to be alone. Maybe he understood because he didn't force her, instead leaving briefly himself to check status on the Omenra retreat and returning with a blanket, pillow, and a makeshift, tent-like shelter for Nicole. Cozy in the warmth of the tent, she soon fell asleep.

When she awoke, it was already bright outside. Nicole stretched and crawled out through the entrance flap. She glanced around and found herself alone. "Diu?" she called out.

"Here," came the voice, and then Nicole noticed him sitting on the edge of the building. His legs were tossed carelessly over the side, and he looked up casually at a sky slathered with clouds. The sun had just crested over the city, directly behind Diu, and etched his outline in pure gold.

Nicole approached, but not too close. Heights weren't her specialty. "Did they come back?" she asked.

"No. Not last night."

"Is there still a chance?"

"Of course. But the odds are greatly lessened." He glanced at her over his shoulder with the semblance of a smile. "What, is the brave Nicole scared?"

"No," she lied, taking a few steps closer to the edge.

"Come on," he said. "You'll be fine."

She slunk over and sank down, sliding her feet over the sheer plummet. "Happy?"

Diu ignored the question and held out a small sack. "Breakfast?"

Desperately hungry, Nicole eagerly shoveled down the food. Her companion waited patiently until she'd finished.

"It rained tonight," he commented. "While you were asleep."

She couldn't find a proper response to that, so a few moments passed quietly by. Then Nicole asked, "Where's Lily?"

"Being properly dressed for cremation, an Aereon tradition to honor their bravest warriors."

"It's still not fair," Nicole sobbed. "She was an innocent. She didn't do anything to deserve this."

"It's hard, I know," Diu agreed. "But we have a job ahead—"

"Are you *serious?*" she spat, suddenly vicious. "I can't believe it!"

"Believe what?"

"That you're still thinking about the crystals at a time like this."

"Me? I believe it's your planet that is in danger."

She stood in a huff. "What's it matter, anyway? Even if we stop the Omenra once, they'll just be back. They're ruthless. Merciless. Murderous! We can't stop them. We can't stop them all."

"We can. And we *will*. But you have to learn to move on. Lily did a great thing by sacrificing her life. Why do you think she did that? So you could get back up, go on, have a second chance—"

"Oh, Diu! You're so wrapped up in this stupid Airioth thing, this stupid war—"

"You think I don't understand what you're feeling." It wasn't a question.

"You don't know *anything* about me."

Diu leapt up, suddenly defensive. "I know how hard it is to lose someone you love."

"You don't—"

"If anything, it is *you* who cannot see past your own blind anger. At least Lily's death was not your fault. I'm commander of the Airioth forces, Nicole. I see my soldiers die every day, and then it *is* my fault. Because *I* send them into battle. Because *I* make the mistakes that kill them. But even then, I find a way to move on."

She chuckled venomously. "Oh, sure. How *noble* of you. Because it's just a bunch of faceless soldiers you're sending to the grave, Diu! Not your best friend! You couldn't kill Malkior, remember? Even now."

"Malkior has hurt me more than you can ever know."

"Oh yeah? *Right.* He couldn't have done worse to you than what he did to Lily."

"You think so? You really do? Then I will tell you what Malkior did to me, if you want truth!" Diu tore the beaded necklace from his neck and flung it to the ground. "He killed Serena, Nicole! Malkior killed—"

"Serena? What does she have to do with—"

"She was my *wife*, Nicole! You want truth? There it is! Serena, the girl I loved from my academy days, the girl I was later sent to assassinate and couldn't . . . I married her. And when Malkior went after me, she tried to stop him. So he killed her. Just like Lily! Only that is not the worst of it. *He* shot her, *he* killed her—in my presence, at that—but the last thing Serena said wasn't to me. I loved her—I still love her, and always will—but the last thing she ever said was to Malkior, and that was 'Never tell. Never tell Diu.' And all this time, I've dwelt on what it could mean. So tell me now that I don't understand! Tell me now!"

Nicole didn't know what to say. She kneeled and scooped up the necklace in her palms. Her fingers tightened around the ends where it had snapped. Standing again, she averted her gaze from Diu. Nicole couldn't stand to look at his eyes.

"I'm sorry," she said helplessly. "I'm so sorry. For everything I've ever said. Everything I've ever done."

He took the necklace from her. "When we made these," Diu said, tying the string ends around his neck, "long before we were married, we joked that so long as we wore each other's, we would both have luck always. She never forgot, even when we were apart between the academy and my assassin missions much later. But sometimes I wonder what that luck really meant."

"I wish you'd never met Malkior," Nicole said. "Then you'd still have Serena, and I would still have Lily."

"That's the funny thing about it. Without Malkior, neither of us would have either."

"What do you mean?"

"I met Serena only because of Malkior, and the only reason you met Lily was because of the Galactera which you never would have gotten had Malkior not started this war."

Nicole had never thought about it that way. "Well," she said for the sake of argument, "in that case it would have been better for you to have never met Serena and for me to have never met Lily."

"Would it really?"

Suddenly the microcom hissed in Diu's ear. He touched his paw to it, tilted his head slightly, and said, "Copy that. We'll be down."

"What?" Nicole asked.

"Sorill needs me back at the palace."

"But what about the Omenra?"

"Patrols are sweeping the city, and there's satellite imagery for the rest of the planet. We will be prepared if they try anything. Either way, though, we can't keep this up for much longer. The city is a ghost town because of the evacuations, but Aereons have jobs and homes to be getting back to, so we cannot keep the city locked down."

He unstrapped the Glider from his back and set it down. "Hey," he called. "Are you coming?"

"Yeah. Just a sec."

"Fine. And you can leave the tent. The Aereons will take care of that."

Nicole leaned against a breeze as it swelled against her back. The sun was full in her eyes, bright like Lily's face had always been. If nothing else, she would avenge that. Malkior had been her enemy from the start. But now . . .

"Nicole!" Diu shouted again.

"Coming!" she yelled, running to meet him. She leapt up onto the back of the Glider, but as they sank over the edge, she glanced back. The sun glittered in farewell, and then was gone.

Chapter Thirty-Five

Unveiling the Past

Falkor met them just past the force-field gate and transferred Nicole to his back for a faster flight. On the way to the palace, he updated them on the situation.

"Arvia is giving us trouble," he said. "Now that Malkior left her, as we all so dramatically witnessed, she's convinced that everyone is in a conspiracy against her."

"I can't believe it," Nicole said. "After all this, she still seriously thinks that the Aereons are the enemy?"

"If I could just get my claws on Malkior—"

"Enough, Falkor," Diu interrupted. "Sorill called us back here. Why?"

"He has some crazy idea, but he wants Nicole. Why, I can't imagine. If our finest experts can't figure out what is wrong with Arvia, I don't know what makes him think she can."

It felt good to know that someone trusted her enough to bring her into such a situation, but Nicole couldn't imagine what she could possible do.

They landed in the courtyard, empty of everyone except Arli. The dracling saw them from a distance yet approached only reluctantly to greet her friends. *I sense pain*, she said.

That's what happens in a war.

Arli's dark eyes roved over the group. *Where Lily?*

A surge of grief told her the story.

Nicole kneeled and wrapped her arms around the dracling's neck. Tears glistened on Arli's dark scales. The baby wrapped her tail around Nicole, and there they stayed for a very long moment, comforted by each other.

"Nicole," Diu gently called at last.

She turned to face him but didn't let go of Arli. "Yeah?"

"Sorill needs you," Falkor reminded, a little more harshly than was merited.

Diu glanced at him rather coldly. "Are you ready?" he said to Nicole with what she recognized as an unusual amount of warmth.

Arli licked her encouragingly, and at last she loosened her grip. "Yeah, I think I am. But only if Arli can come."

"Of course," he said.

Nicole petted Arli's head once more, running her fingers over the baby's ridged brows. Then they ran to follow Diu and Falkor as they proceeded into the palace. Nicole halfheartedly eavesdropped on their conversation.

"We have been trying through the night and all morning but it's no use," Falkor was explaining. "She's very resilient, that girl."

"And Sorill's entire team is on it?"

"Yes. But they all have tried and failed, a first. Sorill's afraid that it's something they put in her bloodstream or some new technology we've never dealt with."

"Have you done a full body scan?"

"Yes."

"And?"

"Nothing."

Diu considered this. "Bio and non-bio scan?"

"Yes."

"And not even a hint?"

"Nothing. Well, actually, a little something. Two Aereons out cold who tried to pin her down with an injection for the scans and a third with a broken wing who brought her breakfast."

"At least we know now that Malkior trained her well," Diu commented.

"Good to know," Falkor muttered.

They came to a large, mist-glass door. It was beautifully crafted, as was everything else in the palace, only Nicole didn't have time to notice because just then it slammed open and shut very quickly as Sorill pelted out, panting. "Rav, I've tried everything," he cried to Falkor. "The last hope now was for a manual search, but she already scratched me a decent cut on the wing and was about to smash a vase against me! Arvia's like a wild animal gone berserk! I can't get near her." Then he noticed Nicole. "Oh, I'm glad you're here."

"Why?" she asked.

"Arvia won't accept any more Aereons, so that leaves either you or Diu to try to talk to her. But since he nearly slit her back on the Farrider, I think you are the better choice."

She took a resolute breath. "Fine, but what exactly am I supposed to do?"

"Work a miracle," Sorill said. "And don't worry. We'll be

waiting on hand just in case."

Nicole didn't like the sound of that but nodded, moving forward to open the door.

Can I go? Arli asked, tail wagging.

Why not, Nicole replied, glad for the company. She opened the door and quickly stepped through. A second later, something very large and fragile hit the wall beside her, showering her with fragments. Arvia's snarling voice wafted across the bedroom.

"If it's you again, Sorill,"—the princess poked her head between the curtains of the four-poster bed and stopped. "Oh, it's someone new. Not an Aereon. Finally. Well, go on, break me. Break me . . . Nicole Sky? You're alive?"

"Yeah, I survived. Strange, how that worked out, after you and your pal tried to kill me."

"Pity, though maybe Malkior might regret leaving me now. I would have finished you off nicely. But anyway, that's not why you're here, is it? So go on, do your job. It's not like they haven't given it a decent enough attempt already, but it entertains me, so do go on."

Arli moved before Nicole did. She wobbled across the room and scrambled ungracefully onto the bed, tearing down curtains with her weight. The princess shrieked and raised a wing to strike the dracling.

Arli, what are you doing?!

Trust me.

Arli curled up in Arvia's lap and peeped happily. Arvia slowly dropped her clawed hand onto the baby's back. She stroked the arched spine.

"She's beautiful," the princess admitted.

"And loyal."

Arvia clenched her fists. "As I thought Malkior was."

"As the Aereons are, and will always be."

Now there were tears in Arvia's eyes. "Malkior," she said, "told me a lot of things about my family."

"Like?"

"That Queen Tári is really my mother and that this was once my home."

Nicole stared blankly. "But . . . but you said . . ."

"I know what I said. It was all tactics. I was told to pretend. Either way, it's something I wish I could forget."

"Why?"

"Because my mother treated me like some royal plaything. She never loved me and would probably have abandoned me given more time. I tried to run away from that, and Malkior found me, and took me almost as a daughter, and loved me more than the queen ever did."

"Don't you get it? You were just a strategy to him. He would have left you anytime, just like he left you now."

"Maybe he left me, but while it lasted he cared. That's something Queen Tári never did."

"Arvia, your mother loves you with all her heart. I've heard the way she talks about you. You just don't know how much she's done to try to get you back. She would have given up Serrona for you. She would have given her life."

"Then why didn't she?"

"Because even if she had, the Omenra wouldn't have returned you. It's all tactics, remember? Hold the princess hostage, and they can get anything they want. Your mother had to find a different way to get you home."

Arvia looked up, and her claws paused over Arli's head. "Then . . . she did care?"

"If you're willing, you can find out for yourself."

The dracling hopped down from the bed and squeaked encouragingly.

"Come on," Nicole said. "Just talk to her."

Arvia nodded tentatively. "Can you bring her here?"

"Sure. I'll be back." Nicole beckoned to Arli to follow, and she shut the door softly behind them. Diu, Falkor, and Sorill were waiting on the other side.

"I assume the lack of breaking furniture is a good sign," Falkor said.

"I've convinced Arvia—with Arli's help—to at least talk to the queen."

"I'll get her right away," Falkor cried, sprinting away. "Sorill, come with me!"

Squeaking, "Okay, rav," Sorill rushed after Falkor. They vanished around a corner, leaving Nicole, Diu, and Arli alone in the hall.

"It must be hard, being Arvia," Nicole said at last.

"Not as hard as you might think."

"What do you mean?"

"As long as she was with Malkior, all she had to do was follow orders."

"Maybe you're right. I guess it would be easy, not having to make decisions and live with the consequences."

"You're wrong."

"Wrong?"

"There are always consequences. Whatever we do, it always impacts something."

Nicole realized he was no longer talking about Arvia.

"I never thanked you for yesterday," she said suddenly.

Diu glanced away. "There is no need."

"You saved my life. You could've left me and gotten help for yourself. You were hurt worse than I was. But you came for me."

"Nicole, know this—so long as I am alive, you have nothing to fear. I will protect you always. And that is not a promise I make lightly."

"Because of the prophecy?" she asked, smirking.

"Halfway."

"Halfway?"

Diu looked towards her, but he would not meet her eyes. "There is much power in hope and friendship," he said. He faltered, and then added almost reluctantly, "For the first time in ten years, you have given me both."

He suddenly seemed very interested in a flurry of movement at the end of the hallway. Falkor, Sorill, and the queen hurried towards them. Queen Tári was in the lead, and she was first to step into her daughter's bedchamber. The others, including Nicole, crowded around outside the door to eavesdrop. All except Diu, who seemed strangely distracted.

A shriek from Arvia alerted them to something gone wrong. Arli restlessly scratched at the door, pleading with Nicole to let her in. Nicole opened a narrow crack and the dracling bolted through, calming the screams with her warm presence. Falkor peeked inside but drew back when the queen stormed out.

"Arvia," Queen Tári said, "does not believe me. It is as if her memory has been altered or erased."

"Or suppressed."

"Suppressed?" the queen repeated, glancing at Sorill, who had uttered the statement.

"That's right, Your Majesty. It could be a blood-infused suppressant, but I'll need a sample and time to analyze—"

Suddenly Sorill's words cut off. His last phrase hovered in the air. Nicole blinked, confused. Sorill's mouth was still moving. Everyone was still nodding. But she couldn't hear a thing of it.

Another sensation overcame her. A wrenching force drove her to drift toward Arvia's bedchamber. Then the world, already set on mute, was paused. Everything around her simply stopped. The door swung in slow-motion when she pushed it. Even the floor seemed half-dissolved, like walking on gelatin. Arvia's movements lingered too, her head drifting in a cocked glance. Arli's pupils flexed lazily in surprise.

Watching them, a wild, insane impulse suddenly seized Nicole. She moved in a flash, snatching Arvia's wrist. The princess opened her mouth in a drawling scream, drawn to Nicole's eyes.

A thing welled up inside Nicole. It seared through her body. It ripped through her heart. It cleaved right through what was her essence and left her shaking with sudden vision beyond what she could see.

A small Aereon child twirled amidst the haze that was her

vision, embraced warmheartedly by a mother garbed in flowing purple. They crooned to each other, and sang, and the child danced away on outstretched wings and curled up in the lush grass, giggling. The mother joined her daughter, and they laughed and spoke in soft voices that meant nothing to Nicole, yet meant the world to this small family.

The mist flickered violently, snuffed out by a wave of dark. Nicole blinked, seeing nothing, and tasted nausea on her tongue. She was holding something—she had forgotten what now—but she clung on, clutching till the thing was ripped from her grasp. Her body curved over and flattened out, and then the nothingness ate into her heart and ate into her mind and ate away the world.

Chapter Thirty-Six

The Queen's Treasure

A dry, bumpy mass wandering over cracked desert earth; that was how Nicole's tongue felt tasting her lips. Her fingers spread in a tangle and groped lumps of fabric. Her eyelids lifted, taking in the red curtain that lined her view. It was woven delicately with alien birds and flowers.

Everything came together in a blast. Nicole was back in her own bedroom. But . . . how did she end up here? She rolled over. Pushing a gap in the curtain, she saw that it was very dark outside.

Nicole?

"Arli," she said, reaching out an arm.

The dracling, who had been lying on the bed, nudged her head against Nicole's shoulder. She licked the extended fingers. *What happen?*

"I don't know. I—"

Wait. I hear when you tell him.

"Him who?"

He has been waiting. To hear you are okay.

"Waiting? Waiting how long?"

Half a sun and through the night.

About eighteen hours, Nicole reasoned. Then again, days and nights, she had noticed, felt much shorter here than on Earth. It brought her back to the infamous question of just how much time she had left in the thirty day cycle of the Terranova. However, before she could dwell on it, another thought struck her. "Wait, who was waiting?"

Arli crooned playfully, poking her nose between folds in the red fabric. *He not leave all this time, but he tired from fighting and not sleeping for long time.*

Nicole pulled the curtains apart, slipping down off the bed. Her feet were silent on the marble. Arli stayed behind, and only her head was visible past the red wall. But both saw an astounding spectacle.

Diu was asleep on a chair by the door. Nicole had never seen him this peaceful. For once he was not tense, not lusting for a fight. He just *was*, plain and simple. He had changed back into his ordinary clothes, the torn and warmly familiar garments he had worn that first night they met. His head lolled back idly against the chair's high back, cocked slightly to one side as if listening. One paw lay on his lap; the other drooped by his side, swaying slightly. His mouth was barely open, and the corners were raised in a smile, pure and easy as if always belonged there.

The Mar strapped to his hip reminded Nicole that this was just one rare, fleeting glimpse of another side of Diu's life, one he never wanted her to see. She thought of waking him but knew that now, just once, he probably wanted to be left that way. They could talk later. And she could pretend that she still saw him as nothing but a gruff, vicious warrior and not the gentle creature Nicole now realized he could probably be.

Come on, she called to Arli, slipping out the door past Diu.

Where we going?

"I don't know. Dining hall, I guess."

Nicole followed the winding hallways she had finally come to memorize, thinking suddenly how dated and obsolete this palace seemed in comparison to the grand metropolis that lay just beyond and the countless other cities that doted this planet. The small, rural villages made little sense, too.

"I don't get it, Arli," Nicole said.

The palace?

"Yeah. It's not any better than a castle from Earth, but the Aereons have way better technology and capabilities. I mean, just imagine! The palace could be incredible! All this just seems . . . too plain."

"Because, Earth child, the queen wishes that her people understand life without wings."

Nicole and the dracling whirled round to face Queen Tári herself. She was smiling warmly at them from several paces away, dressed in sparkling sapphire robes.

"Your Majesty!" Nicole gasped. "Arvia—"

"Is fine. Now child, come with me."

Nicole followed the queen out into the courtyard. Arli tagged along that far but was forced to stay behind when the queen invited Nicole to mount and carried her out past the palace walls, gliding down on the other side. They walked side by side in the darkness, heading nowhere, guided only by pale moonlight.

At last Nicole could no longer keep quiet. "I'm sorry; it's really not my business, but Arvia—"

"She is fine, as I said. And I think you made her that way."

"What do you—"

"If you allow, I shall explain. I don't know exactly what happened, but we were discussing my daughter in the hallway when something overcame you. You went to her room, and we followed. But by that time you had snatched her hand. Arvia succumbed to a fit, and you fainted. Sorill and Diu rushed for you, and I came to my daughter. Her eyes were very blank then, and for a moment I feared she was ill or otherwise hurt. But then an incredible thing happened. My daughter, my Arvia, she recognized me as her mother and accepted it, as if time hadn't passed between us. Whatever you did, Earth child, you saved my daughter. And you saved me."

"I swear, Your Highness, I don't think I did any—"

The queen silenced Nicole with a smile. She reached into her robes and drew forth a small lavender bundle, clutching it tightly in her claws.

"Dear child," Queen Tári said, "you cannot say, with any honesty, that you have done nothing. You risked your life to rescue my daughter. You fought for my kingdom, even though it was not your battle. You took up arms, challenged Malkior and were nearly killed for it, and returned me my Arvia. For that we are indebted.

"I heard, child, of your Lily. I have nothing that can ease the pain of losing a friend, especially one so noble and loyal as to accept sacrifice. But at least take this small token. It is a gift from my kingdom, my people, and from me."

The queen held out the bundle and slowly unraveled the fluid material. "As I understand," she continued, "you came here on a quest. For many years, my family has treasured this artifact."

Queen Tári pressed something into Nicole's hands. "Do not let Lily have died in vain. Save your Earth. Save your people."

Nicole held up a small, yellow crystal. It appeared to be a simple, rough rock. She broke down into joyful sobs mingled with painful tears and stashed the crystal away in her pocket.

"There is something else," the queen said. "Lily's cremation ceremony was last evening. But the ashes we saved for you, her best friend, to scatter to the sun."

Queen Tári offered Nicole a small box. She accepted it, desolately admiring the image of Lily wrought in glowing gold metal on its top. Opening her mouth to speak, Nicole found she couldn't and so merely nodded. She heard the queen say, "I shall return for you soon."

Then Nicole was alone in the valley, clutching the tiny box. For the first time in her life, she felt truly on her own. Her legs began to move, carrying her across the sea of grass to a small hill nearby. A single tree overshadowed the hump. It was an incredible plant with long, swaying strands of tiny leaves like the weeping willows of Earth. The periwinkle leaves flickered rapidly in a slight gust as Nicole mounted the hill. She leaned back against the tree to look out over the land. Breathing the dry, clean scent of the grass and leaves, she wondered what this place would be like when the rains came and left them glistening. Several hundred yards off, the land turned and climbed skyward, rising in a long slope that was nearly invisible in the dark. But Nicole knew that some half-mile above it would level and sweep out to meet the force-field wall.

She hugged the box. "Lily, I swear I'll finish this quest, and when I do, my victory will be for you. I'll never forget you. Never." Hot tears rose in her eyes. "Though you've left me alone now."

"No," a voice said behind her. "You are not alone."

Nicole twisted around where she stood, mouth open, still holding the box. Diu smiled gently at her startled face and strapped the JET Glider back in place. "You are not alone," he said again, "because you still have me."

There seemed to be a thousand miles of grass between them, even as he came right up to the tree and took the small box from her. Removing the lid, he offered it to her silently, still smiling.

Nicole took back the box and scooped into the fine ash that lay within. She lifted a small bunch into the wind and flung it out, mingling ashes with tears. When all the ashes had been swept away she stumbled, crying. Diu came up beside her. There was softness in his eyes.

"W-was it . . . th-this way," she stuttered, "when Mal-Malkior killed . . . Serena?"

Diu took the box again and closed the lid over the top. He slowly nodded, kneeled by the tree, scooped out a small hole in a patch of bare ground that made the grass around it look too lush to be natural. Placing the box inside, he covered it with dirt and smoothed the top.

"What're you doing?" Nicole asked.

"You should see this hill," Diu said, "in the sunrise. When the light touches this place just right, the valley sings. And I think that's a beautiful thing for Lily to see every morning."

Nicole nodded, smiling sadly at the silver streaks highlighted in Diu's fur by the fading moon on the horizon. Indeed, as she looked beyond the tree, she could see the faintest stir of sunlight over the rise.

"Diu?" Nicole said.

"Yes?"

She opened her mouth but couldn't find the right thing to say. "Thanks," she simply said at last.

For a moment they stood in silence. Then Nicole moved across the thousand miles of grass and reached her arms up and hugged him. Diu seemed surprised, but after a few moments he responded. Burning tears rose back in Nicole's eyes in memory of Lily and thought of the future and what it all meant, to be on this quest for Earth and to never be alone because there was always something.

Several soft thumps announced new arrivals. Nicole turned her back to Diu and dipped her head in greeting to Queen Tári and Falkor, who had just landed. To Diu, the queen said, "You are needed back at the palace. Falkor will bring Nicole back when she's finished here."

Diu nodded, hopping onto his Glider and following the queen, leaving Falkor behind with Nicole. She was just about to kneel back at Lily's makeshift grave when Falkor said, "I need a word with you."

Nicole looked back, curious but wary, waiting for him to speak. Falkor shuffled forward slowly, his head tilted down slightly. She took a step back, worried, and then his claws shot out and grabbed her hand. Nicole tried to pull free, but then Falkor did something she'd never imagined he would do. Still holding her hand, he bowed low.

He bowed—to her!

Nicole began to bend down too, thinking this was just another setup so he could call her a savage again, but he didn't give her the chance. He straightened up and said, "I want to apologize for all the trouble I've caused you."

"Why the change of heart?" she snapped, thinking it was a joke.

For once, Falkor wasn't fooling. Solemnly, he said, "You risked your life helping us in that battle. I saw you stand up to Malkior. You would have given everything to protect Diu—and, in turn, the Airioth. And when you shot down that Septaglider . . . you saved my life. That ship was coming for me next. It's been a long time since I've met someone as brave as you. I'm only sorry that Lily didn't make it out of the fight." He paused, and then added, "I wish I could take back what I said. She was never a fat little piggy. She was a true and honest friend."

Nicole felt tears on her cheeks. "Best friend," she countered fiercely.

"Best friend," he echoed and stooped low so she could climb on.

The wind beat softly about them as they took off into the now-faint sunlight. As they rose, the sun rose with them, and far away the palace glowed in the morning light like fire. It reminded Nicole of the queen's gift. She touched the crystal in her pocket to make sure it was safe and glanced back over her shoulder one last time.

Light slowly crept up the hilltop, bathing the weeping tree in gold. The tiny leaves flashed happily in the sun, almost as if wanting Nicole to rejoice for friendship and not grieve for a loss. But she only looked away, suddenly miserable. Then she felt something soft and furry brush her cheek. She turned back, catching a final glimpse of golden hill that cried out to remember Lily, to remember the courage and loyalty of that faithful little companion, to remember the dangers and joys they had faced together, and to remember the ultimate price of friendship. A price that had been well-paid.

Nicole put a hand to her chest and clutched the golden pocket watch that had brought her here from nowhere. Finally smiling, she looked back one last time and saw that Lily's hill, in all its beauty, had seemingly become the sun. She kept looking, on and on until, at last, the courtyard walls rose up to swallow them and the hill sank out of sight.

Chapter Thirty-Seven

The Potion

Nicole tightened her grip around Falkor's neck when he swerved in for a landing in the courtyard. "Watch it!" she cried when he roughly touched down, nearly flinging her off.

"Sorry," Falkor apologized sincerely.

Diu and Arli were already waiting. The latter quickly approached with an eager wag of the tail. *What queen say?* Arli asked.

Nicole rubbed her hand along the dracling's neck. *She had a gift for us.*

Arli's tail danced joyously. *What?*

She gave me—

"Nicole!" Diu called, distracting her. "Coming?"

"Yeah," she replied. *I'll tell you later.*

She followed him into the palace. Falkor tagged along until the dining hall, at which point he excused himself to speak to the queen. Diu, however, led Nicole back to her familiar bedroom, where she was careful to notice that the chair by the door had been stashed away. Grinning at that, she gasped when she saw that the bedspread had been transformed into a feast.

"These are the finest Aereon delicacies," Diu commented. "Queen Tári ordered you to be served only the best."

"And strangest," Nicole cheerfully added.

Starving from her day-long respite and having learned that when one is on a galaxy quest, proper meals are few and come rarely, she dug in, swallowing massive mouthfuls and eating everything she could, including a newfound favorite: a fantastic assortment of velvety red fruit pieces, steamed and cut over some deliciously grilled meat and generously slathered with a slightly spicy green sauce.

All the while, Diu merely watched Nicole—and Arli, who helped clear a few plates—eat, not touching a thing himself. He was again the tough warrior they had come to know. Occasionally, he glanced at the wall behind him, watching the sun clip the head of the valley as morning broke.

Once when he turned away, Nicole slipped out the queen's crystal. "Guess what?" she teased. When he looked back, she held it out, catching Diu in surprise. Twice in one day, she noted. A personal record.

Taking the crystal, he flipped it to see the bottom. He stared for a long time, face creased in worry.

Arli tensed. *Something wrong.*

"What is it?" Nicole asked.

"We have a problem. Just listen to this:

"Only mighty wings of fire
May the traveler's flames tame
In the lone heart of Solrius
Dwells the greatest gift of flame"

"A traveler?" Nicole repeated. "Does that refer to a planet?"

"Not a planet. A comet."

Nicole stared blankly. "You're kidding, right?"

"Solrius," he continued, ignoring her comment, "is a famous and beautiful comet covered with blue fire. But we're not merely traveling to surface. The 'gift of flame'—the fire crystal—is at the 'heart' of the comet."

"You mean the core? And we're supposed to get there . . . *how?*" To "You mean the core? And *how* are we supposed to get there?"

"On 'wings of fire,' according to the stanza."

"On . . . what?"

But he wasn't listening anymore. Diu paced the room. "That's where I've hit a snag. I could probably get one out here, but every string I could pull would take too long, and we only have a few days left—"

"*What?*" Nicole shrieked hysterically.

"I've been keeping count of Earth days, and today is the twenty-sixth day since the Terranova sequence launched. The weapon based on a thirty-Earth-day cycle, which means—"

"Four days!" Nicole screamed. "Four days!" She jumped down from the bed, breathing hard and fast. "We've only got two of the crystals and no idea how to get the one from Solrius," she squeaked. "What're we going to do!"

There was a sudden shuffle of noise just outside the room. Alert, Diu darted to the door, opened it, and glanced out. The hallway was empty.

Nicole barely noticed. A cruel affliction of thoughts boiled through her mind. *Four days left.* How much destruction had the Terranova already caused? What terrible devastation had razed Earth? Were her parents and friends safe? She buried her face in her hands at the very idea.

Diu seemed about to speak when a sharp knock sounded at the door. Falkor let himself in. Nicole glanced up and noticed he was holding a small leather pouch and a pair of black goggles with tinted glass.

"Pardon me for eavesdropping," he said, "but I couldn't help overhearing."

"Bet you could!" Nicole snapped. Arli snarled from her place on the bed.

"If Arli doesn't eat me first," Falkor said, "I might have a suggestion."

"Arli—" Diu gasped, but Nicole interrupted.

"Oh, really?" she shot back, though she immediately regretted the sniping remark in light of Falkor's sincere apology in the valley earlier. Nicole sighed into her palms. Nothing was going right.

"Do you want to hear it or not?" Falkor growled.

"Yeah, and I'm sorry. I didn't want to sound mean."

Falkor's expression softened. "I understand. I overheard you two talking, as I said, and I know it's a hard time. But I came with good news; there is a way to get that crystal."

"Arli," Diu repeated.

"The Drácar," Falkor explained, using the term Nicole remembered meant *dragon*, "evolved from the ancient races. They were some of the first creatures to populate the universe. They were slowly wiped out, taken as pets and killed for their meat. To prevent absolute extinction, the Drácar evolved to live in the harshest conditions, including in the midst of fire. This extreme heat resistance is allowed by a mental shield that protects their bodies—and, consequentially, anyone who is riding—against heat."

"Do you see, Nicole?" Diu continued. "Dragons can be said to have 'wings of fire' as they can adapt and survive in heat."

Nicole stared at them both as if they'd simultaneously lost their minds. "So . . . we're talking about Arli, right?"

"Yes," Falkor said simply.

"Arli? My Arli? My baby Arli who's not even a *month* old? *That* Arli?"

Falkor nodded. "Yes."

"Are you *insane?*" she shrieked.

"Completely," he replied and held out the leather pouch.

"What's that?"

Falkor shook the pouch. A vial filled with an opalescent substance dropped into his claws. "You might have heard a noise earlier in the hall; I'm sorry for startling you. I just overheard and ran to find Sorill to see if there was anything he could do. This is what he proposed; this potion," he continued, "serves to amplify abilities like strength, speed, and stamina. If Arli swallows this, she'll be able to fly, project shields, breathe fire—basically, she'll have the full powers of an adult."

"Any drawbacks?" Diu inquired.

"Well," Falkor mumbled, "there is *one* problem."

"Of course," Nicole muttered.

"The potion allows the drinker to fully amplify his or her abilities, but only for a short time. At the end of that time, it leaves the drinker weaker than the frailest creature—how long varies."

"No!" Diu cried suddenly. "I should have realized this all along!"

"Realized what?" Nicole asked.

"The Omenra took Arli's mother. We wondered why then, but there is some sense in it now. Malkior knows about the prophecy, remember? If he found out the words to the legend without getting the crystal itself—"

"How could he do that?"

"From the source."

"What do you—"

"Later, I'll explain later. Just listen! If Malkior found out about Solrius, he'll be after the crystal because to destroy the Terranova, we need all four. If he gets even one, even I can't help Earth then. And *that* is why he needed a dragon. Even ships with force-fields cannot resist solar temperatures for long, and extremely fast comets like Solrius build such pressure that their very bodies sometimes burn. But as Falkor said, dragons have natural shields that adapt to their environment. Dragons can control the heat and redirect it. They can fly and thrive amid fire." He sank down onto the bed, muttering a string of angry words in an alien language. "The battle," he continued. "I *knew* there was something suspicious about Malkior's retreat. He would die before he would surrender. Unless, of course—"

"He used that battle as a distraction," Nicole realized. "He never meant to finish off the Aereons, only Earth! He was hoping to kill me or the next best thing, to get the crystal before we did! No!"

"Technically speaking, why does he *care* if you save Earth?" Falkor asked. "Can't he just retest the Terranova on some other planet?"

Diu shook his head. "Falkor, you of all creatures should understand. This is not just about Earth. This is about breaking Nicole's spirit. She is the only one that can end the war in our favor. I don't know how yet, and neither does Malkior. But he can't risk it. He knows that if her family is dead, her planet destroyed, then so is her will to fight."

"It's probably too late already," Falkor said. "He has had enough time to find and retrieve that crystal."

Nicole shook her head fiercely. "Even if Malkior's had time, even if he has fast ships, even if he might already have it, there's still a chance he hasn't. And if that crystal is somewhere out there, I'm getting it. At least I have to try. And if Arli takes the potion and we go now, there's still that chance left—"

"No!" Diu said, enraged. "You're exhausted. You will make a careless move and get in trouble or worse! And how will Arli know what to do, even if she has the strength to do it?"

Nicole took the vial from Falkor. "She just will."

"You are not listening. Again. I know your heart is set on saving Earth, but not at the expense of your life! You have done things your way before with near-fatal results. You picked a fight with a Shazgor, left in a snowstorm, went after Arli, and were nearly mauled by the Korrak, stamped off on your own on Serrona, stood against Malkior when he would have killed you—"

"I lived, didn't I?"

"But what if?"

She met his eyes. "Remember the soul of the universe? You told me to believe in it." Her heart thumped as she went on: "Well, I do now. And I have to do this. I know it's right. So you're just going to have to trust me and get over it because Arli can't carry us both."

Falkor cleared his throat. "Excuse me for interrupting this lovely conversation, but if you don't mind, the clueless remainder of us might find it nice to know just what is it you're talking about?"

Diu ignored Falkor. He seemed for a moment to be ignoring Nicole as well. There was just one telltale sign that he had heard: his eyes. There was a moment when the deep brown trembled as if a single ripple had stirred in those dark pools. It was enough.

"All right," he said at last. "Go. But I swear, if anything happens—"

"Nothing's going to happen," she assured him.

"You are *absolutely* certain the potion is safe, Falkor?"

"Entirely yes."

Smiling weakly, Nicole said, "Hey, don't worry. I think I've proved I'm made of tougher stuff than I look. As for Arli, she's stronger than you think. We'll be okay, and we have the Galactera just in case."

"I hope you're right," Diu said, and Nicole took it to mean that he had surrendered. She called Arli, and the dracling stumbled over. The baby stood before them, head tilted high, examining the vial.

I ready, Arli said.

The Potion

Nicole knelt anxiously. *I know you're scared, but—*

Arli lashed her tail defiantly across the marble floor. *I scared, but Lily give life for this. I do anything now!*

Nicole uncorked the vial. "For Lily," she whispered, pouring the shimmering potion into Arli's waiting mouth.

The dracling swallowed, and Nicole released a breath she hadn't realized she'd been holding. Then she was seized by a stroke of tension. Arli trembled, radiating fear. She bowed her head, releasing a small, helpless sound. But that was all. As long moments passed and nothing more happened, Nicole grimaced, disappointed. "Falkor—" she began, but suddenly Arli screeched.

The potion manifested itself in the form of a needle-sharp spike that drove straight into Nicole's stomach. She fell to her knees, cringing. Arli convulsed and squeaked. She swung her head, unfurled her wings, whipped her tail—anything to relieve the pain! Beside her, Nicole writhed and thrashed on the ground, screaming from the intense fury of the force tearing her body apart . . .

Then it was over. Falkor and Diu lifted Nicole to her feet. But it was almost as if she were detached from her own body. She barely absorbed their touch. Somewhere far off, her voice said, "Falkor, what happened?"

"The potion taking effect."

"Quite some potion," Diu said. Nicole followed his gaze to Arli and gasped.

The dracling practically glowed like a fire. Muscles rippled beneath red scales that blazed dark crimson. Massive, powerful wings unfurled smoothly across the floor. Arching her neck, Arli considered them through shining eyes glazed with silver.

"That's incredible," Nicole whispered, and the dracling squeaked humbly.

"You don't have forever," Falkor reminded. "And it's anyone's guess how long the potion will hold out. So get moving."

Nicole nodded apprehensively. This would be the first time Arli carried a rider. Climbing onto the dracling's back, she pulled herself into a hollow at the base of the neck. Tightening her hands around Arli's neck, she held on as the baby dragon pounced forward and struck the air with her wings to show off her newfound might.

Nicole tossed the air crystal to Diu for safekeeping and told him which drawer held the water crystal and the metal disk from the map. Then she fumbled with the Galactera around her neck. As she lifted the cover, she ran over the newest stanza in her head. She stopped at the last line.

"Diu, what kind of sea could there possibly be on a comet?" she asked.

He shrugged. "I'm not certain about that, but I do know this: Keep your hand by the Galactera. Don't be afraid to come back if something goes wrong."

"Thanks. That really helped ease my jitters."

"You'll need these," Falkor added, holding out the goggles. "To see. Solrius is a comet of high intensity."

"Thanks."

He nodded and extended his claws again, this time with a small, white pill. "And this. To breathe."

"Breathe?"

"What do you expect to find on a comet?" he asked wryly.
"Air?"

Nicole placed the tablet on her tongue and felt it dissolve. She felt no different. "So, what's the point?"

"It will help you adjust to various atmospheric contents," Diu chipped in. "I've had some pills like that with me all this time, but the worlds we have visited thus far have had very similar, though not identical, concentrations of elements as compared to Earth. The pills are necessary now because your constant breathing will quickly replace the oxygen stored inside Arli's mental shield with carbon dioxide, which you ordinarily cannot breathe."

"Point taken," Nicole said.

Falkor coughed conspicuously.

She rolled her eyes playfully. "Right, I'm going."

Seeing that the comet wasn't already programmed, Nicole found the button for new planets. Imagining an elegant arch of blue fire against dark space, she whispered, "Solrius."

Arli's silver-scalded eyes closed as bristling blue flames lashed around them. Strapping on the goggles and pressing close to the dracling's neck, Nicole watched the vortex erupt into brilliant, azure fire. She glanced at Diu as the blaze licked Arli's mental shield, but his image suddenly dissolved and was replaced by the sparkling, starry expanse of space. It was beautiful and ominous.

And deadly.

Chapter Thirty-Eight

The Core

Arli spun forward and spiraled into a dive. Though this was Nicole's second dragon flight, it still provided a rush of invigoration. And, in light of the circumstances, fear. She yelled as they plummeted. Then, suddenly, the scream cut off. It was replaced by an open-mouthed stare.

Nicole blinked in awe at the vast sparkle of dust and fire rushing to meet them. Even from a close perspective, the comet was majestically beautiful. They were somewhat above the comet, flying in low over the partly transparent, periwinkle tail that tapered to a rounded, ice-blue drape around the main body. It was there Arli targeted her flight. The dracling's shield kept atmosphere around them, providing Arli with air resistance to beat her wings and allowing Nicole to breathe. It also gave the air a feeling of intense cold to combat the heat of fire. Yet in spite of the shield and goggles, Nicole squinted against the light and comet dust in a struggle to see.

Arli, Nicole thought, *pull back from the tail and see if you can reach the head. And watch the fire. Don't get us burned.*

She knew the shield should, in theory, protect them against

fire. But could extra pressure from a direct hit also affect the potion's duration? She wasn't planning on experimenting.

The dracling closed in on the comet's flaming body and swerved from a wayward tongue of fire. Her keen eyes narrowed at several small, dark splotches staining the otherwise sheer flaming face of the comet. *Look like craters,* she said.

Deep craters, Nicole added, squinting. *Really deep. Let's check them out.*

It too dangerous to go so close!

Come on, just a little closer.

Peeping resentfully, the dracling dove vertically, dodging a trail of fire. The cold amplified as they approached the surface. So did the flames; the comet's tremendous speed spilled more fire from its massive body. Arli was forced to constantly duck out of the way to avoid fresh spurts. And quickly, time was running low.

Once, Arli swerved to duck a flame but twisted into the path of a second lick of fire. It struck the shield from the side and flung them away some fifty feet before spitting them free. Arli's powerful wings slashed the air within her mental shield, trying desperately to regain ground. The barrier flickered pitifully.

How much longer can you hold the shield? Nicole asked.

I not know.

Then we've got to hurry. Dive a little closer so I can—

Nicole gasped. She saw the black blemishes more clearly now; they weren't craters at all. They were tunnels. Tunnels leading . . .

"To the core! They've got to!" Nicole cried. "And I don't

know what's down there, but it looks like our only shot. But how do we get through safely?"

Arli barrel-rolled sideways, cleaving a stray flame with her wingtip. *I go for one dive, fast speed. It only chance.*

What if something goes wrong? What if you can't pull up in time?

I not planning to.

"Arli, are you crazy?"

Her scream was lost in the force of the dracling's lashing swoop.

They dropped like a stone in a sheer vertical fall straight towards the nearest tunnel. If a flame, a strong one, struck them now, it was over; there would be no way to stop in time. Then something occurred to Nicole, too late. A comet was basically a rock, right? Then how could there be tunnels or empty space inside?

Nicole shrieked as a flame blossomed towards them. Arli snapped her wings shut, transforming into a sleek missile that plunged mere feet from the fire and down into what Nicole hoped was not a trick of the light but indeed a passage. Luckily, he tunnel proved to be precisely that—a narrow, smooth channel through solid rock, just large enough for the dracling's outstretched wings.

Diu had finally been wrong about one thing: It was not hot inside Solrius. The temperature did nothing but plummet. The alien fabric of her suit was warmer than Nicole's normal clothes, but it did not prevent her from shivering. Even Arli's scales were glazed with an icy coating, forcing Nicole to clutch on tighter than before to prevent slipping off.

"Are we close?" Nicole called out, her breath misting into a dense cloud.

Maybe. Is light ahead.

At last Arli slowed to swerve safely out of the passage. They emerged into a massive, spherical chamber whose rounded walls appeared to be made of dark, liquid-smooth rock. No; not rock, Nicole realized. Some kind of metal. The room was absolutely enormous, stretching away almost beyond the limits of vision. Nicole gaped. A cold, hollow metal core inside a comet?

This is impossible, she thought. *Completely insane!*

More insane was the light source at the heart of the chamber. A flickering mass of sapphire flames, seemingly hovering in midair, illuminated the room. It was almost like magic. Nicole pushed the goggles up from her eyes to marvel at the brilliant firelight.

Arli banked towards the flames. Shining and crackling like a ball of lighting, the flickering sphere loomed closer. Nicole expected them to round the object, but the dracling's path seemed fixed.

"Arli, where are you going?" she asked uncertainly. After all, as eager as she was to get the crystal, she certainly wasn't all too eager to die trying.

To the core.

Nicole half choked. "To the . . . have you gone crazy?"

Trust me.

"I'll trust you to turn around before you get us both killed!"

The dracling did not waver.

"Arli, turn around!" Nicole screamed.

The ball of flames was too close.

"Arli, the shield won't take it!"

Deadly flames licked at the force-field.

"Turn away! Turn away now!"

Blue fire fully engulfed them. The shield sputtered weakly, barely holding on. But somehow it managed, and suddenly they soared out of the fire and into a second circular chamber flooded with sapphire light. Nicole's eyes grew wide at the sight of a floor carved entirely of glowing cerulean rock, and wider still at what lay at its center.

A small depression, only some ten feet across, was carved into the rock, filled with a clear liquid. Arli skidded to a rough landing, and Nicole, driven by instinctive curiosity, hopped down. She breathed out a misty haze in the cold air of the mental shield and tentatively approached the shallow, perfectly circular pool. On a strange impulse, she knelt. The immobile surface reflected her frightened eyes. But deeper down, something glinted red.

Nicole's heart missed a beat as she angled her body over the water, trying to see. There was something at the bottom. Barely breathing, she stared down, only just managing to suppress a scream.

That's the crystal, Arli! I'm sure!

The dracling did not share Nicole's joy. *This not feel right. Something wrong.*

"It's not anything bad," Nicole said aloud, half to relieve rising fear. "I'll just jump in and bring it out. That's it."

Arli leaned her head over the pool. *This not right.*

You're worse than Diu. Why can't you just trust me?
This not right.

"I don't have a choice, okay!" Nicole cried angrily. Arli's concern wasn't making this any easier. Yet she felt a cold squeeze of emotion from the dracling and immediately felt bad. Arli was, after all, only looking out for her safety. "I'm sorry," she added. "I didn't mean for it to sound like that."

Arli peeped a slightly reluctant forgiveness and turned her attention to the pool. *Is it water?*

Nicole hadn't thought about that. "I don't know. Want to dip your tail in and find out?"

The dracling fastened her teeth carefully around a small portion of Nicole's sleeve and ripped away a strip. Opening her mouth, she dropped the fabric into the pool. The strip landed on the surface, was suspended there for a few moments, and then sank.

"Looks safe to me," Nicole said. But just to be sure she dipped her pinky into the water. Nothing happened.

Then go. But quickly.

"Right," Nicole said. "Quickly. And stay close, Arli. Don't let the shield break."

She stepped to the pool's edge, trying not to image how cold she would soon be. For a moment, she thought of undressing. The water was freezing, and she'd need something warm when she came out. Only there was no time. Nicole shut her eyes and sighed angrily. The whole thing was so stupid. But before she could change her mind, she jumped.

The cold was wild agony, striking Nicole like a fire. The pool was much deeper than it appeared. Her body screamed in protest; she could hardly breathe and trembled violently, vibrating the pool's surface as freezing water splashed against her neck. Nicole was only up to her chest in the water now, and even that was terror. Diving was the last thing she wanted to do in the universe, and for a moment she thought of leaving it and returning with Diu and some high-tech gear later. But Nicole knew that would be impossible. It seemed that somehow she had beat Malkior here. That advantage could not be lost.

Gathering courage, she submerged. Groping numbly through the water, kicking half-frozen legs and fighting to retain air in bursting lungs, Nicole's fingers closed around the object. She felt a tiny prick, adjusted her hold, and swam upwards; she broke the surface gasping. Arli swung her neck out and Nicole grabbed hold, fingers locked in a death-grip upon the crystal in her hand.

"I got it," she muttered weakly, stashing the crystal in her pocket. "I got it."

Arli dragged her out onto the metal floor. Nicole lifted herself to her knees and immediately collapsed. Water pooled around her soaked clothing, but she couldn't move. She was shivering hard enough to frighten the dracling, who could only croon weakly and nudge Nicole's arms where they lay limply in a puddle.

We must go, Arli said.

I know.

Now.

"Yeah." But Nicole made no effort to budge, barely managing to breathe. She focused on that now, sucking the air into her lungs and out—the icy Solrius air that wasn't really air but the stuff Falkor's tablet made it into.

Her body was going limp. Everything below her neck had become a massive, burdensome lump. Her brain seemed to be slower, too. Thoughts sluggishly oozed along. Nicole sighed with sudden apathy and watched her misty breath rise on a current of wind.

Wind? Suddenly Nicole found her arms again and used them to push up and roll sideways. There was something happening to the pool. Arli snarled as the surface began to boil and steam.

And burst into flames.

The fire spread and formed into a creature—a great blue dragon. It was Arli on a much grander and fiercer scale. Fangs of fire curled over its protruding lips. A pair of twisted horns adorned its head. When the dragon roared, breathing smoke, Nicole found the will to jump up and stumble back, terrified.

Arli, we've got to get to out of here, she thought, desperately clinging to the dracling's neck.

Climb on quickly!

Nicole pulled herself into the small hollow at the base of Arli's neck and held on as the dracling battered the air with her wings, mounting higher and then twisting about, diving and leaping again as the fire dragon blasted after them, bright blue wings stroking its weightless body along. It pursued them swiftly, driving them towards the ceiling, cornering them against . . .

A passage! Arli, fly there!

The dracling swooped up, wings pressed close to her body. The dragon writhed up after them, its body molding to fit the narrow passage. Its jaws were inches away when the creature jerked to a halt, its great chest swelling with a sucking breath.

Nicole glanced back in triumph. They had won. Or, so it seemed. There was something wrong. The dragon was neither following them nor turning away. It merely hovered there in the passage, its chest bulging . . .

Suddenly Nicole realized their mistake. *Arli, we've got to go faster, we've got to—*

She never finished the thought because, just then, the very thing she feared boiled up at them—a massive, burning blue fireball.

They broke free of the tunnel an instant before the blast struck. Rolling out of the way, Arli just managed to avoid a total hit. But they did not escaped the fireball altogether.

Nicole pulled on the goggles to see and cried out. *Arli, your wing!*

The dracling wobbled. She fought to stay in the air with a badly burned left wingtip. The best Arli could do was fly lopsided, fighting to gain elevation. In the meantime, Nicole fumbled for the Galactera. It was their only chance.

Another blue fireball ripped past them. Arli only just managed to dodge. Yet as she rolled, she lost precious altitude, hurtling back towards the surface of Solrius.

Arli!

The baby dragon struggled harder, maintaining the mental shield to avoid the flares which, although seemingly cold, were deadly. But then the fire dragon shot another fireball straight at them, and this time Arli could not get away.

They were struck from the side and thrown towards the comet. The shield just barely held, flickering faintly. For a moment, Arli seemed stunned. But she lifted her wings to the stars once more.

Just a second and we'll be out of here, Nicole thought. She was still fumbling with the watch when suddenly it snapped open.

With terror, she saw that the planet names were gone. In fact, all the buttons were blank, and when she pressed them, nothing happened.

Nicole's mouth dropped open in a silent scream. They were stuck on Solrius with a creature that would kill them.

The dragon rose up behind them, its body igniting into a massive blue flame with only the snapping mouth intact. A blaze welled up behind the fangs—a blinding, white-hot glow that swelled to gigantic proportions. Even worse, Arli's shield suddenly died, leaving them exposed to the blaze that was coming, to the fireball in those jaws, and all Nicole could do as she watched the flames rise was sit numbly and clutch the worthless pocket watch in her moist fingers.

But her hands were not the only things wet. Her clothes were soaked through and dripping. It felt as if she had received a thorough soaking in ice water. Now something rough was wetting her face, something that glided back over and over, and a scream burst in her head.

Nicole!

She sat up in a jerk, surging with fear. A terrified Arli reared away from her. Nicole looked down and realized she was sitting in a puddle of water and her clothes were soaked. The pool lay beside her.

Nicole's hands groped blindly towards her pocket where she had stored the crystal, hoping and praying that somehow this much of it had been real. But her fingers touched nothing save fabric.

Are you safe? Arli inquired.

Nicole weakly nodded her head. *What happened?*

You start drowning. I pull you out. But your hand bleeding.

Feeling a prickle in her right palm, Nicole cast her gaze down to a dark trickle winding down her arm.

And, Arli added, *there was this.*

Carefully opening her mouth, she dropped a small metal ball glittering with spikes. Nicole prodded the object with her foot and felt a strange onset of dizziness. *What is that?*

It in your hand when I pull you out. But it not smell safe. Smell like death. Like poison.

So Malkior had beaten them here all along. An overwhelming sense of doom beat Nicole with an iron fist. His plan had worked flawlessly. She had won the battle of Serrona but lost the war. Only with four crystals could she destroy the Terranova. Now that Malkior had the fire crystal, it was all over. They would never get the crystal back in time to save Earth.

Then Arli's words hit her. Poison? Nicole's vision seemed slightly distorted. She shook her head to clear it, but colors retained strange tints; the blues and blacks were more prominent while Arli's crimson scales were subdued.

Nicole?

She clutched Arli's neck for support, feeling her heart hammer. *Malkior . . . his poison . . . Arli, we've got to . . .*

The dracling turned so Nicole could climb on. She groaned at the offering. *I can't climb on. You have to help me.*

Arli's head swung to Nicole and came to rest by her arm. Nicole wrapped her hands around the dracling's neck, and Arli lifted her up. Nicole just barely managed to swing her legs in place, suddenly feeling the Galactera brush her skin beneath the tunic. The watch was warm even now, despite the coldness of the chamber. She thought for a second of teleporting right away, but a sudden thought stopped her. If she left from here, could the watch send her to the core of Serrona?

Arli, fly us out of here, she decided. *Just to be safe. Then I'll take us back.*

The dracling beat her wings and surged towards the ceiling. She climbed higher, sweeping towards the nearest tunnel. Nicole's stomach lurched; she was glad that it was empty. As they rocketed up the passage—this one large enough for Arli's outspread wings—Nicole screwed her eyes shut and strapped the goggles in place. Her legs were beginning to complain from all the riding.

Arli cleared the tunnel and tilted into a steep climb. She thrashed her wings to gain altitude. Cold stars clung to the dark mass of space, glowing with a light that could not warm them. Arli's shield kept away the comet's fire, but she was dodging weakly now, barely evading the flames.

What's going on? Nicole asked, herself feeling a spur of sickness.

I not know. I trying, but . . .

The dracling wobbled heavily as if struck by turbulence. Her wings beat in clipped, painful motions. Nicole shook unsteadily, terrified as she had never been before. She reached for the Galactera, but before she could touch the watch, Arli's wings flailed aimlessly, almost as if she were unable to move.

The potion, Arli said, barely thrashing with the last of her strength.

And Nicole realized their time was up.

They fell into a dizzying plummet. The mental shield flickered like a weak candle around them. Nicole knew they had only seconds left before it gave in and the void of space swallowed them. She fumbled for the pocket watch as Arli tried to angle into a shallower dive, snapping her wings open as far as she could to suspend them in a slower fall.

But Nicole was weary with dizziness. Nausea welled up in her throat from the crazy, swirling plunge and the effect of the poison. The world swam in and out of focus. She clenched her teeth shut to keep from vomiting. Grabbing hold of the watch, Nicole stared blindly at the buttons, unable to see which one to press.

They had fallen behind the comet, and suddenly a vast offshoot of flames blasted off the main body and barreled towards them, massive, wide, and ferocious. From an instant wave of fear she deduced that Arli had felt it too, but neither could do a thing to stop the fire from coming. Nicole slumped weakly on Arli's back, trying to keep from falling into unconsciousness. They'd both die if she did. But seeing the flame coming, she knew they were both dead anyway. The watch began to slip from her hand . . .

Nicole knew she would never forget what Arli did next. It was incredibly brave, incredibly stupid, and no less than what Lily had so recently done. Seeing that the end was near and knowing that a direct blast when the shield was so weak would mean death, the dracling used the remainder of her ebbing strength to turn her body so Nicole was facing away from the fire and her own soft underbelly, the weakest part of a dragon's body, would take the hit. Just like Lily, she was ready to give everything to protect Nicole.

And like Lily, she would die doing it.

Unable to scream, unable to move, Nicole watched the flame come. The pocket watch was still warm and heavy in her hand. Thinking of warmth and safety, an image of Queen Tári's palace flickered in her mind. Then darkness engulfed her vision, the world faded from sight, and Nicole knew nothing more.

Chapter Thirty-Nine

One Last Chance

Nicole was blinded by white light. She tried to wiggle her fingers but nothing happened, so she fought to find contentment in squinting and waiting. Only she couldn't. A surge of panic ripped through her body. She thought she felt her mouth but couldn't get it to move. Nor would her voice function. Nicole's entire world seemed to have become the light.

Then it blinked into darkness. Slowly, the feeling returned to her body. She curled the fingers of her right hand into a fist. The insides of her legs burned slightly. Nicole vaguely remembered bright blue fire, and heat, and space—

She jerked to a sitting position, dragging wires along. Nodes clung to her body beneath a papery smock. Looking around, Nicole found herself in a familiar setting—translucent walls that were dark with night, marble flooring, and grand, dark-brown furnishings, including the regal bed she discovered herself in. It wasn't her usual room in the palace, but close enough. Sizing up the situation, Nicole fumbled with the sheets and crumpled them to the base of the bed, stood too hastily, and collapsed onto the floor.

Forcing herself upright, she stumbled towards the door. The sticky nodes ripped painfully from her body, but she ignored them. Nicole pressed the misty door and it easily swung out, spilling her into the hall beyond. Clinging to a wall, she pressed her face to the cold surface, breathing heavily. Her heart thumped painfully.

"Nicole!"

Her body angled towards the voice. "Yeah?"

Footsteps rushed to meet her. Strong arms held her now, and she allowed herself to relax.

"You have to get back to the room—"

"Diu," Nicole laughed, "*you* have to stop worrying." She suddenly, and strangely, felt overwhelmingly safe.

"Stop worrying?" he retorted with an icy edge. "Arli's severely burned, you were poisoned, both of you teetered on the brink of death, and you expect me to not worry!"

Arli. Nicole winced at the very memory. "How bad?"

"How bad what?"

"Was she hurt?"

"Bad enough."

They were through the door now. The lights flickered on automatically.

"Will she be okay?"

"The Aereon medics claim there is a split chance for her survival. Here, lean more, you are about to fall . . ."

Survival. Arli's very life teetered on the edge of death, and whatever happened, it was all Nicole's fault.

Diu helped her onto the bed. Suddenly feeling clammy, she snuggled beneath the soft covers. She felt Diu's rough and furry paw touch her forehead and then pull back. He muttered, "Fever," and uncorked a tiny vial waiting on the nightstand. "Here, take this," he said. "It will help."

The liquid tasted almost metallic. It was bitter enough to burn Nicole's throat and spurred on a violent coughing fit. Diu sat on the edge of the bed and waited till she fell back on the pillow. The soft fabric cushioned her head.

"Thanks," Nicole muttered, feeling nauseous. But at least she wasn't quite as cold.

"You were extremely lucky to have teleported back when you did. The Aereons were just starting to clear the remains of dinner when you and Arli crashed right into the central table, snapping it in two." He paused, and his dark eyes brushed across her face as if searching for something. "Luckily," he continued, "Falkor and I were there and knew exactly what must have happened—or thought we did. We found out soon enough about the poison and managed to extract it. If you had teleported anywhere else, you would be dead now."

"Good to know," she said weakly. Cold tendrils gripped her spine, but not because of the fever.

"How were you poisoned?"

"Malkior. He beat us there and set a trap. He knew I'd fall for it."

There was a brief silence.

"Diu," Nicole asked at last, fearing the answer. "How long have I been here?"

He didn't answer at first. At last he carefully said, "In Earth time? Two days."

"Two days? Two days! I've been here . . . I've . . . we only have two days left," she finished.

He nodded. There was nothing else to say.

Nicole felt like her throat was stuck. She opened and closed her mouth several times before she was able to get some words out. "It's over anyway!" she cried. "Malkior got the fire crystal, and without it, there's no hope. We won't even know where to look for the last crystal unless we read the inscription!"

She broke down into sobs. Everything she knew. Everything she loved. Everything she cherished, and dreamed of, and treasured. All gone. And Lily . . . Nicole had made a promise to complete the quest. But despite all of that, they had failed.

Diu managed a slight smile. "You're wrong."

"Wrong?" she wept.

"It is not over. Not yet. We can still get back the crystal, and there is more than one way to find out what the inscription said."

"How?"

Diu looked away. "I haven't seen him for a long time. Not since the start of the war. He was always a last resort."

"Who?"

"My old friend, Tibo."

"Oh," Nicole muttered. "That Tibo again."

"Tibo can be useful. After all, he is the one who had a vision of the prophecy. His is the one who warned us from the outset about the Terranova. He can tell us where the last crystal is, just as he must have told Malkior where to find the fire crystal."

Nicole gawked. "If Tibo's known where the crystals were

all along, why did we have to waste time finding the map and searching for them? Why didn't we just go to him from the start?"

"Because," Diu explained, "see, Tibo . . . well, he has incredible power and knowledge, but even ten years ago he was a bit odd, so imagine what he is like now. And to be honest, I don't even know whose side he is on anymore. He used to be with the Airioth, but then turned neutral, and now he helps the Omenra more than he helps us."

Nicole considered their options. "If we leave, will Arli have to stay here?"

"Yes. She is in a critical state."

"Then . . ." She stopped, not wanting to abandon the dracling, yet knowing what she must do.

"We will have to finish this mission alone," Diu said.

Alone. There was something strange about the way he said it. Nicole glanced up and their gazes locked, and then she realized there had been a question in his voice, a question now in the brown-black of his eyes. He had made a connection even Nicole didn't understand, but whatever it was she felt it even there, she so helpless while he sat not two feet away so strong and at the peak of power. She didn't like it, this weakness, and she didn't like the second, more inexplicable and unnamed emotion she sometimes felt around Diu.

Nicole pulled her legs over the side of the bed, disturbing some of the wires. Lifting one by the node, she twirled it and asked, "What're all these for, anyway?"

"The Aereons wanted to monitor you for stability. Surviving a dose of the kind of poison you were injected with without suffering permanent physical damage is exceptionally rare. You were lucky."

"Or maybe the soul of the universe is looking out for me."

"Maybe." He stood, walked to the door, and paused at the opening. "Tomorrow morning, the nurses will perform a last mandatory check. Then we may head out to see Tibo. Don't bother arguing with me about going right now, because you are on your own if you want to go wake him up in the middle of the night, as it is now where he lives."

"Don't worry," she said as she crawled back into bed. "I haven't gone totally mental."

"Really?" he said softly in mock surprise.

"Really, really," she replied, as Lily would have said.

"Sleep well."

"Good night. But, Diu, wait."

"Yes?"

She wanted to ask him something, but then she thought better of it. "Never mind."

He seemed to understand. Turning off the light, he said, "Good night, Nicole."

"Night," she mumbled as he closed the door with a soft thump, leaving her alone in the darkness.

She reached out to Arli telepathically, but the dracling must have been deeply unconscious because Nicole's mind remained full of nothing but her own thoughts. Nicole sadly turned over beneath the blanket and sighed.

She thought about the thing she had wanted to ask. It had been about Serena. There was something strange about Diu's story. Had Nicole been in Diu's place, nothing would stop her from hunting down Malkior if he had really killed Serena. But somehow Diu always restrained himself. He had restrained himself for ten years. It was almost . . . almost as if he didn't want to kill Malkior. Ever.

Confused, she pushed the thoughts away. More significant now was also the matter of this Tibo person. He sounded like a strange character, but Nicole prayed that he'd be willing and able to help them. He was their last hope.

And if Tibo wouldn't help them, who would?

The following morning greeted Nicole with breakfast in bed, courtesy of the considerate Aereon servants. They had also cleaned and folded her clothes and placed them on top of a little nightstand next to her bed, along with the Galactera. Nicole shoveled down the food, set the tray aside, and changed from the papery smock into the leather tunic and pants. She slipped on her shoes, hung the pocket watch around her neck, and walked out into the deserted hallway.

Through the translucent walls Nicole could see a glorious sunrise over the lip of the valley. As she sought a familiar route, the golden light lit her way through a section of the palace she'd never explored before. She heard Aereons stirring and speaking softly to each other behind closed doors as she passed. Sometimes an almost-familiar voice reached her, and she would listen to the snippets of conversation until the sounds fell behind.

At last Nicole recognized the crystal arch that led into the palace courtyard. She knew how to find her way from there, so she hurried forward, only to stop abruptly at the edge of the grass. Standing all alone in the center of the courtyard was Diu, looking up at the last few fading stars.

He heard her coming and pretended to look puzzled. "Thought I saw something," he mumbled and bent over to pick at something in the grass, almost as if he had something to hide. Sure enough, he rubbed his eyes before straightening up and coming over. But she could still see wet stains in his fur.

Deciding not to press the subject, Nicole instead asked, "We're leaving this morning, right?"

"Yes. Right away. Have you already had breakfast? I told the servants to lay it out early."

"Yep. You?"

He nodded. "I knew you would want to leave as early as possible. I also took the liberty of telling Queen Tári and Falkor that we would be going first thing. They wanted to say good-bye, but I don't think—"

"We have time," she interrupted. "Are they awake already?"

"Yes. The queen is having an early breakfast in the dining hall with Arvia. If we are lucky, the others may be there too."

"Lead the way," she said, following him back through the archway.

In the absolute quiet of the morning, their footsteps echoed like gunshots. Nicole was suddenly and acutely aware that there were just the two of them now where once there had been four. Would the final crystal call for a sacrifice as well?

Shaking the terrible thought from her head, she asked,

"Hey, Diu? I forgot to ask last night. Where does Tibo live? Is it somewhere new?"

He slowed down so she could catch up. "It's a very interesting planet. A small place called Earth."

"Earth? *My* Earth?"

"Yes."

"Why would an alien want to live there?"

"Not an alien. Tibo is one of few humans who know the truth about what's beyond your world. Like I said before, he's brilliantly clever."

Diu cut the conversation short as they approached the dining hall. The great chamber was mostly empty. Only the queen sat at the high table, flanked by Falkor and Arvia. She held a tilted cup in her claws and glanced up only briefly when they walked in. Falkor jumped to meet them, followed by the princess.

"We're leaving soon," Nicole said.

"I'm glad you came," Falkor replied. "I was worried."

"No need. I'm fine. So far, anyway."

Arvia's mouth tugged into a smile. "Thank you for all you've done. Without you, I'd still be with the Omenra."

"It was nothing."

"You returned my life, Nicole. That is something I will never forget."

Arvia and Falkor both looked back at the high table where Queen Tári still sat, staring at the cup. Nicole guardedly stepped forward, waiting for a signal. At length the queen stood and gazed at her from across the table.

"Child," she said, "my people owe you our freedom."

"I didn't do that much," Nicole admitted. "I just tagged along and got lucky a couple times."

Queen Tári moved slowly around the table, one clawed hand trailing lazily along the silk tablecloth. "Child, you did far more than that. Your very presence has rekindled hope for my people. Nearly every creature in the galaxy knows the prophecy and sees you as their savior. A great destiny awaits you, a path that will take you to the edges of the known galaxy. And in that journey I promise you the heart of my people. Remember always that the Aereons shall be by your side if you find yourself in need.

"Take care of yourself, child. Mend the galaxy. Bring peace to the universe. You are our last hope."

Nicole nodded solemnly, feeling the weight of the queen's words. "I'll do my very best," she said, bowing.

"Time is running short," Diu reminded her. "If we want to have any chance of saving Earth, we need to leave, now. We'll be in touch, Your Majesty."

"You know you are always welcome here. Both of you."

"Thank you," Nicole said. Her cheeks were moist with tears. Upset that she couldn't have said goodbye to Sorill but knowing they had no more time to spare, Nicole waved a final good-bye. Then she glanced down to hide her face and clicked open the Galactera. There was no button for Earth. But there wasn't really a need.

Roaring waterfalls and silent rains cascaded through her memory. Pyramids towered above a massive spread of desert; the ocean glowed like fire at sunset; night gracefully veiled the sky. Mountains climbed till they vanished beyond the clouds; snowflakes sang as they drifted lazily through the air; volcanoes belched burning lava; jungles teemed with the pulse of life; a cheetah sprinted after an antelope; a dolphin burst from the sea. And closer to home: trees towered and birds twittered; children laughed as they played tag; the school bell called students to their classes; *swoosh* . . . a basketball had made it.

There was no need for a button for Earth. There would never be a need. Because all Nicole knew in that moment was that, after what seemed a long, long time, she was returning home at last.

Chapter Forty

Meeting Tibo

The blue sky was empty, all save for the sun. The orb of fire burned with such heat that Nicole broke into a sweat almost immediately. They seemed to stand in the center of some kind of giant, gently-sloping crater. Silent sands spread around them, washing to the edges of the depression. Nicole swallowed a deep breath and coughed against the dust and dryness in the air. It almost appeared as if they were in a desert. Yet something seemed wrong.

Maybe Diu alerted her to it. He suddenly turned away and wouldn't look at her. But there was something else. The sand . . . it wasn't perfectly smooth. Nicole squatted and picked at several parched, white sticks. Not wood, she realized when she looked more closely.

Bone.

"Diu, what's going on!" she shrieked. "Where are we?"

"A lake," he admitted. "Or what used to be one."

Nicole gaped. This giant, empty crater, hundreds of feet deep, was once a *lake?* What could that mean for the rest of Earth? Pushing away the terrible thought, she picked up several bones. From fish, she guessed; fish that had once thrived in the waters of this lake. She crushed the bones into white powder in her hand. They had thrived, at least until the Omenra intervened.

"We have to find Tibo," she said. "Now."

"Yes, I understand."

"So where we go?"

"I have absolutely no idea."

"I'm being serious."

"As am I," Diu said matter-of-factly.

"*What?*"

"Tibo hardly ever stays in the same place for very long. He could be in London one day and Kenya the next."

Nicole gawked in horror. "So what're we going to do? It's not like we can stop time and go look for him!"

"Hmm," Diu said, thinking out loud. "There is only one way I can think of. Give me the Galactera."

She slid the chain over her head and handed him the watch, waiting for the explanation she knew would follow.

"Remember how you ended up in the dining hall the second time you teleported to Serrona?" he asked, opening up the watch.

"Yes. And speaking of which, how—"

"I will explain. So far as I know, the Galactera does more than teleport the user from planet to planet. It can take you to a *specific* site on a planet. Basically, here is how it works; if you want to go to a certain planet but not to a specific place on that planet, it will teleport you to a randomly selected location. However, if you have an exact destination in mind and think about it as you're pressing the button, the watch will send you there. Of course, I don't know where Tibo is, but I know what his hut looks like, and I doubt he would leave it behind. If I can remember that in vivid detail, this may just work."

Nicole ignored the overwhelming urge to image a tiny, old man dragging a house around on his back. Then she remembered something. "Before we teleport, I have to ask you something that just doesn't make sense. How come Malkior has to use a cruiser to get around? How come he can't just get himself a Galactera and teleport his army from place to place? If he could take them anywhere, instantaneously, he could have destroyed the Airioth a long time back . . . no offense."

Diu's smiled tightly. "Because Galacteras are extremely rare. There is, in fact, only one in the known universe."

Open-mouthed, Nicole gasped, "No kidding?"

"You should have learned by now that I rarely joke. Now, let's hope I can take us right to Tibo's doorstep. I still remember what he looks like, even after all these years. He is not the kind of person you easily forget . . . or *can* forget." He flipped open the Galactera. "Ready?"

"I guess so."

"Good. Just one last thing. Say *nothing* about the crystal until I give you the okay, understand? Tibo has strange ways of testing people, one of which includes how quick you are to get to the point. It is one of the reasons he originally did not trust Malkior. Tibo likes general prattle first. If you pester him right off, we'll be lucky if he only chases us out and not worse."

"Got it."

"And another thing. Tibo loves making deals. If he attempts to pull you into one, make sure you understand *exactly* what the terms are before you agree. He's tricky. I know from experience."

"Okay, okay, can we just get on with it?"

His deep brown eyes flashed to meet her own. "Fine, but remember what I told you. You will only get one chance with Tibo."

As the blue vortex churned around them, salty seaweed scents filled the suddenly moist and tropical air. Waves crashed somewhere nearby, and the next thing Nicole saw was a glorious, white, sandy beach bordered by a range of dark, ruffled cliffs. The sun was low over the water and had the bright quality of morning. Light danced over waves and reflected off shiny shells in the sand. But the water, Nicole noticed, was empty of the tiny fish that usually darted about in the shallows. The sky was silent; there were no seagulls or other birds in sight. And it was dreadfully hot.

Diu chuckled, his voice coming from far away. "Good thing Tibo never leaves his hut behind."

Nicole turned to see where he had gone and saw him standing near a tiny, lopsided structure hidden in the shadow of the cliffs. It was constructed almost entirely of small stones. The roof was made of thatched reeds. A large piece of driftwood served as the door. A bent chimney poking out of the reeds completed the strange array. Coming closer, Nicole was shocked that the hut was actually standing. The stones were simply stacked up clumsily on one another. The door was wedged roughly between two particularly unsteady stacks.

The sight of the crooked hut nearly made her forget why they were there. An unexpected tap on the shoulder brought Nicole back to her senses, though her heart nearly sprang up into her mouth.

"Sorry," Diu apologized.

"Don't do that!" she gasped, panting.

He motioned towards the door. "I just wanted to know if you were planning on knocking any time today. Take your time; I'm in no hurry. We only have the earth to save, you know."

"Hilarious," she muttered.

The sad-looking hut was much more austere close up. Looking at the precariously balanced stones again, Nicole remembered that Tibo had a certain brand of magic beyond normal powers. She briefly hesitated. Diu had said that Tibo helped the Omenras now. If he had helped Malkior find the fire crystal, how deeply involved was he in the Omenra conspiracy?

Curiosity more than anything else drove her to knock on the door. Each bang was hollow but filled with a strange, chilling ring. Nicole had hardly knocked three times before the door swung open seemingly of its own accord. With a quick glance at Diu, she slipped through the doorway, wary for danger. He followed close behind, so close that she could feel his breath on her neck. But no sooner had they stepped inside than Nicole stopped dead in her tracks, shocked and amazed.

The room that greeted her was enormous, and not just compared to the outside of the hut. It was nearly half as large as the Aereon's dining hall. It was also very cramped; every square inch of floor boasted furniture and various ornaments, and every millimeter of wall was plastered with posters, paintings, and various splotches of wild color. Every available surface gleamed with shining artifacts and complex contraptions, jewelry and gems, trinkets and lockets. A narrow path had been forcefully carved through the mountains of objects. It led to an empty fireplace at the far end of the room.

Nicole took a few tentative steps but stopped again when she noticed that the unlit fireplace was smoking ominously. Diu came up beside her and cautiously glanced around.

"You're sure we're in the right place?" she whispered hastily.

"Absolutely. You can always tell by the fireplace. Tibo believes they become bad omens when lit."

"Rightfully so, might I add!" cried a squeaky voice from a place not two trinkets away.

Nicole shrieked and whirled around so fast that she nearly stumbled backwards over a three-legged table. As it was, several worn, leather-bound books went flying off the table and landed in a heap on the floor, raising a cloud of dust.

"Messy, messy, messy!" the voice continued, its source still concealed by a nearby chair piled high with dusty maps. "If you want to come visit, I have no problem with you being here! But why so messy? Watch your feet, please!"

Looking down to make sure nothing was nibbling on her shoes, Nicole scooted over closer to Diu, still searching for the elusive Tibo.

"You're being very bad guests, you know!" the voice chided. "I don't see a single present for me, not even a bunch of fresh-picked flowers or a nice trout. But I'm not being a very good host myself, so I guess the injustice is squared. Everyone loves a batch of chocolate chip cookies in the morning, but it doesn't seem like there are any extras lying around." Then the speaker seemed to lose his train of thought and mumbled a few words under his breath. All of a sudden, the furniture and trinkets started to rearrange themselves of their own accord, creating a new path. Through the turmoil, the voice exclaimed, "Why, I haven't even introduced myself! What a poor host I am, indeed!"

Tables, desks, and chairs slid sideways and rearranged themselves neatly so no books or trinkets fell off. Out of the shifting mass appeared a pair of sandaled feet, followed by a short, squat body wrapped in colorful, exotic-looking robes, and finally the large, wrinkled head of an old man with wide, bright, blue eyes. The man dipped his head in greeting to Diu, and then turned to Nicole. Creasing his body in a bow, he said, "Welcome. I, my friend, am Tibo."

Chapter Forty-One

Making a Bargain

One of the moving tables suddenly lurched sideways and flooded the floor with yellowed papers. Tibo snorted angrily and waved his little arms around, screaming, "Look what a *mess* you've made! What'll my guests think now?"

Under his furious gaze the table cracked in two. Its legs rolled out over the floor. In the meantime, the papers flew into the air and arranged themselves neatly on a nearby cabinet. Tibo nudged one of the table's legs with his toe, nodded in satisfaction, and walked away, scratching his long, crooked nose.

Mouth hanging, Nicole glanced sideways at Diu. "I warned you, didn't I?" he said and followed the old man through a newly formed path, leaving Nicole alone.

"Completely mental," she muttered.

Tibo's voice floated towards her over a pile of musty books. "Ah, let me see now, you must be hungry. Do you like fish? I just made a fresh batch of great white stew, and it's absolutely delicious, or so I've been told . . ."

He fell silent, and Nicole scrambled around a chair that leapt aside to get out of her way, eager to see what had happened. She skidded to a halt at the center of the room.

Tibo and Diu huddled together near the smoldering fireplace, speaking in low voices. The former was holding her Galactera in his veined and knotted hands, examining it with extreme interest. Nicole shot Diu an angry glance for showing the crazy man the watch. "Be careful with that, okay?"

"Hmm," Tibo replied, turning over the Galactera. He placed it on the floor, stood back, and raised his hands. From a corner of the room, a giant stack of thick volumes streamed through the air. They circled around him once and formed a neat pile in midair. Then he dropped his arms and the books crashed down heavily onto the pocket watch.

What're you doing?" Nicole shrieked hysterically, digging through the books.

"Nicole, get back!" Diu yelled and grabbed her wrist to pull her away.

She broke free from his grasp and snatched hold of the watch. Pulling back, she cried, "Tibo, you'll break it!"

The old man clapped in response. The watch jerked out of Nicole's hands, smashed itself against the wall, and fell with a clatter onto the smooth stone floor. Then a massive cabinet lifted off from the ground, glided over slowly in the air, and crashed down in a mass of splintered wood onto the pocket watch. Nicole screamed and tunneled through the rubble. Grabbing hold of the watch, she tucked it safely away in a pocket.

"Are you insane?" she snapped. "You could've ruined it! Thanks to you, it's probably all scratched up now anyway."

With a wave of his hands Tibo restored the cabinet and set it back in a corner. Chuckling, he said, "Look with your eyes, not with your mind."

"What do you—"

"I mean," he said, "that you should look before you accuse. Hold out the watch and tell me, how broken is it?"

Smoldering in silent anger, Nicole shoved her hand into her pocket and tore out the Galactera, dangling it by the chain so Tibo could see. In a snarling tone, she screamed, "It's completely . . . fine?"

Her mouth was hanging again. It was as if the watch had just been unwrapped from its original package. Turning it over, Nicole saw that it was completely unblemished and unscathed. "It's like it's never been touched," she whispered. "But how's that possible? It's been through so much. There's no way!"

"The mist of Tertius," Tibo said softly. Leaving her in confusion, he moved away to tend to a kettle that was hanging over the smoking fireplace and stirred with a wooden spoon.

Nicole glanced at Diu, who only shrugged. Curious, she followed Tibo. "What do you mean?"

"Do you know where the Galactera came from?"

"Diu gave it to me, but before then—"

"No, not who owned this device. I am speaking of its origins."

She had never thought about that before. "Where *did* it come from?"

"The Galactera," Tibo said, "is so called not because that is the name of the device but because that is the name of the race that crafted it. They were an ancient people, the creators of the spoken language that is now the common tongue of many races. Yet the Galacterans also invented fantastic creations with the use of a special brand of magic found only on the planet Tertius, a long-lost world now thought to be destroyed. The magic that allows you to teleport using that watch takes the form of fog, and that is why it is called the mist of Tertius."

Nicole remembered the place out of time and space, the in-between world Diu had teleported them to just before Serrona. "If Tertius did exist," she asked, "would there be a way to access it?"

Tibo threw her an odd glance. "Perhaps . . ."

"Why did you never tell me any of this when I asked?" Diu asked.

"Because you are too nosy. You did not need to know. And still don't."

"If he didn't, why do I—" Nicole started to ask, but just then an independently moving bowl slammed into her stomach and slopped soup all over her tunic.

"Sorry, my fault," Tibo apologized. He held out a spoon and a hand. Watching her shirt magically dry itself, Nicole took the proffered utensil and grabbed the bowl out of the air. She tasted the soup on the tip of her finger and found it to her liking. After draining half of it in several enormous spoonfuls, she asked, "What's it made of?"

Tibo sighed in exasperation. "I *told* you, it's called great white stew. Guess."

The soup didn't taste as great after that, and Nicole could have sworn she saw a couple sharp teeth swimming around in the bowl.

Once they had finished eating, Tibo sent the bowls off

to clean themselves and found a comfortable spot in front of the fireplace where he sat quite still, deeply immersed in an ancient text. Nicole exchanged a quick glance with Diu. He nodded, indicating that it was time.

"Um . . . Tibo, sir?" she mumbled, unsure of how to begin.

The book angrily slammed shut. Dust spiraled into the air. Tibo stood quickly, looking her over. "You've come for the crystal, haven't you, Nicole Sky?" he said, so sharply that it sounded like an accusation.

Diu tried to come to the rescue. "Tibo, I know you warned us, but—"

"Warned you!" he cried, storming across the room. "Ha!" Tables toppled before him, spilling precious gems and books. "I practically spent my days and nights trying to convince you that the Terranova would lead to nothing but galactic chaos, but you all chose to ignore me, so now you're only reaping your just deserts!"

"Tibo, please," Nicole begged. She ducked as a heavy wooden crate flew over her head and smashed into the wall.

"It's too late for that! Your friend should have listened before. There's nothing to be done now."

"If you just tell us where the earth crystal is, we'll be able to stop the Omenra!"

"What a fine chance you have, seeing as how Malkior has the fire crystal. In case you didn't know, you need *all* of them."

Nicole caught her breath, shocked that Tibo already knew. "How—"

"Because," he explained, guessing at her unfinished question, "after I had a terrible vision about the Terranova's future, I sought out the crystals and cast spells upon each one. I ensured my knowledge of each crystal's whereabouts so I could track them down if there was ever need. I *knew* that one day you, Diu, would find me and beg for forgiveness. I *knew* that you'd need those crystals some day! And after Malkior stormed into my hut with half his army at his back and demanded I tell him where to find the fire crystal, I watched out for it and for the earth crystal just to satisfy my curiosity of how this war would end!"

Nicole felt her heart thunder with frustration. "Why didn't you just take the crystals when you found them?"

"Because, Nicole Sky, this is a quest that *you* must undertake."

"I-I . . ." she stammered. Then she broke into tears. "Tibo, *please* tell me where I can find the last crystal! If not to help *us*, at least think about yourself! If the earth goes, so do you!"

"I'll move to another planet."

"You'll be the only human left in the entire universe!"

"Other humans don't care much for me anyway."

"I'll die, and according to your prophecy, without me the galaxy is finished."

"I'll take you with me when I leave Earth."

"No!" she cried, so loudly that he winced.

"No?" he repeated.

"If my planet, my family, my friends—if everything I know and love dies, then I die too!"

It didn't seem that Tibo had expected that. Nibbling on

a fingernail, he muttered, "I should have figured you would want to be brave like that. Just know, it's your sacrifice."

"I *know* that you won't stand for the Omenra takeover of the galaxy. You *won't* let me die!" Nicole retorted. At least, she hoped not.

But Tibo seemed willing to compromise. His small body wiggled towards her, the feet moving in a funny dance-like motion. "I have a deal to make with you, Nicole Sky," he said.

"I'm listening."

"You don't believe that the prophecy is true, do you?"

"I think some bits are true."

"The part where only you can mend the galaxy?"

"Well, no, but only because that's completely insane! I'm just some random person who happened to find the Galactera."

"You think that's just luck?"

"What else could it be?"

"Fate, Nicole Sky. Destiny. But here is my bargain. I will tell you where the earth crystal is and even help you get back the fire crystal, but in exchange you must make an unbreakable vow."

"I'll do anything."

"You must vow to this: No matter what the danger, no matter if hope is lost, you must fulfill your destiny, no matter what the cost."

"Done," Nicole said.

Muttering an incantation under his breath, Tibo held out his hand. "If you're certain, then shake. But remember, you will be unable to break this vow."

"Sure," she assured him, ignoring Diu's wild gestures and pleading look. Her hand lifted slowly as if in a trance, and Tibo snatched her wrist.

The next thing Nicole knew she was on her knees, screaming, right hand stained with her own blood.

Chapter Forty-Two

Kyria Again

The dark liquid welled on Nicole's fingertips and pooled in a small puddle on the floor. The deep gash on her palm pulsed with every heartbeat. Her eyes glided slowly to stare at Tibo, who was just stowing a dagger back under his colorful robes.

Diu's paw twitched toward the Mar.

"Wait," Nicole muttered weakly, swinging out an arm to stop him. "Why did you do that?" She wanted to give him a chance to explain.

"He has changed sides!" Diu snarled fiercely, shoving past her. "I've been afraid of just this for years!"

"No," Tibo assured him as a cabinet door creaked open and spat out a tiny vial, which soared across the room. He snatched it from the air and filled roughly half of it with blood from the puddle. "I am still very much neutral," he continued. "But I prefer to be cautious."

Nicole plastered her lips to the wound and sucked, watching while Tibo whispered some strange words and corked the little bottle. "What's that for?" she asked.

"You pledged to an unbreakable vow," he mumbled. "For such a vow I must take a bloodseal. It is a way for me to assure that you will not break your word."

"So what happens if I *do* break it?"

Tibo smirked. "Believe me, Nicole Sky. You won't."

The vial vanished back inside the tall wooden cabinet in the corner. Then Tibo reached for Nicole's hand. She jerked back, but he said, "I mean only to heal your wound."

As his stubby fingers groped along her palm, Nicole realized that suddenly the old man's voice and tone was completely changed. He had been silly, foolish, and half-crazed. Tibo was anything but that now. This terrible split in personality was unnerving, as was the prod of fingers against her wound. Nicole sighed in relief when Tibo finally pulled his hands away. "I'll just fix that now, no problem," he said distractedly, reaching into his robes.

She pulled back instinctively, fearing he would pull another knife on her. But what the old man drew from the robe's colorful folds was something quite extraordinary. He held it out, and his bright blue eyes sparkled with amusement.

"Phoenix feather," he explained.

Feeling the breath catch in her chest, Nicole reached out and stroked the long feather. Warmth seeped into her fingers, and the throbbing pain in her hand ebbed away. The red-gold plume glowed with a soft light. It seemed to sway in a non-existent wind. Tibo gently turned Nicole's hand so her palm was facing up and stroked the feather over her wound. Where it touched skin, the cut healed close as if nothing had ever happened.

Nicole stared in awe at her unscarred hand. "H-how'd you do that?"

"Phoenixes," he said, "have extraordinary gifts, and a feather combined with just the right spell has incredible healing powers. Diu knows—it has saved his life in battle before."

"True," Diu muttered almost reluctantly.

"Maybe one day," Tibo added, storing the feather back into his robes, "it may save you as well, Earth child."

The word Earth stirred up her purpose again. "I made that vow," Nicole said, "to find out where the last crystal was. We're running out of time, so can I know now?"

"Of course. Here is final stanza:

"Journey far along the coastline
To where mountains meet the sea
The words of magic will guide you
To the final, earthen key"

Nicole pondered the lyrics and repeated them to herself. "The words of magic . . ." Suddenly, she was hit with realization. "I was *meant* to come to you!"

Tibo's lips creased in a small smile. "Fate has strange ways, Nicole Sky. So does magic. Now, Diu," he said, turning away from her, "leave her here with me for a minute. Wait outside the hut." Noticing him tense, Tibo added, "I wish to ask her a question. No more daggers and vials."

Diu slanted his head away. "All right," he said. "But be quick." The old man chuckled as Diu walked cautiously to the door, opened it, and, after a pause, went out.

"Malkior was never vigilant enough," Tibo said. "Your friend, far too much. Sadly, about the wrong things."

Nicole waited, but he said nothing else. "You wanted to ask me something?" she reminded gently.

"Ah, yes. That I did. Where is your friend Lily?"

"My friend—wait, how do you know about her?"

"My question first."

"She's . . . dead. She sacrificed her life to save mine."

Tibo looked puzzled. "Odd. I thought she would be with you the whole way."

"It's your turn to answer my question."

"Certainly. I'm actually glad you asked. It leads to my second question. Whenever I see a vision of you, Nicole Sky, the child who shall save our galaxy—I always see you with Lily. I never spoke of it to anyone for it seems inconsequential, but I wanted you to know. It feels right for you to know. But I have never been able to derive meaning from it, and I am curious—what do you think of it?"

Nicole's eyes moistened. "It means that Lily should still be with me, and if hadn't been for Malkior, she would be! I hate him for it! I hate him!"

Tibo nodded, thinking. "One final thing, Nicole—some advice. You may not appreciate it now, but one day, you shall understand. There is an essential element of evil as well as good in every creature. It is the core of balance and harmony. Thus, you can only truly know someone if you have known them as an enemy and as a friend. Because then you will know the two halves of their being. And then you will know them whole."

"Come," he said at last and gestured towards the door.

Chapter Forty-Two

Logging the strange words away for later, Nicole followed. The door leapt open before them, startling a slightly jittery Diu. At first, Nicole squinted against the bright light of day, but once she was able to see properly, her heart spiked up into her throat. The sun was directly overhead; their precious time was trickling away.

"We'll never make it in time," she whispered to the sky.

"On foot, no," Tibo agreed.

"The JET might help," Diu said.

The old man shook his head. "The Glider cannot help now."

"But there's no faster way!" Nicole cried.

"What if the wind takes you?"

Before she could reply, Tibo jabbed his fingers into his mouth and gave a whistle so high-pitched that the very cliffs resounded with the shrill blast. Then silence fell, broken only by the lapping of ocean waves. They stood huddled together on the beach, watching. Waiting.

"What're we—" Nicole started to say, but a distant sound cut her off.

Mystical music spread across the sky. The very air seemed to absorb warmth. A large, bird-like creature streaked out from atop the cliffs, piping music and beating its beautiful wings, a shadow against the sun. Nicole watched in awe as it swooped in a majestic dive, wings clasped to its body, and landed lightly on Tibo's shoulder, still singing, shining with red-gold light. He stroked the bird's back lovingly.

"Kyria, my dear friend."

The creature's head shot up. Its gaze passed over Diu but

stopped on Nicole. The dark orbs seemed to pierce into her very soul.

She gasped. "I-I remember you! You were the first creature I met after I teleported from Earth!"

"Kyria has followed you most of the way," Tibo explained. "I myself sent her to watch you. Didn't you notice? She led you to the pocket watch, showed you the way to safety during the storm on Lunara, helped Diu track you, led you to Arli—Kyria was always watching and always ready to lend a guiding wing."

Cocking her head, the phoenix examined Nicole curiously. Then she fluttered from Tibo's shoulder and came to rest on Nicole's, her weight warm and comforting. Nicole pulled her arm up to stroke Kyria's feathers. The phoenix didn't pull away.

"Strange," Tibo murmured. "She has never accepted any touch but mine."

"She's beautiful," Nicole whispered.

"But can she help us get to the crystal in time?" Diu interrupted.

"My old friend," Tibo said, "you seem to be forgetting that phoenixes, much like me, have their own brand of magic. Only the wind itself can reach the earth crystal in time, but I alone cannot harness its power. However, my dear Kyria may have the magic to channel the wind into a useful form." Stretching out his hand, he said, "Come, my firelight. You know what to do."

Nicole was sad to see the phoenix leave her shoulder, not only because she missed her warmth but also because she'd briefly remembered the joy and comfort of Lily's weight. Blinking back the dampness in her eyes, Nicole watched Kyria settle in a flutter on Tibo's arm and peck the old man's cheek affectionately. Then the phoenix bowed her scarlet head and piped a mystical, lilting tune. Pressing the tips of his stubby fingers together as if in prayer, Tibo proceeded to recite a strange incantation. His voice rose and fell with Kyria's song.

As they recited their spell, the air churned in a crazed whirlwind, blasting sand and sea spray skyward. Their voices rose higher and the wind roared with them, thrashing like a beast in transformation. As their song reached a peak, the wind screeched in protest, pounding with hurricane force. Nicole dug her heels into the ground, squinting against flying sand, kneeling and clutching the ground to avoid being flung away. Yet despite her efforts, her knees scratched backwards across the sand and she was flung onto her back. Then Kyria shrieked a final note, one so powerful that Nicole's eardrums echoed the sound long after the phoenix's voice died away.

Nicole groaned to a sitting position. She opened her eyelids an infinitesimal amount and cried out in awe. Looming before her, his mane whipping wildly in nonexistent gusts, was a mighty stallion. He snorted and pawed the ground, head held high, and every shifting line of him was sleek with wildness. His translucent body swayed in and out of existence, melting into the sand and air and sea. The stallion cantered forward, his body reflecting the sun's brilliance, and reared against the sky, whistling so the very cliffs shook with his cry.

Tibo stepped forward and placed his wrinkled hand on the stallion's flank. "Nicole Sky, for you the elements themselves conspire. Let the stallion of the wind and my Kyria show you the way. Come, climb on, and don't be afraid."

She threw a glance at Diu, and when he dipped his head in approval, she stood and petted the stallion's nose. It felt strange to the touch, almost like warm liquid. He snorted and bowed his head, sniffed her, and nickered softly. Still disbelieving, terrified yet awed, Nicole glided like a wraith around to the horse's side. Diu helped her up, and she sank down slowly onto the stallion's shimmering body, feeling it shift lightly beneath her. She grabbed hold of his mane, a heavy liquid substance hovering on the edge of reality, and steadied herself for the ride.

Kyria let out a piercing screech. Her wings clipped the air as she soared off along the coast. The stallion sent out an air-splitting whistle and leapt after her, hooves flying over the ground. Tibo cried out something out after them, but his words were lost in the roaring wind.

The cliffs rushed past in a blur, shining in the sunlight, and the brilliant sparkle of the ocean forced Nicole to squint. The stallion's body swayed beneath her like a shadow, not galloping but soaring over the sand. She gripped his sides tightly with her knees and held on to his mane for dear life, not understanding and not caring, knowing only that she was riding the wild wind itself. And far ahead Kyria led the way, buoyed up by the air currents the stallion pushed before him.

As they pulsed across the coastline, Nicole noticed the cliffs mount steadily skyward till they towered like giants. In the far distance, the rocky wall angled to cut across their path. From there a range of mountains, merely a vague outline from here, rippled away into the distance as far as she could see. It was there they headed. Slightly in awe, Nicole wondered where on Earth they could be.

Suddenly, something startled the phoenix. Kyria splintered the air with her cries, her wing beat throbbing. She wheeled away over the cliffs, but the stallion didn't waver. Nicole twisted her head back, wondering what had happened.

The relative silence was rent by a thundering roar. The very cliffs clattered, rumbling with the echo of thunder against stone. Terrified, Nicole craned her neck to search for the source of the sound. A flash of shining scarlet caught her eyes as Kyria dove from the cliffs, sweeping down to soar alongside the stallion. The phoenix screeched, and he broke into a full-out gallop with hurricane-force winds. Another roar wrenched Nicole's gaze skyward, and only then did she understand.

Spiraling down from the cliffs, black scales and dagger-like white fangs glinting in the fierce sunlight, was the dragon she recognized as Arli's mother. Strapped tightly around her neck was a red collar, embedded into which was a tiny, flaming gem. Clinging tightly to the collar, straddled in the hollow of the dragon's neck, eyes flaming with malicious anger and rage, was none other than the creature Nicole despised most.

Malkior.

Chapter Forty-Three

Fiery Pursuit

"**R**un!" Nicole yelled needlessly. The stallion blasted away with all possible speed, challenging the limits of the wind itself. The black dragon swooped low over the ocean, twisting sideways to snap at the horse's legs. Nicole barely managed to hold on as the stallion dodged the dragon's fangs with a powerful leap into the air, ducking again when the dragon barrel-rolled sideways, slashing at the air with her mighty wings. He galloped towards the cover of the cliffs, but the dragon beat him there and smashed her whip-like tail into the rocks.

Nicole screamed as rubble spun down in a mass of dust, but then warmth engulfed her as Kyria swept overhead, baring sharp talons and slashing into the dragon's neck. Roaring in pain, the mother shook off the phoenix but relented, gliding out towards the sea. Snarling in rage, Malkior drew his Sigrá, cocked back the trigger, and aimed for the bird.

"Kyria!" Nicole cried.

The phoenix evaded the gunshot and spiraled out of range. She swung back in an arch and jabbed the dragon's head with her sharp beak. In the meantime, the wind stallion darted ahead, cutting away from the cliff. From the corner of her eye, Nicole saw Malkior turn the handgun away from Kyria, aim straight at her—

The blast sizzled centimeters over her head, singing her hair. Screaming, she ducked low, feeling the rhythm of the horse's sleek body hammer through her hands. Behind her, Malkior cried out with wrath.

"Give it up, girl! *It's over!*"

"Not yet!" she yelled, her voice a roar against the wind.

Narrowly missing another snap of glittering fangs, the stallion leapt seaward, hooves pounding the frothing surf. The dragon spiraled over them towards the cliffs and lashed out her tail, aiming to strike the horse off his feet. But the wind stallion stayed true to his path, sprinting and darting, leaping and soaring, escaping each fresh attempt. Nicole could see that the dragon was tiring, forced to fly at odds with the wind, but Malkior pushed her onwards, too close to give up now.

Knowing the pain the mother must feel, Nicole desperately cried, "Malkior, she can't keep going! If you don't stop, you'll kill her!"

"Fly faster, you beast," Malkior shrieked to the dragon, "and kill *her!*"

The stallion whistled shrilly, and Nicole whipped her head around, staring in awe at the sheer wall of rock rearing straight ahead. She spurred the horse and he galloped forth, his hooves suddenly touching down and clattering against the ground as sand gave way to craggy rock. Kyria came up beside them, her scarlet wings fiery streaks against the cliffs. Squinting, Nicole picked out a roughly hewn passage carved into the stone.

A massive wave of heat suddenly swelled behind them. The stallion bounced sideways like a spring, barely dodging a fireball. A second such blast missed them as well, but the third was perfectly centered; they were unable to escape in time. The force of impact flung the stallion sideways and smashed him into the cliff. Nicole's heart thundered as she scrambled to hang on but couldn't. She skidded heavily across the sand before jerking to a halt face-down, mouth filled with grit.

A nuzzle on the shoulder roused her. The stallion nickered encouragingly and stamped the ground. Kyria landed on Nicole's head and crooned softly. They wanted her to stand, to go on. Thinking of Lily, Nicole forced herself up. Tears burst into her eyes as lightning pain ripped through her arms and legs from fresh, bleeding cuts. She broke into a run alongside the trotting stallion till she gained enough momentum to leap onto his back. Then they were off again, this time into greater danger.

The dragon had gained distance and now flashed past them. She twisted her body around to face them. Her jaws sprang open, and a red glow welled up behind the teeth. Nicole screamed, ducking down, and the stallion lurched forward to cut a path beneath the dragon, just barely avoiding the blast. But there was another thing they could not evade.

All of a sudden, something heavy hit Nicole from behind, slamming her forward against the stallion's neck. He shied fearfully and reared to the sky. Nicole would have fallen except for the fact that she was pinned to the horse's back by none other than Malkior. She guessed he must have, in a feat of sheer desperation, leapt from dragon to stallion, determined to fight her to the end.

Screaming, Nicole wrenched the stallion's mane. The horse bucked, but Malkior wouldn't let go. Cleverly, he snatched hold around Nicole's waist. Now the only way to get rid of him was for her to jump off as well.

Unfortunately, Malkior hadn't counted on one thing: an enraged dragon mother's vengeance.

Finally free and wanting nothing more than Malkior's blood, the dragon spat another fireball towards them. It missed but smashed into the cliffs, just as the stallion darted into the cover of the passage in the rocks. A terrifying crack echoed through the tunnel.

Nicole snapped her head up as cracks snaked along the length of the ceiling. Suddenly, it splintered. A large chuck of rock crashed to the ground ahead of them, and the horse only barely managed to leap out of harm's way. His body glowed to provide light for the pitch-darkness of the tunnel, and the massive boulder flashed silver as they passed it.

"Turn the horse around!" Malkior yelled in her ear. "Turn him around!"

"No!"

"This tunnel is about to collapse, and we'll die if you don't!"

"But the crystal—"

"Isn't worth my life!"

"And Earth?"

"Earth?" he spat. "Earth is just a speck of dust in a giant galaxy."

"It's *my* speck," Nicole countered fiercely. "And I'll fight for it to the death!"

Malkior's eyes flashed red. "I'll see to it you keep that promise!"

Rocks crashed down everywhere around them, blocking their path. The stallion managed to pick his way around them and, when all else failed, forced a trail with ferocious gusts of wind. Malkior still clutched Nicole's shoulder but not as tightly as before, and more than once did the thought of knocking him off cross her mind. All it would take was one jerk in the wrong direction, just one, but she couldn't bring herself to commit cold-blooded murder, not even when Lily's laughing face flashed in her mind. Nicole knew she was being crazy, that the evil Omenra would never do the same for her . . .

Suddenly the horse trumpeted in terror. She wrenched her thoughts to the present, jerking his mane to force him to dodge right around some falling rocks. But as the ceiling buckled and parts of it collapsed behind them, she knew their time was running out.

Just then a splinter of light pierced through the inky darkness. The stallion sprinted faster than ever, scrambling desperately for a hold on the crumbling rock. Nicole clutched his watery mane so tightly that her knuckles turned white, praying against all odds that they'd make it. The end of the tunnel held the promise of safety, of shelter, but getting there was half the reward, and that much she wasn't sure they could do. The exit was nearly blocked with enormous boulders that even the strongest gust wouldn't budge, and they couldn't squeeze through the remaining crack.

Chapter Forty-Three

She felt the liquid mane dissolve into wind as the stallion transformed into a fierce gale. He shattered the boulders into tiny pebbles that clattered to the ground, allowing her and Malkior to burst through, pursued by a screen of dust and rocks from the devastated passage. Rolling over in the dirt, she landed on her back, moaning as bleeding scrapes pulsed over her body. But her groan broke into a full-fledged scream a moment later as a giant boulder, a rock the stallion had missed, tumbled from the passage. It careened over the ground straight towards her. Nicole tried to move, but her body was too battered to comply. After all she'd been through, after all she'd done, she realized that the end had finally, truly come, and nothing lay between her and death.

Chapter Forty-Four

The Second Prophecy

Thrusting her hands out instinctively, Nicole rolled her eyes away, waiting for the boulder to strike. Suddenly she was knocked sideways. She crashed hard onto her stomach. The ground beside her shook as the boulder pounded over it, but incredibly, impossibly, she was left untouched. Not daring to believe her luck, Nicole cracked open an eyelid and saw the rock tumble till it struck the opposite wall. Malkior sat beside her, breathing hard.

"Y-you saved my life," she summed up, mouth gaping.

His face twisted into a look of disgust as he scrambled to his feet. "Not yours," he snapped as if she had just shot him a dirty insult. "I was getting out of the way myself and accidently pushed you."

In spite of the dire nature of the situation, a smile tugged at her face. "Guess there's some good in you after all."

"I should have rolled the other way," he muttered.

"I guess I owe you one."

"I did *nothing* for you."

"You did."

"Did not!"

"Did!"

Silence.

"Hello? Are you paying attention?"

Malkior wasn't looking at her anymore. He was mesmerized by a point somewhere behind her. Puzzled, Nicole turned around. Her hands darted to her mouth when she saw what he had been staring at.

Spiraling up from the center of the floor was a small, flat pedestal. Simply lying on top of the platform, looking very ordinary indeed, was a rough chuck of green rock. It glowed with pale light, illuminating the cave. Malkior's face split in a grin, but Nicole scrambled up faster, skidded in front of him, and reached out for the last crystal.

She was flung back by an invisible barrier and smashed hard onto the rocky floor for the second time in as many minutes. Malkior chuckled and extended his claws for the crystal, only to be thrust backwards by the same shield. Brushing off her slightly scraped palms, Nicole stood shakily and moved forward in a kind of slow dance, holding out her hands till the fingers touched a smooth, curving surface. From there, she found that she could go no closer than three feet away from the pedestal. Nicole smacked the invisible wall with her fists and was shoved back by the protective force.

Malkior was having no better luck. He was doing all he could to break the barricade, but the wall was holding up well. Growling with impatience, he blasted a few Sigrá shots at the shield, but they only ricocheted. One nearly grazed Nicole.

"Hey, watch it!" she cried, ducking.

Malkior began to circle the invisible shield, searching for a clue on how to deactivate it. Nicole backed up too, frustrated. So close . . . *so close!* Furious, she started to wander, hand sliding over the sphere, trying to collect her thoughts. She didn't notice when she came up beside Malkior, accidently brushing her hand against his.

The force-field suddenly burst into light, surface veined with green tendrils. Nicole stumbled fearfully as emerald liquid poured like a waterfall from the pedestal, flooding the floor with shimmering, warm water. The cavern walls seemed to absorb the light and echo back the illumination.

Strangely, Nicole was not afraid. She cupped the water that rose to her knees in her hands and let it trickle through her fingers. Malkior too seemed mesmerized, tracing his claws along the shining surface.

Soft, lilting voices seemed to emanate from the rocky walls. At first, the words were blurred, but then individual words broke through the slurred song. The chorus was composed of a great multitude of languages, so many that perhaps every language in the galaxy was joining in song. In their mystic, singsong tone, the voices repeated a single stanza over and over again that Nicole's translator slowly hissed out:

> "Their voices shall unite as one
> Pure of spirit, pure of heart
> When strings of wrath are all undone
> The ring will return to the start."

From across the emerald pool, Malkior's head shot up. Nicole returned his gaze. For the first time she saw that his eyes were not black or burning red, as she had always thought, but a soft green.

"I think," Nicole said, "the song means that we can't do this alone."

After a second of hesitation, Malkior dipped his head. "Together, then."

They sloshed towards the pedestal, half walking and half swimming. This time when they placed their hands on the shield, the shining sphere broke apart into glistening sparkles that filled the air with enchanting light. Still enthralled by the peaceful feel of the cavern, they touched the crystal simultaneously, fingers meeting claws.

The spell instantly shattered. The liquid seeped into the ground and the voices ebbed away, plunging the cave back into semi-darkness. And almost as if a switch had been turned on, Nicole felt fury pulse through her body. She jerked at the crystal, trying to snatch it from Malkior.

"Le'go!" she shrieked.

But he was equally determined. Malkior twisted Nicole's wrists and wrenched the crystal sideways with all possible strength. Barely managing to hold on, she launched herself at him, hoping to catch him off guard. But he was prepared and flung her backward, smashing her into a wall. Nicole slid down with a groan, feeling blood run over her lips. Breathing hard, she stumbled to her feet, looking up just in time to see Malkior slip back into the crumbled passage, crystal in claws.

She barreled after him. Malkior scrambled into a narrow

fissure between a large pile of rocks. Nicole was quick to follow, crawling deftly through the tiny opening. Struggling to make out blurry images in the dark, she squeezed out on the other side in time to see Malkior round a bend in the passage. Sprinting down the tunnel, she leapt squarely onto his back; they crashed sideways into a wall. He raked his claws down her arm, and she shrieked as blood welled up in the deep gashes. Malkior went for her face but Nicole spun aside, kicking out with all her strength. Her foot caught him in the stomach. He skidded backwards, groaning, and dropped the crystal. It clattered loudly to the ground, rolling to Nicole's feet. Snatching it up, she pulled out the Galactera, fumbling for the right button.

The chain tightened around her neck as Malkior seized the watch from her hands. Twisting her head sharply, she managed to wrench the watch free from his grasp and grab hold of it. Desperately clutching the crystal, Nicole's mind exploded with images of Tibo, his hut, and the peaceful beach as she clicked the tiny button, only vaguely feeling claws grab hold of her wrist.

Stinging saltwater burned Nicole's eyes as she landed head-first in waist-high water. Suddenly, her sight blurred as she was fully submerged. She flailed for air but couldn't free herself from the strong arms keeping her underwater. Water flooded her mouth, and Nicole couldn't see, couldn't move . . .

Then all of a sudden she was free, leaping up and gasping for air. Whirling sideways, she saw Malkior wrestling with Diu, frothing water flying around them. She ran to help, but before she even got close Malkior was raised up in the air by an invisible force and flung away towards the beach. He tumbled over in the sand and lay still.

Tibo strode into the water, his fingers directed at Malkior's limp form. Diu sloshed over to Nicole, making sure she was unharmed.

Cringing as water stung her various wounds, she said, "Today's just a day for life-saving, I guess."

He gave her a strange look, but she was already making her way over to Tibo, who was still observing Malkior's body cautiously, stiff fingers trembling. The old man noticed her approach and waited before setting off for shore, his small stature forcing him to half swim through the water. But before they got very far, a distant rumble of thunder ripped through the air.

The black dragon soared over the cliff and landed heavily on the sand next to Malkior. He rolled onto his stomach and crawled to his knees, grabbing on to one of the dragon's massive wings for support. Pouncing to his feet, he cried out, "It's *over*, Nicole Sky. You may have the earth crystal, but you must have *all* the elements to save your Earth. And you will *never* get the fire crystal! It's hidden in a place far too dangerous for anyone to try to take it back!"

Though the crystal felt warm in Nicole's hands, her blood flowed like ice-cold sludge through her veins. In spite of all she'd done, he was right. Without the fire crystal, it was all futile, all pointless. But one thing didn't make sense. The dragon mother had tried to kill Malkior. Why, then, would she return to him?

Malkior broke into sneering laughter just as the dragon

blasted an earsplitting roar. Nicole looked up as just as the mother bowed her head, nudging the red collar around her neck. Sparkling sunlight illuminated the tiny gem set into its center. The stone glinted with fiery light.

A place far too dangerous . . .

Nicole suddenly understood. She screamed aloud, pointing desperately. "It's the dragon's gem! Diu, Tibo—the gem!"

But it was too late. With Malkior on her back the dragon reared high, spitting fire. Cackling in triumph, Malkior spurred her to fly, and she beat her wings hard against the air, ready to soar away.

Nicole stumbled forward, tears streaming down her face, knowing that it was over. Finished.

Suddenly, a magical sound broke through the chaos. Piping her enchanted song, Kyria streaked through the air, flaming light shining from her wings. She swept down in a flurry of fire, talons bared, and snatched the gem from its clasp. Malkior screamed and the dragon roared, but Kyria was already soaring seaward. She dropped the crystal from her claws, and it fell into Nicole's outstretched hands.

As the phoenix settled lightly on Tibo's shoulder, he stepped forward. "Go now, Malkior," he ordered. Bright blue sparks flashed from his fingertips. "Go while I am giving you the chance."

Feeling his aura of power, the dragon retreated. Malkior screamed in fury but snapped at her to fly. In spite of all his power, all his influence, and all his strength, Tibo's magic was greater; even Malkior feared him. Still, as the black dragon soared high into the sky, he cried out, "You still haven't won yet, Sky! You have won the battle, but I'll triumph in the war for Earth and the galaxy!"

She barely heard his words. Her fingers felt across two bulges in her pockets: the two crystals. Diu stood across from her, the other crystals and the disk from the map strapped to his belt. He was beaming, and Nicole sprang to hug him, crying in joy. "We did it!" she whooped. "We got them all!"

"Then only one thing remains, Nicole Sky," Tibo said. "The Terranova waits at the heart of Earth. Tomorrow is your final day. Rest in my hut overnight, and rise with the morning sun."

"Thank you," she said, tears blinding her, "for all you've done."

Nicole let go of Diu and stepped back. It was nearing evening, and they waited together in the water long enough to watch a brilliant sunset paint the ocean. The waves sparkled, tinged with crimson and orange light. As they sloshed to shore at last and the sun vanished beyond the cliffs, Nicole watched the sky melt into shades of darkness. With all four crystals in her possession and the Omenra powerless to stop her, she knew that all was well.

Or so she hoped.

Arli's Return

The following morning found Nicole sprawled before the smoking fireplace on a colorful, thick, and surprisingly comfortable rug. Twisting onto her back, she rubbed her eyes and yawned, stretching her mouth wide. Scratching her neck and groaning, she heaved her body into a sitting position and glanced groggily around, blinking to adjust to the light. Tibo and Diu were already awake and sitting around a tiny, triangular table that the old man must have summoned from under some pile of trinkets. Both were busy sipping away at fresh bowls of soup.

"New recipe," Tibo announced as she joined them.

Nicole plopped down on a three-legged stool and glared at the murky red soup. "What's it called?"

"Phoenix stew!" he said excitedly, swallowing another mouthful.

Nicole tasted a surge of nausea. Disgust must have shown on her face.

"Don't worry," Diu explained. "This is not actually made from a phoenix. We caught some little red fish this morning, and called it 'phoenix stew' because the soup is red like fire."

"Then where's Kyria?" Nicole snapped, noticing that the firebird was nowhere in sight.

Tibo sipped another spoonful thoughtfully. "Kyria," he said slowly, "is my dear friend and ally, but she has a wild spirit and loves to fly free. She is always near when I need her, but I would never force her to stay. Phoenixes are only truly powerful when they are happy, perhaps one of the few reasons that tame phoenixes are nearly unheard of. A phoenix must choose to help you, because unlike all other creatures, forcing them into submission is equivalent to death."

Curiosity satisfied and nausea abated, Nicole swallowed several spoonfuls and was surprised at how delicious the soup tasted. She lifted and tilted the bowl, guzzling the contents in several large gulps.

All of a sudden, a cabinet in the corner started to clatter. Nicole spat soup all over the table and jumped back, screaming and pointing. Tibo and Diu turned their heads, staring at the jittery cabinet.

"Ah," Tibo said calmly. "Visitors."

The cabinet doors burst open, and a brown blur fell out onto the floor, groaning. "I have *got* to fix that thing one of these days!" it said.

Nicole almost squealed in joy when she recognized the squeaky voice. "Sorill!" she cried.

"Me," he grumbled, glaring darkly at the cabinet. "That thing's driving me crazy! I finally managed to set up a small teleporter from the palace, but I just can't manage to sort out the kinks. I'm starting to get a feeling that thing's intent on killing me. Anyway," he continued, nodding towards the cabinet, "I can't stay long, but I have someone here who really wants to see you."

Nicole peered inside but only just managed to jerk her head back in time to avoid being trampled under Arli's excited feet.

"Arli!"

The dracling bowled her over, licked every bit of Nicole's face she could reach, and joyously flared her wings. *Nicole! Is you!*

I've missed you so much! Nicole clasped Arli's neck in her arms, squeezing the hatchling in a hug.

"That was a close call," Sorill said, grinning at the heartwarming reunion. "You need to be careful. This burn was healable, but next time you might not have such luck. Oh, Diu," he added, "I need to talk to you."

They congregated in a corner, but Nicole didn't pay much attention. She was too busy rejoicing in Arli's incredible survival. It was only as Sorill stepped towards the cabinet that she called to him once more.

"Thank you, Sorill, for bringing Arli back," Nicole said, standing and wrapping him in an embrace.

His scales flushed scarlet. "I'm glad I could help," he said humbly.

"I owe you one," she said softly as Sorill stepped towards the cabinet.

"Don't worry, you'll get a chance to pay up," he joked. But understanding the sincerity of her words, added, "Hey, it's okay. My greatest reward is seeing you two together again."

He was about to close the cabinet doors when Nicole's hand shot forward and clasped his own. "Sorill?"

"Yes?"

"Um," she said slowly. "Could you . . . uh . . . do me a little favor, please?"

"Yes, naturally."

It was bound to be difficult anyway, but the lump welled in her throat wasn't helping. "If you're ever near Li-Lily's hillside, could you leave some f-flowers for her? I-I want her to know that I-I'll never forget all she's done for me. She was one of my best friends."

"Of course," he said gently. "Any kind in particular?"

Thinking back, she remembered the first time she met Lily. "If you're ever on Lunara," she said softly, "bring back a native plant. It'll almost be like she's home again. The closest thing to it, anyway."

"I'll do my best."

"I promise I'll make it up to you some day."

"There is no greater reward," he repeated, hopping behind the wooden doors.

As the cabinet rattled, Arli rubbed against Nicole's leg. Her very presence was a great comfort. Diu came up beside Nicole, watching her with a strange curiosity. All three turned around as Tibo approached, his shiny blue eyes intent on the little dracling, but his words meant for them all.

"Nicole, Diu, and"—he bowed—"young Arli. You have little time left to stop the Terranova. We may have all four crystals, but if you think that Malkior will not fight back, then be warned. He is a force to be reckoned with."

"Don't worry. I have learned that lesson well," Diu said.

"Actually," Nicole said reluctantly, "there's something about him I think you all should know."

As she relayed their adventure in the cavern, Tibo's eyes steadily widened. When she reached the part about the voices, he stopped her.

"So there is a . . . second prophecy?"

"It was just a way to get the earth crystal."

"I think it is more than that. Repeat it for me."

"All right. It went like this:

"**Their voices shall unite as one**
Pure of spirit, pure of heart
When strings of wrath are all undone
The ring will return to the start."

"In any case," Nicole added. "I doubt it refers to me."

Tibo whirled on her, eyes blazing electric-blue. "Do you not realize, Nicole Sky, that *both* the prophecies are meant for you alone?"

"Listen, I still don't see utter proof of that."

"You want proof? Think about this: is there not rhyme to the prophecies as spoken in English? Is there not rhythm? Those words, Earth child, were selected specifically for you."

She gasped, amazed how such a simple fact had never crossed her mind. "That *is* true, I guess."

"There is one further measure of proof. Do you know what the words 'incident arises from circumstance' mean?"

Nicole shook her head.

"That saying means things happen solely based on how one reacts in a particular situation. Have you noticed how perfectly the Galactera has been teleporting you all this time? On Azimar, the watch took you straight to Teradru Valley where the map lay. On Espia, it very conveniently left you by Rayonk's taxi so he could take you to Coralian City. On Serrona, you neatly appeared close enough to the Omenra base so as to shape your argument with Diu and ensure his later capture. And why, Nicole Sky, do you think it happened that way? Mere coincidence?"

Her eyes grew large. "So that things would happen in the right way."

"Precisely. And as for the second prophecy, I will consider it and let you know what I think."

"What I still don't understand," Diu said, his voice icy, "is why Malkior would save her. She's the reason he wanted to destroy Earth to begin with."

Tibo rubbed his chin thoughtfully. "Unite as one," he whispered.

Nicole shrugged. "Given I'm the only one who can stop him, I personally can't see any motive for why he'd want anything except my death," she admitted. "But what I do know is that we can't waste time trying to figure it out. It's now or never."

"Let me just see the fire crystal so I can translate the final stanza," Diu said.

"There is no need," Tibo interrupted. "Of all the prophecy, this is the part I remember best."

> "Air and water, earth and fire
> Mend four powers into one
> And the elements conspire
> For darkness to be undone."

"Meaning," Nicole cried, "that all I've got to do is put the crystals together!"

"Not quite," Tibo said. His fingers groped out towards Nicole. "Give them to me."

She glanced at Diu for reassurance. He hestitatied, then gave Tibo his two crystals as a sign of consent. Nicole did the same, and Tibo softly murmured something.

In his hands, the crystals cracked.

"No!" Nicole shrieked. "What're you doing!"

The rocks shattered into dust that blew away in a sudden gust, disappearing as if by magic. But Nicole stopped cold when she realized that Tibo was holding something else.

"These crystals," he explained, "are merely the guardians of the greater power."

The small things Tibo held now seemed entirely worthless. They were four stone tubes, each the length of Nicole's index finger. Each was the color of its representative element—blue, yellow, red, and green.

"So . . . what do I do with these?" Nicole asked, accepting the proffered tubes from Tibo's outstretched hand.

"When you sought out the map, did you remove the metal disk from the center?"

She glanced at Diu. Tibo followed her gaze, and his eyes locked on the disk clipped to Diu's belt.

"May I see it?" he requested.

Diu passed over the disk, albeit reluctantly. The old man looked at it carefully and nodded. "This, Nicole Sky, is the centerpiece to the key. The four slots in the disk are for these tubes."

She nodded, her eyes wide with wonder as she glanced with newfound respect at the disk.

"I think we had best go," Diu said, taking back the artifact.

Dipping her head, she said, "Thank you, Tibo, for everything."

"Just one last thing," the old man said, extending his hand, palm facing them. He muttered an incantation under his breath, and a wave of cool air washed over the room, so cold that Nicole began to shiver. "This enchantment will protect you from the core's heat," Tibo explained. "It will wear off after about twelve hours, so you had better get going."

"Thank you," Nicole said.

Tibo nodded. "It is time."

She took out the Galactera, storing the tubes in her pocket with the disk. Holding the pocket watch in her hand, she rubbed her thumb over the golden cover, thinking briefly back over how far it had taken her. Through life, through war, through death—and beyond. Beyond the farthest stars. Nicole snapped open the lid and looked up at Diu and Arli, their shining faces a mark of the friendship that bound them together. She could even almost see Lily hovering beside them, fur streaked with silver light.

I won't be gone . . .

"Thanks, Lily," she whispered.

Nicole began to imagine Earth's iron core before remembering that the Omenra had transformed it into something entirely unrecognizable. Not knowing what to think, she pretended to feel enormous heat and saw lava bursting all around her, licking at her feet. Her hair rose on end as the electrical vortex enclosed them and real, scorching heat flooded into the sphere. As lightning roared in her ears, Nicole grabbed onto Arli and felt Diu pull her close. But then the vortex broke apart and everything was still.

Absolutely still.

Chapter Forty-Six

The Only Way

A blast of sizzling, hot air rushed at Nicole's face. She coughed and squinted, peering around tentatively, gasping out loud when she saw the full extent of what the Omenra had done. Earth's core was no longer like a drawing from her science textbooks.

They stood on the edge of a vast, circular iron island that was entirely surrounded by a sea of lava. A bridge-like structure connected the main island to a narrow pathway that ringed the enormous spherical chamber. The curved metal walls glowed red-hot, dripping with the heat.

"I don't get it," Nicole said. "Where'd all the lava come from?"

"The force-field surrounding the core must be keeping temperatures low enough to stop the Terranova from melting, but the iron and nickel still can't handle such heat," Diu explained. "Some of the metal must have melted, forming the island and the magma."

Nicole ventured out a little further, exploring the chamber. The air shivered with intense heat, particularly in a tiny, concentrated sphere at the center of the island.

"What's that?" she muttered, cautiously approaching the shimmering ball.

But even with Tibo's enchantment, she couldn't get close without feeling like her skin was about to melt off. The sphere radiated such heat that she was willing to bet that even a star would have found it a worthy challenger. Squinting to see through the hazy air, she made out a shape that vaguely resembled a spider. Had they finally made it?

"The Terranova," Nicole cried in reply to her own question. She quickly reached into her pocket. "So now I just—"

Suddenly, a flaming red spark sizzled through the air. Leaping back in fear, she watched as the entire chamber began to glimmer with light and electricity that took a roughly spherical form. She wildly snapped her head around, searching for shelter from whatever was happening. Diu made the decision for her, shoving her sideways and into the shining ring. She barely had time to make out the dark bulk of two dark cruisers before they found themselves crowded beneath the larger one's metallic belly, staring out from a narrow gap.

"That's Malkior's *Aphelia*," Diu whispered.

The rear hatch of their ship groaned open, and a dozen Omenra guards filed out. Flaming red light reflected off their Salviras. Nicole caught sight of booted feet marching alongside the cruiser. Wondering how they could survive in the heat, she crawled forward on her elbows, peeking out just enough to catch sight of brand new, red and black, and clearly heat-resistant uniforms. The guards spread out along the edges of the island, their senses intent for trespassers.

"It seems," said a cold voice that she recognized only too well, "that the Earth child has missed her chance." The clang of boots on steel echoed through the chamber as Malkior jumped down from his private ship. "For all her courage, for all her triumphs, she will still lose the war."

Arli fidgeted, radiating sickening waves of disgust. Nicole tried to calm the dracling, but she knew Arli had a bone to pick with Malkior for kidnapping her mother and was eager to teach him a lesson.

Stay put! Nicole warned.

But the murderer is so close . . . I can take him! I can finish him! Arli cried, starting to crawl forward.

She grabbed the dracling's tail and pulled back. *Don't!*

From the corner of her mouth Nicole hissed, "Diu, what's the plan?"

His face tightened into an anxious grimace. "I was certain we would get here before them. I suppose I ignored possibility the possibility of Malkior setting up a temporary teleportation system."

"You mean there's no Plan B?"

"Hang on, hang on—give me time to think! We just have to figure out a way to get close to the Terranova without being noticed."

The initial stages of a plan were already bubbling in Nicole's mind. It was dangerous, but so far as she could see, there was no other way. Her friends wouldn't agree to it, of course, but she'd have to make them see reason.

It was the way it had to be.

"Diu," Nicole said slowly, "you know as well as I that there's only one way any of us are getting near that weapon."

He looked straight into her eyes, sizing her up. Finally he

shook his head. "No," he said firmly. "We will find a way to sneak up on the Omenra, or—"

"It's impossible to get to the Terranova by stealth and you know it! Diu, there's no other way."

"I'm not letting you go out there."

"But I've got to! I've got to be captured. Then, while they're distracted with me, you can sneak around with the key and destroy the Terranova. It's the only chance we have!"

He was silent for a long moment, watching the Omenra guards shuffle around the edges of the island, guarding the weapon.

"What if Malkior kills you?" he said at last.

Nicole's mind pulled away into the past. Images of her home, family, and friends whipped through her mind. This was their only hope, their only chance. And then she thought back to Lily's sacrifice.

"Diu," she said softly, "I accepted that risk the moment I set out on this quest. If that's the way things are meant to end, then so be it. But I've got to try. We've got no other options left. Besides, I was lucky twice. Maybe I'll be lucky again."

Nicole, Arli begged, *stay! I lose Mama to him. I won't lose you, too.*

"I've got to," she repeated.

"Then at least promise me something," Diu said. "Promise that you'll come back, and maybe, with luck, you will keep your word."

"I promise," Nicole whispered, praying it was a vow she would keep.

"But remember, we will be watching. If things start going

wrong, we will be there to back you up."

"Fine. But don't interfere unless you have to."

Nicole pushed the tubes and disk into Diu's arms. She slithered forward, snatching one last look back at her friends, knowing that they'd always be there, always on her side. For a second, she thought she felt something warm on her shoulder and looked to see a shimmer of silver fur.

I won't be gone . . .

Gathering her courage, Nicole sprinted out from under the ship and waved her arms wide. "I'm here, Malkior!" she screamed. "Come get me!"

In an instant, a dozen guns flashed in her face. A dozen claws tightened on cold, metallic triggers. She held up her hands in surrender, hoping against hope that Malkior would stop his guards and that it wasn't the end.

The gunshots ripped off simultaneously, exploding in the air. Gunfire sizzled over Nicole's head, raining sparks. But then the guards stepped back, heads bowed respectfully to Malkior, who now came forward with his Sigrá drawn. Nicole backed fearfully, eyes darting from him to the Terranova. He followed her gaze and sidestepped nimbly so he was between her and his precious weapon.

"Some professional advice, Nicole," he said. "There's a difference between courage and stupidity, and you've just crossed the line. And will someone check under that ship . . . you never know what other company we might have."

Nicole could only tremble in utter terror as two guards approached the larger cruiser. There was absolutely nothing she could do now to prevent her friends from being discovered.

Terrified, she squeezed her eyes shut.

"Nothing here, General Taggerath."

Nicole's eyes flashed open. *What?*

Before she had time to ponder the impossible nature of the situation, cruel jeering called her back to the present. The Omenra guards crowded around their leader, chuckling at the captured prey. Fueled by their racket, Malkior leapt forward and shoved Nicole to the ground, much to the delight of his guards. She fell hard and scraped her cheek against the metal ground. Glancing over, she tried to locate her friends. But the space under the cruiser was empty.

Wherever they were, Nicole had to buy them time. What would a movie hero do? Oh, yes . . . taunt the enemy. She had almost forgotten.

"You're just a cruel tyrant, Malkior!" she cried. "Killing and hurting innocent creatures—it's all a game for you, isn't it? You don't care about their lives. You're blinded by power, blinded by greed, blinded by—"

He cut her off with a sharp kick to the stomach. She rolled over, groaning, and screamed when the sheer drop into the sea of molten metal reared an inch from her face. Nicole tried to scramble away but Malkior pointed the Sigrá at her head, keeping her at bay.

"You, my dear, need some lessons," he hissed, pressing a clawed boot firmly against her shoulder. "Lesson one—don't meddle in things you don't understand." He stepped forward, keeping the gun trained at her head. "Lesson two—don't talk back to grown-ups with guns. You never know what will drive someone over the edge." He pulled back a little on the trigger, and his eyes widened slightly, almost as if he were wondering what would happen when he proceeded. "Lesson three—"

"Never leave your back unguarded," cried a voice from behind. "And lesson four—don't betray your best friend. You never know what can happen."

Malkior whirled in time to see Diu materialize seemingly out of nowhere next to the Terranova. Nicole couldn't believe it. Was this more magic? She glanced at his wrist. There was something strapped there . . . Sorill's wristband! Of course! It was probably the reason, she realized now, Sorill had wanted to talk to Diu in Tibo's hut. Sorill was one to plan ahead, just in case. And he must have given Diu the wristband then.

"No!" Malkior cried out, running at him, but Diu had already snapped the four tubes in place and raised the artifact high.

Nicole shielded her eyes from the explosion of light she knew was coming. Her ears prepared for the blast of sound, the roar of energy. Leaping to her feet, she screamed in joy, knowing that it was all over, that they'd won—

For a long, long time there was only silence, and finally she dared to look. There was no light, no blast. Diu simply stood opposite Malkior, his face creased in horror, the disk and tubes held in his paws. Malkior let out a burst of terrible laughter and sprang forward, knocking Diu to his feet.

"That's impossible!" Nicole cried out. "Why didn't it work?"

As she watched the Omenras surround her again, a vague wisp of memory flared into her mind. Tibo was showing her the wind stallion and saying—saying what?

Nicole Sky, for you the elements themselves conspire.

"For me," she yelled, finally understanding as two guards grabbed her arms. "I'm the one who has to do it. It's got to be me!"

"Too late for that!" Malkior yelled. "There's nothing that can help you now!"

A roar rent the air, and Malkior was knocked sideways by what appeared to be air. Then Arli's band wore off and she appeared next to the Omenra general, snarling. The guards holding Nicole let go in surprise, and she managed to dart away, dodging outstretched claws. "Diu!" she screamed, narrowly avoiding a gunshot. "Diu, where are you?"

"Here!" came a yell as he sprang from the crowd. The Omenra turned to chase him but were distracted again by a livid Arli.

"That was brilliant!" Nicole cried.

"I'm only sorry I didn't think of the bands before you went out to face Malkior."

"It doesn't matter now! Where's the disk and tubes?"

Diu shoved the artifacts into Nicole's hands and drew his Mar.

"Where's the last one?" she screamed, realizing that the fire tube was missing. But in a terrible way she already knew. Malkior was sneaking away across the bridge, clutching something in his claws.

"Nicole!" Diu cried out as she bolted away. "Nicole, come back!"

She ignored him, dodging and twisting through the guards, glancing back to see Arli engage three Omenras at once in battle. The dracling was in a tight spot when, suddenly, Diu blasted into their midst. Together, back to back, they fought to give Nicole time.

Ahead, Malkior was getting away, sprinting as fast as he could across the bridge. A roar ripped from Nicole's throat, and she dashed after him, meeting him at the halfway mark. She lunged and knocked him to the ground. The tube skittered out from his grasp, nearly flipping over into the magma. Dropping the disk, Nicole lashed out with her fists, striking Malkior across the face. He retorted by slashing at her shoulder, tearing flesh like it was origami paper. She shrieked and fell backwards, her tunic stained dark where cloth met blood.

"You will never win!" Malkior cried.

"But I'll never give up!"

"Then you'll *die!*"

"No!" Diu screamed, and Arli and all the Omenras whirled to see Malkior draw his Salvira Sigrá and gun down on the trigger.

"You once said you would fight for Earth till the death," Malkior sniggered, a glint of triumph flaring in his eyes. "And I swore I'd make you keep that promise."

Nicole staggered. Her eyes roved slowly from the tyrant to the dark, bloody stain blossoming over her chest.

"You protected her for so long, Diu," Malkior sneered. "But even you couldn't save her in the end."

Nicole heard Diu yell again, but she could think only of Malkior and the artifact. She stumbled forward, each step sapping strength. Kneeling, she reached for the final tube through tears of pain and groped to find its place in the disk.

Malkior stared in terror.

Nicole wearily met his eyes.

"You've been busy, Malkior Rav Taggerath. You enslaved half the galaxy, tormented the innocent, stole the Terranova, set Earth a deadline, left death and kidnappings in your wake, betrayed everyone who had ever trusted you, tried to kill Diu. Your best friend. And then you came after me."

She prayed Diu wouldn't intervene now. Because she would never be able to do what she had to if he came.

"You've succeeded in a lot of things. Like the Terranova. Like the Omenra conquest. Like Lily. Like . . . me."

Her mouth folded in a grimace. Blood dripped from the corners of her lips. She crumpled to her knees, barely able to speak. Her eyes stared blankly at the ground. It took all she had just to whisper.

"You got everything, Malkior. You won—except for two things. On Serrona, I didn't let you have Diu. And now, you're not getting Earth. Because in life—" she sobbed wearily, forcing her eyes to meet his, "—and in *death* . . . I won't *ever* . . . give . . . up."

In a flash of motion, she shoved the final tube into the disk.

As the artifact began to glow, a terrified scream twisted from Malkior's throat. He leaped at her, intent on wrestling the disk away. But he miscalculated, and the force of his jump drove them over the side of the bridge, hurtling towards the magma.

Shadows ate away at Nicole's vision. The world grew bleary and dark. Her fingers clutched in a death-grip on the disk. But strangely enough, her chest didn't hurt anymore. She didn't even feel heat. Nicole's body curved through the air, hair wiping wildly, and Malkior was close to her, screaming. Curiously, his voice was partially muted, almost as if someone had pressed a pillow around her head.

Each still clutching the disk, their bodies broke through the lava with a soft splash. The force of impact drove them deep beneath the surface. The magma felt thick and slightly warm, but nothing more. The world blurred in a swirl of color. *If this was death*, Nicole thought, *it wasn't all that bad.* Even the pain was fading.

But was this death?

The blood had vanished from her tunic, and she looked down to see her wound heal over with new skin. The Galactera around her neck hovered in the lava, its golden covers shining, the mysterious words etched in blue light. Each tube glowed with its respective color, channeling energy to the disk at the core. The centerpiece burned with white-hot light.

Malkior, too, was staring, his terrified emerald eyes revealing that he understood what was going on no more than Nicole did. But they were spiraling towards the surface now, bursting through the magma, and soaring high over the chamber. Both were caught in a powerful wind and bound to the artifact, unable to let go.

A blazing circle of light exploded from the disk, raining silver sparks onto the gathered crowd below. In a blast of burning fire, sparkling water, raging gusts, and swirling leaves, a vast sweep of white energy erupted from the artifact, forming a protective, shining force-field around the chamber. The magma and iron walls and island emanated pure white radiance, filling the core with brilliance. The light concentrated in a ring around the Terranova, swirling faster and faster until a silvery sphere surrounded the weapon. The ball of light suddenly compacted and turned into a tiny, glistening marble that exploded in a wave of glittering sparks.

And the Terranova was no more.

But Nicole's eyes weren't on the weapon. She now cared for nothing but the small creature that perched on the disk, beaming.

"Lily," Nicole whispered breathlessly.

"My brave, loyal friend," Lily said, her voice somehow different and bearing a soft, musical quality. "You did what no one could have ever asked of you. Sacrificing yourself for your family, your friends, your planet—that is what defines you, what sets you apart. For your courage, for your unconditional love, your Earth will be saved. Me, I am here to reward you for all you've done. When you united the four elements together, you unleashed a power greater than any other in the galaxy. And that power, coupled with the magic of your soul, will grant you a single wish—anything in the whole universe. Choose wisely."

Nicole looked down at Diu and Arli, standing far below. She thought of her family. She thought of all her friends. She recalled the creatures she had faced on this journey, and all her enemies, and all her allies. She thought about the war between the Omenra and Airioth, and then Nicole knew what she wanted most.

"I can choose anything?"

"Anything at all."

She nodded firmly. "Then I know what I want."

Suddenly, both Nicole and Malkior were blasted backwards. They crashed and tumbled across the ground, rolling to a halt at the island's edge. Nicole felt a searing pain in her right palm and looked down to see a shining silver ring etched in her skin, glowing with pale light. Her eyes shot up and saw Malkior stare at his hand, too. She wondered if he now bore the same mark.

Diu and Arli rushed to her side, but she held up her palms and rose like a ghost, crossing to the center of the chamber. She stared up at where the disk was still hovering in the air. Slowly it spiraled earthward till it finally sank to the ground.

Lily was still sitting on the artifact, wedged between two tubes, looking curiously at Nicole. Then she leaped off and landed lightly on the ground. She took a few cautious steps forward. With each footfall silver sparks rained from her fur and purple patches poked through. Convinced that it wasn't a dream, Lily shook herself off and bounced up into Nicole's arms, eyes shimmering with tears.

"What did you wish for?" Lily whispered.

"Lily," Nicole choked out, "I chose *you*."

Arli bounded to them in several leaps, quick to join in the embrace. Diu simply watched them, mouth drawn into a grin. Sparks rained around them, wrapping them in something like snow. Nicole touched the Galactera around her neck, feeling its warmth.

There was no need for words between them. Lily took her usual spot on Nicole's shoulder, and Arli and Diu took a stance by her side. Looking up, Nicole saw Malkior rise to his feet. Their eyes met briefly before he tore his gaze away and mumbled something to the guards. She braced herself for attack, but to her great surprise, the Omenras trooped away towards the cruiser, muttering amongst themselves. They said many things, many of them vile and murderous.

"It's not over, Sky," Malkior said, but there was something soft in his tone.

"I know it's not," she replied coldly, snapping open the pocket watch. "I'll be waiting."

As Malkior turned away towards his ship, Diu whispered, "I think that's as close as he will ever come to thanking you for whatever happened down there."

She glanced at her palm. "It's enough."

"I wonder why he's letting us go so easily."

"Because now we're even. He saved my life, I saved his. It's given him something to think about. His guards don't like it, though."

Diu appeared to be puzzled. "What do you mean?"

"I mean what the guards were saying just now. Didn't you hear them?"

"I did, but . . . how did you?"

Nicole shook her head. "What are you talking about?"

"How did you understand what they said?"

"Duh. I have the translator."

"Not anymore," he said, pointing.

Nicole reached up to her ear and pulled out a piece of twisted metal. The lava must have melted the translator. And yet she had understood every word.

"I-I . . . I don't know," she admitted. "I didn't even notice."

But it was true, Nicole realized. The Omenra voices hadn't been run through a hissing translator. She had interpreted the words on her own. "Maybe," she suggested, "it has something to do with this."

Nicole held up the mark on her palm.

"When we see Tibo again, as I am certain we will," Diu said, "we will ask him. He will have an answer to this."

For now, I think it time to go home, Arli said.

Nicole relayed the comment.

"Me, I couldn't agree more!" Lily said.

Smiling, Nicole pressed the button for Earth.

Chapter Forty-Seven

Dawn of Destiny

oming home was definitely one of those times for the scrapbooks. When Nicole and her friends appeared in a blaze of blue light right in the center of the living room, her grief-stricken father, who had the misfortune of being present in that room at the time, nearly fell backwards over the sofa and her mother shot down the stairs, shrieking something about burglars. It took a while to calm them, but when Nicole managed it at last and told them her story, they stood speechless before her, disbelieving but proud. It took much longer for her parents to warm up to her newfound allies, but after her brilliant rendering of the adventure, jazzed up a little in all the right places, they agreed to let her friends hang around for a while.

Or, at any rate, to not call the police.

Of course, Nicole was very aware of the fact that her parents didn't entirely believe her. Had she been in their shoes, their crazy daughter would have been shipped off instantly to a mental institution. She had a nagging feeling, however, that it was Diu who convinced them otherwise. In any case, whether or not actual threatening was involved, her parents always seemed rather terrified when they were in the same room as Diu. He fixed that problem nicely, though. A ship was soon called up from the Airioth fleet and stationed in the nearby forest (what was left of it, anyway, after the Terranova) and away from prying eyes, under the cloak of invisibility.

Lily and Arli, on the other hand, decided to remain with Nicole in the house for the duration of their stay. That worked out well. Mostly. Excepting, of course, the times when the little Lunaran raided the fridge at two in the morning and received a broom whacking . . .

The episode in the core seemed to have humbled Malkior for a while, allowing Diu a brief respite for the first time in ten years. But as summer faded to August, he received more frequent reports of Omenra mischief. Finally, with full-scale attacks breaking out again, it came time to say goodbye.

It was a pleasantly warm, crisp fall afternoon, mere days before school started, when they gathered in a forest clearing. They already had some plans worked out and were just running through things one last time.

"Nicole, we *will* be back," Diu assured her for the umpteenth time. "There are just a few things that need to be taken care of first."

"Don't worry," Lily said cheerfully, "if he tries to get out of coming back, me, I'll sing in his ears till he does."

"I've never heard you sing," Nicole said.

"There's a reason."

Bursting into a laugh, Nicole said, "Don't worry, you all have to come back. The entire fate of the galaxy hinges on me, remember?"

This time it was Lily's turn to giggle. Diu only rolled his eyes. "Just don't panic if we don't return immediately. It will take some time to sort things out properly. I have been away for a while and things get hectic."

They were near the end, and conversation was growing difficult now. There was a brief silence. Then Nicole pulled out the Galactera and turned it over in her hand, remembering something she'd been meaning to ask for a long time. "Diu," she said, "I noticed this on the very first day I found the watch, but I kept forgetting to ask. I know the front cover opens for the sixteen buttons, but the back looks like it unlatches, too. What's on that other side?"

"I have no idea," he admitted. "I have not worked out all the watch's secrets, and that is one of them. I am sure it opens, but the how is beyond me. Maybe Tibo knows, but he won't tell me. It is one of those things that I 'don't need to know,' according to him. But next time we have to see him, be sure to ask. I do have a personal guess, though. I think it has something to do with the strange language that's on the back cover. If we can ever figure that out, maybe we'll crack the secret."

An engine roar ripped through the forest as a large cruiser slipped over the trees, curving in a ring around the clearing. It stroked down onto the grass in a gentle ripple, and the rear hatch slid open. Diu looked towards it.

"Right on time," he said.

"Pilot?" Nicole asked.

"Auto."

"Sorill?"

"Who else."

"Well," she said, "I guess that's it then. I'll see you all . . ." Nicole turned, concentrating on each leg to move it. It was a struggle to fight tears. After all they'd done, after all they'd been through, she didn't want it to end.

"Lily, Arli," she heard Diu say. "Get on the ship."

"Going," Lily said. "But what about you?"

"It will wait."

Nicole stopped and spun around. She flashed a glance at Lily, who shrugged, and at Arli, who meekly ducked her head. They scrambled onto the ramp, Lily riding Arli's crested back.

Then Nicole and Diu were alone.

"I should be getting home," she said, her voice shaky. She didn't understand why he had to make it harder than it already was.

"I know," Diu said. He moved across the clearing, pausing directly before her. "But not yet." He unstrapped the JET from his back and placed it in a hovering position a few inches off the ground. He stepped on, his feet locking into place. Nicole waited, unsure, until he stretched out a paw. "Get on."

She still wasn't sure, but then she looked into his eyes and saw a softness there she had never seen before. Maybe it wasn't something he wanted her to see, but Nicole took his paw and hopped on behind him, arms around his waist. The Glider was small, contracted, and gave her very little room to stand. Her shoes bent at the toe as she pushed herself slightly away from the edge, still keeping space between their bodies. Diu smiled at her efforts, almost laughing.

"Now give me the Galactera."

Nicole didn't argue, didn't think about it twice. She pulled the watch off her neck, passed it to him. He closed his eyes, thinking, and then suddenly the vortex channeled them to a new and strange place. It was very dark and foggy where they were, but at least there was some dim ground below them.

"Where are we?" Nicole asked, thinking of Tertius.

"It doesn't matter where we are," Diu said. "What is important is this—planets such as this one are very rare. This world is completely untouched and isolated, a land at the edge of the known universe. Few, if any, creatures dwell here. This planet itself is a legend, and there is only one way to access it."

"The Galactera?"

"Yes. And if explored properly, this land is fantastic and brimming with secrets."

"Can't I know what it's called?"

"This planet was named in the Galacteran's ancient language from which the common galactic tongue sprang. It is called Cárine Galactera. It means 'heart of the Galacterans.' Along with the place on Espia, this is another of my secrets. Malkior showed it to me, and I showed it to Serena, and now I'm going to show it to you."

"Malkior?" Nicole repeated. "How did he know about this place first?"

"The Galactera was my wedding gift from Malkior. He probably didn't fully know what it was or he would not have given it up. But it was his originally, and we often played with it as kids. It got us into a lot of trouble, that watch—but I'm getting away from my purpose.

Chapter Forty-Seven

"I took you here today so you would always remember this day, no matter what is destined to come. Remember this day, this planet, and this journey you and I are about to make. Remember always that we went where there were no bounds, no limits, no expectations. Remember that we stood together in a place where no others have gone before."

The Glider shuddered, a current of air washed against Nicole's body, and she saw the ground drop away in the fog. They were rising quickly, the mist growing lighter. Streaks of pale silver streamed past her. Long trickles of pink sank away. The fog lifted, and she could see craggy cliffs surrounding her, descending down, out of the way of their flight.

Cliffs became sharp wedges, rolling away into a haze of sky, framed by mountains that raced the two friends and were left behind. Thick clouds bubbled around them, silver splashes against the blue, soon falling away. The land below them, wild and virgin, spread in a tangle of rainbow squares and lines.

Nicole felt the height press against her eardrums. The air was thin, sparse, and hard to breathe—yet still it beat against her arms. In the distance, a winding stretch of water rose to meet the sky. The ocean spread in a blanket, swallowing the farther half of the world, sweeping higher as the mountains fell away.

Gazing out across the sun-drenched sky and hearing the faintest whisper of water lapping a far-off shore, Nicole suddenly realized that the sky seemed bigger, and grew bigger, the longer she stood there. Looking into that expanding sky, she suddenly felt very small, like the whole of the universe was there before her and it was only a matter of reaching out and grasping it.

Nicole was terrified and invigorated, gripped by a sense of extreme. Her heart pulsed in a swirl of fear and ultimate freedom and a vague, fleeting peek into something past reality. It was an inexplicable feeling, a sort of a momentary experience out of her body, an instant in which she was suddenly separated from herself and from everything that bound her to the material world.

Nicole Sky did not know what she was feeling. But the fact that she was here was enough. Feeling lightheaded, she whispered, "Thank you, Diu, for everything you've done. You saved Earth. You saved my friends and family. You saved me."

He laughed, very softly. "No, Nicole. It is you who saved me."

She didn't understand, but maybe she didn't need to. Leaning back, she let one arm go, touching the stuff of freedom on the rising Glider in the breaking dawn.

Diu looked back at Nicole, the girl who thought she knew the world but hadn't mastered a thing yet. He knew her type of innocence, her skewed sight of things. Years back he had been no different with Malkior, and that had cost him. Next time he would have to be tougher. More distant. Maybe that would send a message.

He didn't want to hurt her. Not Nicole Sky. But there was another destiny waiting for him, and she had to know, now more than ever, how to go it alone.

Soon he would take the Galactera and wonder about the

second cover he had never managed to open and the inscribed words in the ancient language he still couldn't translate. The vortex would flash them back to Earth, momentarily illuminating the silver-scaled ring that was still bright on Nicole's palm. He would close the Galactera and return it, pulling the chain around her neck. He would cross the clearing, join Lily and Arli on the ship, glance back one last time at the beaming Earth child, her glowing face tearstained.

Eventually, at Lily's stubborn insistence, he would enter the cockpit, disengage the autopilot, and initiate the launch sequence. He would do this without thinking; it was a reflex that had become instinctive after so many years of training. As the ship roared to life he would throw it into hyperdrive, barely feeling the lurch that would upset Lily for days.

As the hours slipped away he would grow distracted, anxious at last to be alone and to return to his *Orellion* cruiser waiting at the edge of the galaxy along with his fleet, probed for constantly by Omenra intelligence yet still undiscovered. He would think back to Serena, to his former best friend, to his new ones. When the first of his ships appeared as a blip on the radar, his craft would automatically blast out from hyperspace, and he would be home. At least, as close to it as he had come in a long time.

But for now Diu gazed out across the ocean, past its boundless rims that stretched to the end of the world. He smiled and looked again at Nicole. And he knew then that no matter what was to come, the galaxy had a new hope.

Epilogue

In a tiny hut at the base of a cliff bordering the ocean, a wrinkled old man picked up a pinch of blue powder from a worn sack and tossed it onto a fire. The flames fed on the magic and burst into a brilliant shade of violet. Tibo leaned over the flickering mass, searching out an image in its heart. A small, purple creature twirled among the flames, giggling musically. Swooping down, she perched on the welcoming shoulder of an Earth child. They stood together, laughing, the best of friends.

"As always, Nicole *and* Lily," Tibo murmured. "I wonder."

He lifted his arms. A quill and parchment hovered to him, and he scratched down a few words. Then he glanced to where Kyria perched on a pile of heavy books beside him.

"My firelight," he summoned, and the phoenix glided to his outstretched arm. "Firelight," he said, "a favor, if you will. Take this to Madam Banda. Return quickly with her answer."

Kyria pecked his cheek with affection, spread her wings, and vanished in a blaze of brilliance.

Sighing, Tibo blew out the fire and stood.

Epilogue

He shuffled outside and watched the great sun sink. Shadowy clouds fused with scarlet crept up to consume the golden sphere. The old man reached into his robe to retrieve something—a tiny vial filled with dark, red liquid infused with silver sparks. To himself, Tibo whispered, "What you survived, Nicole, was only the beginning. The time for confrontation is at hand. You were lucky this time. Lucky that, by destiny, you did not have to die."

He paused, stared up at the bloody sky, and swilled the liquid around in the vial.

"Not yet."

KEEP WATCH FOR

THE GALACTERAN Legacy

Equinox

Prologue

Malkior was dreaming.

The beginning was simple: a mission accomplished. Only things had not gone according to plan. Now Serena, barely nineteen, knelt with Malkior beside a Diu more dead than alive. He had taken a shot to the chest, and there was so much blood . . .

"Diu!" Serena cried. Her slim body trembled as she sobbed, "Malkior, what do we do?"

Malkior folded a thick cloth across the pulsing wound. "We apply pressure and try to stem the blood flow," he said. It was a fight just to keep his voice steady. He was close to tears, but he had to be strong for Serena. She couldn't know. Not yet. Because if she realized it was hopeless, if she knew that such a wound was fatal . . .

Tears glistened in Serena's soft, brown eyes as her slender, delicate fingers pressed against Diu's neck. "It's not working. His pulse is weakening."

A lump welled in Malkior's throat. He swallowed, hard, and said, "There's nothing else we can do."

The liquid brown of Serena's eyes hardened. "That's a lie."

"Serena, please!" he begged. "You must understand—"

"I understand, but you're wrong. There is always one way."

"What do you mean?"

"Tibo," she said resolutely.

"Tibo!" Malkior spat. "He is never fair, Serena! We can't trust him."

Her eyes, piercingly cold, met his. "Diu can't survive a wound like this, can he?"

Malkior's heart thumped painfully in his chest. He looked away.

"Can he?" she repeated, louder.

"No," he admitted.

"No," she repeated. "Not this way."

"But Tibo—"

"I don't care! Malkior, if there's a chance he can help, can't we at least try? Can't we try?"

The dream blurred into a swirl of color, leapt ahead through time, and solidified once more as a terrified Serena pounded the door of a sad-looking hut secluded in the depths of an ancient forest wreathed in mist. Malkior stood a little behind her, holding Diu in his arms. Gripped tightly in his claws was the Galactera.

The door slammed open of its own accord. Serena ran in first with silent footfalls. Malkior walked in slowly after her, taking care not to jostle the heaps of thick, musty volumes stacked around the hut. He hoped against hope that the old man would help them.

Prologue

"Diu is in trouble again, I see," said a coldly familiar voice from the far side of the room.

"Tibo, please," Serena begged. "You must—"

"I must nothing!" Tibo thundered, suddenly appearing from behind a table laden with trinkets. "I warned you against this mission. This is the reward for disobedience!"

"Please, Tibo. Please! I'll do anything!" she cried.

"Anything," the old man said. "I have heard that far too often."

"But others did not mean it as I do! I will truly do anything. I swear it."

"Serena," Malkior interrupted, troubled by the sparkle in Tibo's bright blue eyes. "I think we should—"

"Wait," Tibo said. "Allow her to finish."

Serena motioned for Malkior to lower Diu to the rug stained with color spread across the floor. Diu's breathing was labored, and he barely had the strength to wince when his body touched the ground. Serena knelt beside him and cradled his head in her lap.

"Tibo," she said, "if you save him, I will do anything you wish."

The old man's mouth twisted into a cruel smirk. "Serena, child, I have always loved you as a father would his daughter. Please, go home. I don't want to see you hurt."

"You're hurting me now!" she screamed. "Nothing could hurt me more! Tibo, I love him! Don't let him die!"

"Serena, it is true that I have powers. But everything has a price. For Diu's life, I must have an equal sacrifice."

Malkior instantly discerned the meaning of the words.

"Not her," he warned, darting forward to stand between them.

"No," Serena said, her hot tears glistening on Diu's ragged fur. "Malkior, this is my decision. I'll be the one to pay."

Tibo laughed grimly. "It is not so simple. The cost of a life is determined by the impact it has upon others. Your Diu is more important than you know. If he lives, the galaxy and all its creatures must suffer for it. And you, Serena Airioth, will suffer most of all."

She nodded. "I accept."

"No!" Malkior yelled. "Serena, you can't!"

Tibo clucked his tongue. "You would be wise to listen, for your suffering will lie in death. The worst of all deaths."

"I don't care!" she cried. "I choose Diu. Now save him."

Reaching into his exotically-colored robes, Tibo withdrew a phoenix feather that glowed like the crimson sun. He brushed it across Diu's chest. Tendrils of fiery energy sealed the bloody wound.

"It is done," he said.

Years into the future, Malkior jolted awake. Across the galaxy, on a small planet isolated on an outer spiral arm, so too did Earth child Nicole Sky.